T0374401

O'
Darkness, Darkness!
My Son Shall Pass

A novel by

CARLTON JORDAN

WESTBOW
PRESS®
A DIVISION OF THOMAS NELSON
& ZONDERVAN

Unless otherwise indicated, all Scripture quotations are
from the Authorized King James Bible.

Scripture quotations marked (ESV) are from The Holy Bible, English Standard Version® (ESV®), copyright © 2001 by Crossway, a publishing ministry of Good News Publishers. Used by permission. All rights reserved

WestBow Press books may be ordered through booksellers or by contacting:

WestBow Press
A Division of Thomas Nelson & Zondervan
1663 Liberty Drive
Bloomington, IN 47403
www.westbowpress.com
1 (866) 928-1240

ISBN: 978-1-4908-9076-0 (sc)
ISBN: 978-1-4908-9077-7 (e)

Library of Congress Control Number: 2015914348

Print information available on the last page.

WestBow Press rev. date: 09/26/2018

CONTENTS

DEDICATION

To families in search of a why

ACKNOWLEDGEMENTS

I am thankful to God for sending Barbara Scott, a little woman by the well, who provided clarity and direction with a word from the Lord before, during, and after my divorce.

I thank God for Christy and Conwood Seymore, my sister and brother-in-law. They provided shelter when I had none, and my sister, Christy, proved to be light in the darkest of times.

When I fall, I shall arise; when I sit in darkness,
the LORD shall be a light unto me.
Micah 7:8 KJV

CHAPTER 1

I am out of God. This realization took shape as Max noticed the final position of cars all around him, cars forced into action as drivers ignored road decorum and dotted lines in full-blown accident avoidance until stopped. One car neatly behind the other one second and positioned sideways across two lanes the next, some unscathed, some not. He sat amid the chaos unharmed with his wife, Sylvia. Heart pounding, mind racing, he did not pray. His mind, a trained one, parsed text, reveled in a beautifully turned phrase, felt secure when meditating on chiastic mysteries such as "Many that are first shall be last; and the last shall be first."[1] He cared about linguistic logic, hidden meaning, coherent paragraphs, conclusion to story, but there was no beauty or coherence in this mess, and the comfort and order he enjoyed moments earlier while enveloped by the words coming from the car stereo abandoned him.

The accident unearthed fault lines in his spiritual walk. He never noticed until now that he stored an allotment of God, and the reserve he took from the eleven o'clock Sunday service emptied with the initial realization of an imminent crash. He had no prayer for the injured or shocked who survived their loved and unloved dead. Nothing. Accidents are never plotted like stories, never planned, so he could not internalize the details and speak peace into the chaos to impose order. He realized his reserve like manna did not keep.

Max gave God only so much of himself with infrequent, ephemeral exchanges of flesh for Spirit, but routine tithing, incessant volunteerism, and generous offerings fed the illusion of growth in the Lord. Twenty years of tithes, ten years of children's church, and six years of a building fund commitment, he gave what clergy called time, talent, and treasure. Their strategic use of the phrase placed giving on par with obedience for many. Since church leaders never dispelled this misconception, the committed gave more in any one of the three areas while they prayed less, read less, and remained unaware that their giving accessed no true benefit of the work wrought on the cross, that sacrifice was never God's first choice. Max acted as if he forgot this, forgot that works that appease the flesh war against the spirit.

Forgetting made it easier to walk with those who believed themselves savvy enough to separate superstition from fact. They would interject "Well, I believe" or "You do know that" into discussions about the Bible and follow with their views on holiness or descriptions of God's demonstrations of power. They considered dying daily an ancient, outmoded concept in the era of technological advancement and modern comforts, and many took the forty days of flooding and seven days of creation for compelling reads and nothing more. They knew lightning would not strike them dead for thinking and saying so.

Max went along with their repudiation of routine bouts of crucifying flesh, opting as they did for the annual twenty-one-day Daniel marathon of raw vegetables, lemon water, and unseasoned cooked vegetables in rotation to accomplish a year's worth of crucifying the flesh in three weeks. Why crucify the flesh privately over the course of a year when a concentrated communal stint accomplished the same? Why fast one or two days here and there since skipping breakfast when running late or working through lunch when behind happened regularly enough and could, if repurposed, be used to know God more?

For many, knowing God in the United States today differs greatly from what it meant to know him while walking through ancient occupied streets. With no Roman or Assyrian soldiers to worry about, deciding to unwind in the recreation room, sitting room, or family room after a long day governs most evenings. For many, abundance renders dying daily obsolete.

Twenty years, three states, and three pastors and the last two never made clear the ineffectiveness of this Christian approach as the accident did in a matter of seconds. Max never had a need for spiritual rationing, but with this accident came a frightening revelation that now he did and a more chilling revelation that one who served an omnipotent God never should. In truth, it had been some time since he showed a need for God in his ordered comfort. Amid the growing clutter of things, he displayed no need or earnest appreciation for grace, and he remained unaware until now that he and many like him transformed the Spirit into fuel and church, a filling station. He thought Tuesday and already empty, as if he pumped too little at the Sunday altar and bought only enough God to last a typical week. Perhaps attending the two earlier services along with the eleven o'clock service would prevent running out amid crises, but he suspected the current church had little to impart spiritually. Yet, it was his church and Sylvia's church and the church of their two children. He remained silent. While other Christians might have praised God for the accident protection, the awareness of the exhaustibility of God as he and possibly many, many others experienced caused a spiritual crash far greater than the natural one before him.

Max lived off grace in the absence of fear. The two Virginia churches he attended never considered the fear of the Lord or meditated on lyrics such as "Look and live, my brother live, look to

Jesus now and live." Never once. So the lyric and those of its kind that ministered in his first church never forged a connection in churches two and three between the Lord's anger with his chosen people and the grace he extended them.

Grace was not a New Testament concept. Abraham's negotiating exposed it, and the story of Nineveh proved one could not thwart it. Still, church members never considered the story of fiery serpents and a brass likeness set on a pole to deliver the children of God from the deadly venom. A look was all it took to reverse the price of murmuring and scoffing at God's provision. Just one look accessed God's grace during their moment of need in the wilderness, and an introspective look nowadays with each rendering of the song or Scripture read could lead to a better understanding of the fear of the Lord in an era of grace, and it could, if one opened up to the Spirit, jumpstart wisdom. Yet his current church never pondered anger and grace side by side through preaching, through song, through Scripture. Never once.

Never once did music remind the congregants that bitter water turned sweet, and a most merciful God admonished his chosen to seek his face, to look to him, to diligently hearken to his voice, to do right in his sight, and to keep all his statutes. If they saw God and not the tree, if they sought the agent of the sweetener and not miracles, then the Lord would heal them and their land. They needed only look and live then as some believers look to the Author and Finisher of their faith today and see beyond the spiritual largesse to the benefactor, the life giver, the chaser of darkness, the Father of lights.

His most recent church and the one before it never juxtaposed grace and righteous judgment, and grace without the fear of the Lord left Max powerless. As it stood, he could not speak the name of Jesus into the wreckage with any degree of confidence that Jesus would heal the wounded, calm the sea within the nervous, and raise one if dead.

God, he knew, would not right the car now turned upside down. Mountains moved only in the pages of books or through metaphor granting power to a worthy wielder, one who had the wherewithal to give the metaphor meaning and make it live. At this moment, neither the power he ascribed to words nor the faith he possessed ministered spiritual assurance. This epiphany, a stark counterpoint to the non theatrical voice reading the Word of God over the car's stereo system, frightened him more than the previous revelations.

Fissures formed in his heart, but he neither listened closely to the words read over the car stereo nor tried to access the transmutable power within them that could turn rock to flesh, fissure to wound. He simply sat in the post-accident stillness reeling and having not quite shaken off the surprise of it all, a fragile quiet fed by shock and relief in most cars and partial revelation in his. Gathering himself, he thought of a long-distance race horse sprinting much too fast from the gate, an exhausted tennis player with no more to give in the final set, a soul on empty.

CHAPTER 2

Two weeks before the accident they visited a nascent church that asked Sylvia to sing a solo. That Sunday they sat next to each other; their children sat on either side. In their home church both were busy, but Sylvia was extremely busy. She worked in the music ministry, and he, in the youth department. While he directed children's church, she sang on the praise team. If he sat in the congregation, she sang in the choir. He understood God to be a jealous God who would not share, but leaden eyes prevented his seeing the busyness during service was neither God's doing nor work assessed as marvelous in God's sight.

In this young church, Max sat with an expectation of God's rain. He believed he and Sylvia touched and agreed as one without any hint of lingering disagreement. Then Sylvia rose to sing. She walked toward the makeshift pulpit in the school gymnasium. She took the microphone and called forth an angelic, soft, unaffected voice to deliver beautifully rendered lyrics that reminded all listeners that he, the Lord and Savior, the Messiah, could not come down from the cross. She sang of unparalleled love and sacrifice reminiscent of ministering in their first church.

With the song's conclusion, Sylvia walked back to her seat and sat next to Max. He leaned toward her and took her hand. The combination of his nod and smile said beautiful. The music moved him, but while the voice aspired to reach heaven, her spirit bearing the weight of cares and imagined slights had not. She looked away from him as she flicked her wrist discreetly with a quick, sharp move that broke the connection. His hand returned to his lap. Her hand landed within a sea of errant pleats she realigned while shifting in her seat. He sat still.

The rejection of his touch emanated from a disregard of God's plan. Through music, friends' stories, and imagination, Sylvia ingested trace amounts of leaven from the edge of lies. It only took a little here and a little there to start an evolutionary change—a subtle, slow, imperceptible transformation ten years in the making. Now it impacted their commitment to each other and their vow to persevere as one for and in the cause of Christ.

Spiritual evolution proved an effective, widespread satanic tool. Very few in the church could see the inexorable march from the eternal toward the temporal, but spiritually weary visitors could. Those desirous of a life changing experience in church sensed something a little too familiar in an usher, deacon, or minister and muttered to the one seated next to them, "He's saved? She's saved?" before a discreet elbow pushed the wonderer into silence. In times past those not claiming Christ could tell by a look, "She's saved; he's saved," could tell by actions not taken, weekend places not visited, or when entered under the direction of the Lord, the stranger moved as pilgrim passing through, fishing, as it were, for souls in need of lifeline and hook. Cigarettes snuffed out, drinks hidden, and dance suddenly less suggestive because the Spirit of the Living God cast invisible lines of spiritual invitation tied to a hook of "Heaven or hell? You decide!" while the obedient fisherman never spoke a word.

That was then before the current understanding of freedom and grace blurred distinctions between saints and sinners and beclouded the radiance in ardent believers and anointed churches. Each at one time moved unfettered through the world under the protection of the Lord's wings. Now many believed more in what was seen. Desiring the deceitfulness of riches, many convinced themselves a life of ease was promised them. Churches and individuals joined the world, embraced its trappings, and ignored the weightier matters of judgment found in the last five verses of the twenty-second chapter of Revelation.

Church leaders approached ministry like project managers selecting personnel for time-sensitive projects. They took from God the responsibility of completing spiritual tasks that seemed to move much too slowly. They appointed talented people with proven track records in the workplace to the detriment of the more important move of the Spirit through work and workers ordained by the Father. Leaders preached the promise inherent in a David, but repeatedly opted for the safety the natural eyes read in the selection of a Saul. This transfer of responsibility from the Eternal Refuge to earthen vessels in Max's church reflected the shift away from the spiritual which is not seen to the natural which is, from the invisible that lasts forever to temporal things that yet once more will one day pass away.

Teaching abetted the shift. Preachers offered a malleable gospel with little discernible impact on contemporary life. Messages rarely became a scourge for the soul that needed one. Sermons overthrew no internal tables, drove no animals out of earthen temples, and spoke little of crown-worthy acts that last forever and much too often of those reflecting financial prowess that eventually fade away.

The more popular sermons avoided temporal and eternal comparisons central in understanding pure, unadulterated scriptural history. Few beyond the biblically literate came to see God as God and believed deep down in the city of their souls, for example, that by his Spirit a stone wall crumbled on the seventh day with a shout after six days of silence, and a red rope tied to a God-given promise saved an extended family alive because of an oath of secrecy concerning the whereabouts of spies. All this occurred through faith and waiting; no interpretation, no time, talent, or treasure could replace a willingness to follow and wait on a patient God who endorsed an unnatural tendency toward waiting.

God worked on the hearts of those in the army outside the wall wanting desperately to get in while he worked on the heart of a woman ruminating on the veracity of the promise "our lives for yours" inside the walled city waiting anxiously to get out. Because they waited as directed, a move from the throne of God made actionable through Joshua, two spies, and Rahab accomplished what God pleased and prospered, prospered in moving a waiting Israel closer to the prophetic promises of inhabiting land and bruising a serpent's head under heels. Inside the wall, the Lord drafted an unsuspecting woman in a spiritual war before she hid spies in a natural one. Most likely she never knew God wove her into the Messianic history of his Son who saves to the uttermost those who wait on him in cities and towns under the pall of darkness.

Waiting on God guarantees success because nothing can disannul or turn back his hand. Waiting apportions time for listening, an essential element of discernment. The faithful learn to wait and come to understand that forging ahead, tantamount to an army shouting on the fifth day and expecting seventh-day results, courts disaster. Two days too early or two days too late, any adjustment to a divine plan requires continual alterations to keep the work afloat. Crowded out, the Good Shepherd steps back until the sheep finally notice, admit error, and repent for moving too quickly, too slowly, or taking partners on a solitary assignment.

Max's church tinkered with its divine plan; it forged ahead in an attempt to build a church that doubled in size from the ordained vision. The revised blue print included a coffee house and credit union. Leaders sought ample space to keep pace with the changing needs of ministering to God's children. Lending institutions approved additional loans and bonds, resulting in the completion of the shell of the building and the laying of the subfloors. The church celebrated the progress and publicly attributed their good fortune to the favor of God, but appropriating the pace and adjusting the square footage proved costly.

The changes took the project out of eternal hands and placed it squarely in temporal ones, yet no one noticed the transfer took place or considered the staff called Favor had been broken. They seemed shocked initially when the building campaign suffered, and then reacted by soliciting more from their faithful. Church leaders asked congregants to dig deeper and more often into their pockets. Still, the church paid a price for its lack of biblical understanding. While some gave more, leaders could never call an end to giving as Moses once did. The funds never equaled or surpassed the rising monthly debt, and catering to desires more than ministering to the spirit, construction stalled. The amount failed to multiply as fish once did, as the bread did too when placed in the Master's hands and covered by a prayer of thanksgiving followed by breaking and distributing.

Many failed to understand the very contemporary lesson embedded in antiquity: God brings forth the impossible not by might, power, or any natural means available to the realm of creation. All is done by his Spirit, and while Egyptian magicians replicated the first two plagues wrought through Moses, they were clearly out matched and ill-equipped to reproduce plagues three through ten. A few spiritual feats are allowed duplication by effort and worldly knowledge, but most are not.

The progress in the construction of the church building stands as contemporary example that spiritual principles hold fast, and twenty-first century skills and knowledge cannot supplant the will of the Holy One. Each architectural decision amending the ordained plan pushed the spirit of Bezaleel further and further away until the flesh completely shut the spirit out, saying, "No thank you" to the anointing that oversaw the replication of the heavenly tabernacle on earth and the building of the Ark of shittim wood overlaid with gold, shunned the spirit that directed the construction of the blessed mercy seat of pure gold made by one in the shadow of God for worship in a most lowly, arid, harsh place. The shift to the flesh stood as a rejection of the Sovereign, a repudiation of his peculiar ways, and a belief the church given ample time would be completed through talent and treasure.

CHAPTER 3

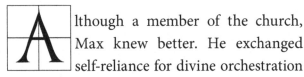lthough a member of the church, Max knew better. He exchanged self-reliance for divine orchestration during his sophomore year of college. While studying Arnold and pondering two worlds: one dead and one powerless to be born, Max gave it all to Jesus, and Jesus gave him life. While reading Nathaniel West, he agreed life was sometimes like a movie set, but Jesus could capture it on film, edit it, and turn it into something new, something award winning and worthy of a well done my son well done. "Jesus is the Everlasting Yea," he wrote in the margins while studying Carlyle and followed it with "Jesus is Lord."

In other texts deep down near the binding, he wrote longer scriptural messages, encouraging the future reader not to faint or give in to weariness. He admonished those tried with raging fire or bedraggled by torrential rain to run on because nothing could separate a child from the Father's love, not height or depth, not gain or loss. Nothing could, nothing.

At the end of the semester, Max sold those books filled with stealth witnessing and biblical aphorisms back to the bookstore with the hope that some soul in the semester to come who needed the stirring of water and the promise of change would find the path leading to both in the pages of the books. While he stood in the buyback line with books containing words of life within them, he noticed Sylvia. She smiled, and when he returned the smile, she spoke to him.

Pointing to her shopping basket of books she asked, "You wouldn't happen to have this would you?" She bent down and lifted up *The Complete Works of Shakespeare*. It took both hands. She pushed her basket along the floor using her foot when her line inched forward, and then replaced the massive text.

In the line across from Sylvia, Max pointed to himself and said, "Me?"

"Yes you."

With a smile he asked, "What makes you think I go for that sort of reading?"

"You're holding *The Collected Works of John Donne*. It's probably safe to assume you're majoring in English, and you've read Shakespeare."

He looked at the Donne text. The others he brought into the store lay piled in a basket he pushed along the floor with his feet. He struggled with parting with Donne. Donne provided a foray into holy sonnets and the most interesting conceits of enduring love. He held it in his hand as the internal debate between sell and keep continued.

"Nice powers of observation and deduction," he said to her. "I've taken courses that required the text, and yes, I still have it. It was one of the few I couldn't bring myself to sell back, but for you, if so directed by the Lord, I'll let you have it."

The church he attended in the Bronx emphasized waiting on the Lord for one's mate. "Wait!" they would say. "Wait on the Lord for your mate." He needed to gauge her reaction to his statement before pursuing a possible relationship and relinquishing that Shakespearean tome. The depth of her knowing Jesus remained buried under mystery that required uncovering through revelation and time, so he opted for a mutual kinship in Shakespeare right away. He quoted, "Love is not love/Which alters when it alteration finds,/Or bends with the remover to remove:/O no!" He got a smile instead of the next line, so he stopped quoting "Sonnet 116" and looked sheepishly at the John Donne text in his hand.

Donne offered insights through metaphysical poetry. If this, their union, were ordained to be, then eyes would lock and create a world all their own where love would be like a piece of gold beaten to airy thinness, stretching, stretching, stretching but never breaking or like a stiff pin compass, the pin on one arm and the pencil on the other joined at the top, and no matter how far the pencil roamed, it would never detach from the pin. "A Valediction: Forbidding Mourning" and "Sonnet 116" had much in common as he hoped he and she would in their love of Jesus.

"And what do you know about Abba?" she asked.

Smiling he said, "Well, I know he knows my name, and since you called him Abba, it appears he knows yours?" Max looked around, stepped toward her, and leaned in like a spy preparing for the exchange of classified information. She stepped over her basket, moved toward him, and leaned forward for his playful use of Deuteronomy 29:29. He whispered, "It's apparent that our names are secret things belonging at this time to God. Perhaps they might be revealed?"

She straightened up and laughed a little. "Perhaps," she said. Playing along she returned the smile and leaned forward. "Sylvia, Sylvia Black," she whispered.

"Max," he said smiling and thought of Donne's line "My face in thine eye, thine in mine appears" from the "Good-Morrow." He held onto Donne.

CHAPTER 4

His sophomore year was more than twenty years ago. While Jesus did not age, their marriage and Donne's metaphysical conceits once characterizing it showed the effects of aging. Graphing calculators and tablets usurped stiff pin compasses. The modern world dubbed Donne too esoteric and replaced his metaphors and conceits with less beautiful, less thoughtful, less weighty images of love. The fire fed by hand-in-hand walks around the school's lake, eyes locked together forming a private world, and voices from husband and wife raised in harmony as they drove hours to church gave ground to things and bills resulting from the acquisition of things that could do nothing more than fan embers of a waning fire, a condition far too common in treasure bearing couples.

A shaking from God years before the accident which now lay before them ignited the family move from New Jersey to the DC area. God pried them out of their first home and all it represented. Their gold-colored, split-level house backed to a yard that sloped upward. Its massive boulders eventually exposed by the cyclical beauty of trees unleaving year after year along with flocks of wild turkey, herds of deer, and the occasional wandering black bear until covered again in spring's green foliage. From the road it appeared the house sat atop a hill, but, in fact, it was ensconced in it and reached by a curving driveway flanked by moss covered boulders and rocks that gave way to a small lawn. The lawn followed the driveway to the one-car garage and gravel bed next to the house between the porch and garage. Max parked alongside the road in a parking spot in front of concrete stairs that once he crossed the driveway led to stepping stones in the lawn which led to the porch. When he turned toward the street before opening the front door and looked toward the car, only the roof was visible. He thought it the perfect house and yard for teachers, able to hold forty people the weekend they celebrated ten years of marriage. He needed little else, having moved from farmhouse in Long Island to ownership in New Jersey with his wife and two children. He was content, so God allowed upheaval with the promise of an end to it all, a churning complete with beacons bright and impossible to miss, pointing to a restored peace after the storm.

The heart of the storm rose inside the job he loved. Nominated for teacher of the year, Max turned deaf to his orders and chose spiritual stagnation over movement. The Lord wanted Max and Sylvia's gift elsewhere in his army, but wooed by temporal noise, they chose things over obedience. Neither truly grasped the idea that no being directed God. No one! No one made of flesh could weigh mountains and hills or measure the waters in the palm of a hand as he. The Lord took counsel only with himself. Neither challenged God in this. They had too much respect and had learned enough to avoid that inexperienced overt slight, but like many who stopped seeking God for direction and no longer declared through word or action that they were merely pilgrims on this earth seeking the divine city whose builder and maker is God, they missed his face without deliberate attempts to seek it.

When reading the Word of God neither asked, "Am I where you need me to be?" They failed to realize that their careers were intricately connected to the work of Christ, not separate. Subconsciously they turned the light of God up in preparation for Sunday service and dimmed the light of life Monday through Friday during work just low enough to negotiate the work world but not too low to be mistaken as worldly. Their current employers, church, and geographical location fulfilled God's expectations five years in the past. Satisfied, they ignored any communication about the Father's current plan, so God blew. He forced spiritual waters to churn and waves to roar. He blew on Max and Sylvia as one flesh, blew on the contentment and security with teaching and singing, and blew on the collegiality with colleagues and acquaintances until their contentment, security, and connections withered.

In the middle of the turmoil, Max and a colleague prepared for a weekend presentation in Washington, DC. Sunday while dressing for church, Max reminded Sylvia of his trek southward. Silently he thanked God for a day of reprieve, a little peace away from it all. He thanked Sylvia for getting the suitcase she stored.

"Where are you going?" Sylvia asked.

"DC," Max said, thinking it small talk around the capitol city.

"You forgot to tell me you were traveling so soon."

"I told you I was leaving Friday and coming back Saturday night."

"You didn't tell me."

"Yes, I did. I'm a teacher. Teachers rarely travel. I think you'd notice if I didn't come home Friday. You pulled the suitcase out for me." He looked at her somewhat perplexed. "What's this really about?"

"You didn't provide all the details." She dressed their youngest, a toddler, on their bed. "I wouldn't forget because I don't like it when you travel. I don't like being left in the house alone with the children. I'm afraid."

Max had no answer. As he looked rather puzzled at Sylvia, the enemy's camp watched them both. It noted the couple's handling of the storm to better target future attacks. It saw the value of hurt and fear as levers and recorded communication lapses between them.

The camp of darkness observed a yearning in Max for distance and clarity in the temporal when The Lord provided superior distance and transparency and was more than enough. These enemies noted Sylvia's sense of rejection fed by loneliness, and they exacerbated these feelings through anxiety surrounding Max's travel plans and the slight of friends. Notes captured the couple's carnal nature. Neither husband nor wife had any idea that the Spirit did not lead every facet of their lives or understood that he should. They had yet to engage in recursive spiritual reciprocity in which God's children privately offered struggles, fears, worries, all spiritual dross that only rose to the top as one walked closer and closer with the Consuming Fire who gave in return a cleaner heart, clearer sight, and rescue or sufficient grace.

Sylvia and Max gave to God, but they failed to give those secret things that accelerated spiritual growth. Although not lost by any means, neither fully engaged working out one's soul salvation with fear and trembling, using the light of Jesus to expose areas within not seen by the naked eye, and then allowing the Holy Spirit to cut out that which needed excising. Their bodies and souls still had their say. Desires needed taming; wills required breaking, and independence, rooting out. Christ had more to say to these warriors, but they could not yet bear it all. More awaited them in the spirit, and while much depended on wisdom and knowledge, much more depended on their transparency with God, on an anointing not predicated on any natural law of acquisition or extended study. The Sovereign simply chose whom he chose, a Samuel, a Barzillai, a Gideon, a Phinehas, a Deborah, a Micaiah. He required humility and "Here am I" from some and "What the Lord says to me that will I speak" from others sometimes preceded by a fleece test and other times accompanied by an offer of help, but always, always reflecting an "I will surely go with thee."

As deacon and deaconess, Max and Sylvia worked the prayer line near the end of service in their first church. He stood behind those receiving prayer, and she stood in front of them to the left or right of the minister. He caught them as they fell, and she draped prayer cloths over them once down. They joined elders and evangelists in the spiritual fight with silent prayer. However, on this Sunday at the height of the prayer line when both were needed, one of two evangelists working the prayer line called them over for prayer, together, as husband and wife, one flesh. The unusual timing of the request pulled them from their work, and reminded both briefly of the morning altercation they brought into the sanctuary with them. They entered quietly as they normally did, but the motivation feeding the silence did not engender reverence and expectation; it sullied it.

They looked quickly at each other. Then beckoning to the Spirit's lead, they stepped over bodies as they moved toward the one who called them. They stood in front of Evangelist Carter not as morning foes, one to travel and one to stay behind, but husband united with wife, holding four hands up in the natural and standing before the Lord with two up in the spirit. In the eternal, they stood as one, and readied themselves for a dialogue with *El Roi* who witnessed their morning conversation and chose the prayer line to address their current concerns. They stood with hands raised and eyes closed, and the Lord spoke a word.

"I told you not to worry about the money. I told you not to worry about the money. You know this," she said poking Max in the chest a number of times. Each poke from the evangelist took him back to the all-night prayer of New Year's Eve. Max never forgot those early morning words, but now he repented over the lack of faith surrounding finances in his home and his ineffectiveness in championing the message of the All Sufficient One made clear with "You know this."

Turning to Sylvia the Lord said, "But you have forgotten." The evangelist continued with the word from the Lord. "You will not be afraid when he travels because I will be with you, and I am more than enough! Indeed, Max will travel to take care of you. Your husband will travel for his job." The surprising word of knowledge forced eyes and brows to ask and answer the simplest nonverbal questions.

"Did you tell her?" eyes asked.

"No, did you?" brows replied.

It took the body and soul a moment to process, but the spirit knew the answer; it had no need to ask. The Lord spoke from his holy temple, and the spirit of husband and wife bowed down in reverent silence. Travel, the heart of the morning's conflict, was deprived of its edge because the omnipresent God intervened.

"Did you tell her?"

"No, did you?"

Evangelist Carter pulled Sylvia aside for private prayer while Max worshipped and waited. Once deacons guided Sylvia to the floor, the evangelist turned to Max. With fingers previously dipped in anointing oil now on his forehead and the other hand on his back, she began, "The Lord said you already know this, but you have chosen to resist his direction. You chose to turn left when he needed a straight path, so God will move you, and you will obey!" The thunder and authority in her voice made clear God's displeasure, but God plated the rebuke with a paternal love. "Difficulty awaits you two because you both hold on tightly to yesterday's blessing and ignore those growing out of my morning mercies. The familiar should be and will be behind you! This is a faith walk. You must walk it by faith, but know I will not leave you alone."

Evangelist Carter saw what awaited him on Monday, but the Father forbade disclosure or a prayer that the storm be averted. He permitted a prayer for strength. Like Jesus who prayed for a disciple who at the time stood confident and completely unaware of what it really meant to be sifted like wheat, she prayed for Max. She knelt down beside a slain Max after fellow deacons placed him on the floor. Granted a glimpse beyond Monday, she prayed and prayed over one already tossed about. She prayed that his faith fail not.

CHAPTER 5

Hosts of hell seized the opportunity to amplify the disquiet churning beneath the couple. Where the Lord purposed realignment through planned relocation, they aimed to bring Max to the brink of destruction, to marginalize him and drive deep within a desire for stability. They sought to shape a Christian who would send roots down deep, who would stay put and be grateful for anything the school conferred upon him from the bounty previously taken.

The school leaders had no idea darkness moved them to act as they did. Smarting from unwanted policy and curricular changes led by a team of three that included Max, they sought revenge at year's end within a short window of transition between an outgoing superintendent and an incoming one. Without a leader of their own to provide oversight and tighten reins, the principal and department chair eliminated a significant portion of Max's summer income when they removed him as summer school director on Friday, two days before the Lord reminded him not to worry about the money.

Monday, the day after he heard from God, the principal and chair called another meeting. He entered the principal's office and took a seat around the conference table. His department chair sat at one end, and the principal sat at the other.

Pointing at him she began, "The district created a monster in you, and you have forgotten your place." She paused. "I'm here to remind you of it." She read a letter aloud, and then slid it across the table for his signature. Her finger lingered on the letter a little longer than necessary to make clear the seat of power. "I'll have a copy placed in your mailbox later today and the original put in your personnel file," she said.

At the end of that meeting, he followed his chair to the English office for a private meeting where he received a forty-five-day notice. This reprimand would carry over into the new school year, and in education when most things September promised new beginnings, Max's after Labor Day start would be tainted by the previous year and would remain marred for weeks, turning his walk down the school's wide hallways into one on a balance beam that practically invited a slip leading to termination. The department chair placed the forty-five-day notice in his file. Walking out of the chair's office, he thought to himself over eight years in the district and not even a verbal warning, but in one day I signed two letters of reprimand.

Hosts of hell assumed that after an initial fight, Max would accept the verbal and written parameters for continued employment. In gratitude for kindnesses extended, he would remain ineffective in the ways of spiritual warfare, bind and loose in word only, and continue to embrace ambition as blessing. They assumed Max would avoid the appearance of discontentment, and live with the fear that even the perception of stirring trouble would abrogate the unspoken, soulish pact that if he behaved like one who had learned his lesson, he would be left alone.

Sylvia's life evidenced storm damage as well. Without warning or visible provocation, her closest friend from work ended their friendship. Sylvia's attempts at reconciliation failed. The friend rebuffed all advances, refused all calls, and answered collegiality at work with a cold professionalism. She offered no explanation at all.

As the divine induced storm grew in intensity, the demonic kept both under surveillance. Hosts of hell noted behavioral patterns and vulnerabilities in the spiritual walk of the two.

When they first met, they waited patiently for God's leading. Under the direction and power of God's anointing, they walked as one, but the current intense pressure exposed hidden vulnerabilities exacerbated by choices they made over time. During the storm, Sylvia moved inward and prayed silently. She would sing of God's goodness. "I've got a home, a building not made by hands." She sang of God's power. "Lord I don't know where, but I'm sending you there." The singing doubled as prayer. Dressed as song, she spoke to the Father publicly about the demise of a friendship without anyone noticing the personal nature of the song that doubled as prayer.

Max cried outwardly. He prayed kneeling, sleeping, and walking. He told God, family, and friends all about it, all about the wind and sea. He solicited their prayers and advice. The demonic watched as Sylvia turned inward and Max turned outward, and neither inquired about the source and timing of the storm.

While the Sovereign pruned Max, he never ceded him to storm. The wind and waves wrought by the Husbandman cut through roots of relationships, careers, and desires. God cut away dark roots that brought with them a false sense of security, a simple but effective lie that Max and Sylvia stood on their own and owed much to their hard work, education, and talent. The wind forced the realization of the need for a healthier attachment to the true vine, a need to look the storm in the eye and ask, "Lord, is this from you?"

Although the storm did not yield the right question, it wrought waiting on God, and the resulting patience brought with it a sense of peace as a viable buffer to the storm raging about. Once Max internalized the grossly undervalued command to wait on the Lord, the researcher who arranged the conference presentation called him and said, "I know someone who wants to hire you. I don't know much about the organization beyond what we gleaned during the conference, but they're interested in you. The director of the organization called me and wants to talk with you about employment. Call them tomorrow."

He called and arranged an interview for the following Monday. The director gave very little information about the position over the phone except that once created, it would require a great deal of travel, including a monthly visit to the west coast. "Think about a salary that feels right to you for this work," she said.

Twice my age he thought to himself immediately after the call and then again while at the dinner table with Sylvia, Mark, and Sarah. "Twice my age," he answered when Sylvia asked, "So what will you ask for?" Sylvia wanted to move to Virginia or further south when Max considered graduate school. The love of four seasons prevented his searching further south than Virginia, and the desire to escape the northern winters made any state above it a temporary option in Sylvia's eyes. "Twice my age" made the move a possibility.

Sunday morning they prepared for church and held onto the hope that Max moved according to the Lord's direction. During the prayer line, both Max and Sylvia took their positions to work as they had countless Sundays. While working on the prayer line with Evangelist Robinson, she waved him in front of the one standing for prayer. He moved forward, raised his hands, and closed his eyes. She then looked around for Sylvia. Finding her, she pointed until one working the line with Sylvia got her attention and pointed to the calling evangelist. Sylvia walked over and stood next to Max. He felt Sylvia join him. They stood side by side with bowed heads and hands held high again, but this week they stood on one accord to hear a word of confirmation or redirection.

When they settled in the spirit as one before the Lord, the word came forth. "Fear not, for I have made it so. You will travel from the east to the west to take care of your family. You will travel from the south to the north as I direct. The work will include both state and federal levels; they need to know who I am. Name your salary, and watch what I do." Max fell to the floor. She moved onto Sylvia. "I will be with you. If you walk up right before me and submit to me as sheep submit to their shepherd, I will withhold no good thing from you. Use the time Max is away to know me intimately. This is my will for the two of you." With that deacons guided Sylvia to the floor.

Knowing some of life's next steps as the storm dissipated comforted the two, but it also unnerved them with its unspoken message that the weighing of faith was not yet over for two groomed for and enjoying independence. The Lord's unveiling of next steps reinforced Jesus as Shepherd and Lord of his sheep. It reinforced the basic command to depend on the Lord, the only one who sees yesterday and tomorrow as today.

The words of the Lord did not alleviate the current financial strain although both were told not to worry about it, but worry they did. Sylvia tried to adjust the plan. She forgot God planted in Max the draw toward metaphysical poetry and satire and tilled his like of authors from Pope to Ellis. She forgot God made possible his experience as an adjunct lecturer at the university in Albany. Yet bills mounting confirmed within Sylvia that Max's destiny lay in university life, and working with public schools even through a nonprofit served as a detour that became a distraction for him. More, much more, remained hidden in Max. If no one else saw the untapped promise, she certainly did, and she found it difficult to heed the words of the Master.

"I married you for your potential," Sylvia once said to Max before they both gave up their careers to enroll in graduate school. He gave up on business, and she gave up on state politics. Each chose education. They knew financial struggle lay ahead for a while until they accepted jobs in their careers. Now nearly twelve years later with summer approaching, struggle once again appeared on their horizon.

She thought of a future stalled and dreams placed out of reach by two administrators determined to teach Max a lesson. She believed he needed prodding to move his vision beyond the high school students he so enjoyed. Sylvia thought to rekindle old dreams of a professorship before time rendered them an unrecognizable, dusty regret. As they prepared for bed, Sylvia found an agreeable way to tell Max that he, so full of promise, still came up short. "I think you need to go back to school. You need a doctorate," she said.

"You think so?" They took turns using the bathroom sink, he brushing his teeth, she removing make up, applying astringent, face cleanser, and moisturizer.

"Yes, I do. If you had a doctorate, if you continued with your dream, the one you had before we moved here…" She paused. Weighing the words of the evangelist, she brought forth a measured response. "When you taught at the university, you had your eyes set on a doctorate. Things would be easier for you, for us, if you had it. You'd be respected, and you wouldn't have to experience this craziness. A finger pointing at you to remind you of your place, you are so much more than that. You need the certification for administration." Looking at him through the mirror with a cotton pad in hand as she dabbed her face she said, "You should have the option down the line to be a professor if you like. There are a number of universities in DC. You could take a class here and there as you travel." She closed her eyes and bent over the sink while filling her cupped hands with water and rinsing her face. Dabbing her face with a towel, she looked at him through the mirror and continued, "A doctorate can only help you in the work in DC. All nonprofits like to have some employees with doctorates." She smiled.

Max returned the smile as he thought about the craziness and the divine orchestration behind it. Whether the Lord's hands stirred things directly or he gave Satan room to meddle remained unclear, but God's sovereignty, God as director and editor of their lives was undeniable to Max. They stood as one before two evangelists and received answers to less than public questions that only Sylvia, Max, and God could know. He wondered why after he scheduled an interview in DC that Sylvia dismissed the Lord's workings and his demand for dependence, blocked out the power and spirit behind budding rods, dismissed the exactness of the divine optometrist who touched for a second time one seeing men as trees, blocked out fire eating rock, and ignored the plan from the one who ordered life. She shut him out with an ill-bred boldness of an independent kind.

When first married she whispered menu orders to the wait staff at restaurants. Waiters and cashiers would lean forward, "Excuse me, Ma'am." Holy Ghost boldness meant little to Sylvia.

Max's family wondered about the quiet one beside him and constantly asked, "Are you ok? Would you like water? Is it too hot, too cold?" One never knew, was left unsure. Was it the food? The hug upon entering the house?

Now something rose up within and questioned direction from heaven. "He will travel to take care of you" dismissed as if a colleague proposed a preposterous lesson plan in a café over coffee. He rinsed his mouth. Placating Sylvia, Max promised to give the idea some thought. He walked to his side of the bed and climbed in it, but his mind refused to shut down. Although God shared his plans for them, Sylvia began a trip in the opposite direction. "No!" conveyed by a running Jonah guaranteed his story would be told and retold. Swallowed by a large fish, an unwelcomed rescue from a raging sea, Jonah spent three days and three nights in its belly wrestling strangling seaweed as his body remained unharmed by digestive enzymes. God waited for the right prayer and right spirit before the fish brought him up to complete the task previously refused. Jonah found out the hard way that a godly directive did not invite choice. God does not accept "No" when he delivers verbal instructions. Kicking against the pricks is futile. After denying the power behind hail, frogs, boils, and blood,

Pharaoh found the children of Israel would indeed leave Egypt in the face of his staunch "No!" The powerful leader learned that when God speaks, the only answer is yes and amen. Heart and mind racing, Max could not sleep.

Just before morning the Lord spoke through two dreams. In the first he found himself on the campus of his alma mater.

Pulling a suitcase with his briefcase attached to the handle, he walked against the flow of the pedestrian traffic across large squares of pebbled pavement that caused a rhythmic and predictable sound as he crossed each gap. It was noticeable. As the oncoming foot traffic increased in number as well as pace, he began to weave and dodge those walking against him. The rhythmic predictability disappeared, and then without warning he lost his grip on the handle. The luggage dropped to the pavement. He immediately turned around and tried to grab the handle, but it moved in and out of view as if the foot traffic moved it along the ground with its movement forward. When the traffic cleared, the luggage and computer case were gone. A long exhaustive search availed nothing. With eyes closed, he rested for a moment. Finally, Max settled down and sat upon a raised concrete slab and prayed. "Lord, I need your help." He calculated the costs of replacement clothes, luggage, computer, and computer case. He prayed hoping God heard. Once he reconnected with the Lord through total reliance and humility and then gave up his sight for God's, he opened his eyes to see the luggage and computer case on the ground where they had always been.

He woke up with a sense of relief having found something never lost and able to trust in someone who had always been there waiting, waiting until Max yielded.

Later that night, the Lord put an even deeper sleep on Max and confirmed *El Shaddai* as *El Shaddai*. He sent the second of the two dreams just before the morning.

Dressing for work, Max put on a button-down shirt, pullover sweater, and corduroys. Then he reached for hospital greens. He forced the hospital shirt over his sweater. Although he was able to pull it on, he could barely lift his arms. He reached for the hospital pants and struggled to put them on over his corduroys. With much effort he succeeded, but he could barely move his legs. He turned to look into the full-length mirror leaning on the wall and noted the spectacle staring back at him. He tried to make it work, but the evidence again was right before his eyes. As he said, "Sylvia wouldn't like this," he sat up. He kept the dreams to himself.

CHAPTER 6

Max made the trip to DC, and after a series of interviews, he noticed a number of employees writing and working hard although not rushed. It became clear that senior associates and principal partners at the nonprofit thought, problem-solved, and wrote. Few phones rang, and the teacher in Max constantly on the move wondered about the writing and thinking taking place. Before leaving the office, Max asked, "Just what do you folks do?"

"We get paid to think, and we have more time now to do that since school is out for the summer." With that he left with the charge to consider whether or not the job was a good fit for him since it required a week a month in Los Angeles and every Thursday and Friday in Philadelphia when not in California. He used the train ride back home to think about the job, knowing he would work little with students if he took it. His focus would shift to teachers, school organization, and state and federal policy as promised on a Sunday afternoon. A *rhema*, not additional schooling or a doctorate, positioned him to walk through the door God created. God, a single voice in the sea of many dispensing advice, created access.

There was little to think about. The storm realigned spirit, soul, and body, and it facilitated listening to God and following his plan. His walk needed more alignment for sure, but that would come through prayer, fasting, and walking more closely with the Lord. The interview confirmed what Max already knew. He would travel to take care of his family. The high school no longer had a place for him; school leaders made that clear. He would call with a yes to the offer and watch all unfold as Providence ordered. With his acceptance of the position came yes to a salary twice his age, and working in California with a partner nonprofit every month covered the cost of one fourth of his salary. This, the Lord had done. The God of Glory renewed hope, and Max praised the Lord.

Assuming travel apart from Los Angeles meant driving from city to city, Max and Sylvia decided to replace their three-cylinder hatchback with something more substantial. They believed they could make this decision without divine intervention, so they remained seated when the call, "It's prayer time" went forth across the pulpit. They chose to avoid the evangelistic duo that pierced mist and fog to reveal godly direction. All went according to plan, and they made their way to the basement after service to fellowship and share their relocation news. Deciding to skip the evening service, the two along with Mark and Sarah ascended the stairs to head home. As they reached the landing, the family ran into Evangelist Robinson.

"Well hello. You didn't work the pray line today," she said, looking from one to the other.

"No, we both decided to sit it out."

"Yes, I could see. It was noticeable." She paused and looked intently at them as if looking into them. "You can't avoid the Lord."

"We know. We thought that we'd sit and enjoy the incredible things the Lord has already sent our way."

"Three arrows in the ground should never be enough." She smiled as they looked at her. "Tell of his work."

While Max and Sylvia told their story, they realized that Evangelist Robinson had no recollection of any of the prophetic words given. They continued to fill her in and recounted the tag team nature of the evangelists' role in their changing lives. They assumed wrongly that absent the fire of the prayer line, they would control the conversation. While they spoke, the evangelist interrupted and asked a direct and simple question.

"Which one of you needs a car?"

They looked at each other. They ignore the budding inquiry, knowing there was more behind the simple question. Before leaving the house, they agreed to avoid hearing more. Sylvia and Max continued with the fulfilled nature of the words they received, and then Max provided a job description as he understood it.

When they finished their story and the visible wonder of God's hand in their lives, the evangelist not moved from her course said, "You didn't answer my question. I'm picking up in the spirit a conversation about a car. Who needs one?"

"The job requires a lot of travel."

"You still haven't answered my question."

"I have a three-cylinder car which most likely won't hold up to the rigors of travel."

Unmoved. She said, "Ok."

"We talked about getting a larger car, a four cylinder. I'm thinking of a used car. We'll have to sell our house, and then rent for a short time before buying one in the DC area. We don't need any new debt as we make this move." That last sentence crashed into the clear directive from the Lord not to worry about the money.

A man of words, Max heard the crash and cringed a little with the conclusion of his sentence. He knew that while Evangelist Robinson might not remember the word, God did. He gave it to Sylvia and Max along with "Name your salary, and watch what I do." Max saw the perennial pattern from the Red Sea to Marah, from manna to quail, from don't worry about the money to selling and renting. He thought of Hamlet's, "What a piece of work is man? What is this quintessence of dust?" For years he thought how could the children of Israel? How could they? If I saw the cloud, the hail, the parting of the Red Sea, one supernatural manifestation after another, I wouldn't have participated in the making of the calf, but the sound of his independent clause butting against a *rhema* about the job and seeing the proof unfold before him proved otherwise. So he paused.

"The Lord said get a new one; don't get used." She began to walk away, but sensing a spirit of independence within them, she turned around and looked both in the eye and emphasized, "The car is to be new." Then she headed down the stairs.

At home the two continued in silence. God heard the thoughts imperceptible to the natural ear, even those thoughts in the early stages of formation during the car ride home, thoughts that ignored the sound of the crash of his sentence into the immoveable directive given on the church landing. Their thinking betrayed the fact that neither learned to hear from God with both ears. Thoughts gave away unspoken secrets, told on them to God that neither learned fully to trust the words that entered the spirit, that neither will gave obeisance to the Master's.

Max broke the silence and gave birth to the unspoken. "The Lord confirmed that we need a car, but I think I'm going used. New for a teacher during the summer, I don't know; I think that was flesh talking." They willingly accepted God's directives concerning the job in DC with its travel across the country and the need for another car, but they chose to believe that the deliverer of the word misspoke. She got the car part right, but not the year. Sylvia sighed in relief as Max revealed her monetary fears as his concerns. Sylvia followed the heavy sigh with a deep breath in which a haunting loneliness joined as stowaway and quickly began to rework the assurance created by God's promise, "I will take care of you when he travels." Loneliness turned into a deep emptiness dressed as good sense. It posed as a natural substitute for complete utter trust.

Max should have remembered the words only came through Evangelist Robinson; they were not her words. They came from The One who could premier a thought picture of what is to come, not what one could afford. Sylvia should have known that the words came from the Lion of the Tribe of Judah who could tame hell within, settle a stomach, and realign a digestive system without a noun, without an article, without one superfluous word. The car's description limited only by verb and adjective, "Get new," was more than enough. When God spoke the scale of the directive did not matter. National or local, it was never partial and never included the word but.

The Lord had a plan for their lives, all four of them, and God revealed enough to realign the adults since their eyes adopted as anchors what their salaries afforded them. Too much revelation banished faith, an essential requirement for a just life. The storm put them back on track and led them again to hope, the true anchor of the soul, but the silence broken by Max proved that while the two Christian soldiers were on track once again, they were not totally sold out.

CHAPTER 7

Work began immediately in July. Max drove to DC and stayed in hotels around the city through Wednesday each week when not in California. He drove to Philly Thursday night and returned home Friday evenings in his four-cylinder used car. Sylvia stayed in New Jersey with Sarah and Mark through Thanksgiving, the deadline she gave herself for moving south if the house remained on the market. Max thought best to accept the self-imposed deadline. When the house did not sell, neither asked, "Lord, is this your doing?"

Renting in July reflected faith, a dependence on the Lord absent contingencies or any assumptions that his plan needed adjustment. It acknowledged God controlled finances, and Max and Sylvia trusted God to oversee theirs. Both failed to realize that partial acceptance of the Lord's plan was in essence a rejection of it and a lack of total surrender. The decision to disobey the directive about the car opened a spiritual portal in which darkness entered as host to two-thirds the inhabitants and began service with a spirit of independence as appetizer. Both ate the familiar dish, and Sylvia's decision to move the family in November allowed the host to serve soul and body an entree of rebellion since God made his plans clear Sunday after Sunday. He emphasized that he would take care of family and family finances.

Max ready to live in the DC area walked with one reluctant to join him there, one who then dined on sides of loneliness, imagination, and fear.

The demonic knew the futility of a direct assault on any plan the Master laid out. The two as destined by the Lord could get back on course in the location of God's choosing and rear godly children destined to deliver more damage to Satan's kingdom than blows resulting from the inconsistent walk of their parents. As Jacob followed Isaac, as Elisha followed Elijah, as John followed Elizabeth— the coming work promised greater returns than that which proceeded it if all (mother, father, brother, sister) stayed on plan.

Although both would have denied it, in the spirit Max and Sylvia still required milk along with solid food, but the time would come when the Lord of All would demand more of Max and Sylvia. They had benefited so much in the spiritual realm through teaching focused in the centrality of the death, burial, and resurrection, a simple gospel that remained sincere year after year in its focus on the exchange that took place on the cross. God gave keys: prayer, fasting, and faith and numerous examples of the power of each, how they moved him, how he dispensed angels on behalf of his children, how he gave unlikely battles to his own, and how he required a much higher, more sophisticated continual combined use of prayer, fasting, and faith over time. Nevertheless, with Sylvia and Max, indulgence encircled prayer, and doubt posed as common sense from time to time once they left college and even more so when they moved from New Jersey and attended two churches in Northern Virginia.

The area had no shortage of anointed churches, but the two simply grew weary in their search and never asked, "Lord is this church the one?" Though they prayed for a church, the short list attended included those serendipitously found as opposed to the one God had for them. They landed in two houses of worship where their spirits suffered from the unequal yoking of acquaintances and kind people who had a zeal for God but did not know God deeply. They acknowledged the ill-fit of their first church in Northern Virginia after Sylvia told Max the pastor wanted Mark and the other children to teach bible study. Max said, "No," believing a bible study taught by his fourth-grade son or any child not clearly identified by God was unthinkable.

"Then you tell the pastor," Sylvia replied.

"Sure."

That night the Lord gave Max a dream. The simple dream ended almost as quickly as it began. Sitting on the edge of the bed, he pieced it together in the morning. He recalled Elder Williams from the church in the Bronx appeared in the dream. He remembered a fruit basket sat on a credenza at the end of a hallway. Walking toward the basket, Elder Williams asked, "Any oranges?" When they reached the basket, they found it was empty. He remembered they looked at each other in surprise before Elder Williams said, "I think the basket needs fruit."

Later in the day he told Sylvia about the dream. Both were perplexed. He prayed over it, but received nothing.

Wednesday, immediately after bible study, Max met with the pastor to say that Mark would not teach bible study.

"I believe the children need to be brought up in the Lord and studying at home to deliver a message in bible study is the way to go here," she said.

"That sounds interesting, but my son will not participate, and when the young children teach bible study; we'll stay home."

"This is my church and the vision the Lord gave me. Are you telling the Lord no?"

"Not at all, I'm telling you no. I expect the one teaching me in church to know more than I do. I think that's a reasonable expectation. I'm a teacher, and asking students to teach a lesson or two is an effective strategy, but this is the Word of God. It's not based on interpretation but on study and revelation. That can't be crammed a couple of nights before the delivery. Generally one needs years of listening to the Lord and reading God's Word before entering the pulpit for Sunday service or bible study. That level of intimacy with the Bible is too much to expect from a child in the fourth grade not explicitly chosen by the Lord for the task. I'm one hundred percent behind the young speaking and presenting a message during evening programs after church or special weekly programs, but I can't stand behind their speaking during church service or bible study."

As Max spoke he thought of Elihu, how in God's reprimand of Job's accusatory friends, he, the youngest, was never mentioned by God, never called out for pretending he heard from the Lord. The lack of acknowledgement spoke just as loudly as did the Lord's singling out the elders.

"If this is not the place for you, then you can leave, but God is here, so be careful if you choose to leave," the pastor said.

"Thanks for the warning," Max said as he rose and walked to the door to meet up with Sylvia and the children. He continued, "Most of us will be shocked on the other side when we find out some we thought wouldn't, make it in, and some we thought would, don't. Granted, my statement assumes we'll recognize each other in heaven though many believe otherwise, and you may be one of them. If so, take the spirit of the comment. Even if we recognize each other, we'll be so carried away with the centerpiece of our affection it won't matter. Anne Ross Cousins' beautiful hymn about sand and time, you know it. We are our Beloved's and he's ours. We will care little about garments and crowns and glory—the stuff that preoccupies so many down here—but we'll look on the King of grace, taking in the Bridegroom's unveiled face. Seeing the pierced hands, nothing and no one will distract us there. I'm hopeful that when I come to church I'll get to eat fresh fruit like the wisdom of Cousins, and it will sustain me when I leave until back again for more." He thought of his dream and paused slightly. "There's something about age and wisdom; the young generally have moments if God grants them, bursts if you like, but the moments are hardly enough to sustain a sermon or bible study." Finished, Max left.

After his meeting, the meaning behind the fruit in his dream became clearer, but like many Christians, Sylvia and Max had not quite learned to hear from the Lord in a way to make sense of cryptic dreams or wait patiently in silence during and after prayer until the Lord talked back and then bade them move. Max and Sylvia, willing to find a new church prematurely and end their work based on feelings, had not sufficiently crucified flesh to move spiritually into the eternal and benefit from the fullness of a holy relationship where he who knows tomorrow ordered their steps today. The ordering could appear whimsical for those needing but not getting a subsequent because clause. "Go here because if you don't, tomorrow.... Pray this right now because an ocean away a soldier.... Gird up your loins at this time because in three years you will...." For those unable to hear directions for an immediate and essential task, God sent a peculiar treasure who carried his message, one instant in season and out and not swayed by a voice or a look, one who could dispense pleasantries and reproofs cities, states, and oceans away without adding or taking away from his directions. These soldiers waited before the Lord and remain open to his voice throughout the day. No need for the because clause to spur movement; they acted as directed. They boldly and assuredly pick up the phone not knowing what would be said as they dialed, believing that a message not yet received would come their way and the call would not end before "Thus says the Lord" for those not spiritually aligned.

God weighed in on the duration of Max and Sylvia's stay through a call from Evangelist Carter.

"Hello."

"Sylvia. This is Evangelist Carter. How are you?"

"Doing well. We were just talking about you the other day and our move to the DC area. How are you?"

"I'm good. I'm calling because the Lord has a message for you. He's not told me what it is yet, but I'm to give it to you and Brother Max. Where's Brother Max?"

"Max!"

"Yeah!"

"Pick up the other line. It's Evangelist Carter."

Max knew a message was forthcoming. He wondered, even worried a little if he was out of line after bible study.

"Hello."

"Hi, Brother Max. How are you?"

"Fine. What's going on?"

"I have a message for you two. Now that you're on the phone the Lord is telling me you had a dream you've not been able to figure out. I'm seeing a fruit basket. What did you dream?"

"Just that, an empty basket on a counter and then Elder Williams asked, 'Where's the fruit?' He followed with 'the basket needs fruit.' Then I woke up."

"Hmm. How's church going?"

"Not so well. We most likely will not be going back."

"The Lord said you are to go back, and you'll stay there until he moves you, which he will do, but now is not the time to leave. You two know much, and since you chose that church without asking him, you have to share some of what you've learned over the years and be open to what the Lord reveals about the church to you. You've not been open to hearing him, and he needs you both to listen."

"But, they don't like us. They think we think we know everything, so it's not the church for us. We're not getting fed. They even wanted Mark to teach."

There was silence on the phone.

"The Lord said there are times in which you feed. He said you're right. Some don't like you much, but we're not in this walk to be liked. You two should know that. Popularity should never be a factor when the Lord has made plain his plan. You two signed on to do his work. He never said it was easy. When you leave it will not be a smooth break at all. Your presence threatens many there, and they'll talk about you and start trouble, but the fact remains that at this moment, the church's basket is empty. While you two have some of what it needs, many will not appreciate that you do. They'll see your value once you're gone. Anyway, you can't leave until God releases you. God says that he'll let know when that time comes."

CHAPTER 8

"They don't like us" revealed flesh ruled spirit and prevented Sylvia and Max from seeing the future work of their young children as targets. In the Bible some attacks on parents were strategic weapons designed to stunt progeny's work, to bring an end to the lineal fight or at least minimize future damage godly seed were destined to inflict on Satan's kingdom. Very few understood this; their thoughts sullied by the spiritual parlance of the day such as the devil tried to keep me from my destiny, and he should have killed me when he had the chance obscured this reality. The sentiment and use of the first-person possessive did not reflect a denial of self and the picking up one's cross essential for heavenly assignments here on earth.

This dark trick, this most subtle entrapment that encouraged Christians to focus on themselves moved an inexhaustible spiritual power meant for expansive work into the narrow field of wants and feelings. Milk behavior so long after receiving the spirit of adoption left them spiritually exhausted with little to show from any expenditure of talent or time.

Mark and Sarah were to see their parents work selflessly. See Max pray prayers that touched heaven's door and wrought deliverance on earth. They were to see their father as all others in the congregation should, praying and laying hands with the expectation of evidence: a sign, a wonder. They were to hear Sylvia sing with a voice steeped in humility that reached heaven's throne and offered itself like a cloud to seat Jeshurun who moved in majesty and power, driving the enemy out before his own, the beauty of her voice realized through obeisance to the Spirit that rode upon it saying, "Destroy him!" Praying and singing needed no earthly audience. Praying like preaching was meaningless if bloated with enticing words of man's wisdom and singing useless if appareled in flesh. Mark and Sarah would learn singing and praying under the anointing brought deliverance. It sunk deep within the soul, and then exploded into light that destroyed dark strongholds. They would come to understand that a beautiful voice absent anointing was merely a beautiful voice and with a little luck might leave its signature pressed on a compact disc or digitally recorded for streaming and downloads, a beautiful voice for posterity of which the world and the church had many, voices that left nothing which impacted eternity. Mark and Sarah were to see their mom and dad working in tandem, see the harvest basket that housed evidence of their labor overflowing with the production of fruit, and note that who God put together no one was to pull apart, that under the anointing the work of two who became one was a force.

Much depended on their training. What they did or did not see and how each learned to prepare in the spirit before offering a sacrifice. What did their dad do before he taught or prayed? What did their mom do to ready herself to minister through song? When did the preparation with prayer and fasting start? Hours, days before? Did it ever end? How should one live publicly and privately months before offering a sacrifice to God? The two along with all other children attending church would confront any manner of worldly diversions meant to derail them as they traveled a course designed by God and watched their parents and other adults live godly lives as they carried light before men.

The enemy assumed Mark's years of lessons would lead to playing the piano in church, and Sarah's nightly routine of books on the floor as she studied artifacts, paintings, and literature since elementary school might place her on the teaching end of the spectrum. If they stayed on God's paths, there was a limit to what Satan could change, but he could affect how well the gifts ministered based on their relationship with the Holy Spirit or the level of carnality in the church. His two-pronged attack of darkness directed at the child and darkness festering in the environment increased the odds of elevating flesh to hamper spirit, ensuring music and insights offered would not minister or that which did landed in an arid atmosphere in a fleshy church.

The phone call gave Sylvia and Max a nudge for work today and the mentoring of workers today for a harvest measured tomorrow. While the parents could not see this, Satan suspected as much. Experience taught him present disruption sometimes derails tomorrow's promises. He taunted Hannah to break the lineage pointing to one yet to be born who would abide before the Lord forever. He entered Korah. He reminded Nazarenes Jesus was a local son. He clouded Jesse's sight in an attempt to prevent the selection of a shepherd destined to pen songs and poems for readers not yet born who would battle despair, failure, and loneliness. He drew Demas. There was always a chance through misdirection, always. The devil sought to stunt the destinies of Sarah and Mark. He could limit the demonic wreckage each would exact on his kingdom by ripping in two the spiritual scroll that first appeared the morning Max and Sylvia said, "I do."

Satan would turn off the light as it were. He would eventually end Mark and Sarah's reading of the epistle mid-sentence with Mark fully situated in adolescence and Sarah approaching its threshold, but for now he would wait. While Max and Sylvia's unified yes and amen to God's immediate demands appeared sound and created a pathway for

Sarah and Mark's individual yes and amen to God's army, he would exhibit patience. He knew the unfolding body of the parental letter foreshadowed but had not yet realized the conclusion written in light and the salutation, the salutation of the best of their marriage wine only appearing toward the end of their journey as godly libation, a drink offering to the Lord if I remained interlocked with I over the decades and their voices spoke as one at the finish line to say, "I have finished my course." Foreshadowing it currently was that he, the father of lies, targeted to be edited out.

Chapter 9

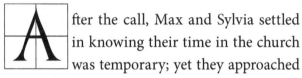fter the call, Max and Sylvia settled in knowing their time in the church was temporary; yet they approached the work there as if the stay were permanent until Sylvia received a phone call while Max was in California.

"Sylvia, can I talk to you later today?" the pastor asked.

"Sure. I'm at home. What's this about?"

"Well, I want to talk to you about the children and how you two are raising them."

"I don't understand what you mean."

"I'm not sure you two are raising them to love the Lord and be sold out for him."

Ire began to rise in Sylvia. The previous conversation that involved the children almost caused Max and Sylvia to leave the church prematurely, and this conversation promised to do the same. "And you gathered information about our approach to rearing the children from...?"

"We'll talk later; what time works for you?"

Later never came. When Max entered the house after a week in California, Sylvia said, "We no longer go to that church." Max went along with the decision in spite of a godly dream shrouded in mystery and interpreted through a messenger who explained the Father's plan and emphasized his will.

When commanded to stay, they chose to leave. When directed to impact the lives of Christians in a young church of their choosing, they ignored the divine directive and held the cuttings prepared for grafting and the eventual production of much fruit that would fill an empty basket. The "We no longer go to that church" reeked of stubbornness and said, "No" to the Lord. Responding negatively to a divine directive shifted their anchor from hope back to things where Max held on steady to what he had, and Sylvia sought what she thought she lacked.

No edited the living letter with darkness. It replaced peace with evil, stunted a future, and revoked hope. Satan camouflaged the exchange through the pretense of helping others. It began with a call from Sylvia's estranged friend. The call shocked them both although they were happy to receive it because neither asked when the soul tie was cut in New Jersey, "Lord, is this your doing?"

It became the pattern that Max or the children answered the phone and turned it over to Sylvia. The calls were sporadic at first, but soon increased in frequency and length until darkness prepared caller and called for the giving and receiving of the news. Sylvia's former colleague sought a divorce. No infidelity, no drunkenness, no abuse involved, the marriage of over twenty-five years now described as a relationship no longer felt right. With mothering redefined by college, Sylvia's friend found marriage stifling. It gnawed at her sense of self since no longer militated by mothering a child in the home.

The caller required and expected more and more advice to navigate the ordeal, and never claiming a personal relationship with Christ beyond church attendance and grace over meals, the calls to Sylvia elicited less and less prayer when off the phone and never any direct line to the Father while on the phone. Then one from the music ministry called. Darkness framed the discussions, ensuring little to no prayer coverage over the caller to stay the grip of marital distress when on the phone and fewer and fewer prayers when off the phone.

As landlines gave way to cell phones, the role of husband and children in the "it's for you" handoff disappeared. With a direct line to Sylvia, callers and calls increased. Driving to work, at work, and driving home after work, Sylvia counseled. Doing laundry and watching cable, she advised those in need. The Bluetooth earpiece meant both hands free and the opportunity to talk comfortably when cleaning or playing Sudoku. Ascending the stairs from the garage, the phone demanded her attention. Descending the stairs to the garage, she held consultations. Before choir rehearsal and after, Sylvia listened, and then dispensed marital advice. Initially with a passion to save marriages, Sylvia eventually counseled with a heart to help the callers find themselves through their marriage, find their resolve as some purposed in their heart and soul to tear apart what God put together years ago. Darkness ensured well-intentioned conversations never crossed the boundary that separated eternal and temporal advice.

Church, counseling, and work kept Sylvia busy and contributed to spiritual exhaustion. With Tuesday bible study, Thursday choir and praise team practice, Friday night classes, and all-day Sunday worship including evening services, members saw a committed servant. Max and the children saw one who complained of exhaustion. At times, Max and the children would answer Sylvia only to find out she never asked them a question. She spoke to someone on the phone.

They invited her to join the family fun as she passed by the kitchen coming up from the garage. "You want to play a board game with us?"

"Not now," she would tell husband and children. "Not now, I've a lot to do." She turned her attention back to the one on the phone, and walk heavily up the stairs unaware that she courted exhaustion, that if God were the travel agent of her current path, he would build in breaks for the body and spirit; he would include time to shut down and rest. God would drive her over "to the other side" away from class and work, away from the phone and earpiece. Instead Monday through Friday she worked, counseled, studied, and counseled some more. Saturday, she doled out advice and studied. She failed to realize her exhaustion was linked to losing faith in the union God sanctioned.

CHAPTER 10

Satan swept through the music ministry without opposition. Not one with a collar rose to say, "Who God has put together, let no man put asunder, the Lord has spoken." No one stood as bulwark to say, "Thus saith the Lord, don't marry him or don't marry her. The marriage will ruin your music ministry." Not one. Two of the more stable members of the praise team divorced spouses before joining the team, and then left the group and church amicably to marry pastors in different cities. The spirit of divorce followed as unseen dowry in need of maturation before embracing a new church home, but the harvest was ripe in Max's church. Two tenors separated from their spouses, the base guitar player his wife, a camera woman left by her husband, an usher divorced by his minister wife, and on and on with teachers, elders, singers, laymen, and evangelist revealing the not so hidden cost of a church eager to modernize its ways.

The acceptance nearly imperceptibly replaced the living spring with stagnant water in need of agitation by stellar singing, liturgical dancing, and rousing preaching. When the door opened and who opened it was never a concern since few knew a door existed and served as gateway for the switch. Max thought little of when, how, and who. To him it mattered that the door remained opened, not that the pastor unknowingly wove an invisible snare of foolish and hurtful lusts when he told his daughter divorcing her first husband, "Take him for everything he's got." It mattered that Max's marriage began to crumble under the sheer weight of the open invitation. But who actually did matter, for the body follows the head in word and deed. "The door was opened by a minister high up in the organization," a New York pastor told Max when he visited the church. "Demons have gained control of your wife, but you didn't fight in the spirit to stop them." The pastor continued, "God is not pleased with you for this."

Max was not alone in his spiritual malaise, so few fought with weapons able to pull down strongholds. Contemporary leaders understood and accepted the costs of growth. Ministers studied and taught from books on effective leadership and preached on the change process. They invoked metaphors involving red wagons and yellow buses, passengers and drivers. Although behavioral science displaced more and more of the Word in sermons and deliverance yielded to counseling, the shift from the eternal to the temporal was hardly evident.

Max, Sylvia, and the church packed away their spiritual banner. The church put away its admission of unabashed, total surrender to God and lowered hands in the spirit, exposing itself to the spirit of Amalek. Where once members sang, "I'm a Soldier in The Army of the Lord" and lived it, attacking in the spirit with hands and the rod of the Lord held high, Max and Sylvia like so many in their church laid down helmet, sword, and shield and reneged on praying coverage for watchmen and those on the frontlines. The pastor did not intercede, did not stand in the spirit with weary arms held up by the prayers of a spiritual Joshua or Hur. The pastor simply accepted the devastation wrought by darkness and allowed the invisible warriors to swarm upon his congregation like a plague of locusts on crops, those ripe and those young, tender, and so full of promise.

Satan plowed through leaders who should have been resolute in their commitment to family to reach congregants who believed the house of worship they chose an ark of safety. Dark spirits glided through aisles and churned the ground as they moved among seats in the absence of spiritual covering. No invisible wall of defense prevented their brazen entrance or restrained their movement once inside. No angels stood guard because they were simply not asked to do so and therefore not charged to do so.

With an eye on Mark and Sarah, Satan placed the idea in Sylvia that her current life or more precisely her marriage barred self-determination and stymied her sense of self. He easily wiped from memory the attraction to musicals that led to enrolling in an acting class in New York City; Sylvia never auditioned after the course ended. The enemy edited from memory the desire to sing professionally for the Lord. He pushed just behind automatic recall Sylvia's cassette tape recording of herself singing the female part of a chart-topping duet. Encouraged by Max, she entered the contest with hopes of winning a chance to sing with the male artist during the concert. Although the concert promoters chose someone else, Sylvia continued to hope, continued to dream as she delivered anointed leads for the choir in the Bronx. A recording artist invited Sylvia to sing as part of a large choir he put together for a live recording. After the album's release, he whittled down the choir to a handful of sopranos, altos, and tenors. Sylvia made the cut, but she refused to travel.

The search moved from ministry to career. She enrolled in a medical transcription course. After the course, the machine sat unused until it became obsolete. Real estate complete with course and fee tossed after five months in the business. Satan convinced Sylvia this never-ending search for the right ministry and career resulted from an unfulfilled Christian duty to support people through listening and providing advice.

She now believed God's ultimate plan for her never included the heartfelt gift of song, and the current church believed this too. Satan erased from memory the connection between her voice and the anointing that fell in their church in the Bronx once she closed her eyes, removed self, and yielded to the Spirit. Deep down within the enemy called into question yokes broken as she once ministered through song. He made sure the current church never tapped that anointing, but fed the congregants' craving for showy voices and vocal gymnasts who delivered rifts that entertained the flesh, soothed the soul, but left the spirit flat. Absent the outlet of anointing, Sylvia's soul sought a sense of usefulness as doubts grew that her voice ever rose with anointing, that her lyrical delivery ever resulted in anything more than a building full of emotion.

Though the singing never stopped, the Northern Virginia church failed to tap the gift of song within her, and this led Sylvia to believe that singing provided cover, a hovel for hiding from the more difficult work of deducing issues buried within some since childhood and using the love and grace of God to set those captives free. Counseling she believed was God's plan for her life, not singing. Marriage and family responsibilities hid this, and singing kept her sated, busy, and off track. She dampened the desire to sing and gained control over that need rising out of the inner man to open her mouth as if directed and led by some other power. Dispensing advice provided friends comfort, a needed respite delivered through spoken words that she called up from the inside. Sylvia learned that she could do without the expectation of yoke-breaking song.

Then the enemy suggested to Sylvia that Max who traveled far too often to take care of wife and children on the departure side of the flight kept a strange woman on the arrival end of the monthly cross-country visits. With the enemy's deception accepted, Sylvia found she could do without Max. She reconnected to siblings and family friends from her youth who thought her a victim of brainwashing by a husband who believed God demanded a different lifestyle than the one she embraced as a child. She gave up drink and adopted a genre of music to the near exclusion of all others, including the music she sang and danced to as a child.

Siblings thought Sylvia an active member of a cult. They believed she lost her identity when she joined the church in the Bronx. Then she married Max, and she gave up even more of herself to keep him. They believed the Lord never required all that Sylvia relinquished. Manoach's wife who carried and reared a judge saw an angel before renouncing drink. Sylvia saw no angel and carried no Nazarite. In their eyes, she had no contemporary foundation that the call on her life required turning down rum and carrot juice, beer or Bailey's. She had no need to embrace an austere life removed from such earthly pleasure. Mark was no Sampson, no John the Baptist and Sarah no Esther, no Deborah. Max erected a wall and kept Sylvia separate from family in their eyes and now in hers. It was he who stood in the way of frequent familial visits. Sylvia had no legitimate need to pull away from brothers and sisters; it was better to pull away from Max and remove antiquated distinctions between those called elect and those not.

Her siblings ate what they wanted and remembered as a young child she did too. They willingly gave up what she once had trouble digesting during high school and college. Being able to eat pork and beef was not a blessing at all, and they left Sylvia to wonder why one might be delivered to digest that which she and her family deemed unhealthy. By one's own volition, such meat should be shunned if one wished a long and healthy life. While alone with the children, the enemy suggested that her life was not her own, but it could be, and she listened. Having given him access, she leaned toward his voice to the exclusion of the Lord's.

She had given up much for her husband. She left a cold, lonely city she did not love and wanted to leave to move closer to her adolescent home in the Bronx all because of a job opportunity for Max. Satan convinced Sylvia she moved, left all behind for her spouse. He blotted out that God gave her a job teaching which she enjoyed more than the one in Albany. For Max she moved to New Jersey, and then for him she moved to Virginia. She gave up a life in New Jersey she did not crave for the more moderate clime in Virginia, a place that met her warmer sensibilities away from the constant promise of snow if not snow itself. Once a mutually agreed upon target destination when Max considered a doctorate, it was now tainted by him, a move controlled by him and only for him. With the enemy's help, Sylvia convinced herself she once again gave up something they both agreed held nothing for them. The enemy soiled their decision with the thought of too much one-sided sacrifice, the notion that only she submitted, not Max, that only she lost herself to yet another move while he gained. Sylvia refused to believe that a plan in the spirit for half a married or betrothed couple was a plan in the spirit for both, that Sarah walked with Abraham, that Zacharias was silenced until he wrote upon a writing tablet acceding Elizabeth and Gabriel's selection, that Joseph fled with Mary visiting a number of provisional places until the Lord settled them in Nazareth.

CHAPTER 11

Sitting in traffic with no one to talk with, Max's mind jumped to the choices he made, the sacrifices for family which seemed to matter little now. He left the organization that brought him to the DC area primarily to support Mark who stumbled academically. When Mark's academic performance stabilized, the economy faltered. The money schools used to support their work with independent consultants disappeared. Max worked very little, but led by the Lord, he advised the afterschool student-led Christian club at the high school. He hoped the depth of the relationship he experienced with God in college might be replicated to some degree in the young he advised once a week after school, and to some degree it was. He thought of a word given to him from one of the students. "The Lord said, 'Don't you stop running, Brother Max; keep on running,'" the student said.

He sat behind the steering wheel knowing that he stopped running like his life depended on it. He settled for contentment and lost the spiritual edge that began to surfaced again with the students in the after-school club. God admonished him through a member to keep running, to remember that he and Sylvia were once members in a church that fought with prayer, the name of Jesus, and his blood before they traveled from Northern New Jersey to Northern Virginia to join a church extremely active in advancing a kingdom of God here in the flesh. Now they sat holding hands in traffic caused by a wreck ahead because neither could invoke the excuse of church busyness to get away.

Looking ahead for the cars involved in the accident Sylvia said rather mechanically, "Thank God. We have not lost our savor. For if the salt...." They looked at each other. In a moment of fear Sylvia grabbed his hand, but after her rendering of Scripture, she let it go and looked deliberately forward leaving him to focus on the word, "savor."

The two had not been jettisoned like ineffective salt. Tare or wheat, he could not say, but God's mercy granted another day. Max looked at Sylvia as the voice from the MP3 player became noticeable. She still looked forward. How long had they been driving for him to miss the entire book of Malachi, which included the well-known controversial verses on robbing God and loving Jacob, lesser known verses he knew on shutting the door and refusing to kindle fires in vain, and the verses he did not know that spoke to the Father seeking godly offspring. This was a tall order for a shaky marriage. Life overshadowed the hearing of it, so once again an important spiritual truth of families in Christ was missed.

Although he heard none of the verses delivered from that even keel voice providing an interesting backdrop for the accident, he decided the book of Malachi still counted. After "Surely I come quickly" followed by the final "Amen," he would be able to say he listened to the entire Bible this year. He was ahead of schedule with the transition from Old Testament to New Testament amid crash and mayhem. Surely God understood his lack of concentration as the MP3 player moved from Malachi to Matthew. The dispelling of the hand weeks ago and the unfolding of the accident moments ago would be reason enough for a reasonable God.

As Max focused in on the words of Jesus with hands held, hands dropped, and all the symbolism imparted, hope grew. He appreciated the focus Matthew demanded. One worked through parable and metaphor for a nugget of meaning, a revelation unearthed out of secret things. He settled in needing a washing, a renewing of the mind that surely the red words spoken audibly could provide. Already the accident resulted in a touch from Sylvia. A hand tossed one week and clutched another. He believed God moved to shore up their tenuous territory, and the spoken words of Jesus would seal those gains.

But the unstoppable Word moved ever forward beyond the lame walking, daughters healed, and blind seeing. The reader marched on through wine in old wine skins and plentiful harvests and a search for worthy laborers. He moved through sheep saved on the Sabbath and restored hands. The Word spoke of divided houses and demon expulsion. Red letters unfolded into words of the Master rendered evenly and without theatricality until finally they told of camels, eyes, and needles. Max zeroed in. Paid close attention to words not written in red at all. They were stark and hardly an inspiration for the crisis survived on the road moments ago and the harbinger of pleats that told of the presence of darkness weeks ago.

Darkness infiltrated Sylvia and Max's marriage and even blighted marriage's precious metal symbol. Gold once elevated in metaphysical poetry for its ability to take a beating proved less accommodating to unauthorized changes to God's union. A broken prong gave up a hard-won faceted symbol of love never to be found by Sylvia.

The Spirit used the lost stone to reveal the hidden thing happening in their marriage. Max refused that message as he had others, not out of stubbornness, but through the cumulative effect of the choice to ignore his early day's teachings that flesh and spirit war, that the temporal obscures the eternal, that embracing excess in the form of selfish prosperity for family did not reflect a church seated in kingdom principles. His first church which embraced temperance and moved in the spirit was not legalistic. It understood God still roams the earth looking for those who will keep his commandments, and while he roams, the enemy does too.

Sign after sign, jigsaw pieces of revelation tossed Max about. He could calm the storm brewing with just a word, a word from the Lord Jesus couched in parable spread about for easy digestion. Just a word from the Lord would do, a word in red, yes, a word in red, but the disciples spoke instead of Jesus, and they raised a question through that even, nontheatrical voice. Max settled in for a washing, a calming, but unable to control the surge about him, he experienced a massive flood. Although seated and belted in behind the steering wheel, he was not left standing in the spirit. These were not words from the enemy to bowl him over, but words to start the process of raising him up out of the temporal and once again placing him firmly in the eternal.

This would be a long and painful journey that his spirit, not his flesh, requested. God required that Max and all others following him willingly crucify the flesh and engage a process of self-denial deeper than outward appearance that consisted of routine sacrifice and fasting. God who changes not still asked for this, and when the cry of a spirit that once knew the Father intimately rises through flesh, sin, and independence to reach the throne, God who dwells in unapproachable light after waiting patiently for the call answers it, burning away in the spirit as much as the earthen vessel can bear, burning away what should have been willingly crucified year after year, but was not.

A verse ignited the long process when Max heard what he was meant to hear. It was no coincidence that he heard the disciples asking Jesus a question that cut through the distraction of modern life as sharply as it did their ancient one, needing only an exchange of foreign cars for camels and the absence of a garage door for the needle's eye. The disciples asked simply and earnestly, "Who then can be saved?"[2]

CHAPTER 12

He glanced at Sylvia. More than forty minutes passed. He thought who could feign sleep when surrounded by all this chaos mixed with an odd sense of bystander curiosity. Some people walked around outside, stretching, peering, hunkering down for the long wait, and hoping for a glimpse of the macabre. Three lanes each way and not one moved in either direction. Forty-five minutes. There had to be a death. His "O Lord" was not Lord have your way; it was a filler, a mental reflex and nothing more. Drivers turned off engines and opened windows to conserve gas, and passengers waited. Fifty minutes. Appetites returned. Thirsts reemerged and cravings resurfaced. The smell of cigarette smoke entered the car from those on hoods and sitting in front and back seats. Sylvia shifted and unsuccessfully tried to roll up the passenger window that no longer received power from engine or battery. Annoyed that she had to speak to him and suffer the smell if not the smoke, she asked, "Could you please roll up the windows?" She waved her hand in front of her nose to displace the smell. Her eyes never opened.

He thought car on, AC on, windows up, smell out. Cigarettes. Even with all we know, Cigarettes? He watched as two stood atop the guardrail for a glimpse, a piece of news. A young truck driver moved from hood to cab to trailer for an unobstructed view. "If we had microwaves in cars, some people would fix popcorn and melt cheese for nachos; this is insane."

"What?" Irritation seeped through the letters of her speech.

He looked at her. Then he asked, "What was Sunday's sermon about?"

"Weren't you there?"

"Of course I was, but I can't remember the text, do you?"

"Why is it important?"

"It's odd. I don't recall the sermon, and it's only Tuesday." He remembered the pastor's gestures; he remembered the pastor's hand going over his head from front to back; he remembered the pastor was convinced no one got the full import of his insights. He recalled clapping congregants, hallelujah, and amen pastor. He thought but dare not say that God spoke through the play performed on Sunday. Everything afterward to his mind was flesh and needless, sermon included, but a sermon was delivered as they generally are on Sunday morning, and as he sat behind the driver's seat with nothing more than his thoughts for company, it occurred to him he had no idea what was preached.

Assuming there was more to this, Sylvia said, "God help me. Does everything have to be analyzed? This is why our friends don't like you. You never know when or how to turn it off. You intimidate everyone we know. They think they have to be smart around you. This was just a big mis—"

Her cell phone rang. He glanced at it, then at her. He believed cell phones contributed to emptiness. Few people knocked on doors, sought coffee or tea in each other's homes as an excuse to talk. Talking face-to-face kept the community alive. Now people called or sent texts. He snorted at the thought that the death of family would be the cell phone.

"I am not your child, and your rule about cell phone use in cars doesn't govern me," she said. He never thought of it as a rule in the

Draconian sense; a welcomed principle of etiquette was more like it, one to help negotiate a world fractured by constant communication. There was something terribly disconcerting about being in the car with someone who was elsewhere, not through imagination, daydreaming, or reading, but mentally and emotionally elsewhere with someone on the cell phone. Max believed talking on the phone sent a message that the one on the other end was inherently more interesting than those currently sharing the car. He found the message unacceptable and communicated such. This message he could see, yet he remained oblivious to this message sent by Sylvia to him.

With the ear piece now in place she said, "Hello," and an animated conversation began.

He turned off the Word since he no longer listened to it. Max figured her vivacity was part of the anything but you vaccination. It proved terribly ineffective. It had to be repeated often through deeds that communicated I want nothing to do with you. I will talk with anyone but you. I will extend grocery shopping rather than be with you; I will enter the house on the cell phone rather than say hello to you. Headaches will envelope me rather than sleep with you. I will talk on the cell until you fall asleep when I've reached my quota of headaches for the week. He just did not see.

He looked at her from the corner of his eye. She caught him, and she returned his stolen glance with even more exaggerated laughter. He made out, "Favor, um hum, pastor says favor's not fair. It could have been us in the crash." He thought of favor and how those who think they enjoy it today equate it with the avoidance of difficulty. Quite unlike Paul whose life might best be characterized as one surrounded by difficulty. Paul's life reads as one full of God. He wondered whether the troubles: vipers, prison, betrayal, and shipwrecks resulted from such a life or resulted in such a life or merely highlighted a life full of God. Imagine a viper's bite in which the venom never enters the body or that which does is rendered innocuous by the lack of attention given it by the man of God or the hedge of protection given the bitten by God. Lord to know you like Paul he thought.

"Elijah!" Darkness pulled him out of the book of Acts with a name.

"Huh?"

"Sunday's message was about Elijah." Her eyes widen with vocal emphasis placed on Elijah. He thought of the many ways the human voice and body communicated disdain. The body often betrayed the speaker, but she had nothing to hide. "You can go now."

"I'm sorry?" he said, asking for more clarity.

"You can go now." This time the body more animated than the voice. She raised her right hand slowly to point to the growing space between their car and the one ahead.

After driving for a while, he asked, "Sha or Jah?"

"What?" She asked with a puzzled look.

"Elijah or Elisha?" A second or two passed. "The sermon."

"I-d-o-n-'t k-n-o-w; I don't remember." She squinted as if trying to look into him.

So he began, "I was reading an article about crows. They mate for life, and when the mate dies, the surviving crow goes back to the mother to help raise siblings. Though pilloried in novels and periodicals as farm pests and devourers of corn crops, they also eat insects that destroy the crops."

Arms folded, she turned from gazing out of the window at nothing in particular to look squarely at him. Her head bounced and remained slightly bowed. Her eyes peered from the top left corner of the lids. "Just where is this going? Better yet, just where did it come from?"

"The provision of the Lord." He paused. Realizing the clear connections lay buried inside him, he said, "Sunday's sermon—if in fact the sermon was about Elijah hunkered down in a cave or near the brook Cherith when told to go hide himself, he was fed by a raven, the cousin of the crow. I love the excerpt of that sermon we listen too."

"You mean the one you listen too."

"Well, all right. It says something like I commanded the raven to feed you here, by the brook, and the woman to feed you there, in the widow's home. Elijah was full of God, a man of faith and included in the transfiguration." He gathered himself and continued, "God is sovereign, yet Elijah went through a lot that caused him to wonder. I sometimes struggle with the reconciliation of sovereignty and chance. It's, it's…I mean the accident just down the highway—"

"Tell you what, you drive quietly and concentrate on the road. Bible study will start shortly, but we should be on time and in the right frame of mind if we make it there in peace."

He looked quickly at her, and then placed eyes back on the highway. Peace to him meant thinking. Thinking at this moment meant dwelling on Elijah and his time by the brook and in the cave with only himself and God. How did he do it? He continued to think about Elijah and weigh whether time alone or time with God was the more difficult. He drew parallels with his current life and realized neither he nor Sylvia spent extended quiet time alone or as a couple with God or waited after earthquake, fire, or wind for a voice small and still. He continued flitting and fleeting and alighting on the most fragile of unspoken connections until broken by hello after she answered her phone.

Eventually she turned to Max. "The Reeves are inviting us out for a night at the movies this weekend."

"Ok, what's playing?"

She sighed, turned away from him, and said into the phone, "I'll call you back." She turned to look at him again. "Can you just for one moment have fun? Do we always have to think a movie through? My God. Can we just have fun with people we like? This is why our friends don't like you." She then added emphasis through a broader base. "This is why nobody likes you! They think they have to be smart around you all the time. You never allow them a break. Nobody can be themselves when you're around, and I'm sick of it. I can't do it anymore. I can't! I just can't! There are a lot of people who want me. I shouldn't have to settle! I knew the day I married you I made a mistake. I knew from that day it was all wrong."

They sat in silence for the remainder of the drive.

CHAPTER 13

Those comments answered Max's anguished prayer with clarifying fire. The Lord's many messages were in fact not inscrutable. The call from California, incessant cellular use, a thrown hand, and the lost diamond were now framed by words delivered in traffic. The framing resulted in seeing things previously not seen for one of two people in a car not a cave, surrounded by darkness and drought but not in any position to call fire or rain down from the sky.

He thought about the church's position on divorce recounted by a deacon he ran into while walking through the mall. During a Friday night leadership meeting, a concerned member asked the pastor to address comments that the church was considered the divorce church within the county. The pastor said, "No one focuses on the marriages the church saves from divorce; people only focus on the divorces." The pastor said that the verbal attacks came from the enemy who wanted to stop what God destined for the church, and the members should turn a deaf ear to the rumblings because they had a church to build and a vision to birth that no devil in hell would stop. With that the associate pastor walked into the pulpit and began to teach on divorce.

The associate pastor said that the church misunderstood God's stance on divorce. God's prohibition stemmed from inequality. Women in those days could not earn a living. Once divorced, prostitution became the most viable option for survival, but women work today and that invalidates the prohibition surrounding divorce if couples desire one.

Max waited for the deacon's reply, and the deacon waited for Max's. Finally, Max asked, "And you said…?"

"I said, 'Show me that in the Bible.' That's what I said. If you say something that bizarre, you have to have proof, and the proof has to come from the Bible. I can't remember what Scripture he asked us to turn to, but there was no support."

"So what was the support?"

"Whatever it was, it didn't work, so I said, 'I still don't see it, and I'm confused. If you want me to believe we've been wrong all these centuries, you must show me why in the Word.'"

Max said, "If we accept this as wrong, what other tenants will the body, not just this location, but the body of Christ be asked to throw out? More frightening, how many will throw them out without reading the Bible for themselves before dismissing truth as tradition?"

"It makes you wonder, Max, what else will change without scriptural support. What, a circle of leaders read a work by a researcher who concluded those who stood tall and those cowering near the base of Mount Horeb, one blinded by a light on a road, and those crucified upside down got it wrong? We believe this, why?"

"Wow, what happened next?"

"The class took a break, and the associate pastor walked me to the overflow room where he tried to explain the church position. I told him that I wasn't interested in the church's position. The only, and I meant only, position that mattered to me had to come out of the Word. He tried to show me another Scripture, but it wasn't there either. Finally, he asked if we could agree to disagree. I said, 'No!' Max, this is not literary theory! This is not a debate about how best to stimulate a sluggish economy. This is the Word, and the support for such a position is either in it or not, plain and simple."

"Wow!" Shaking his head in disbelief, Max wiped his face, and then said, "My God. I should tell you that my wife and I are having problems, and this teaching doesn't help. Come to think of it, way too many couples are having problems."

"Be vigilant, Brother Max. God is not in this mess, and he can't be pleased no matter how much we tell ourselves he's leading us. We'll pray for you and your family. Are any of these folks teaching this lie thinking of the children? It's a trick of the enemy, and we've not seen the worse yet."

Sitting in the family room after his trip to the mall, he heard Sylvia's voice through the ceiling dispensing advice from the master bedroom. The carpet from the bedroom and the sheetrock of the ceiling muffled the voice so that he could not make out the content of the discussion, but he heard the sound of a counselor in overdrive. He shook his head. Spiritual sewage poured continually into her ear from the callers, making in her body and soul a nest for what claimed residence in theirs. Spirits landed emboldened with a legal right and building permit since they were not uninvited. They entered and waited, timing the perfect moment to attach to a soul no longer anchored in hope.

The counselor bound no spirits within the counseled; as they slept at night, she soaked none in the light of the Lord to pry loose and expel roots of darkness in preparation for deliverance on the next phone call. The Holy Spirit within her was not consulted. The anointing left untapped. Having opted out of the spiritual fight, Sylvia's weapon of choice became advice—an ineffective weapon against darkness that moved in and out of unprotected flesh at will. Had Max, had Sylvia stood like Christians dressed for battle as they did in their first church, they would have noted the spiritual attack on their marriage and fought it off with weapons of Word and faith, of cross and blood; instead, each accepted what education, science, and their own flesh told them was real.

Before the accident, the Lord sent a phone call followed by a church play to say, "Wake up!" A few days ago, First Lady Rita called from Los Angeles and asked, "Brother Max, what is going on in your home? While I was with the Lord in prayer, he showed me a black insect whispering in your wife's ear, and he told me to tell you that there's a constant stream of evil pouring inside her through her ear. What is going on?"

"I'm not quite sure," he said. "I can't put my finger on it. It's more than the ups and downs of married couples." Then to himself and under his breath he said, "More than a dry patch."

"Have you prayed about it?"

He was a little irritated with the question, and his response reflected his annoyance. "Of course I have."

She said, "Well I'll keep your family in prayer, honey. The Lord has a job for you and your lovely family, and the enemy is trying to stop it. Open yourself to the Lord. Be aware and be ready."

He thought prophetic folks are often cryptic, but for once, Lord, just once could the message be direct and clear. No mystery God, just straightforward and clear?

After the call he opened his computer and pulled up the Bible. Aiming for Psalms twenty-seven and ready to seep into the Lord as light of his salvation, he read instead "Boast not thyself of to morrow...."[3] He paused and realized he read Proverbs, and although Psalms twenty-seven was a click away, he continued to read, stopping after "The full soul loatheth an honeycomb; but to the hungry soul every bitter thing is sweet."[4] He meditated and read verse seven over and over, but nothing came to him. He reflected on the phone call. He got the insect reference. That was clear to him. He heard a number of one-sided conversations as he drove, as she drove, as she ascended the stairs from the basement garage, as he ascended the stairs to the second floor, as he entered a room or exited it. The insect metaphor presented no problem, but the message encased in the deep structure of the verse would not yield its secret.

While cooking dinner Saturday night, he thought of the call earlier in the week and his subsequent reading of the Bible. He wondered why the Lord spoke to him as he did with a call from California and an impenetrable proverb. It nagged him as he called the family for a meal of salmon, spinach, and rice, a meal to be eaten together. All came to the table. Then after sitting down, Sylvia's phone rang. Surprised, Mark and Sarah quickly looked at Max, then each other, and finally down at their plates. Before the pervasive use of cellular phones, the family never answered the house phone when it rang during dinner, and cell phones were not allowed at the table.

Sylvia answered the phone, and the family could see something rising within her. It peaked with "I'll be right over."

That night before bed Max said to the Lord, "I need clarity. Why are your messages so hard to crack?" He got into bed and prepared himself for a night of warring in the spirit once Sylvia made it home and then to bed. The battle would be practically all night followed by a calming down for the morning ceasefire and pretense of happiness while in church.

Before the preaching, the drama ministry performed a play during the service in which one woman dressed in white and another in black descended upon a family of four sitting down to dinner. The two representing an angel and demon were not visible to the family. Max, ready to dismiss it as an unimaginative cliché of good and evil, white and black, gave himself over to the eerie likeness of the previous evening in his home.

After the grace, the woman in black whispered in the ear of the mother; the secret message interrupted only by the ring of the mother's phone. She tapped her earpiece and began offering advice to the one on the other end. She seemed unaware of the effect on the children. Eventually she stood up from the table, paced a bit, and then said, "I'll be right over." She turned to the children, "I have to run out;

my friend needs me." The children responded, "We're eating dinner." The woman in white ran over to the children to comfort them. "We need you," the husband said, and an argument began. The woman in white ran by the side of the husband to calm him and pull him out of the exchange as the one in black stood whispering in the ear of the wife to fuel the argument. The wife against reason and visible hurt of the children grabbed coat and keys and left the house to help her friend negotiate a crumbling marriage while ignoring the cracks developing in her own.

Max never encoded the sermon on Elijah in short-term memory because the play grabbed him, took him back to Sylvia's ringing phone and her leaving on the front end of dinner. She dropped fork and knife on the table and with earpiece still in ear ran to the aid of a friend. The supplication of the children did not stop her, and the suggestion from Max that she leave after dinner only annoyed her. Then he said, "This is a trick of the enemy. We're together as a family, and once again he pulls you away."

She stopped midway between the basement and main floor landing, but never turned to look back when she said, "Everything is not spiritual, and you will not tell me what I will or will not do. I won't let other people go through what I've been through."

Turning away from the table toward the basement he yelled, "Just what have you been through? Tell me what have you gone through?" There was no denying the foothold the enemy had in their marriage. Without specifics, there was no way to address them.

"Be a man and figure it out," she yelled as she continued her descent.

Shaking his head, he looked at Mark and Sarah and was pulled back to the meal with the sound of the garage door lifting. The grace was quick. "Thank you, Jesus." They ate in silence a meal prepared with Sylvia in mind who gave up poultry, beef, and pork while it became quite clear that a hamburger or hotdog anchoring the Saturday night meal would have been more than enough.

Little seemed spiritual because the choice to not walk in the spirit left them to fulfill the lust of the flesh. Before the wreckage in the pew and the one on the highway, each grew deaf to the Good Shepherd's voice. For Sylvia, a sincere desire to hear what she wanted to hear made listening to the wrong voice easy. For Max, accepting a lack of anointing and rampant divorce resulted in hearing snippets of answers to prayer which rendered a number of divine messages enigmatic, so he questioned the effectiveness of prayer, but sitting in the congregation after a night of war, the skit confirmed prayer as the preferred mode of communication with the all-seeing God, and answers to prayer took a variety of forms.

Mark found out a little more about a God who took the role of Father seriously and relentlessly pursued those who lost their way. He sat behind the piano in awe. His mouth and eyes wide open. He looked at Max and said with his eyes, "Wow! Dad, can you believe this?" And Max, who once said yes to a light ambling down a well-lit but darkened college dorm years ago and then attended a viewing of a private thought video of what was yet to be, used facial expressions to say, "Yes."

Crying out from his heart in wonder and bewilderment last night preceded a skit delivering a message too grave for one family and too important for a Sunday sermon geared to selling compact discs. His mind followed the timeline of events, and for a moment he believed his prayer could not have wrought this because someone or everyone on that team sought God's direction when penning the simple yet sincere skit days ago, and all were open to its debut. Or could it have? For God sees outside of time and knows thoughts afar off making it possible for a drama ministry listening to his voice to rehearse last night's dinner days before Sylvia walked out on salmon and family to be with a friend, and then perform it less than twenty-four hours as a warning to the family unraveling and the congregation at large that God watched the fraying of couples and the unauthorized rewriting of covenants. God saw all this, and he was not pleased.

Sylvia, eyes closed, sat with the praise team, and Mark, eyes wide open, sat behind the piano with the band. The play's message, the private delivery in a public arena, the family's open and closed eyes grabbed Max and refused to release him. The call from the west coast a couple of days ago and the drama on Sunday morning revealed God's concern for his family and all others teetering on the edge of destruction. God sent a resounding, "No!" to share his displeasure with the teaching propagated by church leaders and to confront the action of members where husbands and wives were calling it quits just because, just because.

The play pointed to Malachi who warned all to take heed to their spirits, and it highlighted the message reflected in the life of Jesus that people entered covenants to keep them. Breaking such for many resulted from the misalignment of spirit, soul, and body and the misalignment thrived in selective hearing and hearts hardened like stone where body and soul put the spirit in its place. When asked about the play after church, Sylvia said she slept through it during the two services. She ended any discussion of the message, the message neither one of them heard again while in the car waiting. "And did not he make one? Yet had he the residue of the spirit. And wherefore one? That he might seek a godly seed. Therefore take heed to your spirit, and let none deal treacherously against the wife of his youth."[5] The discussion of marriage in Malachi floated past them, and they heard none of it though the Bible came through the front and rear speakers of the car as they stood still on a highway impacted by an accident which turned them into a captive audience.

Once the accident was cleared, puzzle pieces began to fall into place. A level of clarity previously lacking in Max's spiritual life emerged. "I shouldn't have to settle" fit perfectly into "I didn't come home because I didn't want to see your face" which snapped tightly into self-exile and church busyness. The lost diamond snapped perfectly into place with incessant headaches and "No, I didn't see it; I slept through that play." "Friends don't like you" connected to "You should know I never liked that." Telling Max where he could spend eternity connected to "be a man," and fit neatly around two tossed hands. All combined with the play, the call from the West Coast, and the meeting at the mall as if the Lord said, "Does it need to be all the livestock from a thousand hills? What more do you need me to show you?"

For the spiritually hard of hearing, God sent a message to the church body, to the souls of husbands and wives, shepherds and under-shepherds, the betrothed. A play voiced his displeasure since reading the word alone had not resulted in any tangible proof of comprehension. The word stood just beyond the hard-hearted deaf, a reminder "Crash follows hard on crash."[6] The play spoke to those with uncircumcised ears who do not listen, to those with whom the Word of the Lord has become an object of scorn. "Hear, O earth; behold, I am bringing disaster upon this people, the fruit of their devices, because they have not paid attention to my words."[7] "Incline your ear, and come unto me: hear, and your soul shall live."[8] The play was a call today to fear the Lord and entreat his favor like Hezekiah and all of Judah once did. They moved God and averted disaster pronounced through Micah. To heed the play's underlying message was not a request.

CHAPTER 14

They made it to bible study in time for praise and worship. Moving quickly, Sylvia got out of the car and ran into the sanctuary. She placed her purse and sweater on a chair in the third row of the sanctuary and walked hurriedly onto the stage to join the other praise team members rendering song. Max, following slowly behind, found his seat next to Sylvia's things. He sat with a look of unwelcomed realization made possible through words intended to presage the ripping apart of family and lighten her a bit before extending the communal invitation to Jesus through harmony, tone, and pitch, inviting him to the sanctuary here below.

With the end of the final song, praise team members left the stage for their seats next to their spouses. The director remained behind as usual to render a transition song that bridged the singing and the teaching. Sylvia stepped across couples and children to take the seat next to Max. They sat next to each other in church for the last time though neither knew it, and neither did those around them having become inured to the signs of impending estrangement and taken in by the mask of the spiritually employed that busy, unhappy Christians use. None saw the sign except the two children who missed the wreck, the one inside the car, having ridden to bible study with friends. As psalmist husbands found their wives and psalmist wives found their husbands, Mark and Sarah, the two of them, caught a glimpse of their family's seemingly inescapable march toward disrupted lives seconds after Sylvia sat on the row with Max after praise and worship ended. The brother from behind the piano had a front view, and the younger sister in a row behind the parents saw more than anyone else who looked in that direction saw. While, they watched their mother take her seat next to their dad and muster a smile of spiritual contentment, the brother and sister saw something ethereal never seen before by either of them.

They were offered a glimpse into the spirit, seeing, as it were, the spirit of dad reach toward the sitting spirit of mom. Both reached for each other and became as one filling the space that existed between the two natural bodies. This was not discernible to the natural eye, to the pastor, those enrolled in round two of the Friday class, ministers on staff, and certainly not those seated in the rows or behind musical instruments. For a moment the Spirit drafted the two children as watchmen on the walled city called family, seeing briefly as never before but all too clearly that the natural body did not follow the leading of the spirit.

Neither knew what to make of this sighting. The sister, the keeper of a journal of dreams, learned to distinguish between spiritual dreams and those that grew out of business. She, however, was not asleep. This was no dream. Yet, she understood its spiritual significance in the middle of the sanctuary recently prepared by the songs of the praise team inviting Jesus with "Hosanna to the Son of David," and "Come Sweet Spirit."

Those songs besought heaven for a visit from Jesus. He sent an emissary in his stead. And although the church pleaded for a visitation each week through song delivered by a praise team of eight, the invite sunk to ritual and routine. Most singers and listeners never sought an actual visit of the invisible and missed the eternal during previous calls as it did now.

Each couple with private struggles failed to notice the fraying of family ties was much bigger, much larger, and involved more people than anyone made of flesh could know. He who invited brother and sister to glimpse reality sat next to each of them as they watched and noticed the spirit weeping, weeping, praying and calling, calling to an implacable mother and an overwhelmed father to yield and lay it all down.

For a spiritual second the watchers, all three, caught sight that all four (mother, daughter, father, son) would succumb and be crippled under the attack from a worthy opponent. While that was more than enough to take in, what the siblings saw next staggered them. Sister and brother saw the bodies of married couples moving further and further apart as their spirits still joined as one writhed in agonizing pain for what the flesh had begun to do. The ripping apart of husband and wife transcended all words, and where the union began to fray a darkness formed, a growing patch of darkness overtook the light of their spirits. A deep darkness already sat between a number of couples purporting to be happy and posing as stable. The spirits of a few rumored to live separate lives away from church were completely surrounded.

Unable to penetrate the oneness of some, the darkness proved relentless. Bursting out of itself in frustrating anger, it moved all around the couple and enveloped them as it searched for a vulnerable spot within the union to separate one flesh into two. While some held fast, the success rate was overwhelming. For those pulling apart, the desire of one appeared headed toward the opposite end of the row, leaving the other spouse blindsided by the current state of marital affairs. The initiating spouse grew ever darker and more determined. In the pit of anger, the body tested grace. The victim sat perplexed, torn, exposed, and fraying as wounds filled with darkness. Each grew darker as the darkness between them intensified while those resisting the darkness grew more brilliant still.

The parents of the young watchmen grew darker, so the daughter stopped singing, and the son stopped playing. Neither child looked at each other. They locked in on the event unfolding before them at times with eyes nowhere in particular because of the pervasiveness of the darkness appearing at will and the scarcity of light, but then they rested from time to time on mom, on dad, on the consuming darkness overtaking them both.

I don't believe this Sarah thought. I really don't believe this. She knew she saw a truth at this moment, a shocking but believable truth; teachers, deacons, musicians, and faithful church members sat unaware they entertained hell's hosts. I can't believe it she thought. Like living smoke moving, encircling, and inspecting possible spiritual prey: chairs, aisles, singles, children, it was everywhere, growing and billowing effortlessly about.

God had prepared her for this moment weeks before he allowed her to see it with spiritual eyes. God placed a reading in her dad's hand for a future round of the game they played at dinner. The game included Scripture, vocabulary, movie clips, and literary passages used to stump the opponent. They asked, "Who said...? Who wrote...? What is the meaning of...? In what film did...?" Each amassed points if they stumped the others. Max gave both of them lists of vocabulary words and excerpts from time to time or directed them to passages of novels, bible verses, plays, or poems.

Earlier in the month he gave them excerpts from *Ascent of Mount Carmel* by St. John of the Cross and quotations from Soren Kierkegaard to add to their arsenal of material for the following month's game. Sarah began with St. John of the Cross and found herself locked in on a series of thoughts describing darkness. She never moved on to Kierkegaard, and even though points were at stake in the game, she felt compelled to share with Mark portions of the book. She began with "The soul that is clouded by the desires is darkened in the understanding and allows neither the sun of natural reason nor that of the supernatural Wisdom of God to shine upon it and illumine it clearly." They continued reading excerpts *from Ascent of Mount Carmel* although they remained a little unsure about what they read. "Darkness and coarseness will always be with a soul until its appetites are extinguished. The appetites are like a cataract on the eye or specks of dust in it; until removed they obstruct vision."

Until now, Sarah believed nothing in particular drew her to chapter eight and moved her to point this reading out to Mark. Both thought it deep. Neither would have believed that God would show them the spiritual cost and extended reach of independent, private choices, that he would orchestrate for them a visual image of a reading written long ago and dismissed as superstitious nonsense today. What was deep to Sarah and Mark only weeks ago because they could not fully understand its import was deep this night because they could.

Sarah wondered briefly if her dad read and understood what he asked them to read. She wondered if he saw what she saw, but given the look on his face, the weary look of one coming to a profound but unwelcomed awareness which changed little after entering the sanctuary, she assumed his sight had not been altered. It was probably for the best, for she saw more than enough. Mark too. Both closed their eyes but continued to see families that displayed wellbeing and unity fractured, broken, destroyed by the invisible and unidentified dark cloud-like force. In the city of their souls each knew it was only a matter of time that the state of unions fraying in the dark would be brought to light.

Their vision returned to normal with the announcement from the pastor that the church would add to its current mission, "Building the community of God's kingdom" the phrase "through strengthening families one by one." To actualize this amendment, the church would increase the number of marriage seminars to be led by a couple who recently received degrees in Christian counseling. The couple would assemble a team of other degreed volunteers. The announcement resulted in applause from the adults present. The couple, pillars and founding members of the church, stood and nodded to the congregants. The highly regarded husband and wife were a solid couple by all accounts, but to Sarah and Mark who caught a glimpse in the spirit, the couple selected to lead the seminars was indistinguishable from many in the crowd that night in that husband and wife appeared as dark as night. At the conclusion of the announcement, brother and sister rose out of their seats along with a number of unsuspecting, unaware children to attend bible study classes. Ushers, ministers, and other adults lovingly and spiritually tapped or hugged both on their way to class, believing the singing touched them. The look Mark and Sarah carried to class stood as proof that God moved in the building. They remained unaware that a spirit lurking just beneath their smiles and praises now controlled many including themselves, some of whom once knew but had since forgotten how to make the soul's appetites and desires yield to the spirit.

Neither mom nor dad was granted a glimpse of the spiritual in the sanctuary, but they felt the weight of the darkness on their everyday, natural lives. They moved accordingly, avoided eye contact when possible, and seldom spoke to each other. Max never understood why, but Sylvia convinced herself she did. She chose to take a stand against a life of unhappiness and correct a lie forced upon her that a woman in the church could not redefine a twenty-year life without reasonable cause. The self-proclaimed state for lovers said a year apart was reason enough to re-imagine the parameters of marriage, no need for death as parting ticket, no need to hang around debilitating sickness or a sudden bout with penury. A year and imagination and a shroud of invisible darkness was enough to say goodbye. Max's travel schedule made it easy. Sylvia's increasing travel made it feel right.

Max focused on Kierkegaard's writings that spoke to a life stripped as worked dried up and Sylvia self-exiled. These held him, and he readied himself, initially, with quotations for the game, but he found himself pondering his relationship with Jesus and a need to die daily so that Jesus could increase. He thought on his excessive church work as busyness, a "temporal distraction" as Kierkegaard named it that fed the illusion that a Christian relationship could be a healthy one when Jesus remained at a distance.

Max thought of their first year of marriage, their uncomplicated life more a product of finances than a godly desire for simplicity. No matter the reason, their first year was lived simply: a one-bedroom basement apartment, few pots, and little furniture. That was then, the two woven tightly together over four years in college, the light of the Lord as thread ensured the Father remained at the center and darkness kept at bay. That was then when the music of the house ranged from Michael Card to New Jersey Mass, when the two sang themselves hoarse driving from Albany, New York to a church in the Bronx where they talked about Jesus in Sunday school after singing with him and to him in the car.

But that was then. Now, the ride home from church was quick, twenty minutes and quiet particularly this night with the exception of the noise from a vibrating phone quickly silenced. There was nothing to say. The children drafted as temporary sentries reporting to an emissary could not shut out what they did not want to see, and Max's spiritual eyes were forced open by a pattern of events in order to see a large platter arranged with the content that could cover a thousand hills. There was nothing to be said.

Max felt eyes on him that came from the back, but he refused to look in the rearview mirror. Sarah though not asleep sat still with eyes closed after counting five bodies in the car where four entered. She remained calm. What appeared to be a sleeping child to all others in the car was in fact a weary seer, a middle school child who would have welcomed a vision of sheaves of wheat or astral bodies in obeisance as she sat in church. What she saw instead wore her out and left her resting her head on the shoulders of an angel sent at this moment to reassure and remind her that she, a seer in a line of seers, was not alone and would be comforted through what was to come.

The Lord granted Max's son sight for a moment and that moment only. It was not a gift he operated in. He tried hard to actually see what caused the hurt, but he could not. The vision in the sanctuary was granted by he who sits the throne to one, a son, a student, a piano player, a member of the church band, which accompanied the praise team, which ministered to the congregation more than song.

CHAPTER 15

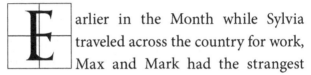arlier in the Month while Sylvia traveled across the country for work, Max and Mark had the strangest conversation, and though Max avoided the rear view mirror, he knew Mark gazed intently at him. He linked the depth of his stare to the conversation earlier in the month.

"What's up? You look heavy. Want to talk about it."

"Well yeah. It's kinda weird and a surprise."

"What is it? Do you want to say?"

"Yeah, Steve told me that he and his wife were separated and headed for divorce."

"Steve from church, music director Steven?"

"Yeah, who else?"

"Oh well umm, they just appeared to be happy and this seems out of the blue." Separated, not separating? My goodness. How devastating for those poor girls."

"You didn't know?"

"What makes you think I did?"

"I don't know. I just thought you knew."

"You and your mom, given your music ministry connections, know him better than I do. Much better than I thought you did since he told you about this impending divorce." Behind his voice were

83

thoughts that his son, a high school student, acted as confidant to an adult in a divorce. He was unsure, not clear how to think about it.

"You really didn't know? Mom knows."

"She didn't tell me." He paused. "Will he continue to direct the choir and lead the band?"

"She told me she knew when I called to tell her, and why wouldn't he?"

The conversation was a bit much for a teenager he thought. Stepping down, being sat down, such decisions involved nuance, long-term thinking about the ramifications of propping open spiritual doors that most could not see and very few understood. Two churches ago, his church embraced deliverance and believed in fighting Satan and his demons head on. He knew he settled with his current church, the unadulterated word replaced by cliché, cadence, and organ music during the last ten minutes or so of the sermon. No walkers, crutches, or wheel chairs hung around the church. No bags of pills or inhalers adorned the walls.

Once, in the middle of a sermon on David and Goliath the preacher in his first church spoke of one having been besieged by a spirit of asthma in the past and held onto it once again. You befriended it, welcomed it back, "but God wants you to let it go and lay it down," he said. The preacher continued, "I don't know why I am going in this direction, but the Lord does, and the Lord knows who you are." His college bible study teacher seated on the second row turned around and gave him the "this is for you look." Max believed the Lord knew about his asthma and that he brought his inhaler with him to church. He had asthma as a child. Took spoons full of what he called "yellow nasty" to facilitate breathing, help it normalize, find a workable rhythm. Some seasons proved worse than others. He could not remember what triggered attacks because he outgrew the asthma in late elementary school, but the color and the taste of the medicine stayed with him, and when he roomed with an asthmatic his sophomore year in college, his old companion came running back.

The sermon ended as always with great solemnity that the message was life and death urgent, knowing tomorrow was not promised. On the prayer line he received deliverance from a spirit of asthma and turn over his inhaler, not at the conclusion of the prayer but after getting up off the floor. Breathing freely, he walked over to the preacher. No wheezing, no delayed whistles, no feeling of air squeezing into unknown chambers of the lungs and refusing to come out, he was delivered from a spirit of asthma and any damaged to the lungs healed, so he handed over his inhaler. On campus if he felt a wheeze, he would gather himself before it gained a foothold and claimed full rights on his breathing. He bound up the spirit and pleaded the blood of Jesus.

The enemy tried in other ways to knock him down. His knees long scarred from growing pains kept him out of gym and sports for a better part of a year in middle school, and kept him off his knees for prayer during communion at times. On a subsequent prayer line, Elder Morris looked at him or through him and said, "I'm sick of you." He opened his eyes in shock only to have his ears do double duty at the next ten words, "Spirit of infirmity, out in the mighty name of Jesus." With that he fell backward into the arms of the deacons and placed gracefully on the floor. While sitting in the third row of the station wagon heading back to college, he listened to the story of one on the floor spewing phlegm as sickness left. He missed that, so asking, "Who, who?" during the conversation elicited playful laughter. "You," the driver said. "It was you." A half smile masked embarrassment, but embarrassment turned to awe when he knelt to pray that night.

He did not answer "why wouldn't he?" when talking to Mark. It required a conversation of spirits and demons and doors and invites.

In the old church there would be no need for a conversation like this. His son would know why, and in the spirit the church would close the door before it opened. Before stepping down or being seated there would have been prayer and oil and blood pleaded and Jesus. Demons would flee and flesh would yield in the old church two and a half to three hours away from his college campus. The blood still flowed was more than a song. The lyric "It never lost its power" did more than move a church. It chased demons. When the prayer line hit its stride and the preacher gave a specific look, it meant, "Blood songs. I need blood songs in here," and the oil flowed and the blessings came down. Demons fled in that old church he attended with his bible study teacher, a sophomore with a nascent prophetic gift, and two other bible study students willing to make the drive. Not all people changed, however. Those who were led by the soul and loved their fleshy choices left the service with the demons in tow.

Those led by the Spirit yielded and celebrated in a variety of ways. Young girls danced and then fell and a cloth was laid across them. Older women shook, called Jesus, and laid it down body and soul. A cloth was draped over them. Men jumped up and then down, removing the cloth as they rose. Elders in prayer at the altar spoke in tongues; they spoke to Jesus. Fathers, daughters, mothers, and sons at the altar spoke to Jesus in tongues and in English like a savor sweet and rising with the songs of blood and victory, weeping for the lost and crying for promised rest.

When one of the evangelists of the church who attended a different location in the city made a surprise visit one youth night, members grew still as she walked in the door. She, a seer, gave brief messages she never remembered giving. Teachers became teachers not because she said so, but because it was meant to be. Preachers became preachers, and she knew and told them often confirming the path before them. In an evening service filled with the young faithful and not so faithful, tensions rose as she walked the aisle. Too late to leave, all sat quiet, some prayerful and some with quiet fear they would be called out of secret sin as she walked. Fornication, she called it out. Pornography called out too. "Thus saith the Lord, turn away from those pictures or I'll call you to an open shame." She moved on. Skipping some and tapping others here and there. Those hiding in the center pew feeling safe called to the aisle as she doubled back. "Thus saith the Lord…." The darkness kept at bay in the light of the message, and the spirit within made ever stronger as the soul's hold weakened in the recipient of the public or private message received.

Then she approached Sylvia and shared for a moment her personal struggle with food. Food went in but could not stay. Ham in, ham out. Fish in, fish out. Fries, wings, vegetables, nothing took; cornbread, pasta, potatoes, nothing. After calling out to Jesus and calling him earnestly, finally Sylvia received a touch light as a feather on the left shoulder with head bowed as she sat on the edge of the pew struggling privately within. A touch and then a whisper reached beyond the outer earthen vessel to the internal part of the temple. Six pews from the front of the small, red carpeted, heavily wooded church, Sylvia sat in conflict, her body in a brawl with death itself. Then insight, access granted, a glimpse of the benefit of the exchange on the cross captured, "Satan has desires to sift you like wheat. I have interceded and said no. Eat. Eat. Eat."

And then the next shoulder and another and another until the evangelist sat down, unaware of anything said or anyone in particular touched. She took a seat near the front of the church drunken with the residue of virtue having passed through her to reach the seeking, the bulimic, the disaffected, the unredeemed. His children blessed with a touch and a word made public sometimes for a moment only to convey healing, deliverance, or a warning to his children and then forgotten by the messenger moving under his anointing. There were no theatrics, no large or national audiences, no monetary partnerships, just a private message from Jesus delivered through one of his own to those who needed both a touch and a word.

There were the Isaiahs and Jeremiahs who spoke to the nation and then those including the one hundred hiding safely in caves that spoke to everyday folks about everyday struggles absent scribes and epistles for posterity. They gave a correction here and spoke life there. "Eat, eat, eat," soft spoken words given through the evangelist to one in the throes of demonic ire and words to others abusing a limitless grace. A *rhema* for a hungry body and a weary soul to eat in the natural: meat and grain and vegetables and fruit, yes, and to eat in the spiritual: the Word of God in public and private, to eat the living bread and never hunger again. Lives were at stake, battalions impacted based on Sylvia's actions, but the unmarried freshman in college who worried about food, weight, and college requirements thought nothing of children and the expectation that children of godly parents should one day enlist in the army of God. "Before I formed you in the womb I knew you," God told Jeremiah, "and before you were born I consecrated you."[9] The evangelist said, "Eat, eat, eat" in the natural: meat and grain and vegetables and fruit that she might live, yes, and the children she did not yet know, Mark and Sarah, had not yet conceived, children seven years into the future would survive through her eating in the natural and be prepared for battle through her meals in the spiritual. The children not yet a thought were to live and grow and fight in the army of Christ.

The answer to Mark's question made sense only with context, and context would not hold at this time because churches two and three did not serve family meals of Word, signs, and wonders. Children dined isolated on Sunday in children's church and spent an inordinate amount of time on crafts and games, and adults dined in the sanctuary on meals sullied more and more with entertainment involving white gloves and painted faces, leotards and liturgical pirouettes perfectly rehearsed and timed like the music too, all beautifully rendered and soothing to the soul, so he left Mark's question unanswered. Spiritual context governing spiritual warfare is not learned through conversation, lectures, or online; it is experienced through a song that goes on much, much longer than planned because the anointing says so, through a sermon hijacked by the Holy Spirit who dismisses the three points outlined on paper to meet the needs of the congregants sitting hungrily in the pews, through unplanned deliverance that ignores the order of service to set free and heal those bound and elicit thunderous, genuine praise. He had no answer.

"Are you and mom gonna get divorced?"

"No! Why would you ask that?"

"Cause you're having problems."

"Well, that's not the problem at least in our case."

"I don't understand."

"Every couple has problems. Our problem is not discussing the problem, staying busy, talking to anyone but each other. We'll figure it out."

"You sure?"

"I'm confident we will."

And then the question came, the one that caught him by surprise. "Are you having an affair?"

Sylvia asked that very question, so he asked Mark, "Where did that come from?"

"Are you?"

"No. I don't know if you are aware, but one has to be out and about to meet someone to have an affair. Where have you see me most? In the garden. In the kitchen. At your school. Wow! I'm home before your mom gets home, and now travel less than she. I was the advisor to your Christian club on Thursdays because I'm home. I attend the church business meetings Tuesday morning because I'm home working out of the house. Where did this come from?" Hedges trimmed, trees fed, beds weeded, perennials tended, and annuals planted, the yard was stunning display of color, height, and texture because he had time on his hands.

Mark gave no answer.

Even with that question which took place before the accident on the highway, confidence remained unshaken, no divorce in his house. He missed the signs because he chose not to see or listen to them, and the puzzle pieces formed an incomplete picture. Seeing with natural eyes and hearing with natural ears, he missed the growing darkness his children saw and missed the Spirit's voice—the call to arms, the call for sword and shield beyond song lyrics and exhilaration. The sifting like wheat was not time sensitive and not confined to Sylvia alone.

Though delivered more than twenty years ago, the words proceeded by a touch did not expire, but Max and Sylvia lived as though they did. They fell asleep in the spirit, withdrew from battle as if the spiritual war could only be waged if they chose to be present and active. Being saved gave them access to grace and power, and they chose passivity, to enjoy the saved life and its kingdom benefits while others, mostly collared and titled waged a public war on Sunday and a couple of hours on Tuesday. They chose stolid Christian lives. They willed themselves out of battle, and the soul regained dominance over the spirit. The light which brought with it access to healing and deliverance began to recede within them and many, many others like them.

CHAPTER 16

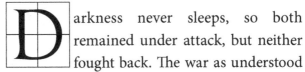arkness never sleeps, so both remained under attack, but neither fought back. The war as understood in churches two and three centered on riches. Quickly amassed riches and an enviable bounty indicative of battles won. Warfare in the current church meant negotiating, rubbing shoulders, blending in to get ahead, taking back what most assumed the devil stole. All of which obscured the view of heaven and God's directives that included persevering, resisting, evangelizing, remaining sober, and being wise as serpents while shunning the serpent's ways.

Max entered the battlefield against Satan three churches ago. Before meeting Sylvia, he attended campus bible study regularly. One bible study night during the closing prayer a voice he never heard before, a man's voice, came out of one of the women attending. After a discerning look, the bible study teacher pounced. "Out in the name of Jesus," and the voice became a groan, an eerie, unnatural sound that tapped depths once unimaginable.

He and most of the other students watched in wide-eyed fright that the dark spirit world whose very reality seemed to rest on the faith of its existence revealed itself to the unsuspecting group. Amazement tempered the fright somewhat because at the name of Jesus the unworldly voice that inhabited a body in bible study caved as the inhabitants of bodies submitted in the Gospels and Acts. None of the students had ever seen this before, and understandably it wrapped them up like spectators who were anxious, amazed, and willingly separate from the action. They watched as the teacher demanded a name, and when the voice refused she said, "The blood of Jesus," which elicited a frightful scream. From the depth of entrenchment to the heights of eviction, the unnatural voice traversed spiritual terrain until now understood only as parable and possibly metaphor by the students. Not by might or power, the strong man understood it would be evicted that night, for this bible study would differ from all their previous worship and study in that it was a night of spiritual gathering. One regularly attending would be set free, connections to the kingdom fortified, and words of Jesus, "Neither shall any man pluck them out of my hand"[10] made real. All present would witness the power of the blood of Jesus through the battle that went on for some time until the name was extracted and the vile demon cast out.

The bible study teacher asked the young woman, "Can you say Jesus?"

"Jesus."

"Say Jesus is Lord," the teacher commanded.

"Jesus," the woman said.

"Say Jesus is L-o-r-d," the teacher commanded a second time.

"Jesus," she said.

Sensing the fight nearly over, victory within reach, the bible students watched intently for the inevitable conclusion.

"Nobody calls Jesus Lord except by the Holy Spirit! Who are you!?" The voice let out a scream, revealing the victory within reach precious moments ago as spiritual rouse. This was war, a spiritual battle of cunning and deceit, a back and forth waged in the spirit that rendered temporal sword and shield, temporal knowledge and learning useless. The knowledge amassed as economics majors, accounting majors, psychology majors, English majors all ineffective in this fight, but the name of Jesus, the Word of God, the cross and his blood, insuperable.

The intensity with which they watched this perennial battled was broken by the voice of the bible study teacher yelling, "Don't just stand there. Help me!" Her voice and the urgency it carried broke the trance, a trick employed by the enemy. The scheme was devised to keep them all off the battlefield, but the Spirit through her voice pulled them onto it and gave the students momentary sight and an awareness of the enemy's nearly imperceptible but effective machinations to transform cadets into spectators. The budding awareness of this subtle trickery kindled fear. "Just how did the enemy immobilize us?" Max wondered before noticing another bible study member coughing and moaning. He heard the voice of his teacher once again and more commanding this time, "Help me!" as she wrestled with demons, calling out names and pleading the blood of Jesus.

"What do you want me to do?"

"Join the fight! Plead the blood! Cast out demons in Jesus' name!"

The two, teacher and apprentice, worked well into the night, which ended with a lecture on the seriousness of this walk followed by a prayer of coverage to accompany the new-found awareness and understanding that as they walked, spirits walked, and as they planted, spirits uprooted. At the conclusion of the prayer, a single voice emerged, not at all like the unwelcomed voices, and all others went silent. Max had never heard a message from the Lord like this, a message through a person not unlike himself, but at two in the morning, he and all others heard unknown tongues followed by "My children, I love you with an everlasting love. Follow my ways this day. Live righteously and pure, and I will bless you. Walk up right before me, and I will bless your goings and comings. You are mine, and I love you. The Lord has spoken."

Around two-thirty in the morning, a long night by any standard, the students walked as if gliding back to their respective dorms. Solemn and focused, they learned this weekday night that while a number of students slept, the invisible world was bustling and plotting how best to avenge the blow it received earlier from a bible study teacher and those under her tutelage learning spiritual warfare firsthand. They walked covered by the Father who loved them so and guided each one in a new level of understanding of the name of his Son and the power of his blood.

They no longer pined over a college experience restricted by can't and won't because with the fight came a new found understanding. "Can't" at last had been replaced by "can" through battle experience. "I can cast out demons in Jesus' name." The longing surrounding "won't" exiled because they carefully embraced an understanding that the choices they made reflected the true object of their faith and allowed God to activate gifts planted within them. They found the rate of activation, their stirring up those gifts, commensurate with holiness, and holiness a peculiar choice; I "will" know God more. True, no one worked for salvation or any of the nine, unearned gifts, but daily walking deeper into a more meaningful relationship with the Lord brought with it clearer sight in the spirit and clearer sight brought with it seeing and experiencing the activation of gifts within that in many others remained locked without a hint of their existence.

They read that Jesus loved them and empowered them, and they believed it too, but this night, they heard God speak. They saw him triumph, and they understood this night what it meant to place the enemy under their feet. Earlier that day, they served a baby born amid hay and straw, but with the long battle, they discovered Jesus grew up. No longer a baby, the lamb reigned as majestic lion and had a face brighter than the noonday sun. Between seven-thirty that evening and two-thirty that morning on a Tuesday night of bible study, Jesus grew up in their eyes, and they came to an understanding that the secret of the Lord is with them that fear him,[11] and having gained a better understanding of the awesome, awesome treasure dwelling within their earthen vessels, they grew up too.

CHAPTER 17

T he enemy lurked about, but they stood at the ready: fasting before bible study and church, crucifying the flesh to see more and more of Jesus. When their language or thoughts were less than godly, when the desires of their college bodies raged and the spirit waned, when their walks got sloppy and they read less, prayed less, and fasted less, and when they longed for a life apart from the highway, God spoke through the one who gave the word on that long night of battle, calling them out individually and collectively at bible study or when fellowshipping at the bible study teacher's house. God reminded them that "can't" and "won't" important stones in the path to holiness mark the gait of his peculiar treasures that see the task ahead and their role in his army. The faithful pause, listen, and hear victory when others fearing what lies ahead more than their distaste for the life they left behind abandoned the path, block hearing, and go backward. The faithful move ahead toward the fight and say, "For they are bread for us: their defense is departed from them, and the LORD is with us: fear them not."[12]

The members of the bible study stole inside the enemy's camp and witnessed. They invited friends and strangers to their dorm rooms to pray and talk about Jesus, and almost always, almost always a knock at the dorm room door would reveal the bible study teacher with

Bible in one hand and pocketbook in the other. She placed either on desk or bed, extended hands, and prayed as she had been invited by the Spirit to trek to the dorm and join the two. Tears would flow from the one witnessed to and with job done, the bible study teacher packed up and left.

Christians on campus sought them out for prayer and deliverance, and those needing help but not wanting God sought them out too. God directed the bible study members in witnessing in the dorms, and often just before prayer in their rooms with one seeking Christ, a knock at the door would occur, Bible and purse put down, and prayer would begin. Some of the invited left healed and some filled with the Holy Spirit. Some left delivered. Their walks made straighter, study more focused after a visit to the dorm rooms of those enlisted in the army of Christ who understood after that long winter's night when darkness dared show itself that knowing God was more than a life style. It was a life or death commitment that did not go away because someone ignored it. God never granted passes because one wanted only a part of God. While God drafted some of them as watchmen back then, he drafted all of the bible study members from that first year as frontline warriors who learned how to fight under the aegis of the bible study teacher who never drew a natural weapon.

The weapons were spiritual and available to any who coveted the best gifts. One night in a dorm room, Max and a fellow bible study student engaged in prayer with a new member. Max believed any minute the knock would come. As the anointing rose in the room, both heard a groan like the one that Tuesday night of deliverance and prophecy. No knock announced the rescue of the novice warriors standing alone to fight an opponent much older, much wiser than they. Committed to the fight, the two quieted the fear attempting to rise within and continued by binding the enemy and forbidding it to enter either of them in the room. Then they said, "Out in the name of Jesus."

The voice in the one being delivered held firm. It howled loudly and unnaturally bringing with it knocks at the dorm room door followed by shouts. "What's going on in there?" Students on the outside yelled through the door, but neither Max nor his fellow bible study member answered. "Open up! Are you all right in there?"

"This is a trick of the enemy," the one praying with him said; "We have to keep praying." And they did, more fervently as the pounding on the door increased, and they realized God would not send their teacher to pick up where they left off, to finish what they believed they could not. They were on their own in the natural and needed to step into the spirit to see an army awaiting orders. The two fought earnestly. Fought hard mimicking what they heard and saw. Each called out names, bound and loosed, and burned with their tongues. Little happened until they moved out of the natural, out of what they had seen. Little changed in the spirit until they came to the understanding that victory was not by might, mimicry, or by power; victory came by the Spirit. By the Spirit, the name of Jesus and the blood of Jesus gave them inexhaustible authority, and they used both until the one receiving deliverance though exhausted in the body answered their question with, "Jesus is Lord," to the glory of the Father and followed the answer with high praise. The pounding at the door ceased.

Max answered his son out of this experience. His assurance in the natural emanated from a lack of deciphered information in the spiritual though God sent warnings continuously to his enlisted. Mark caught a glimpse of something in the church that shook him to the marrow; something dad through his spiritual malaise would not see—a languid body, a head hung down, a sullenness seen from piano to chair, from son to mother, a weight lost on all others. While, he saw their spirits reaching toward one another, he also saw their bodies and noticed one in particular at that moment visibly hurt and rejected, moving further down the row of chairs in the spirit and overcome by darkness. Neither Sylvia nor Max nor any adult in the sanctuary for that matter could see in the spirit or hear the weeping of the emissary vying for their attention. After praise team members took their seats and before the minister of the evening took the podium, the emissary with a sparrow in hand laid wet eyes on Max and Sylvia and other couples ripping, ripping, ripping in the spirit what God had put together. The church had unwittingly endorsed a bewitching branch of mathematics in which a single soul tie made by God and God alone becomes two.

As a toddler and young child in the family's first church, Mark preached in the living room of their rented two-bedroom apartment. He would don a T-shirt of Max's, pick up brush, comb, or paper towel cardboard cylinder and preach with the fire he saw in his pastor. With every "Glory to his name" and "Hallelujah!" hell took notice. John 3:7 he would say with conviction, "Marvel not that I say unto thee, ye must be born again." He preached to invisible, heavenly hosts sitting, standing, floating, bestowing upon Mark a spirit of encouragement to continue in season and out, in the days of his youth, and beyond. "Speak life, speak truth," they said while Mark's praise joined that of angels in their continuous worship, "Holy, Holy, Holy the Lord God Almighty." That was then when a young boy watched and listened to his pastor, and then preached in the living room three churches ago.

In the current church, the young made no makeshift microphones. If children received glimpses of the spiritual, they exhibited limited visible evidence in their play. The Holy Spirit once asked to take control in the development of godly children waited for an invitation. He watched and waited, wept and waited as the current church implemented new activities for the young.

It lost sight of the holy, re-purposed the temple into a part-time art studio for the young and weekend coffee house for those older. Late night board game tournaments replaced all night prayer before sinking into a communal sleepover for those who brought pillows and blankets fighting heavy eyes across from an opponent who said, "King me" or named the candlestick as weapon. The environment moved the Father to the margins in his own house where a house leader's dream church would someday be surrounded by tennis and basketball courts for the young, and fitness classes, origami classes, yoga, and karate offered sweet enticements to bring in and keep the lost, but nowhere in the course selection was a class offered on "How to Live Holy," "How to Walk in the Spirit," "How to Pray without Ceasing," or "How to tell the Flesh No!"

From the backseat after bible study, Mark looked at his father because he wanted to but also because he was directed to. While he saw other couples tearing apart, he focused on what mattered most to him, his family. Because of the sight granted in the sanctuary, he thought he might catch a glimpse of his dad's actions that caused the current crisis. He failed to understand that the initiator was spirit, not flesh, that invisible actors can force natural reactions. The realm he moved in as a child atrophied over time with his family's attendance in two churches. He forgot about those early days and relied on implanted memories from mom and dad who lived off memories themselves after packing up much of what it meant to be active, fighting, battle-driven Christians.

Packing up deliverance was difficult when visiting the second church. It was who they were, delivered saints on the front lines in a continuous war between light and darkness. Each had been delivered from some power that lived within them and claimed residence for a time before being cast out. No one packs up all at once a war not only winnable but already won by Jesus, the Paschal Lamb, so pure and full of light his death tore the veil, rent rock, and brought the dead back to life. In college Max was told often, "We are pilgrims passing through. We are peculiar in that these worldly trappings fall off us, stick only if the Father chooses. We are peculiar treasures, carriers of an unspeakable gift, a Holy Ghost magnet."

But that was then, and Max now emerged as a conquered, defeated, retired frontline fighter who having been with Sylvia throughout her four years of college forgot that she was not a member that first year when the group fought darkness without manuals or how-to videos or seed money planted in a television ministry directing them. He forgot the real-life experience, and she willingly forgot the stories about it. Having felt a sense of being left out, she felt relief when his "remember when" stories faded. The price was steep. In their hands the Word of God became a historical book that shaped stories for children's church and sometimes assumed the role of muse for the interpreting of song lyrics that entertained the congregation. The stories and songs served as reminders to both of them that once not so long ago they were active warriors who knew if no one else at the current church did that the stories of old were real.

They once fought and had the battle scars to prove it. Knotted knees allowed prayer without pain, deep breathing lungs worked in silence, and a digestive track yielded to whatever the hand placed in the mouth and dared not fight back. By the third church, "It doesn't take all that" had worn them down, and kneeling to pray became a memory. Max prayed while standing or walking or lying in the bed. Eating became a task once again, so Sylvia gave up pork, then beef, then chicken. This was war in which they enlisted through repentance and conversion, but they had grown weary in spirit and befriended many who knew God in name, not experience and who encouraged the placating of a growing weariness with things.

By church three although changing, they were odd, serious, spiritual folk who were reminded again and again, "Yeah, but it doesn't really take all that." The first church's message of warfare with helmet, sword, and feet shod contrasted with two and three's message of prosperity and kingdom living in the here and now. "We are holy rollers," an elder from the first church would proudly say. "We are sanctified people, tongue talking, a holy church!" Where the first church sang about giving all to Jesus, the current church sang about getting things back. The contemporary speech made the devil a target because of theft—the things he stole, not the souls tortured or those traveling as companions on a one-way trip bound for hell. While their first church embraced hymnals like "By and By" and those about solemn, solitary morning strolls through dew-laden gardens where generally by the third verse most needed to read from the hymnal, the overhead in the two most recent churches provided ditties of grace, big lettered phrases needing one slide possibly two to appear helpful in the assistance of the congregational song. Clearly it didn't take verse three to really reach heaven, and folks had grown to believe it never took verse four. Verses three and four faded away because "it didn't take all that." Eventually the hymnals remained untouched, a repository for dust until moved from behind the wooden pews into dank storage rooms where the revelation of godly men and women of days gone by remained locked from view and heart. Few heard William Reed Newell's lyric "Mercy there was great and grace was free/Pardon there was multiplied to me,"[13] as a place for souls to find liberty. Most never sang "When I see the blood, I will pass, I will pass over you."[14]

Possessing too much character and telling an antiquated story, pews followed the poetry of song and were sold. Churches replaced them with chairs that worked better in the contemporary, multipurpose sanctuaries. Clearly, clearly it didn't take all that dark wood.

Max would remain silent when people from the church contrasted what they identified as traditional church ways with the contemporary move of God, restrictive can't and won't with freedom, judgment with grace, Old Testament with New Testament, and solemnity with merriment. The savvy had many ways to build a case against the severity and shortsightedness of the old ways and communicate their support for the love and grace of heaven reflected in the contemporary church. Churches that championed love and grace boasted huge memberships, and the numbers they believed proved the godly inspiration behind their approach, but the new understanding of church lost something in translation for Max.

The increase of merriment resulted in shallowness, superficiality, and zeal. While it did not have to be this way, few asked the Lord how to make it work. People talked as they entered the sanctuary. They caught up on each other's lives as they exited. Members understood church as an obligation, a duty for an hour and a half in one of three services on Sunday before the building assumed the roles of community house, recreation center, and school. The notion of reverence in the sanctuary fizzled and became ritual, a legalistic barrier that unnaturally capped socializing in services that lasted much too long in a formal setting that waited for a visitation from the eternal that only a few ever claimed to receive.

But a formal invitation drew Max, and his heart RSVP'd before he stepped into the church in the Bronx to dine on bread and wine. Absent video, absent voice, absent confirmation, Max could not be sure he would have converted. He knew deep down within that a walking light approached him on a weekend, which led to a fateful, unforgettable Tuesday night at the movies and a Sunday afternoon in a free museum for a photography exhibit. For him to eventually say yes to the Lord, it took all that.

CHAPTER 18

Max wondered about the roles of solemnity and honor in church. One was in the presence of a king, in fact the King of Kings or presumably should have been; honor and respect were due. A bowed head, closed eyes, silence, all signifier of humility sunk to empty ritual. He wondered, but never questioned aloud that if it took all that back then, why not now for The One who is the same today, yesterday, and tomorrow? Bowed heads and closed eyes, reverent supplication and humble requests, and silence and waiting mixed with exuberant, boisterous praise in preparation to hear from and spend time with Jesus; it took all that. Kings deserved this. Throughout school, the study of countries with monarchs told us so, and movies with emperors showed us so. Therefore, why not with God who stood as the blessed and only potentate, the Lord of Lords, he who had all honor and possessed eternal dominion?

Early in the marriage they drove either Saturday or Sunday from Albany to the Bronx two and a half to three hours over hills, down windy roads, and sometimes through snow on the Taconic Parkway to enter the sanctuary with Jesus with expectancy that he would do a new thing in an atmosphere teeming with due reverence. For Max, this experience came about and his life forever changed because a friend returned from Christmas break and plowed the area of the soul harboring seeds buried deep within him. Walking down the hall she, a letter written by Jesus to Max and his friends, shone, a letter with a majestic, regal, spiritual crimson seal shining, a beacon in search of souls capable of believing the call of living writing comprised of spirit and light composed by Jesus himself. She walked down the hallway apprehensively to meet the young men of the corner suite. They sat on the floor in their usual position at the end of the hallway near the exit, three on one side and three on the other. She said looking from side to side, "You probably won't want to be my friend anymore. I'm saved. I won't do what I used to do. The drinking, the partying—I've found Jesus." These words tendered an invitation to read with heart and spirit that which cannot be seen or read with the natural eye.

Five sat dumbfounded, but Max trained as a child in the way he should go said, "I want what you have." He had no idea that Sunday school prepared him to read that light destined to stand before him at that moment when he and his friends sat in a hallway.

Destiny placed him there. The fateful January call from the university personnel asking, "Are you in college?" And his simple reply, "No," resulted in a ticket to Albany and temporary housing on the downtown campus with seven other young men and four sets of bunk beds. He stood at a spiritual gate called Bethesda on one end of the phone, and the offer made by the voice on the other end lifted him and placed him in blessed water at the time of angelic stirring one year before he sat in the hall where he read peace and wanted that, read away rumors, talk, worries, and pressures, read a walking epistle, a newly penned preface to eternal life that unearthed seeds long since planted and forgotten. "I want what you have," Max said. He alone, one out of the six, read just enough to allow the Holy Spirit to draw him. There were no bushels to diffuse the light, no hiding, and no words of explanation. He read pure sweetness; he felt a bright light wooing, "Come if you are weary, if you are ready. Come unto me beyond the soulishness of yesterday." A small voice called, ageless and lasting, a sweet enough voice wrapped in an unworldly expanse, wooed an earthen vessel to exchange unsustainable highs and fleeting happiness for inexhaustible and inexplicable joy.

She, the walking letter, had her orders. "Just extend the invitation; disturb the planted seeds lying dormant, and another that I choose will water. I, the great I Am, will give the increase." So she, new to this life, invited Max and his companions to bible study. Max alone took her up on the offer.

At bible study he found out what it did take to satiate a hunger and a thirst unquenchable by all save the Living Water, the Bread of Life. Max found it. Like a weary traveler needing rest, a traveler who searches for a remote tavern in that place where it always was, waiting for the one who admits finally to being lost. Max reached the seemingly elusive destination as he prayed and pressed. He found it. Unsure what he looked for, but found himself opened up to, drawn into a quick courtship in which he would learn more than enough about *El De'ot*, the all knowing who knew all there was to know about Max, who Max was and who he would become. The incomprehensible idea of that alone was enough to move him toward commitment.

At the conclusion of the bible study lesson, the teacher prayed for Max. While she prayed, the Lord showed him his college girlfriend wearing a peach sweater he had never seen. She sat confidently on his bed with legs crossed, absent glasses, and sporting a new haircut. She spoke to his roommate while she waited for Max's return.

They had many conversations about God. She simply did not believe, but intrigued by *El Kanno* and leaning toward the pursuit of a relationship, Max knew he would have to give her up unless she changed her view. He would talk with her, pray the Lord draw her as he drew him. Only then could it work, for she proved adamant in her position in past discussions.

"I think it's a weak mind that believes an outside power is needed for fulfillment. I think all we need is inside us already," she would say.

"Do you?"

"Yeah I do. It's simply, well it's not so simple, but it has to be tapped. My family was never religious. We were brought up to be caring and involved. My parents pushed us to think about how we make this life a better one, not just for ourselves but for others who can't make it better for themselves. You don't need a god to make this life, the only one we know we have for sure," eyebrows raised and eyes widened to emphasize that point, "a good one, a life worth living."

"I'm not religious either, but I believe in God. I've felt him and been helped by him. I know he's there, but I'm not fanatical about him. To each his own."

The two agreed to disagree when it came to matters of God. The pact held because neither one walked with God, and neither one understood before that bible study the granular level with which an infinite God who all day long stretched forth his hand toward a disobedient and gainsaying people stooped for one he elected, one called according to his purpose. He would split seas and rivers. He would replenish reserves of wine and bread. He would use video and voice in pursuit of earthen vessels ordained to carry his glorious treasure.

Their pact to disagree amicably made in the natural and not easily broken collapsed in the spirit under the force of a mental film followed by a word from the Lord, "What will you give up for me?" Hearing an audible voice, Max looked around the bible study and saw no other man there. A silent film played in his head followed by that question. He saw no body; he heard only the voice.

Max thought who is this? What is this? One who can talk without a body and show film without a projector.

Who? What?

He walked slowly across the campus to his dorm after bible study trying to process what happened during the prayer and weighing how this life he considered saying yes to would change the life he accepted most naturally. He needed more time and would think on it throughout the night. I'll send my roommate the message I don't want to talk, he thought.

After entering the dorm, he removed his coat. It was February, an upstate New York winter night illuminated by the snow on the ground and the lights on the campus, but the illumination reached much deeper; because he chose to attend bible study and while there agreed to prayer, light backed up darkness around him. God placed him under protection and forbade darkness to meddle directly with him. This allowed him to walk down the hall with a running movie and the color of peach still very clear in his mind as he reached and then opened his suite door leading to his room.

His room was the largest of the three, an L-shaped room and the first room on the left. Directly across from his room was the bathroom, and at the back of the suite were the two remaining bedrooms opposite each other. He stopped and stood by his door trying to make out the voices he heard. Before he could open the door to his room, his roommate opened it, smiled, and left. No words exchanged, just a college glance coupled with a rather strange piercing look that Max initially interpreted as see you in the morning. Max entered the room, and as he rounded the corner there she sat with legs crossed on the top bunk, his bed. He stood in disbelief. His tongue stuck. His body motionless, staring as if viewing a high-quality bootleg film of his girlfriend in the second most vibrant peach color he ever saw.

"Speechless?" she asked, "I got contacts today. You like?"

His eyes widened in disbelief. The God he read about in Sunday school as a child was all too real, courting him, composing an individualized marriage proposal unlike any other ever written for Max and Max alone because he saw the light emanating from a contemporary herald days ago as she made her way down a spiritually dark hall. Max saw what roommates and suitemates could not see, and then with heart and spirit said yes to the beckoning light.

"I bought this sweater while I was out today. I've never worn this color before. What do you think?"

He wanted to say that I already know. I saw it on you before you entered my room. He wanted to say that I've seen this entire look, the haircut, the jeans, the sweater, the contacts; I've seen this all before. He wanted to say to her that God is real, so very real, and he wants me. He told me so, asked for my hand with spiritual film. He would never say that God asked, "What will you give up for me?" Made clear with a perfectly edited thought picture and simple question, "How can two walk together if they don't agree?" He had no answer for that question standing in his room Tuesday night after an unbelievable bible study and when it confronted him again Wednesday and Thursday and abbreviated itself for expediency, "How can two, how can they?" It bungled his thinking for the remainder of the week as he thought on God and life, considered a spiritual marriage proposal to one who knew everything there was to know about him, those things that happened that he no longer remembered and those things that would happen in the future. God already knew, and still God proposed. As a sophomore in college, Max knew the cost would be high, and since God was a form of weakness to his girlfriend, a result of brainwashing, a stumbling block which all intellectual, savvy people overcame and moved beyond, he would take this walk without her.

To her, Max got stuck. He pondered and listened when he should have ignored the call and moved forward, and he might have had he not viewed a short reality film, a recording of events yet to take place that eventually unfolded right before him, and he heard the voice, the body-less voice. Either alone was more than enough to grab him. Finally, the turn of the doorknob to a door he did not open revealed a roommate's slightly sinister glance and mischievous smile that perhaps was not his roommate's at all, for the look suggested this was much, much larger than saying yes to the Lord. The light prevented a direct attack on Max, but a roommate who refused the invitation and a girlfriend who would have walked away before it were ever tendered could be used to sit on a bed as if to say through a pool of imperceptible darkness, "Here I am just for you," announced by a conscripted herald unaware that the smile rose from a deep darkness he never knew he carried, a darkness announcing victory with a smile and a squint of the eyes that said unequivocally to Max, "See if you can say no to this."

She would never know that Max saw her sitting on his bed waiting for his return before she saw herself there in the reflection of the mirror over his chest of drawers. How could he just move on and spurn the Lord, not return the calls that went on in heart and head? The pull of the Father who drew with intangibles, elements of the eternal including a protective, invisible field of light was irresistible. He needed to find out just who could get inside his head and show a movie of life yet to happen. Just who could do that? He knew it was God, but after years of Sunday school which brought him to the edge and taught him to read light, after years of church, Christmas and Easter programs, recitations, hymns, and things he called miraculous, Max unaware he had seeds growing within him understood very clearly that he did not know God.

CHAPTER 19

T he members of the bible study invited him to attend church. He said yes and rode with them as they passed church after church in the area and along the route to meet God in the Bronx who obviously frequented their bible study in Albany.

During church, he listened to a sermon about sheep and goats. The preacher stated that sheep respond with yes when The Good Shepherd speaks while goats generally ignore his voice or respond with "but" when a simple yes will suffice. Through the sermon's message, Max heard Jesus plainly, "You are not mine until you submit. One must choose to walk with me. You are still a goat, and I only lead sheep." Max realized that if God came while he sat seeking, inquiring, and pondering spiritual technology but not fully committing, hell would be his home.

He, one lost, was sought by God, and since he read the light of one walking down the hallway in a college dorm when no one else dared to see and read, God would be relentless in his pursuit of him. Max, not a bible scholar, did not know the words of Jesus, "And this is the Father's will which has sent me, that all of which he has given me I should lose nothing,"[15] but he did know Edmund Spencer's *Faerie Queen* assigned reading in high school. He committed a quotation to memory. Currently a goat, one lost, made ready for a spiritual transformation into a sheep. God tagged Max for the elect and pursued him relentlessly through spiritual celluloid, voice, and sermon, giving Edmund Spenser's words, "For there is nothing lost, that may be found, if sought" new import, a stopgap until the literary which fell in and out of favor submitted within Max to the Word that would never pass away.

After the sermon and prayer, Max walked to the altar and knelt as best he could to have a little talk with Jesus. Nothing happened, so using the solid wooden altar which spanned the front of the church a step or two down from the pulpit, he pulled himself up and walked back to his seat.

"Well?" the bible study teacher asked.

"Well?" Max inquired, not sure what had been asked of him.

"Feel any different?"

"No, not at all."

"Then not good enough. Get back into the prayer line."

He did, and still feeling no difference after prayer, he walked back to the altar to kneel once again. This time he chose the bottom tier of the two-tiered altar, but no words came initially.

He stayed there, silently with eyes closed, thinking it was the best he could do. He had no formula for prayer, so to start the conversation he said, "Here I am, Lord. I'm yours if you want me." Then the Holy Spirit showed Max stills. No movie this time, just photo after photo of what needed to be addressed and released before he claimed God as his own. Still after still he said yes, asked for forgiveness, and moved to the next until the final picture of a dad since gone who contributed a chain, socks, and underwear his sophomore year of college and nothing else. Max delivered two words in brazen candor. On knotted knees on the bottom tier of a two-tiered altar covered with crimson carpet, he sent through the spirit the equivalent of an unequivocal no! He tapped the fading remnants of goat, resuscitated a withering old nature and called it back to the fore. Max who found yes getting easier and easier with each image shifted the tone and mood and shocked himself but not God.

He could understand the potential of the earlier photography requests building a personal barrier to grace, so he tabled the feelings that fed hurts too strong to wrestle with at the moment and decided to trust God to heal them. He forgave and moved forward, but then the picture of his dad engaged the brakes on a seemingly continuous process of forgiving and receiving forgiveness and moving ever forward. The image called up a "but," to the running list of "O' God forgive me, and I forgive…." The current request asked much too much of him. The force of a single phrase, "Absolutely not!" brought the process to an abrupt stop. Max confronted the Holy Spirit. He would not betray the memory of walking to school through a mud racked potato field in the dead of winter with only two hand-me-down sweaters for warmth and no money for a coat. He clung stubbornly to the "I can't believe he left" and refused to let it go. He chose not to betray the memory of missed classes and failed geometry to take a sickly mother to the doctor because dad disappeared. Max sent a spiritual telegram for the lack of financial support through high school and college, "Absolutely not!" Then the imperceptible bubble of light faded, the photo screen prepared for his eyes only rolled up.

The floor that fought his knees disappeared too. Fire engulfed him as he descended toward a home that enlarged itself, a fiery unquenchable lake not meant for him or others but willing to take in more, to make room for more. He dropped in the spirit and cried out loudly and urgently in the natural, falling deeper and deeper in the spirit through the root of unforgiveness and an emphatic "Absolutely not!" The cry aloud drew the attention of those already ministered to who now sat in the pews and the members of the pulpit who sat prayerfully vigilant as four other elders and evangelist worked the prayer line, one at each corner of the church, two in the front and two in the back. He discovered God needed a yes for all of it.

Ninety percent, ninety-five percent fell short of eternity when what was needed was a yes, a yes and amen to continue the God-directed process of forgiving and forgiveness, a not so simple yes, but a yes nevertheless.

Falling, falling, falling and embracing the realization of a different kind of video, he cried out for forgiveness first and then forgave to the degree that he could at that moment, he surrendered. Words of reverence dropped in his head. He read them before, a golden text from a Sunday school lesson maybe. Although where he read them remained a mystery, they poured forth as if from his belly through his lips: O LORD, I will praise thee: though thou wast angry with me, thine anger is turned away, and thou comfortedst me. Behold, God is my salvation; I will trust, and not be afraid: for the LORD JEHOVAH is my strength and my song; he also is become my salvation.[16]

His body went limp, and Max fell sideways onto the floor where he spoke with his new-found love, the Paschal Lamb, who had a number of years in the past said yes through stripe and thorn. Drinking a new kind of wine and talking, drinking and talking, Max took his time to draw out the yes to a future wedding in a language that only God knew in a conversation years overdue, he said yes and yes and yes in tongues.

THE GROWING DARKNESS

CHAPTER 20

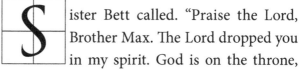ister Bett called. "Praise the Lord, Brother Max. The Lord dropped you in my spirit. God is on the throne, and he is who he said he is. Praise the Lord, darling. How are things?"

"Things are fine."

"No they're not, Brother Max. I've been with the Lord all morning. Although I've never been to your house, the Lord showed me you sitting on the end recliner portion of the brown sectional near the fireplace in your family room. I saw you on your phone sending an angry message to Sylvia in response to one you received. The Lord also showed me you sitting at a public table in an open restaurant or something. I saw people walking by as you listened to the phone company explaining that Sylvia is no longer on the family plan, that she created a separate account for herself and left the children on your cell phone account. You didn't eat your food."

"That was the food court in the Atlanta airport."

"You were trying to hold it together just before you caught the flight. The Lord also said an insurance agent called you to tell you that Sylvia removed you and Sarah from the insurance policy. The enemy is trying to stack one thing on top of another to distract you as she prepares to...." The little woman by the well pulled up short. "My God, Max, my God."

Max listened.

"The Lord showed me parts of the conversation between you and the agent. 'What are you talking about?' You said. He tried to answer you nicely. I could see him rehearsing the call before he made it, knowing it wouldn't go well and would catch you by surprise. You refused to play along. You hung up after telling him you had two children and would not continue the conversation without knowing the insurance fate of both. He told you he could not discuss Sylvia's finances, and you asked, 'How is Mark part of Sylvia's finances and Sarah not?' When he didn't answer you, you told him the conversation was over, so he called Sylvia after you hung up. The Lord told me she called you. You two argued, and he let me see Mark and Sarah's expressions as they sat in the family room with you, both on the sectional on the long end of it listening and trying to make out what was going on. You couldn't understand why Sylvia didn't tell you about the phone and the insurance face to face since you both live in the same house. Is this from the Lord?"

"Uh-huh."

"God wants you to hold your tongue, darling. Stop the back and forth verbally and through texts. It won't get any better for you, but the Lord said that you have to be swift to hear and slow to speak."

"Ok."

"The Father said he's told you this before, but you're not listening. He showed you pictures in the past that you couldn't see and dreams like movies that you can't remember. He's showing you now, but you're still not walking in the spirit to see and hear what the Holy Spirit needs to tell you and show you, so I'm calling you, darling. He wants you to know that she's keeping a record of all you say and write. God said she's keeping a record of all you do as well. She doesn't record what she does to make you react, but your reactions are being recorded. Do you hear me?"

"Yes."

"The Lord wants you to see in the spirit what she is planning, but you have lead over your eyes. You have to remove it and see with spiritual eyes. If you lay before him, God said he'll reveal all to you."

Sister Bett paused. She took a deep breath and continued. "I'm just a messenger. I can only give you what the Lord tells me to give you. I know you want it to work out with Sylvia, but I'm just giving you what the Lord tells me to give to you. Can we say thank you Jesus?"

"Thank you, Jesus."

"Can we say thank you, Jesus?"

"Thank you, Jesus."

Sister Bett continued, "The Lord said for you to hold your temper. The enemy is out to destroy you. Stopping you stops the children, and he will try through a temper you didn't know you had. That old man will try to rise up inside of you, but God said not so; you need to know this, this day." Though Max knew the little woman by the well saw much more than released to share, he knew not to ask particularly when she said, "I can only give you what the Lord tells me to give you," as if answering directly his desire to know more. The Lord gave those who spoke for him permission to share only what he allowed. Max understood this and even shared the principle with the students in the Christian club he advised. When directed to share what the Lord revealed a prophet shares, and when told not to share the prophet remains silent. A person provides the voice, but God orchestrates, reveals secret things that only he can know, that only he can change. When the urgency of a message such as "What have I done unto thee, that thou hast smitten me these three times?" reaches the throne, the Lord God bypasses the natural order of things for speedy delivery. Max did not ask for more even though he wanted to ask.

The little woman by the well sighed when released to say, "She wants you out of the house and out of her life, Brother Max. She's not listening to the Lord. She wants you destroyed. I didn't say it, God said it. Anger and bitterness fester within her, and she has no idea the source is the enemy because the feelings are so real to her."

"The Lord wants you to know that the enemy is angry that I told you this, so he's going to try to take you out. The Lord said get oil. Anoint your hands and feet every day. Do you hear me, darling? Pray your hands and feet move to do his bidding before you leave the house. It's going to be rough, this road ahead of you. The enemy thought he had you and believes there's still a chance to derail you. Do you hear me, darling?"

"Yes."

"The Lord said you have this little prayer you say when you're on the plane. You know what he's talking about?"

"Yes."

"The enemy will try to get you while you travel. If on the day you are scheduled to travel and the Lord tells you, 'Not today, son,' then don't go. Pray before you get into the car even if your trip is around the corner to the grocery store you always go to or the bank, the one in that shopping center of the home improvement store. The Lord showed me these buildings for a reason. The enemy is trying to take you out. The Lord said when your car doesn't start, when it is not drivable just sit in your car and say God is all right, all right, all right three times. He's all right. God said that he will send an angel to see you through. I see you in the car wanting to cry, but God sad suck it up, suck it up! And know that he is all right, all right, all right. Help is on the way. I didn't say it, God said it."

"It's a journey the Lord has you on. No one but you can walk this one. 'No one,' he says. When you emerge on the other side, you'll have found your first love again; you'll be a demon chaser; you'll be able to see and hear in the spirit consistently, and you'll be a mighty man of God speaking to disease and death and lack, and you'll be able to tell them all to move. The Lord said, 'This is why people don't like you. It has nothing to do with what Sylvia said to you. You intimidate people in the spirit, and they cannot put their finger on it because you're a peculiar treasure, and I have chosen you. Sylvia spoke out of evidence gathered from sight with natural eyes, but this is spiritual,' the Lord said."

"Can we say thank you Jesus?"

"Thank you, Jesus."

"Can we say thank you Jesus?"

"Thank you, Jesus."

"The Lord said, 'Beware of the man with the collar.' If you lay before him this night, he will reveal it to you. A trap is being set, Brother Max. A trap is being set. The enemy meant to surprise you with it, but God said, 'You will not be surprised this day.' Lay before him; he will make it plain to you. He keeps saying beware of the man with the collar. Do you know who he's talking about?"

"No."

"Well lay before him then, and he will tell you. Can we say thank you Jesus?"

"Thank you, Jesus."

"Can we say thank you Jesus?"

"Thank you, Jesus."

"I'm not going to hold you any longer. You be blessed, dear. You hold on; you hear."

"Yes, you be blessed too."

CHAPTER 21

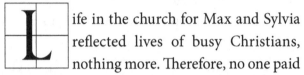ife in the church for Max and Sylvia reflected lives of busy Christians, nothing more. Therefore, no one paid any attention when Max slide into the sanctuary and took a seat near the back after walking through children's church or the nursery at the start of service and exited the service to head back to children's church and the nursery for dismissal, and Sylvia appreciated the disjuncture between public and private lives.

"Maybe we should talk with someone at the church?" Max once said.

"No!" Sylvia was quick. "I don't want anyone there knowing my business."

Max, a man of words, missed Sylvia's choice of pronoun. Perhaps he heard "our" or was anesthetized by the speed of the response. From Sylvia's perspective no one needed to know he slept on the sectional in the family room and then on the futon in his office when it became apparent the move back to the bedroom would not be quick. All this bothered Max, and questioning one's ability to run a ministry effectively while failing so miserably at home, he stepped down as co-director of the youth ministry. Now Max found himself in the sanctuary at the start of the service and chose to sit left of the center aisle near the rear. No longer in charge of bible study, Max

O' Darkness, Darkness! My Son Shall Pass

entered the sanctuary during the Tuesday night teaching and sat in the rear on the right side, not in the third row from the front with Sylvia and other praise team members and their spouses.

The choice painted an unauthorized public picture of their private lives. With a whisper from one sitting near Sylvia, she would turn quickly to see him sitting alone in the back of the sanctuary on Tuesday, or she would shift to straighten a skirt and readjust a jacket just enough to look askance to the left and see him sitting among strangers left of the center aisle on Sunday. He never told her he stepped down as co-director of the youth. He refused to yell from the family room up to master bedroom or send a text to deliver the news. It caught Sylvia by surprise, and she believed shifted the point of control out of her hands and into his, but Max thought nothing of control. He simply found duplicity and sham distasteful.

Though warned by God, "She wants you out of the house," he chose to believe Sylvia who said, "I want you to fight for me," so he fought. In fighting, he sent flowers. She never acknowledged receipt but chose instead to let them lose bloom prematurely from neglect. He cooked pasta. "Tomato sauce gives me heartburn," she said. He built a mushroom cream sauce. "The white sauce sours in my stomach." She ate neither. He fixed coffee for two. "I don't drink coffee anymore; it makes me jittery." He sat next to her on the bedroom loveseat. "I'm trying to watch this." What he assumed was space needed to reassess, realign, and renew a love, she envisioned it was a permanent moat that she controlled and could eventually deny reentry and even parental access.

Sylvia initiated the changes in the cell phone account. She removed Max and Sarah from the life insurance policy. She would decide when their marital problems became public knowledge, and Max capitulated. He moved to the living room and then office after the shock of "If you want me to just lie here and you act like a pig, then so be it." Their last time together meant she would have to start

123

counting again for her goal for marital destruction through Virginia threshold of a year apart. That comment, however, succeeded where excuses and quips just short of invective failed. "I knew from the day I married you it was a mistake," she said. "I didn't come home because I didn't want to see your face," she said. "Men much better than you want me." Such comments resulted in his going to bed later and moving a little closer to the edge on his side. None forced him out of the room entirely until "if you just want me to lie here" drove Max to the main level, picked him up and carted him to the family room first and then office, which meant no more feigned headaches or elaborate excuses from Sylvia to put in motion a plan for divorce in the state whose public relations campaign claimed it as a state for lovers. A year apart and a witness to verify that time was all it took. She could now move forward with clearer conscience, no longer having to bother heaven for forgiveness over headaches imagined or abnormal menstruation cycles concocted. Sylvia's plan included public awareness after Mark's graduation, but Max's simple decision around sanctuary seating exposed the timeline's weakness and revealed to Sylvia that attempts to control others had limitations. She needed to throw the plan into overdrive and began by garnering support from those with influence in the church that now knew a little something of her private life.

Sylvia spoke to the pastor. Sunday after service he called Max to the front of the church, placed a hand on Max's shoulder and said, "I can see your pain. Would you like to talk?" Max nodded, and though he said nothing, he felt finally pastoral intervention to bring about godly redirection. "Come by the church Monday at eleven. It's my day off, but I'll come in just for you." He tapped Max on the shoulder twice and moved on.

Max arrived, sat in the lobby, and waited until called. "Come have a seat," the pastor said. As Max sat the pastor continued, "The Lord dropped you in my spirit." Max, looked at him, and having grown a little skeptical of how often the Lord was dropping and telling, he said nothing but thought to himself how anyone could believe that such heightened activity from heaven could indeed accomplish so little. He wondered too about God's indiscriminate dropping. Since when did God drop the obvious? Daniel, not those around him, had an understanding in all dreams and visions because God gave him that. The magicians, enchanters, sorcerers, and the Chaldeans, well versed learned men, showed their inability to pierce divine mystery and crack the code of secret things.

Separate cars to church, maybe not that obvious, but opposite sides of the aisle during Sunday service and sitting in the back row on Tuesday during bible study seemed quite clear. Just when did God use the supernatural to reveal what any observant person could see with the natural eye? Gravediggers who threw the dead atop a prophet's bones knew without supernatural revelation that the dead came back to life. They could see it. Descending Mount Sinai Moses knew what Joshua could not because Joshua had yet to receive the declaration that began with "As I was with Moses." Moses talked with God, and the Lord told him the noise rising up the mountainside came from the people below who gathered ingredients for heavenly bread in the morning and drank the purest water from a rock; it was not the sound of war. He had no need to see them.

"The Lord dropped you in my spirit" was followed by "I spoke with Sylvia and got her perspective, and she said there was no hope." With that Max's guard rose up. The Holy Spirit brought back the *rhema* given through the little woman by the well. She delivered a nearly inscrutable clause saddled by words that were direct and meant to reveal providential foreknowledge and support during this marital struggle. "The Lord said" preceded "Beware of the man in the collar" which was followed by "I can see it, Max; I can see it." This Max heard after Sister Bett said, "The Lord dropped you in my spirit." Her drop preceded his sitting before one with a collar. Max fought to make sense of the warning when first heard. He thought of many ministers in the church to whom the statement could apply, but fought internally against the meaning leaning toward his pastor. He lost.

Sylvia's call to the pastor which gave her a sense of regaining control led to the meeting with Max in the pastor's office where hearing "no hope" revealed a flippant use of bound, loose, decree, and declare. "No hope" exposed them as ineffective money-making ideas for Sunday morning compact disc sales. It turned them into pulpit clichés that looked the part of battle ready but proved evanescent when darkness engaged the church in direct spiritual combat. "No hope" revealed that neither Sylvia nor the pastor had control to lose, that their actions were merely variables in an equation of demonic division, rising from a dark, dark eternal place.

Max struggled with the chain of events—a call, an invite, a visit to hear what the sectional and futon tried to tell him. The struggle moved him to wonder why the Lord took the time to "drop" him in the pastor's spirit only to hear there was no hope. Did the drop include a script? Did the script include a talk with Sylvia? Was it God's plan for the shepherd to hear "no hope?" If so, did the script include a spiritual response? As he sat across from the pastor, Max received a natural response and answered questions knowing that he would never again grace that office.

Max listened as the pastor spoke about the fastidiousness of Sylvia. Never a hair out of place or suit wrinkled when she stood to sing with the praise team. "Sarah must give her fits," he said. The pastor contrasted mother and daughter, and then asked, "What's Sylvia's mother like?" He followed with, "What's her parents' relationship like? We reproduce what we know."

Max endured the pastor's textbook knowledge on issues and relational psychology absent discernment and anointing. Never once did he hear that marriage is a covenant and a covenant requires sacrifice, a life laid down. Not once did he hear that history began with a covenant, a rather small, quiet, somniferous affair where a man woke short one rib to find a wife in the most idyllic of settings, and they were not ashamed. They were not ashamed. Max did not hear that history would end with a gloriously large wedding feast after the Bridegroom returns for a bride without spot, wrinkle, or blemish. The gaping hole, the spiritual emptiness spoke most loudly, not the earnest speech or psychosocial knowledge. The words highlighted the lack of anointing and discernment that might have pointed an unmoored marriage to the location of its anchor, halted the drifting if not bobbing at least by reattaching the marriage to hope and dropping that hope into a cleft in the Rock there to stay until the remaining despondence transformed into hope and months and months of doubt into a godly, inspired, eternal yes.

The pastor dismissed Titus's warning to hold firm to the trustworthy word as taught, so one could give instruction in sound doctrine and rebuke those who contradict it. He chose instead worldly understanding over spiritual wisdom and a word of knowledge from the Father of Righteousness able to germinate a mustard seed size of faith. A shepherd walking in the spirit would have spoken a word of encouragement, and then looked for hope to emerge on the other end of endurance. One in the spirit would have interceded for Max and Sylvia, slowed things down, tried to outlast the darkness and the stubbornness of flesh with just one seed of faith and an ounce of endurance until hope rose, but there was no understanding communicated to Max during the meeting that suffering wrought endurance and developed in us character that led to hope, a glorious hope that never put us to shame. He did not admonish Max to endure until hope showed itself or rebuke Sylvia and remind her that a Christian's life is one built on hope and a godly marriage a covenant, not a partnership, a covenant where soul merged with soul.

His pastor did not share any kernels of what could be, and Bible verses invoked during the meeting mixed little with the world's knowledge without the rousing shaking of the music department whose zeal ensured vinegar and oil, the natural and the spiritual mixed and separated again only when members and visitors went home and the zeal finally subsided. On this Monday nearly twenty-four hours after the last song by the praise team, Max, given the weight of hopelessness to add to the spirit of rejection, left much lower than when he entered the clergyman's office.

The pastoral deposit of "no hope" clung to the spousal gift "people feel they have to be smart around you, and this is why nobody likes you." Walking to his car he searched his memory for words from Solomon, an uplifting bit of wisdom to lighten the load of the visit, but Jeremiah found his way to the fore instead and Max thought, "He has filled me with bitterness; he has made me drunk with wormwood. My soul is bereft of peace; I have forgotten what happiness is. My endurance has perished; so has my hope from the Lord."[17] Counseling without the Spirit left him dry. He found firsthand the cost of worldly wisdom, compromise, and abandoned solemnity much too high.

He got into his car, sat for a while, and thought a little baroque virtuosity to lift a heavy soul. Max opted for Bach, "Partita No. 3 in E Major, BWV 1006. I, Preludio." He plugged in the MP3 player, found the piece, and closed his eyes. During the second pass, the music drove his mind to Rilke's "The Neighbor" where a deep river would have succeeded in its call to the heavy hearted save for a violinist playing so fearfully beautiful it reminds the speaker in despair, "Life is infinitely heavier than the heaviness of all things."

Life is infinitely heavier he thought. He sat a little longer in the church parking lot held by the verve of the violinist and pace of the music which kept moving, kept marching toward an end only to start over on the player. His spirit moved from the weight of life to the incomparable Father of all so vast that the weight of his train filled a temple, so powerful that a glory cloud descended and filled one too. The all-encompassing weight of the glory of the Lord stood firm while the voice of angels crying, "Holy, Holy, Holy" shook the temple with their praise, but they could not move God. Who is the king of the *Kavod?* Yahweh strong and mighty, Yahweh mighty in battle. The music sunk deep within Max as if, as if fishing for praise beneath hopelessness and rejection to pull exhortation out of a sinking heart and drag it upward through the river's dredge and silt of darkness, pull it upward until his praise merged with the continuous praise of angels in awe of The One who is holy, righteous, and pure. Thank you, Jesus, the Alpha and Omega." He praised God for being God. "Holy! Holy! Holy! to the Lord God Almighty, the Root of David who prevailed to open the book!"

"Hallelujah to the Lamb who sits on the throne who sent warning by way of New York to one in Virginia in a bout with darkness who had forgotten how to hear. Hallelujah, Glory to your name, Jesus." He praised the Lord of all and drove to the bank, praised him while making a withdrawal from the ATM machine, and praised him as he pulled off. He drove past the home improvement store he no longer frequented since times demanded he retrench. He looked at the flowers and shrubs on display, none of which he planted in his yard this year. As he approached the stop light to exit the shopping center, he continued to praise God, "Thank you, Jesus; glory to your wonderful name." The light turned green while Bach played quietly in the background; he waited for the traffic on the left and right of him to come to a complete stop. "Thank you, Jesus," he said again as he yielded to oncoming traffic. He entered the intersection to make the left turn when in the third lane to his left a driver seemingly unaware that two lanes were stopped at a red light drove through the intersection. Max slammed on the gas to avoid a direct hit to the driver's side door. The onrushing car struck Max's just above the rear tire, turning it one hundred and eighty degrees. He sat facing the shopping center he tried moments ago to leave. The impact bent the rear driver's side tire so that the top leaned into the car and the bottom angled outward. A little shaken, he was all right.

A driver stopped at the light ran over to Max. "Sir, are you all right?"

"Yes. I'm good. I had the green, didn't I?"

"Yeah, she ran the light. Are you sure you're all right? That was pretty nasty; it spun your car around."

"Yes, I'm fine."

"I called the police." Shaking his head, he continued, "It makes no sense. How could she not see that two lanes were stopped? I can't understand it."

Max understood. Nothing natural here, she did what she was told to do. Perhaps having listened for so long, it seemed natural that an accident resulted from distraction. "I appreciate your help. Can you stay until the police arrive and give your statement?"

"Sure."

The police arrived, and had Max move his car into the shopping center which he did slowly. Then the police took statements and called a tow truck. Max waited in his car and began to praise the Lord for moving his car enough to avoid a direct hit to the driver's seat. With his car not drivable beyond the very slow crawl into the parking lot, he had no way home. Sylvia would be a little shocked initially, but that shock would give way to indifference. He had no injuries, no soreness. He remembered he was to say, "God is all right, all right, all right." He cleared his mind. He thanked God for the warning about his car and then for ensuring the impact landed behind the driver's seat. The impact's position had nothing to do with reflex, but the actions of angels who pushed the car forward and then around to minimize the enemy's vehicular missile. "God," he said, "is all right, all right, all right." He would live beyond the enemy's attempt to take him out. "God is all right, all right, all right," he said. "God is all right, all right, all right." After the third time, Max sat with eyes closed until he heard "Sir, is there a body shop you prefer?"

He opened his eyes, said hello to the tow truck driver, and gave him the name of a body shop. Then he tried to figure out how he would get home as he got out of the car and watched the driver prepare to pull the car up on the flatbed.

As if reading his mind, the driver looked across the flatbed and asked, "Do you have a ride home? Is someone coming to pick you up?"

"No, I guess I'll walk."

"I'm not supposed to, but I'll give you a ride. Our orders are to go straight to the body shop, but I'll drop you off first. Where do you live?"

"Not far by car. I really appreciate this."

As he pushed the button to lower the flatbed with the car firmly on it, the tow truck driver said, "When it's darkest, there's always hope. Let's get in."

Max, a little shocked by the alignment of the message said, "What did you say?"

The driver looked at him and smiled. Then embellished a bit, "When life seems at its darkest, there's always hope my friend."

"Thank you and God bless you." Max climbed into the cab and strapped himself in.

"God is good," the truck driver said as he buckled his seatbelt.

Max looked at him and said, "That he is; he's all right with me." Then he gave the driver his address.

CHAPTER 22

Satan continued to move uninhibited in the church while marriage after marriage collapsed. Members spoke of God's influence in their lives, but when pushed could point to very little evidence of the miraculous able to halt the stride of dark things. They told how God moved them from around the country to Virginia and placed them in the church they now called home. None ever stated that they heard him say, "You will travel to take care of family" and never saw a thought video that ended one way of life and began a godly one. Most disconcerting of all, when hearing that God still had plans for the lives of his children and made those plans known today as he did with Elijah, Abraham, Mary, and Joseph—told them when to leave and when to stay, told them when to hide and when to be bold—upon hearing stories from friends and acquaintances that God directed their relocation efforts with a message from on high, it frightened them.

Sermons confirmed few walked in the Holy Spirit and many failed to understand the spiritual nature of growth and popularity, that neither could flank an eternal yes as if all three agreed in the spirit. Church leaders believed their preaching could change this; their messages could make the path more palatable and popular by igniting soul and body with a gospel that kept people comfortably in their seats. Few made the connection between the adjuration of the seven sons of Sceva and the emerging enjoyable but ineffective gospel that bound nothing on earth and loosed nothing in heaven. The enemy found no need to say, "Jesus we know and Paul we know, but who are you?" when preachers and elders declared, "Satan, you should have taken me out when you had the chance; you should have killed me while I was down," no answer of the kind acknowledging Jesus or Paul needed since darkness moved unabated. With discernment leaders and members might have heard the demonic response to the crowd rousing, frenzy inducing statements about being taken out, turned around, broken, or killed. With discernment those divorced and those barely hanging on to a fraying marriage where one spouse embraced darkness would have heard the enemy instead asking, "Why?"

But none heard, and as the darkness spread and the number of divorces rose, the church fought back. Nursery and children's church workers sat through protocol training on new standard operating procedures conducted by ministry leaders. The adult signing in a child for children's church or the nursery had to pick up the child and sign him or her out without exceptions because the church was too large and could not keep up with the changing membership of families. Youth workers implementing these new procedures grounded in risk management reflected a church fighting in the natural while Satan and his team fought in the spiritual realm.

Having begun in the spirit, the church unknowingly sought to gain strength apart from the spirit. It could ignore the impact on families because of a seemingly never-ending stream of people joining the church as families moved in and out of the DC area. New members meant new workers and new voices. While the clergy could not put a finger on the trouble, they decided to wait the evil out as veteran members who had developed an increasingly high tolerance for flesh provided continuity by helping those new to the church adjust.

Sylvia ate little spiritually because little went out. Leads and solos that might have comforted the bereaved, broken yokes, and become signature songs in the first church were given to new voices identified as vehicles to minister to the congregation. No anointing flowed through Sylvia as it had in their first church where it moved along her voice to bring forth deliverance, healing, and bended knees. Darkness reigned quietly, unnoticeably. The whispers by way of insect left festering deposits of bitterness and disenchantment, and they lodged deep in the city of her soul. Marriage seminars and women's retreats could not dislodge the tenants at home and comfortably in control within a body that forgot its life was no longer its own.

Amid darkness, Max walked out his request for help. He engaged prayer walks with God who sent messages from the eternal in the form of the play, the Word, and the prophetic. While they helped him endure, they did not alter the course he and Sylvia seemed destined to take, so he walked the more. Thirty-minute strolls became forty-five-minute walks and in a short period of time, walks lasted a couple of hours or more. He walked alone; he stepped out concerns and worries, and then placed them neatly at the feet of Jesus. The more he walked, the less he spoke amid ravaged finances and canceled contracts.

He rose in the morning to walk. When he returned, he cleaned the house and then walked again. Max cooked, and then he walked. Spiritual songs gave voice to prayers in his heart his lips would not let escape. They told Jesus all while he moved in and out of neighborhoods now repositories for an imperceptible billowing darkness that flooded them and tried its best to drown God's own. Through song he prayed Psalms forty-six as he walked while his spirit and soul yielded to the lyric and found rest. They stopped gasping for air and found they could be still and know that God is. Max selected songs that gave voice to confronting rising waters and his sense of drowning until an unwavering conviction grew once again that water gave way to the Lord of all, so "let the waters rise" the lyric proffered and settled his breathing with each step. Lyrics spoke of being carried by God and pointed to the vastness of I Am through notes rising higher and higher. Songs told Max he had been invited. They reminded him to praise God through the storm. They spoke for him as lyrics entered his heart and became silent prayers rising unassailably through darkness toward heaven to reach the Son of Man seated at the right hand of power, a priest without beginning or end who because of his death and resurrection could intercede for Max and take the request for forgiveness for opting out of the perennial fight and cover Max's failings of self and marriage with his blood and pass it to his left along with any tears or moans, pass it left with love and empathy to the one seated on the throne. All this was a benefit of the college yes and the word that no one, "no one gets to the Father but by me."

The scourge of darkness was felt in all areas of his life. Max and Sylvia could no longer keep their building commitment, promised funds that moved through their hands into those assumed to represent Jesus in the building of the Lord's house. Members watched the cost of the building increase with the burgeoning vision delivered through the pastor. From five to seven to ten to twenty-one million dollars, the vision blossomed and costs rose at the same time divorce razed the flock and burned ferociously, leaving the newly singled picking through ash. Some feigned happiness; others reeled from burns. Funds following scattered bodies dispersed and dried up.

The pastor spoke to pen and ink copy and web-based magazines blaming the economy for the marriage troubles. During an interview he noted a three hundred percent increase in the request for marriage counseling in his church. His comment betrayed a lack of faith and portrayed an image of God ineffective at holding his own, families and capital, as evident in the reconstruction of families and foreclosure knocking at the door of the unfinished church.

The church amassed excessive bond debt and high interest loans then cut back aid to the poor and foreign missions, but what did

God say? What was the Father's plan to reverse financial blight and bind the hand of primary and secondary monetary disease? When told to cast its bread, the church held it moving on worldly wisdom instead of lending to the Lord by caring for the poor and investing in a recession and inflation proof account with a high rate of return because the Lord said so, and he could not lie. Tithes dwindled too because an ark built of pitch and wood designed by the Lord himself to transport pairs of animals proved more effective than an ark of safety built of brick and mortar to transport families through this life and souls onto glory.

CHAPTER 23

week before Valentine's Day Max walked upstairs to the master bedroom to find Sylvia at her dressing table. "Can we talk?"

"Talk," she said fixing her hair; she chose not to look at him.

"How are things for you?" Max asked sitting on the side of the bed he slept in before moving down stairs.

"Not good," Sylvia said.

"What do we need to do to make it better?"

"Nothing you can do."

"I don't understand," Max said.

"I don't love you anymore." She continued combing her hair.

The comment wedged silence into an already strained conversation that never found its way. Then Max said, "Well I think some couples fall in and out of love over the course of a marriage—"

"I don't believe that." Sylvia paused immediately after cutting him off. She fussed with her hair, and finally turned to him. "I can't remember one day of happiness with you. I have no memory of ever being happy since I married you." As if anticipating his thoughts that in the past they both stated God put them together, she said turning back to look at her face in the mirror, "Perhaps God made a mistake."

How easily that fell from her lips, Max thought. He twisted inside. She sat at her dressing table looking determined and in control, and he sat on the bed he no longer slept in, not at all at home in a room that invited him to ponder divine error. "I don't have time to talk about this any further today. We can talk about what you'll need to do next Thursday."

"Ok."

"Good. I'm busy now." She continued to comb her hair.

That following Thursday, Sylvia compiled a list of bills complete with a column identifying the contribution Max needed to make for her household to run smoothly in his absence. She gave him the list one hour after throwing a stuffed bear and a hand size box of chocolate candy at him on Thursday, Valentine's Day, the only day her calendar showed availability to discuss ending it all. At the bottom of the list she totaled the sum, and it equaled a little more than six thousand dollars a month.

The next day he walked. Donned earphones and music device and walked down the undigested six thousand a month that mingled with I don't love you and never will again. He walked down the comment I think God made a mistake and the miniature valentine teddy bear and candy thrown in his lap as she said, "I didn't think you'd get me anything; here this is for you." A bear. A miniature tote of candy. A card. A spread sheet totaling six thousand dollars a month worth of irony. Max threw them away later that night and walked the meaning of it all down the following morning. Although he never opened his mouth, Max placed the message of those misused symbols of love at the Rose of Sharon's feet. The meaningless card, flung bear, the confectionary, and feigned hurt for the lack of reciprocation in the face of, "I don't love you," and the message I never will again walked down with mouth closed amid intercession through song.

On February the fifteenth his musical choice asked God to hold his heart. A hard song for him at first, it spoke what he could not.

He had asked for guidance for some time, but God gave him nothing tangible to hold onto. His soul cried out and questioned whether or not God heard him. "If you're everything you said you are...," the lyric put forth by Tenth Avenue North spoke that buried thought from deep within that he could not bring himself to say. "If you're everything you said you are...." But nothing. No answer came as he ambled across town, and then entered his house and sat in his office. Saved from a vehicular missile only to stumble about and wonder if the everyday was also worthy of the Lord's attention and a rescue through divine intervention. "If you're everything you said you are won't you come close and hold my heart." Max wondered if perhaps it was time to go since no longer loved by his wife and tolerated by friends who really did not like him anyway. Perhaps without six thousand to contribute it was time to go.

Later that night, the little woman by the well called. "I was telling your sister that I had to call you. This is my second attempt; I dialed the wrong number. As I was leaving a message, a woman picked up to say that I had the wrong number, and I could pray for her, but you know to walk in the spirit, you have to be about the Father's business. The Father told me to call you, not her, so I got off the phone and tried you again. How are things?"

"Good."

"You sure?

"Yeah, I'm good."

She paused as if listening like an interpreter before giving the translation. Then she said, "God will tell you when to leave, darling."

Max was silent. His first thought was God heard me, heard what lips never spoke. His second thought moved him from accident to everyday. God cares.

"Did you hear me? God will tell you when it's time. God said that he's just who he said he is. He told me to tell you that he is everything he said he is and more. Though man changes, he changes not. While in your house, he may tell you not to go to the church; a trap is being set. Listen to the Lord. If you lay before him this night, he will reveal all to you. If you're in your car on the way to church and he tells you to turn around, then you turn around and say hallelujah over and over and follow God's lead. If you arrive at the church, put your hand on the doorknob, turn it, and God tells you to turn around and not to enter the sanctuary, then you say hallelujah, turn around, and follow his lead. If you enter the Church and God tells you to turn around and leave, then you do what God says. You be obedient to his voice. A trap has been set. I don't know why I'm telling you this, but he wants you to know this; he said you need to know this, this day. The Lord said she is trying to get you angry, to push you as she forms a case against you, but you don't want to see it. The Lord said be wise and don't fall for it. Can we say thank you Jesus?"

"Thank you, Jesus."

"Can we say thank you Jesus?"

"Thank you, Jesus."

"He said there is no need for you to play those four Psalms you've been playing over and over to help you sleep. He says they've done their job, and he's honored your seeking and your drawing closer. He said the trials have led to the walks, and the walks have built you up. Do you know what he talking about?"

"Yes."

"He says, 'I have carried you, my son, and I have heard your silent prayers. You're on a journey, and it is not yet over, but your walking has put you in a place where you can endure.' He said that you forgot him and were busy, busy, busy, working, working, working. You forgot him. This trial is bringing you home again, and it is not quite over. My God Max, I can see it. Whew! The Lord is showing me you walking it down, walking it down. Praying through the music and walking it down."

Max wrote and cried. Body shook as he listened and captured in writing that something more would befall him.

"The Father said that you have given much to brothers, sisters, friends, and those on the street you didn't know. He said your generosity will be paid back double and triple according to your faith. He said he really is who he says he is. His word will not return unto him void. Do you understand that?"

"Yes."

"He said he's opened travel for you. It's like a whirlwind. You get out, and it sucks you back in. You work, and then you don't work, but God has heard your prayer not from your mouth, but it rose from the depth of your spirit. My God, my God. I see a mighty man of God, Max, a faith walker on the other side of it all. If you could see what I see, my goodness, don't give up. Thank you, Jesus! Hallelujah! Thank you, Jesus! There is a release, a much larger release that needs to happen according to your faith, and the Lord said, 'You will soar, my son; soar like the eagle. Soar, my son; soar like the eagle. You are moving in the flesh, and you need to see in the spirit.' God said that when all this is over, you will understand what it means to walk in the spirit. There was an old you he's bringing back, a first love. There was a faith the old you had that he will uncover. Do you know what he's talking about?"

"Yes." Max thought of college, witnessing and laying hands. "Yes," he repeated.

"God is so good. He said that he really is who he said he is, and that you need to know this, this day. He said, 'Continue to be still and know that I am God.' He said that you've been turning around quickly when you see something out of the corner of your eye. He says that those are the angels he's sent your way. Can we say thank you Jesus?"

"Thank you, Jesus."

"Can we say thank you Jesus?"

"Thank you, Jesus."

"He said that you felt a hand on you last night you while you were asleep. You sat up quickly and looked for Mark and Sarah, but they were not in the room. You were a little frightened. You know what he's talking about?"

"Yes, I felt an arm around me last night, so I jumped up and looked to see who it was, but no one was there. I know there was an arm around me."

"God said it was his hand, darling, holding your heart? Can we say thank you Jesus?"

"Thank you, Jesus."

"Can we say thank you Jesus?"

"Thank you, Jesus."

"I'm picking up your son. God said that Mark is traveling soon. Is this right?"

"Yes, for a senior trip."

"Ok, well the Lord wanted me to tell you that your son really loves you. God said you need to know this, this day. He really loves you. God needs you to be ready to see beyond Sylvia's influence which is strong on him, but God said he will break it if you remain patient and walk up right before him. You hear me, darling? The Lord said that she has refused to listen to him and has chosen her own path, choosing to dance with darkness when she destroyed the family God ordained for great works. She's been trying to rally the children against you, but God said not so. None of what she's tried works with your daughter, but your son is a different story."

"God said that he will shake her, and you will not be able to recognize her. Loss will come her way when God shakes. She will look at you to ask you to stop it, but all you'll be able to say is that it's between you and my Father. It is out of my hands. My God, my God. It's a fearful thing to fall into the hands of the living God. You are not going to see this right away, but hold on and pray for her as he commands we are to do. You might not want to, but he commands it. God said that you have to begin to see with your spiritual eyes. If you lay before him this night, he will make it clear to you."

"There is a trap being set, darling, so beware of the man with the collar. God will tell you to shake the dust off your shoes as you go the way he directs you to go. It won't be easy, and when you feel like you have no one else, remember you have Jesus. I'm going to be praying for you. I'll carry you in prayer. You be blessed and hold on. More is coming your way, so hold on to God, and know God is who he said he is."

CHAPTER 24

s promised God opened travel again, and placed Max in Ohio after Detroit and New York trips. Thursday before heading to the airport, Max called Mark from Cleveland.

"What's doing?"

"Oh, I'm on the bus to Florida right now."

"Today? I thought you left tomorrow?"

"Yeah, I had my dates mixed up, but we're heading down now."

"Oh, all right. I'll keep it short since you're on the bus. Traveling mercies your way and call me when you're in Florida to connect while you're traveling."

"Ok."

"Bye. Have fun."

"Bye Dad."

Max called Sarah. "Hello Princess."

"Hi, Daddy."

"What's doing?"

"I'm studying Spanish. I've a test tomorrow."

"All right, I'll let you go; keep studying. I'll see you later tonight."

"Ok, bye Daddy."

While Max could not yet see the strings in the spirit, he could sense Sylvia's influence. He received no calls or texts during the senior trip, and when Mark returned the following week, Sylvia picked him up from the school. He walked into the family room after entering the house and gave Max a hug. After the hug, Max said, "You didn't call."

Out of Mark's growing sense of independence and strings pulled in the spirit, he said, "You don't call when you travel."

Initially shocked by the brazen nature of the response, he wondered how much was natural boundary testing and how much grew out of the current spirit of the house. Max knew Mark was wrong, but did not see that his son spoke out of something far greater and older than himself, that his words in fact were not really his, and the tone of voice he mustered came from an ancient place, a dark place.

Max said, "I called while you were traveling on the bus. I called while I was away."

"It was on accident," Mark said.

"Come again."

"It was by accident you reached me on the bus."

"I think you're missing the point. Whether I got you in the house, at a friend's house, or on the bus, I called to say hello. I was away; I called expecting to catch you in the house, but you had your travel days mixed up. Now, you were away, and you didn't call." Max paused. Looking at Mark he said, "Don't you think you should have called?"

Mark said, "No!"

"So I pay for a trip, but don't get a call. It's as if I get treated like an ATM machine, and once the money is dispensed contact ceases."

Angry, Mark said, "You didn't pay for this trip; Mom did." He turned to walk away.

"Come back here! You need to show some respect. You need to realize that spending money while on a trip is different from the money spent that secures the trip."

Mark stomped away. His anger building as he ascended the stairs peaked after he entered his room. Standing in front of the wall he punched a hole in the drywall dead center between two studs.

Seconds later Sylvia enraged by the power that set all in motion came down from her bedroom. Four words fell from her mouth, "What have you done?"

Max began to explain before realizing this was a trap although he did not understand the depth of it. For while Sylvia had schemed during the better part of the year how the marriage would come to an end, the enemy planned the marriage's demise since the directive from the prophet of the Lord to an unmarried college student to Eat! Eat! Eat!"

"Why am I explaining this to you?" Max got out of his chair and walked out of the family room which meant he walked in her direction.

Sylvia said, "Just run away like you always do." He stopped. With nearly twenty years of marriage, she knew what it would take to stop him. She continued, "You can't stand to see anyone happy. You are just miserable, unhappy, and hateful."

"You need to go back to your cloistered life upstairs. You never come down for anything family related, but you come down for this? You may intimidate your friends and those people at that church, but I am not afraid of you," he said.

"What are you going to do? Hit me big man! Hit me! Huh, hit me!" She tried to goad him into a swing, a push—accidental or intentional—either would be enough for the police or a visit to the emergency room for pictures and a restraining order and infuse a bit of speed into a methodical, timely process which could leap forward with even the slightest touch or sense of threat.

He furrowed his brow knowing the woman speaking was not the one he married. "You're nuts," he said. "Perhaps you have me mixed up with the spouse of someone you counsel. I don't beat my wife. I don't hit women. In fact, I can't remember the last time I hit anyone. You're crazy! You want me to hit you, but it won't work. Try another trick. I won't make it that easy." Max walk away.

She ran ahead of him up the stairs, and yelled, "You disgust me! You're pathetic! Why don't you just move out?"

"You move out!" he yelled back and started up the stairs.

"I pity you! You are less than a man!"

"That one's an old one; you've used it a couple of times now." You need something new, but need I remind you that beauty fades, and in the end what will you have?"

"You disgust me. I should have never married you!"

She headed into Mark's room still ruminating over the exchange and its current failure.

Throughout the swift downfall of the marriage, she had accused him of poisoning the children against her, and as she spoke to their son, Max decided to use the words he heard over and over from the children. "Mom says you are poisoning us against her."

He entered the room and said, "So now y-o-u'-r-e trying to poison our son against me."

Inflamed, Mark said, "No one poisons me and tells me how to think or what to do! No one can be happy here!" With fists clenched and down on either side, he walked over into Max's chest. He continued, "This is my senior year, and you put us through all this!"

"You must be losing it kid," Max said, and stood in Mark's chest, backing him up, "You better take it down."

Mark walked backward, but followed the exchange with "Why don't you just leave!" The three of them stood in the son's room, but they did not stand alone. Hell bound hosts stood victoriously. They celebrated the gulf they created between God and the offspring of Christians. Sarah stood on the front porch in tears refusing to stand as witness and legitimize the victory of the indefatigable darkness she saw in bible study. Though she could not see in the spirit while she stood on the porch, she knew it had overtaken the house as it had the church, and like the families that disappeared after splitting, she knew one if not all members of her family would not return to the church this coming Sunday.

The explosive exchange among mother, father, and son broke through leaden eyes, broke through to Max in a way all other messages could not. While the simple question from father to son as impetus for a volatile argument was unexpected, the goading for physical contact with "hit me big man, hit me" was not. The argument was too explosive to dismiss and made visible the extent of the trouble within the household that a thrown stuffed animal and a six-thousand-dollar request could not.

CHAPTER 25

On Monday, no one spoke to Max. Mark and Sarah left for school without saying goodbye, and Sylvia, not unexpected, left for work without a word. After a night of playing "Grace Flows Down" low on the MP3 player to invite sleep in the natural and minister to a soul nearly worn out, Sarah's was the first voice he heard Tuesday morning. Sarah said, "Goodbye, Daddy," kissed him, gave him a drawing, and left for school. No words came from his wife, none from his son. Only Sarah spoke. "Goodbye, Daddy," she said with a kiss, handing him a manila folder with an angel drawn on one side and Satan drawn on the other. "Goodbye, Daddy."

She and her brother saw the vision in the church, and they watched accompanied by an emissary. She sensed but did not quite understand the unseen battle depicted on the folder. One flap representing angelic forces and the other demonic. The battle she rendered was not fought with tangible weapons. In a speech bubble next to the angel Sarah wrote, "Satan you are defeated!" This eternal message delivered lovingly through the depth of her spirit came from a much deeper place to serve as balm. "Goodbye, Daddy" and the manila reminder through her hands and words through her mouth like a biblical scribe declaring what was not yet in front of the senses, but because it grew out of divine promise, it had to come to pass. She walked to the door and spoke "Good bye, Daddy," two words stretched into three delivered through human voice and accompanied by an illustration broke through a spiritual wall of silence.

Sleep was futile after her loving voice and her rendering of the battle taking place in their house. Sarah caught what adults did not, so he rose, showered, and prepared to teach bible study as he had done throughout the ordeal. During his preparation, the Lord Almighty spoke. Came running to him, breaking through flesh, hurt, and carnality to hold him and whisper. God dismissed the silence that bound mother and son. He answered the prayers walked out with song, answered the extended telegram delivered through the Psalms played at night, and like the lyric of the song he played last night, the anointing flowed down to cover Max. The Lord's answer gave clarity to Sister Bett's message. He told Max that he would leave more than his church this day; today he would leave home. He would pack up and shake the dust. He would leave today for a trap had been set.

Unsure of what he heard, Max tried to refine the bible study lesson, but the Holy Spirit was not in it. Instead the Spirit moved him to clean his office. He vacuumed and dusted. He recycled old papers and emptied desk drawers. Needing money at the beginning of the year, he sold most of the books he collected since college to a used bookstore, so he dusted empty shelves. While dusting Max heard more clearly, "The trap has been set."

Still a little unsure of whether the Spirit spoke or his mind reacted to silence, he continued to clean. He waited for Sarah to come home, but when students walked by the house after school without Sarah, he knew. The Lord spoke, and although he tried to deny it, tried to will the message and the reality it spoke away, Max knew in his soul that a trap was indeed set. His stomach turned. Twenty years of reshaping, compromising, and adjusting, twenty years of becoming one was rapidly being undone.

He scrolled through old emails to find the one for the New York project that contained all the contact information for those team members. He met Cynthia on the plane, and the Lord moved both to share their stories: her story of untimely spousal death and his of marital disintegration. Neither knew each other beyond that moment, but both knew God. Cynthia offered her basement when first hearing about his trouble, and now over the phone, he asked if the offer still stood.

Surprised she asked, "What's going on? Do you want to talk about it? Are you sure this is the right thing to do?"

"I didn't ask for therapy; I asked for a room," Max said.

"Of course, it's available. Let me just move a couple of things to get it ready. When will you be coming?"

"Tonight."

Max followed the call for the basement with one to a storage facility. Once secured, he began to move his belongings from office to Subaru to storage facility, trip after trip after trip.

In the middle of packing and moving, Max called the director of bible study to say he would not be teaching today, and in fact, would not be teaching there at all from this day forward. While on the phone, students from the late bus walked passed the house without Sarah, and he knew for sure. He hung up the phone and continued to pack. A trap, a trap had been set. He recalled, "Beware of the man with the collar." Without thinking about it, Max called a friend and fellow bible study teacher. He did not know why he called. He just dialed, and after each said hello, the deacon said, "Your family's here. They were here early. I think they're still in a meeting with the pastor. They've been in his office for a while. What's up?"

"Nothing much. You popped into my head, so I dialed to check in with you. What are you doing at the church?"

"I didn't have to work today, so I thought I'd come in early and get a few things done. Staying home is not good you know. Are you coming later?"

"Not tonight, I'm a little busy. We'll talk later."

"Thank you, Jesus," Max said. "Thank you for having me make the call. Teach me how to listen, Lord; teach me how to hear."

The little woman by the well said, "Beware of the man with the collar." Not a collar but "the collar." God often speaks to us in our own language of experience Max taught; farmers get farm metaphors and boatman get sea metaphors. Max, a word man, received messages in which verbal nuance, in this case the subtlety communicated by the selected article, proved the difference between hearing and "hearing now hear." The warning identified the pastor who previously spoke to Max privately, and now held a meeting with his family without him.

Packing took longer than anticipated. Bible study would be over soon, and he wanted to avoid a face-to-face meeting when the family returned. Max prayed, "Lord, extend the bible study" over and over with the simplicity of early adolescence, and the Lord who destroyed the wall of silence to reach Max did just that.

Max believed time apart might allow dour feelings to dissipate and a fresh start to emerge. A number of couples reevaluated decisions and rekindled love after time apart. He thought the same might be their story though a pastor's message of no hope and the Lord's directive to shake the dust had him wondering. With the last load stuffed into the back seat, he turned and walked into the house for one last look around his office. Then he placed his house keys on the kitchen counter, left the house, and closed the locked door. He stood on the front porch and looked around at the neighborhood. He lifted his right foot and shook it, and then tapped it with his right hand. He lifted the left foot and shook it, then tapped it with his left hand. Max walked down the steps, sent Sylvia a text, programmed the GPS with the Maryland address, and then pulled out of the driveway.

Mark called while he drove to Maryland. "Call me back in about fifteen minutes. I'm looking for my rental. It's dark, and I've never been here before," he said. Max found the house, spoke little to the landlord as it was late, and unpacked enough for a night's sleep. He left the rest for tomorrow.

His basement rental, a sizeable enough portion of the seven thousand square foot home, proved he was as important as lilies and birds, if not to Sylvia, then at least to Jesus. The lower parts of a sprawling home were better than hotels and certainly cheaper. As a child reared in a farmhouse, adults pumped water from an outside pump and carried it inside before the installation of plumbing brought the ease of running water to a household secretive about its antiquated ways. Still the lack of a hot water heater meant boiling bath water on the stove every morning and carrying it to the bathroom to wash before school. Kerosene stoves in the kitchen and living room heated the house, and opened windows and doors cooled it. Flies that entered the screen-less kitchen door frame and investigated the stillness of their kind eventually mimicked their immobility on a fly strip. Porches were cement squares and beds slept four.

In this current place like his Virginia home, the back door opened to a deck, but unlike his house, the kitchen boasted a morning room with a fully extended dining room table. The family room stretched till it spawned a rarely used furnished sunroom.

The house had space where the desire for it outpaced the need for it, where cathedral ceilings soared, soared as if in a futile attempt to touch the hem of grace. A move from farm house to the basement would be a cause for celebration, but not so. Max owned a house though now a sprawling basement fulfilled the basic need of shelter.

Mark never called back, so Max, once settled in the basement, called him.

"Hello," Max said.

"Hey, we spoke to the pastor before bible study, and he said that you shouldn't have said what you said to me. I just got in from my senior trip—"

"Wait, wait, wait…. If you think I called you to have you tell me what your pastor said, you're sadly mistaken. I called—"

"Well you said—"

"Listen young man, the last time I checked I was grown," Max cut in. Mark's voice communicated that it was unsure, and it reminded Max that Mark was an adolescent pressured into a journey. Only now was Mark aware the itinerary was not his, and the destination until now remained a mystery. Max continued, "Your pastor does not tell me how to run my life, and if you continue not to listen and cut me off as if you are telling me off, this conversation is over. Am I clear?"

Mark more calm said, "Yes."

"Good. Now apart from right and wrong, the real issue is how a simple question about a phone call triggered a chain of events that resulted in my moving out of the house preceded by some secret meeting with three members in a family of four. Time is sometimes all that is needed. You think of your actions; I'll think of mine, and we'll talk again about this when tempers are no longer part of the equation."

"Ok."

"Where's your sister?"

"In her room."

"Put her on."

Through tears and the audible sound of crying, Sarah said, "Hi, Daddy."

"Hi, Princess. So you know I've moved out."

"Yes, mom told us on the way home from bible study that you might not be here when we got home."

"Well, we'll still connect regularly. I'm in the area." Max could still hear the sobbing. "I've put a couple of things in your room here and there, and I left the camera and books and such in the office for you. The bike in the garage is probably best for Mark."

"Ok." With loud sobs she ended the call with "Love you, Daddy."

"Love you too, princess."

CHAPTER 26

T he following morning while he prayed, the Spirit revisited proverbs twenty-seven. "The full soul despises a honeycomb; but to the hungry soul every bitter thing is sweet."[18] He meditated on the verse; then waited silently for clarity. In this short time of estrangement from children and wife, he learned to devote time to listen to Jesus. Often he sat or knelt in silence with nothing out of the ordinary happening, but this morning the Spirit offered insight into sweet and bitter things.

He and many others stood as busy, busy, busy bees working for the Lord. Their nonstop work left no time to rest and gain nourishment from the sweetness of living bread. As God questioned the nature of fasting in Isaiah, Max felt in his spirit God question the nature and motivation of the incessant work performed in the church he recently left. "Was that work I chose? Were the workers placed in those positions by me?" Flitting and buzzing from project to project and walking after the imagination of their own hearts, workers ingested bitter morsels from the enemy as if heavenly bread were set before them at the Father's table. They ate and convinced themselves it was sweet.

Continued ingestion bewitched even the very elect within the congregation. God warned them not to love the world and the many,

many things in it. "Repent," he called to them. Repent. "Then shalt thou delight thyself in the LORD."[19] With honest concern for the hungry and afflicted, "Then shall thy light rise in obscurity, and thy darkness be as the noonday."[20] Hearing dulled, they heard only part and believed that delighting themselves in God obligated him to fulfill the desires of their hearts. Many desired things: bigger homes, multiple houses, or fur coats in southern climes. Gain became a unit of measure for godliness. Much gain, much godliness so it seemed, yet noonday remained hidden. Many church members desired to know God's ways, believing their anchors held fast to righteousness while hearts remained submerged in the temporal.

Praying that morning, Max found God used the afternoon of the accident when the world for him and Sylvia came to a stop to remind them of temporal and eternal differences and say emphatically that all things temporary pass away and cannot promise permanent security and protection. He wanted to break through to Max, help him see the spreading darkness, see sprawl claiming uncharted ground because he, Sylvia, and others chose forgetting and opting out of the spiritual fight at an alarming rate, and the results of this choice reached well beyond their generation.

The choice to live in peace with darkness exposed families to spiritual famine, and no dreamers availed themselves to make sense of the lean devouring the fat within the many iterations of that basic dream God sent. Peace at all costs was not the Lord's will, and he never changed his menu to accommodate the faddish tastes of the masses. When the disciples brought Jesus food while he spoke to the woman near the well of Jacob, Jesus told them he ate already. They looked at each other in surprise having gone for food because they had none, but Jesus spoke of eternal food, food not susceptible to rot, mold, or times of drought. "I have meat to eat that you know not of,"[21] Jesus said to his disciples. "My meat is to do the will of him who sent me and to finish his work."[22]

Hearing the unadulterated Word of God nourished and directed one's spirit and doing God's will served as meat while seated at the table of God. Hearers dined on God's orders to dip in their Jordan seven times instead of three or five in Abana. Only a few in the church could name their personal battle site the Valley of Berachah because they maintained courage and waited on the eternal source for victory when fear and anxiety seemed rational. The independent like Max and Sylvia gravitated to strange hosts who served them meals of rebellion. A few believers, however, humbled by circumstance allowed repentance to make a holy reservation with previously spurned hosts of heaven who without the slightest bit of hurt, anger, or spite graciously reseated them at the table of the Lord, reseated them with joy.

Max and Sylvia were seated at a dinner table of their choosing when they found themselves in traffic the day of the accident. No prayer rose up within them for those physically or emotionally injured from the accident because he was stuck in emptiness and she wallowed in favor, so God strategically placed others there willing to eat the meal he prepared for them as they sat surrounded by cars.

Some simply felt the desire to take a drive, and others said yes when Jesus called them as passenger to nowhere in particular it seemed until their car came to a sudden stop, and they instinctively grabbed each other's hands out of a deliberate urge to pray and persist as directed by the Most High Priest. Husbands and wives, sisters and brothers touched and agreed and stood in the gap by speaking out of certainty according to God's will things which were not. Those who sat alone and knew the Father well held hands with his Son and prayed. They dined until the words spoken in Max's car, "You can go now" which they did not hear coincided with the spiritual fact that they were full.

Max availed himself to the Father's will in the past; he could chase demons, fix plumbing, pray healing, and call for rain through a move of the Spirit and power from on high, but darkness quietly descended and changed this. Darkness touched lives imperceptibly here and there, a nip, a nick—continuous hits, but always making too small an alteration to notice. The darkness rarely spoke and seldom revealed itself, but God granted insights into the invisible to some soldiers of the pen who captured what they glimpsed as best they could, and while in prayer, the Lord revealed to Max the dangers of church busyness through one such work.

The Screwtape Letters by C.S. Lewis read while in college seemed to presage these dark times. Wormwood's progress exceeded avuncular expectation. Nicks and nips resulted in mothers on one side of the church aisle and fathers on the other till many families crumbled or imploded under the straining weight of darkness.

Better busy for the Lord than fighting. Many thought but never actually said if you sit on the right side, I'll choose the left. If you enter the sanctuary, I'll sing in the choir. If you come down to the chairs, I'll work in the overflow room.

Spouses separate during the day Monday through Friday remained so completing house cleaning and yard work on Saturday. Now Sunday provided endless opportunities for husbands and wives to pull apart. Large church buildings required a vast number of volunteers. Nursery rooms, children's rooms—space; chapels, sanctuaries, wedding rooms—space; overflow rooms, offices, coffee bars—space and more space. Hallways had benches; nooks had chairs. Counseling rooms, ministry rooms, classrooms all provided space where nicks and nips easily hidden in game rooms, media rooms, gymnasiums festered and became serious, unattended wounds. Rooms needed workers, and workers craved space.

Better busy for the Lord, for the Lord's work. Busy meant spousal avoidance, and avoidance aided the work of darkness. Some left the church before the problems of their marriage became public. Former congregants thought it the place because sloganeering from the pulpit never portrayed the gravity of wrestling with something spiritual, something invisible, wrestling with something not preferential to architecture or geography. It moved with those taught bitter and sweet water could not come through the same fountain.

Many who remained in the church and worked hard for God believed Satan targeted them through husbands and wives who were either too spiritual and thus legalistic or not spiritual enough and thus carnal. They were either Pharisee or Philistine, a mistake in the pairing ten, fifteen, twenty years ago before those targeted came to know their destiny.

Members of the church enjoyed sermons that addressed hard personal choices such as Hagar, Sarah, and Abraham, moving too quickly in their desire to assist a godly promise. Sermons planted the idea that an impetuous marital choice needed correcting. A decision made in their younger days yielded their current Ishmael when God commanded they bring forth Isaac, and sermons implied a method for rectifying the error. They heard many times from various preachers that Abraham put Hagar and Ishmael out!

A life in the service of the Lord not fettered by his voice but given to soul-stirring preaching and twisted rhetorical devices turned the biblical Ishmael into stalled dreams and derailed destinies prime for abandonment. Problems surrounding the metaphorical child overshadowed the basic relational needs of real daughters and sons. Stirred by a spirit to lay aside weights that so easily beset them, many moved as each imagined the father of faith would. They put their Hagar and Ishmael out!

The praise team, the most visible ministry in the church, supped with Wormwood unawares. The lead pianist-director and his wife, an emerging lead soprano, divorced quickly by all accounts. Both sung praise and glory to God for his goodness on Sunday and opted, it seemed, for separate lives on Monday. Then a tenor on the praise team and his wife in the choir called it quits. Who was the weight was impossible to tell. The bass player and his wife left the church before ending it all. The swing alto-tenor and her husband a bass player-sound engineer threw up their hands while their children clasped theirs. The lead soprano divorced her spouse and took the not recently divorced pianist turned director as mate; surely God saw the potential of blessed duets and sanctioned the initiatives to correct past wrongs.

Within their church grace paired with freedom and many called anything smacking of holiness, legalism. Wormwood's name would be a household one in the world of all things demonic where husbands and wives absent the cry of an Ezra or Nehemiah brazenly exchanged spouse for spouse within the congregation. Some chose for the second round a spouse seated in the same row they sat in during Sunday service, and others selected from the same ministry.

God spoke, but none listened when he asked through heavy, heavy heart words spoken and recorded in Hosea, "What shall I do with you, O Ephraim? What shall I do with you, O Judah? For your love is like a morning cloud and like the dew which goes early away.[23] For I desire steadfast love and not sacrifice, the knowledge of God rather than burnt offerings."[24] Darkness continued unabated and resulted in great numbers treating marriage covenants like cellular phone contracts and struggling as so many do with whether to upgrade or keep their current phone and ever wonder, ever wonder.

Just who spoke to whom when a lead soprano left husband and three daughters to follow heart and desire and a most talented band member left wife, son, and daughter to play privately for the heart and the desire of a most melodic voice. Who spoke to whom? Just who? Who spoke to the five children, the son, the daughters? Was it the woman dressed in white? Who spoke to them? Was it the associate pastor who taught the church stood in the wrong by prohibiting divorce when following the heart, when driven by desire? Who spoke to them? Was it the pastor who received the dark insights, who told the associate pastor, who taught the church leaders, who spread the revelation? Just who? Just who? Was it the woman dressed in black?

The children never experienced a bible study or Sunday service where the demonic thought it worth it to show itself. How could they fight against what they never knew for sure existed? They sat in a sanctuary shrouded in darkness and participated in and watched their pastor counsel one parent over the other through the dissolution of the marriage, and then remarry those recently divorced to each other. How could those children heal when asked to stand to honor a King with songs sung by their new mom, their new dad, to give honor to the One God who in some inscrutable divine wisdom chose not to honor the initial paring that brought them forth? How could they celebrate with songs of praise anchored by a key board player, a bass player who played with skill and made the instrument sing of the goodness, the goodness of the Father and the unconditional grace of the Son who sanctioned strange beginnings for a contemporary version of Abraham without his Sarah, a young Naomi without her Elimelech, Elkanah without his Hannah, for a Mary without her Joseph? How? Their young eyes understandably so questioned this version of Jesus, a foreign and unrecognizable son of God to all save the adult members of the church.

Choice ravaged the ministry tasked with ushering in the Spirit and inviting the parishioners to touch the hem of his garment. Melodic voices that once raised hands, turned dry eyes wet, wrought bowed heads, and transformed unaffected bodies into worshippers were relegated to entertainment. Harmonies were spot on and chords delivered with precision, but congregants remained seated until told to stand, silent until told to sing along. The spirits floating on practiced voices and instruments left body and soul flat. No Holy Ghost fire stirred. The holder of the microphone found it helpful to push the congregation into praise and worship. "Say praise the Lord. Say hallelujah." The request moved to command. "Open up our mouths! Open up your mouths! God has been too good to sit down on him! Say glory to his name!" Commands soon betrayed annoyance. "We're not here to entertain you! If you know who God is, then stand on your feet and praise his name!" Polished voices, rousing beats, and the talented band tried to stir the glowing embers of the listener until flames rose, but the spirits unleashed upon the congregation by the ministry of music banked most fires.

Members and church leaders made selfish, soulish, life shattering choices that mattered in the short term and resulted in blindness and deafness. Members missed the building of a sepulcher, a dark grave posing in the spirit like a raised garden bed, a holder of wheat and weed. The church stumbled toward spiritual demise as it replaced the anointing with zeal, which sent an invitation to spiritual beings. It was not the quality of the voices, the perfect pitch, the band, or points covered in the message that extended the invite. The heart, the aggregate character of the souls sent out the invitation for a meeting on the spiritual plain. Demons always accepted. The Spirit, a jealous guest who once sent an emissary to two drafted as watchers, sent a strong delusion in which wheat and weed kept company.

CHAPTER 27

The trap Sister Bett spoke of occurred in the pastor's office. She warned Max about "the one with the collar" and Sylvia's desire to get him out of the house. On that afternoon when students walked past his house not once but twice and no one entered his, he knew.

Sylvia told son and daughter, "Don't take the bus home today. I'll pick you up and we, the three of us, will eat before heading to church. Just the three of us, we need some happiness. We need peace without any tension so just the three of us." They ate an early dinner in silence and to Sarah and Mark's surprise the three followed their tension-free main course with a talk at the church with the pastor.

After entering his office and sharing in a quick prayer, the pastor said, "Your mother brought you here today so that we could talk. You always have my ear, and the next time we meet," glancing at Sylvia and nodding but attempting to endear himself as friend and confidante to the children, "we'll meet alone."

"Mark, do you want to tell me what happened Sunday night when you came back from your senior trip?" Surprised, he looked around until his eyes caught Sylvia's. She nodded, giving him permission to talk, to tell all, and he did.

"He shouldn't have spoken to you that way. Fathers have a history of being hard on their sons and not showing love to them, but he loves you." He went on talking about father and son relationships.

"Sarah, where were you?"

She remained silent. Sylvia sighed heavily, and then she cleared her throat as she sent the nonverbal message: Look at me now and answer him, but the message was not received.

Sarah looked straight ahead. Staring forward she caught a glimpse in the spirit of the dark math taking place. She felt the ripping and braced herself. She had no idea what was coming in the natural, but she could feel in the spirit that the damage if unchecked would be irrevocable. Spiritual healing was the only option, and she had not learned enough to engage it, and the adults in the room seemed to shun it. The rushed meal surrounded by a perversion of peace sat heavily on her stomach. She felt devastatingly unsure while Mark felt vindicated, and Sylvia, determined. As she looked beyond, a rather large piece of parchment growing darker and darker unfolded before her to reveal a dimming inscription written in light. Grabbing it, Sylvia stitched it into a much larger monochromatic quilt.

Still, Sarah who stood outside on the porch the night of the argument sat firm in the spirit. With arms folded, she refused to participate as tears that fell never reached chin or jaw line. They dropped into a small vial which disappeared as quickly as it appeared, perceptible to the spiritual eye only and then for a twinkle before gone; it was unseen by all, Mark and Sylvia who sat next to Sarah and unseen by those across from her.

Sarah cried silently as she looked forward trying to reconcile within the meaning of the visit in which a pastor to mother, father, sister, and brother took part in a clandestine meeting of five to redefine family without two important members. Where is Dad in all of this? Where is he? And where is Jesus? The humble and well-mannered omniscient guest still required an invitation. Did they ask Jesus?

Did anyone who called this meeting ask him to join us? She who entertained angels, reviewed living film with an eternal emissary, and rested her head on the shoulder of an invisible minister lamented that no invitation was sent to heaven, that the prayer uttered before the meeting was not a request for divine direction.

As bible study approached the pastor said, "Let's plan to meet again when you're both ready to talk, all right?" Sarah remained silent, and Mark with a growing awareness that something much larger than telling on Dad was afoot, that he had done what Sylvia asked him to do, that he in fact ingested spiritual poison and followed directions without seeing the entire plan fell into silence. Neither answered the pastor, so he closed the meeting with a quick prayer, and all five left the office and headed to the sanctuary for bible study. None aware Max had been warned of the trap.

A second meeting occurred the following week to ensure Max now out of the house did not find a way back into it. It required less furtive planning than the first. Still, neither Sarah nor Mark saw it coming. The talk meant to be a therapeutic counseling session between empathetic pastor and gentle lambs concerning familial surgery doubled as a fiery barrage to separate cadets from their Captain.

God had not ended the days of the marriage. No hand, part or whole, appeared and wrote upon kitchen cabinets as Sylvia spoke to Mark or on the bedroom wall when Sylvia told Sarah to come home immediately after school. No finger appeared and then wrote that the marriage had been weighed in the balance and found wanting, that the days of the union had been numbered.

A week ago Max moved out. Left two days after Sylvia said, "What are going to do hit me?" Stood at him, but failed to bait him with "hit me." He did not go to bible study Tuesday or church Sunday, so Sylvia matter-of-factly said to both children as if a replay of the previous week, "Your father, if he chooses to come to bible study, you will see him there." The two sat in the pastor's office for a short meeting, knowing they would not see their dad that evening. He told them so when he called. Sylvia enlisted the pastor as messenger. She made arrangements for him to say to the children what she could not bring herself to say in the bedroom, "It's over Sarah," and in the kitchen, "Mark it's over."

After a quick prayer, the pastor began, "A man and woman, two individuals, join in marriage, but it doesn't always last a life time. This doesn't mean that either is a bad person or at fault or that it was your fault; it sometimes means it's time to end the marriage before it really affects the children. I know you're both hurting, but God is able to make it better, take the disappointment away." He paused, moving his eyes between them both. "You probably prayed and prayed that God would bring about a change in your mother and father, but he didn't. He has a bigger plan we can't see. I can't, and your parents can't, but God is in control. I've spoken to your mother, Sylvia, a lot lately, and she is clear that the marriage is over." He looked at both.

Mark said, "But I believe—"

"It can't be salvaged," the pastor broke in with eyes closed and shaking his head no as he spoke. After a deep breath, he stated as caring as he could, "Hope of reconciliation vanished some time ago." He paused.

"How are you feeling, Mark?"

Mark remained quiet. Pushed into silence with "It can't be salvaged," he winced inside. His church spoke of miracles, but it produced none; it spoke of following the Lord, but then it chose an independent path; it spoke of raising the dead, but it buried his parent's marriage—buried the covenant alive.

"What are you feeling, Sarah?"

Sarah held her peace. She understood the outcome of their meeting had already been determined. The perfunctory prayer, a clearly crafted announcement more than a request for Abba's aid, served notice of that. Behind the feigned humility of the supplication, Sarah heard, "Lord, this is what will be done." It was clear to Sarah if not Mark that God who was everywhere at once watched again as uninvited guest; therefore, this counseling session could in nowise begin spiritual vinification to turn the tepid water of Sylvia and Max's union into splendid marriage wine.

During the meeting, Sarah glimpsed the ubiquitous enemy always present these days somewhere between the leap from five hundred members to more than a thousand when the youth pastor divorced her church elder husband and reclaimed her maiden name, and the pastor's daughter divorced her husband and implemented her father's advice to take her husband "for everything he's got and wipe clean the memory of his name."

The fourth guest directing the ego and will set it all in motion. Sarah saw Sylvia in the spirit during last Tuesday's meeting seated like a marionette along with others, male and female, stitching in unison half of their once living letters into a dark patchwork quilt with darkness serving as needle, thread, and batting. In the natural, Sylvia acted it out. She told son and daughter a week ago, "Don't take the bus home today." This week she told them to come home immediately after school. She never said why, but on the drive to the church, Mark figured out what Sarah already knew. Heads spinning, they retained little from the time they heard, "It can't be salvaged" while their mother as directed sat outside the office door until they heard the pastor's voice again as he spoke across the pulpit. Both remained in the sanctuary after refusing to leave for class to hear the pastor's lesson mined from Ezekiel thirty-four called "Restoration and Supply."

"God," he said, "would restore all that was taken and supply all one's needs" through Jesus, a brother, mother, friend, a meek and mild lamb of a God. "It's never over," the pastor thundered. He gave three points, but Mark caught in the snares of contradiction never reached them. In the meeting before bible study, he learned that family as he knew it was over. He contrasted the pastor's brusque statement, "It can't be salvaged" delivered in their private meeting with his teaching from the pulpit. "God has the final say, and he says it is not over; surely the dry bones of your situation can live. It's never too late, never over with God." The stirring lesson brought congregants to their feet, but in Sylvia's case and the case of the two children, the message in the office precluded the message from the lectern. The contradiction fought Mark from within, and he questioned the effectiveness of prayer, his prayers. Any timber he sent up to the Father would remain stacked because he peeped behind the curtain and found dry bones lived again in the pages of the Bible, not in the individual crises of church members at least the church he attended now.

Mark uncovered an inconsistency with a private God plated for two youths who could not do all and a public one presented to adults who could. God could raise the dead in Ezekiel and in the Gospels. He could add sinew to bone and place respiratory, circulatory, and digestive systems in flesh that once stunk of decay, was picked clean, or fell off bones to become dust. In public God could do this, but in private conversation preceding or following public preaching or teaching, he was limited. The God of restoration and supply worshipped in this church was not immutable, leaving his sons and daughters exposed and placing them in grave danger; his power waned during the week, and he, the God of all worshipped in this place, had to get over the midweek hump, had need of bible study to move him from limited to limitless, needed to hear what could be done as much as the congregation had need of it.

In contrast Ezekiel's God spoke and death moved into submission. What counseling could not bring forth on Tuesday in a private meeting, the simple words or acts of God directly or through his chosen could. Had the pastor studied Ezekiel thirty-seven until it sunk deep down in his spirit before his talk with the two children, would the private message have matched the public one? If steeped in Second Kings and hiding the move of God in his heart, might he have cast the Word about his congregation like meal once tossed into a pot of stew to neutralize the seething poison of wild gourds as well as that already ingested? Through a thundering performance, constant movement, and self-proclaimed revelation, the pastor created for the listeners a portrait of the Good Shepherd that did not exist for two of those in earshot. Their Good Shepherd depicted earlier that evening did not pursue and oversee the restoration of sheep that wandered far away; he did not move through the preached word as refiner's fire or fuller's soap for the spirit of those crying out through contented flesh, "How shall we return?"

The pastor failed to dine with the only interpreter of the Word and hide divine insights within until authorized to distribute them in messages for storm-tossed souls and weather-beaten lighthouse watchmen. He had not eaten "O ye dry bones, hear the word of the LORD"[25] along with chapters thirty-four and eighteen, reminders of the fate of sinning souls. Had he, he might have received revelation that had time to uproot and destroy perverse interpretation, embed itself in his heart, and create flawless pearls to cast before those members willing to gather, string, and knot them with the double thread of self-assessment and repentance.

But no conviction, no self-examination preceded the teaching since he denied the very words spoken across the pulpit time to work within him first. The performance of teaching or preaching well to grow a church no longer anchored in the eternal sapped his spiritual hearing and sight. He failed to see that Mark struggling with God's inability to change some things would play his final song for the church and would leave among rampant divorce and a pastoral lie. He could not discern the absence of spirit in the piano playing as Mark hammered out his final tune in a church ablaze with inconsistencies. No one rose in the spirit like Hananiah or Mishael or Azariah to speak a word from the Lord in Mark's ear beginning with "if it be so" and continuing with "but if not." This might have settled him while sowing deep within the seed that God is able and if he chooses not to change circumstances, he is still able before the world had a chance to sow words and sentences that germinated into a dark, twisted narrative. No one from the church placed an arm around his shoulders and walked with him under an anointing that stayed the destructive forces of heretical flame. Could God or could he not do all things was not rhetorical for Mark who could live with divine mystery, but not theological ambiguity.

Sarah called Max after bible study and found the idea behind restoration and supply as delivered told only part of the story for the armor bearer-less class of scattered and lost sheep. It sidestepped the cause. Sure God would restore. Sure God would supply the needs of his own, but verses one and two provided context for God's grace. Max flipped to Acts twenty and read a portion aloud to Sarah. "Take heed therefore unto yourselves, and to all the flock, over the which the Holy Ghost hath made you overseers, to feed the church of God, which he hath purchased with his own blood. For I know this, that after my departing shall grievous wolves enter in among you, not sparing the flock."[26]

He paused. Then said, "Interesting, no?"

"We didn't get the context in bible study."

"No, I'm afraid not. Broken families are scattered abroad and suffer great loss, particularly if they lose faith, but your pastor is doing well having sold a rather large house to buy an even larger one with a pool and stocked pond on quite a bit of acreage." He paused. "Back to Ezekiel, oh, forgive the search for the obvious, but what shepherd did the purchasing with his own blood?

"Jesus."

"All right then, let's keep reading. Turn back to Ezekiel chapter thirty-four." Max read aloud:

Son of man, prophesy against the shepherds of Israel, prophesy, and say unto them, Thus saith the LORD God unto the shepherds; Woe be to the shepherds of Israel that do feed themselves! Should not the shepherds feed the flocks? Ye eat the fat, and ye clothe you with the wool, ye kill them that are fed: but ye feed not the flock. The diseased have ye not strengthened, neither have ye healed that which was sick, neither have ye bound up that which was broken, neither have ye brought again that which was driven away, neither have ye sought that which was lost; but with force and with cruelty have ye ruled them. And they were scattered, because there is no shepherd: and they became meat to all the beasts of the field, when they were scattered.[27]

"Wow! It talks about the shepherds of Israel, but it could be us," Sarah said.

"In many ways it is us. There is a selfish, greedy spirit pervading leadership these days, so few pastors preach on the warning that precedes the restoration. There are those that hold fast though. They're all over, but we seldom hear about them. There is much to think about here. Finish the chapter on your own. Call me if you have questions or need to voice a comment."

CHAPTER 28

The spirit of divorce circulating across the land tore blessed quivers and left arrows exposed and unprotected. Some ended up scattered senselessly on the ground. Yet, of the watchmen who saw the destruction, none blew a trumpet to call attention to the insidious march against long standing holy covenants. Life coach sermons failed to address the rhetorical nature of the question about brothers and keepers. "If they knew me as Lord, my son, then they would know my word from Genesis to Revelation." But members avoided the hard words of the Old Testament during private reading and never entered the sanctuary where the preached word built a tablescape of Ezekiel replete with warnings against turning blind eyes and deaf ears when fellow members and leaders opened doors and walked boldly into the darkness.

Sylvia never thought twice about their quiver of two and the ramifications of divorce when she brought her lawyer into darkness and worked incessantly to solidify with written summons her verbal call to break her covenant with Max.

The pre-midnight court summons delivered on Mark's prom night with "What did you do to her?" caught Max by surprise, and the messenger's knowledge of page one suggested late-night reading as compensation for the drive from Virginia to Maryland. Delivering the summons, the messenger met Cynthia, the woman in the summons dubbed "strange." She stood at the front door with one hand over the other pulling robe together over pajamas. It did not occur to the messenger boy that she descended stairs to reach the front door, and Max, the recipient of the legal missive, ascended them to reach the main floor.

The clause on page one "He has moved in with a strange woman" proved words were not sacred. Christians once believed they would give an account for every idle word spoken, but no longer, not anymore. No, the woman was not strange, and Max did not move in as implied by page one, but the implication strong enough in the idea of impropriety prevented Sarah overnight stays with Max.

Legal moves from March through July hastened the dismantling of the Lord's path for Sylvia; they blurred the seasons for Max with no winter into spring and no spring into summer. He endured call after call from his lawyer with requests as he reacted to Sylvia's lawyer as both amassed billable hours. Even the distance brought by teaching a writing course in California could not dull the legal noise of two lawyers engaged in a sprint on a track of green maintained by Max.

After three weeks of teaching in Los Angeles, he could only recall Sarah making her desire for joint custody known a week before he landed at Thurgood Marshall Airport to address a request to increase the monthly sum to Sylvia an additional five hundred dollars. Sylvia wanted two thousand a month as well as the house. After nearly twenty years of marriage to a teacher turned consultant, Sylvia, a teacher turned nonprofit employee, knew summers were lean, that experience taught Max to shun the ways of Aesop's grasshopper and work like the industrious ant as if April and May were autumn and he, Max, prepared to hibernate with a presentation here and there in the summer.

Back in Maryland on the basement floor he sung the refrain of the communion song from his first church. "O Lord is it I, who betrayed thee today? Please forgive and wash all my sins away. My soul looks up to thee I pray. O Lord, O Lord is it I?" Max sung the short lyric over and over. The words though repeated were not repetitious in the spiritual sense. They turned the light inward and called for weeding, continual spiritual gardening with each turn of the refrain. On bended knees, the song transitioned into prayer as he cried out.

That night ignited through a communion memory and face on the floor marked the transformation of a life impacted by dark evolution. Max called out to the Lord, "Help! *El Elyon*, come see about me." He told God about two feet in Los Angeles one day, two feet in Maryland the next, and two feet expected in family court in three days. "No time to readjust," he told God. "No time to rest." Max told Abba how he withdrew seven thousand five hundred dollars from the bank to pay his lawyer. He spoke to the Father until he fell asleep. Waking on the carpet, he began again in the morning where he left off, praying until his phone alerted him to an email. After reading it, his spirit craved sunlight and church.

Max lifted himself off the floor, showered, dressed, and drove to a church in Woodbridge, Virginia where after the service and friendly greetings, darkness spied him from behind teary eyes of division. He left the church having met Jesus there and darkness too. He tried to process it all while sitting in a grocery store parking lot back in Maryland. He stared at the automatic glass entrance opening and closing with contents on the other side he could not afford. His metaphorical winter bounty was draining fast. Sylvia wanted more, and his attorney would not counteract hers until he received more. There in the parking lot with windows down in the stifling July heat after a night and morning of prayer and a visit to a small Virginia church, he sat deflated by empty pockets and an imminent court date. He wondered how all this could be when both husband and wife called on Jesus.

Wormwood, O Wormwood who implemented avuncular advice to drown out God's call succeeded unlike spirits before him who tried instead to stop the unstoppable. The choice to mix the Shepherd's call with others confused some sheep. It became difficult for anyone slightly wavering to hone in on divine direction and fight against the lust of the flesh, the lust of the eyes, and the pride of life, a warning embedded in the history of creation and then reiterated directly in the epistle of John. The Word warned believers to fight against a love of the world and the promises such love tendered, but some refused the warnings. Jesus called out to them when asleep and while awake, but they would not hear. Their prayers sought divine intervention to ensure a satisfying career and a financially sound life here on this side while ignoring the sobering reality of the great spiritual forge where one's works on this side would be tried by unearthly fire on the other.

Being grace, God called. In dreams women on swings dressed in red swung above alligators and crocodiles just slightly out of danger. He called. Men in red cars crossing rickety bridges found themselves falling, falling toward a raging sea only to drive away safely across waves and whitecaps. He called. Women and men lived through twisters and survived raging fires. Upon waking they sat reassured of their righteousness but remained lost in a labyrinth tailored for them and them alone.

Over time they could no longer hear the loving Word calling, "Incline your ear, and come unto me: hear, and your soul shall live."[28] The constant wooing during the day and earnest pleading through dreams at night dismissed as a mind overtaxed and in desperate need of a vacation. As chains snapped and bridges gave way, believers called on him mighty enough to split a sea and stopped the mouths of animals. Trapped in submerged cars and gasping for air in dreams, men jumped suddenly and fearfully awake. Falling after chains broke, women screamed themselves awake.

The power in the name of Jesus mighty to save became a found memory pieced together from old dreams retold, a vestige in modern church entertainment, such as mimes, dancers, color guard, steppers.

The voice, the power, the mercy lost in a sea of spectacle embraced by churches attempting to make more palatable the Rock that was and will never be ashamed to offend.

God became daddy to some and a best bud with cap turned sideways and T-shirt stained to others. This caustic process of familiarizing deity stripped away the great mystery of godliness along with the fear of the Lord to produce an amiable, elemental god out of air who could not go before believers in times of struggle and could not stand as rear guard. Wormwood, O Wormwood, his success pushed theology, ritual, and cliché until they usurped divine mystery and all but buried the revelation behind John's writing, "In the beginning was the Word,"[29] and Peter's profession, "Though art the Christ!"[30] Men and women grew too comfortable and too easily dismissed the image of those dreadful winepress stains and God's stance toward a hardhearted, stiff necked people.

Max's ringing phone interrupted his thinking. "Hello," he said.

"Hey what's up?"

"Nothing much," he told his sister. "Just sitting."

"Where are you? Sounds like your outside."

"I'm in my car in a grocery store parking lot, just sitting."

"What are you going to get?"

"Air."

"What?"

"Air is about the extent of my purchasing power." He and his sister laughed.

"You're a goof."

But the laughter faded as he told her he had nothing. He worked hard in Los Angeles in July for a check that generally arrived in October and was forced to pull from his savings to pay legal fees, an estranged wife, and mounting debt. Max told her of his search for peace at a church in Virginia earlier that morning only to be greeted by darkness and learn he was not alone. The dark reach which had an affinity for musicians now had a desire to teach spiritual division to media ministry volunteers.

He was strapped, on empty. He spoke with Jesus the night before, and it gave him peace, but between the setting of the sun and rising of it, anxiety returned. He left the basement after rereading an email and attachment from his attorney. Before entering the church, another email arrived with an amended invoice that grew two thousand dollars before the sun shrinking all shadows had a chance to grow them again.

With tears in her eyes, she told him it would work out. Think it not strange, she thought to herself, but she never imagined such a fiery trial, and she shook her head in disbelief at the story unfolding on the other end of the call where one who called on the name of Jesus moved incomprehensibly in the destruction of another who called on him too, and she felt a heavy disappointment with the body of Christ that friendships from Sylvia's most recent church and relationships that survived the distance between Northern Virginia and the Bronx remained intact because those Sylvia knew well did not accept the challenge described in Proverbs 27:9; friends refused the Spirit's call for iron to sharpen iron. If you don't come soon, dear God, if you don't come soon, she thought.

She said again, "It'll work out." They sat in silence for some time until the solace of one to the other completed its work and all that was left was goodbye. "Much love," she said.

"Much love," he replied.

After the call, he continued to sit silent and alone as his mother often had. He found her words coming out of his mouth. "Nobody told me there'd be days like these, nobody," and he screamed out, "Where are you? Can you tell me where you've gone?" He wiped his face with his hands, turned on the ignition, and headed to the basement. "Why do people do such things?" he asked. Stories about custody battles that ended terribly for one parent abound, and it frightened him that a rising anger within tried to rationalize why.

Before "What are you going to do, hit me?" he rarely sat alone. He spent time gardening with Sarah, cooking with Sarah, and watching quirky movies with her. Unlike Mark, she had yet to reach the point of expecting a parent-free adolescence, but these days of isolation read like a different chapter revised by a hideous editor who cut out Jeremiah 29:6. Satan's revised draft attempted to blot out the relationship between father and child and create a new reading of the chapter where verse five slide into seven without six, and those embracing darkness gravitated to the amended script that directed one spouse in the destruction of the other with an honest expectation of peace covering the restructured family.

Empty and feeling abandoned in the silence of his car, he turned on the radio in time to hear the final line of a song composed in 1990 for this moment twenty years in the future when the storm surge threatened to take him under. The song traversed two decades to deliver its eternal telegram of hope placed in the last line under the direction of the Holy Ghost. Max heard, "Christian, if you could just hold on till tomorrow everything will be all right." At that moment, July 1990 met July 2009 in the spirit. He turned the radio off. He arrived at the house, entered it, and descended stairs to the basement. He opened his laptop, downloaded the song, and wrote an email to Jesus. The song played low in the background.

Jesus—

I know you hear me though as of late the doubts do grow stronger. I'm caught in a divorce which seems to be the order of the day in the church I left and sadly Christendom at large. Too few it seems consider the messages this sends to the next generation. I felt you directing me to the church in Woodbridge this morning. A camera woman from my former church recognized me and spoke to me after the service.

I'm sad to say that I knew her by face only. She cried shortly after the hello. I suspect you saw that. She said she couldn't talk about it when I asked if she were all right. And then she said, "I just don't know why" as she wiped a tear away. My eyes asked, "What do you mean?" I should have verbally asked for her name. "I just don't know why," she said again. "He couldn't tell me why he wants a divorce." Is that why you wanted me there? To see a reflection in a dark mirror. What is the toll on a body in need of a why? He gave no verbal reason for wanting a divorce except he just didn't want to be married anymore. Why remained elusive. I know it's because he worshipped, she worshipped in that place. I told her as much. I told her I never wanted to be in a church again where I knew a face but because of the size and the incessant need to work toward growth, I didn't know the people. I told her it was demonic, not the size, the rampant divorce, and she needed to fight in the spirit. Then she asked if I were visiting the church, and I said yes. I told her I had arrived from LA and needed to meet you on this side of the country, and I couldn't go to that church where congregants knew each other only in passing. Embarrassed, I asked her for her name. She said, "Ivory," and when she asked, I said, "Max." Then I told her I too was caught in the snares of divorce. I didn't tell that Sylvia hoped for adultery, but there was none to find; she tried for physical abuse, but I wouldn't hit her. When I told Ivory my estranged wife whom she knew as one who sang on the praise team also thought me not worthy of a why, the composure she tried best to hold onto fled, and she walked hurriedly away. So here I am. Due in court for money without any, and like Ivory, I don't know why? I'm disappointed in you, but I trust you are in me too. I want so badly to have more than last minute rescues you've perfected, but I'll gladly take them since that's all there seems to be these days. Thanks for the last sentence of the song. I've downloaded it, and will play it as I sleep. I really need a nap. I'm not sure where to send this email, but since you read it before I wrote it, that's not really a concern, is it? Will you join me in my sleep? I hope so. Perhaps I'll find you there.

Love,
Max

CHAPTER 29

Max adjusted his pillow and stretched across the plastic deflated mattress after he said, "Amen." Once he drifted off into a deep sleep, he walked in a garden alone searching, searching until he sat and leaned wearily against the Rock for support where he told all to Jesus. When describing the loneliness camping within because his children lived in one house and he in another, he whispered to the Son. Settings shifted, but the gratefulness remained. In a grocery store as darkness fell upon many who walked unaware of the spiritual siege, Max shared the story with God. Folding laundry and considering he had a roof over his head, he thanked the Father. He maintained his balance under crushing weight with a promise that holding on every day until tomorrow would bring relief. He turned slowly in his sleep. Already as low as he could go, he remained aware at some level that the floor at least would not give way.

Three hours into sleep with a mind now ready to listen, he had tea at home with John Bunyan. *They discussed journeys and the progress made in the face of nonstop trials with each more taxing than the one before it and strong enough to erase from memory the sting of the previous trial if not the trial itself. Max closed his eyes and breathed deeply and slowly. He opened them to find they now sat in the back seat of his car. It moved along as if driven although no one corporeal sat in the driver's seat. The view outside the car shifted from trees to mountains to quarries to rivers to fields, depicting a different geographical location every few moments unrelated to the progress of the car. While in the trees a red-tailed hawk flew in front of the car. A beautiful sight, its fully extended wings and striped tail were clearly visible as it glided across the hood. Max pointed looking at John with a smile who nodded but whose facial expression seemed to say, "Yes, yes I see, but do you?" The hawk entered the trees along the side of the road. They sipped their tea.*

The setting changed to quarries. Cranes on either side of the road lifted and trucks transported heavy stone. After a good look, Max closed his eyes again. The shifts unsettled him. The view outside the car made John think of marble, and he said, "Sometimes hammer and chisel work takes years when an artist carves a masterpiece. Pumice and sandpaper bring the shine." They sat silently drinking. Max respected the wait time. Words in the mind of some writers danced before given life through speech or paper not unlike marble in the hands of a sculptor awaiting the release of what lay buried deep within. John took time to extend the metaphor. "The sanding cannot be easy either, but the stone never cries out." Max opened his eyes and looked at John. He raised his cup and laughed a little to himself. "I think the sculptor likes that about the medium, don't you?" He took a drink. Max smiled which masked surprise that the cups appeared full as if miraculously refilled. They never ran dry. His guest occupied by the setting or lost in his message appeared not to notice and continued, "Stone carving is an intense, lengthy process in the hands of the Master." He looked directly at Max and knew from the frown and heavy look of recognition that Max felt the surge of honor the article bestowed upon the noun as Master supplanted master and by extension Max, the marble. This setting seemed to linger a little longer than the others had, so Max closed his eyes again as he digested this. He took another sip and sighed. John's spirit tapped into the perimeter of struggle and weariness surrounding

Max. Thinking of Christian, his literary character, and the progress of that pilgrim, John sighed revealing discomfort caused by an immediate need to release the little weariness, fear, and anxiety he siphoned off Max. John wanted to help Max with the weight and ensure room for what was to come. Although not nearly enough, he could bear no more than he did. Spiritual journeys are specific in that way; they resist tinkering. Max continued to sit with eyes closed. John smiled an empathetic one accompanied by a paternal shake of the head from one who knew there was more, much more to come but was powerless to alter the plan.

"He's a stickler you know, given over to absolute precision. In his hands, the stone must obey. Unfortunately finding that which is buried deep within can't be rushed." He sipped his tea. "Art history tells us many a marble block lay broken on an artist's floor, having succumbed to rush and haste." The smell of salt and the sound of gulls entered the car. Max opened his eyes to see an ocean replete with sailboats from the view of the bridge the car now crossed. The sight soothed him, but as they continued the inexplicable shift to high rise buildings brought a vertiginous whirl in mind and stomach, so he closed his eyes again, listened to the fading sound of gulls in the distance, and held on as long as he could to the faintest smell of ocean air. With eyes still closed, he drank his tea enhanced by a growing stillness that enveloped the car.

"Consider Michelangelo," John said as the sound of cars and birds became noticeable. "David took three years, and Carrara marble unlike flesh is not peculiar." He leaned over toward Max and said, "It is not alive." He smiled and sat upright leaving Max a little unsure of where all this was going. His eyes remained closed to combat the vertigo induced by the sudden shifts in scenery outside and John Bunyan's wisdom on trials as hammer and chisel, the Sovereign as artist, and anything else this allegorical tale offered. He heard barking and the sound of kids at play. He heard birds. He kept his eyes closed until he honed in on one bird chirping. Thinking this strange, Max opened his

eyes to find they now sat upon the blacktop of what appeared to be a rest stop, and though no longer in the car, the distant settings around the rest stop continued to change. High rises became mountains with low lying trees where chirping gave way to song and the occasional bark to gekkering. Much was in flux. Even the white lines that delineate parking spaces transformed. Parking accommodated cars one minute and eighteen wheelers the next. Most odd, here and there in a parking spot, Max saw a person asleep on a cot with wheels and a steering wheel attached.

People walked in and out of a brown brick, cement, and glass building where the design spoke loudly to the functionality of the place and masked the absence of beauty characteristic of utilitarian architecture. It stood without fanfare in the middle of the lot, and John and Max sat a short distance from it picnicking on blacktop. A thin winter coat spread beneath saucers, sugar, spoons, and honey served as blanket for all things ceramic and silver. Cars sped along the highway to the west and east of the parking lot. The scenery no longer changed. Max gathered himself and John watched him intently as if encouraging one last sip. Max obliged taking a big gulp from his full cup, but with this last gulp his entire body shook from the shock and surprise at the sheer bitter strength of a tea strong enough to release tears from marble, months and months of tears. John breathed in and out deeply holding his cup as his unseen spirit reached over to comfort the Max buried deep within the one before him. He put his cup down and nodded his head as if to say, "I know, I know." He glanced skyward quickly as his head moved up and down with his eyes in one quick move to land back on Max as he said, "He knows." Resigned to his cup, Max opened his eyes, wiped his face, and reached for the honey dipper to sweeten the drink and perhaps life if possible. He held it just above the pot as the excess fell back in. He moved his cup closer with his other hand, but before he could place the dipper above his cup, John grabbed his arm and not taking his eyes off Max held it firmly, shaking it with each

184

word delivered. Quoting a line from one of his poems he said, "He that is down need fear no fall." Immediately Max sat up.

The following day while sitting in his car in the back of a parking lot, his lawyer called.

"Good afternoon, Max. I just spoke to Sylvia's lawyer, and if you'll agree to two thousand a month, there will be no need to appear in court this week."

"I don't have an additional five hundred a month to give to her."

"Look, her lawyer has bank statements that say you do."

"The May-June work as reflected in the bank statements carries me through the summer when schools are closed. This is a case of looks being rather deceiving, and Sylvia knows this."

"If you argue an inability to pay in court, it may cost you more, and you don't have the money readily available to pay me to join you. It's up to you."

"I should stick to coffee."

"What?"

"Never mind, I'll accept it. I know you don't believe me, but I don't have the money for the extra she wants and to be able to make it through to the fall. You'd think she was a stay at home mom and had no income of her own. This won't be good in the long run, but I'm not up for the courtroom this week, so I'll agree to it."

CHAPTER 30

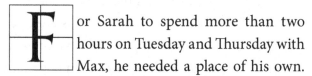or Sarah to spend more than two hours on Tuesday and Thursday with Max, he needed a place of his own. "You have to see it," modern spiritual wisdom said. "Pull it down; pull it down out of the spiritual realm." Max lifted hands and reached. He pulled. He saw money for a security deposit and first month's rent needed to move from the basement of the woman dubbed strange and into a Virginia rental alone. "Write it down and post it on the bathroom mirror. Say it every day and claim it," his former pastor said. He wrote it down, and having learned through travel to keep himself company, saying it every day to himself in the mirror posed no problem.

He spoke, wrote, and posted those needs in faith, yet nothing changed. He asked for and claimed what he needed, still no change. Max wondered why God worked on behalf of some and not others no matter how earnestly those who needed him asked him to move on their behalf. While he thought on these things, his phone rang, and seeing the name of the one he spoke to the day he left his house, he answered enthusiastically.

"Why hello, Deac! It's been awhile. How are things?"

"All great, all great living in the blessings of the Lord. How are things with you?"

"Fine, can't complain."

"I haven't heard from you in a bit."

"Well my conversation is rather limited these days. I assume others get a little tired of hearing new twists on a seemingly intractable topic."

"Friends never get tired. We're here for you. What's specifically pulling you down?

"What isn't?"

"Well, tell me about it."

"Look, I've got to come up with five hundred additional dollars for Sylvia each month, and I can barely cobble together the fifteen hundred I started paying her. It's the summer; I'm in education. On top of this, I need a place so Sarah can stay over, and I can fight for physical custody, but of course I have no rent or security, so I'm a little low at the moment."

"Have you prayed about it?"

"Are you serious?"

"Well the Scripture says that you have not because you ask not. We've got to ask in authority and power in Jesus' name, and he has to give us what we ask for. Be specific in your request. People ask, but they don't give God specifics."

"What about that thorn in the flesh that—"

"That's a lack of faith on your part. Don't dwell on that."

The comment reminded Max of a cartoon he watched as a child. A brother and sister put their rings together to call a powerful genie that appeared and saved them each Saturday morning. The genie called them young masters, but how, just how did one command a sovereign God whom he called Master?

Max said, "Ok. I'll accept that, and now I'm going to ask with you as witness. We'll touch and agree." Max began to pray, "Lord, in the name of Jesus please give me rent and security for a house. Lord, will you cancel my debt which has been exacerbated by this divorce. I give you the glory and the praise for doing this right now. Amen." Max paused and then said, "Will you call back tomorrow to see if I got what I asked for? If I don't get my prayer answered, you can instruct me, you know, walk me through the correct way to ask, add deadlines, proper inflection, more specificity, and anything else I need to tweak."

Deacon Thomas tried to cut him off, "You—"

Max a little annoyed refused the interruption. "If I continue to show a lack of faith, inadvertently mind you, put me out of the room and take it to the Father on my behalf without me. Remember Jesus once cleared a room because of an ensuing quibble over dead or sleep. He said sleep, but all others said dead including the dad. You know that scripture; Jesus even put the father out before telling the maid to rise, and she rose from a rather intense sleep I might add."

"You need to be serious."

"When one has been where I have and is left staring down a path that seems to disappear into the horizon, serious at times is all he has."

"There are spiritual principals that hold firm if you belong to him. He cannot lie."

"Wow, not sure of the implication here, but you might want to reread Job."

"You can't begin to compare yourself to Job."

"Wouldn't dare think of it. Eponymous comparisons seldom enlighten the way one imagines they should, wouldn't you agree?" However, the insight to be gained from the sources of the advice given, not Job, the inspiration around him, now—"

"Whatever. I have to go."

"All right, take care." They never spoke again.

CHAPTER 31

He sat in the media room in an oversized black chair night after night, using his phone to calculate the cost of moving out and walking on solid ground. After a couple of weeks of trying to devise a plan for his way out, the little woman by the well called. She jumped right in with a message. "The Lord said, 'Stop sitting in that black chair trying to calculate your way out of debt and into a house.' He said, 'Put the calculator down. You're putting brakes on him, and he has so much more for you. I'll be your money,' he said, 'and I'm more than enough.'"

Max not quite sure what that meant wrote down what he heard while thinking we don't barter for houses these days; we pay for them.

"The Lord said that he has a house for you, and he'll furnish it, according to your faith. You must wait on him. Can we say thank you Jesus."

"Thank you, Jesus."

"He'll put a deep sleep on you tonight and drop a hymn in your spirit while you sleep. The Lord said that you'll be singing it when you wake up. Can we say thank you Jesus?"

"Thank you, Jesus."

"You be blessed honey, and wait on the Lord. Wait on him. He is who he said he is, but his timing is not ours because he sees tomorrow while we see only today and remember yesterday."

As he prepared for bed that night, he tried to figure out which hymn the Lord would give as glorious morning alarm. He knew them all, God did that is, but Max assumed God had to pick one he knew. Max ran through a number of hymns in his head, but which one would the Lord select? He seldom sang for people since middle school when the music teacher suggested general music after a disastrous chorus tryout, and though skeptical of his chorus teacher's opinion, he trusted his mother's. While pouring a glass a water and singing "Water" by Graham Central Station, his mom called him. "Max," she said, but he was lost in his music. "Max!"

"Huh," he said.

"Hum, dear." Shaking her head and squeezing her face lovingly, she repeated, "Hum, don't sing."

Since then, only on occasion would he sing, and he could not imagine the Lord of all enduring his noise, joyful or not. But he was told his voice would be used as the alarm in a divine wakeup call. While many Christians gave God credit for waking them up in the morning, few could claim an internal singing alarm, a selection from the Master himself, a selection God kept secret until the morning.

He forgot all dreams that occurred during the night until just before waking up. Bowing in absolute silence in the dream, he got off the floor and began to sing with hands raised and head bowed. He stood in total surrender to the Lord Jesus. Surrendered to the Spirit of the Almighty God, his body no longer fought for control. In the morning, Max stirred; bridging the world of sleep and awake, he continued in unadulterated praise and worship. There was no break. His eyes opened, and absent thought and will, his mouth continued what the Spirit began. He was fully awake singing the second verse, "And purchased my pardon on Calvary's tree. I love Thee for wearing the thorns on Thy brow; If ever I loved Thee, my Jesus, 'tis now."[31] Tears flowed as he continued. Max knew if ever he loved Jesus, if ever he did, surely it was now.

The day moved quickly, and late afternoon a teacher from his former church's youth department called. In the middle of the conversation, Max said, "I need to move back to Virginia so Sarah can stay overnight with me. It's bizarre that a dad is forced to use the phrase stay overnight, isn't it?"

"Sarah loves you and doesn't look happy these days. You two were always together. It's sad."

"That it is. What's also sad is that people go on as if nothing has happened."

"Well divorce is everywhere. Life doesn't stop because of it, and you can't expect the church to be exempt. The best you can do is to hope your church can weather the storm."

Max paused. "I disagree. Weathering is acceptance, and we're called to resist, not embrace wrong. It sounds too much like giving in, and we have no examples that giving in to the enemy contains his work. We know it doesn't overcome it. In fact, I'd argue that we have evidence that it emboldens it, speeds it up. What's the point of creating a dynamic youth ministry that attracts families if the pastor and elders encourage family destruction through inaction? Do you see the contradiction?"

"You know before Elder Jones moved to Atlanta, she said that a spirit of divorce had been loosed on the church. She said it right from the pulpit."

"I didn't know that. We've never talked about that. Where was I?"

"Probably in the back working in youth church."

"How did the ministers in the pulpit react?"

"I don't know?"

"One of your own says something like that, and there's no attempt to address or refute the claim. Interesting. Perhaps reaction is the wrong word. Was there any response during the Tuesday morning staff meeting or Friday leadership training?"

"I didn't hear of any."

"No wonder I'm heading toward divorce with a host of other couples from that church that we know about and those we don't."

"It's not just our church; it's everywhere. Many churches are affected. I think you have to be realistic about what's happening in society."

"Like a cake unturned."

"What?"

"Never mind. To accept that more than half the praise team is divorced or immersed in the process of divorce is spiritual and caused by beings outside of time. Even the unsaved would have to admit something inexplicable is going on here. You and I can't claim Christ if we don't believe Satan stands for all that is opposite of Christ, right? The question isn't whether or not he's targeted families in the church. It should be why hasn't the church fought back with spiritual weapons. Paid seminars and annual retreats are hardly adequate weapons against principalities, powers, and rulers of the darkness. You can't fight against spiritual wickedness in high places through a session at a weekend conference."

"You're right."

"Working nonstop in a ministry is not fighting either, and there's no such thing as spiritual sportsmanship toward an enemy that wants his keys and the sting of death back. I don't think we're hearing God, but I can say that the spouse who prefers cruises to skiing and uses the courts to avoid the slopes has learned to listen to the spiritual, but it is not the voice of God."

"Definitely something going on."

"He's destroying families!"

"You didn't know this, but my sister is divorced, long before moving here. Her ex-husband was physically abusive to her and the kids."

"I didn't know."

"It was long ago. She rarely talks about it, but it might have been easier back then had there been a ministry for those divorced like we have now."

"But I'd argue there still isn't one in your church. It's a club filled with many who just walked away from commitment, and it's an affront to the abused spouse frightened within an inch of her life or the one cheated on or the one protecting abused children who runs or needs to disappear secretly. We're in the world, not of it. Your church needs to call a solemn assembly, accept its role in the destruction of families, and repent of the error. Otherwise, it will never see the inside of its new church."

"Well the church had to stop construction on the building a couple of times."

"Not a surprise, not at all a surprise. Anyway, change of paragraph. I need to get back to the Virginia side of the Potomac, any suggestions?"

"Actually yes, I don't know why I didn't think of it before."

"What?"

"Kim and James have a house they need to rent. Former tenants moved out, and they need another one. I think they have to make some repairs before renting it again, but it's a nice house. I've visited them in it when they lived there."

"Where is it?"

"It's just off Dale Boulevard near the firehouse. You know where that is?"

"Yeah, but it probably doesn't feed into Sarah's middle school. Anything else?"

"Look. You need to get back here, don't you? That area off Dale to your old house is less than ten minutes by car. What's the problem? You have Kim's number since she worked with us in the youth department. Call today before they rent it out if they haven't already."

"I don't have security or rent. It's the summer. I'm in education and just finished California work. That check won't arrive until the fall."

"Well call them anyway; they'll work with you."

CHAPTER 32

Max called and met Kim and James on the weekend while they cleaned the rental. Unoccupied during late winter, the house smelled closed and dank. Busted pipes needed repair, and a gray, powdery film on the kitchen cabinets required removal.

Max asked James, "How much is the rent?"

"Fifteen hundred a month."

"We'll I don't have it yet, but I need a place in Woodbridge."

James looked at him, and then said, "Well it's not ready at the moment, so that's not a problem. When will you have the rent? I have to pay the mortgage by the fifteenth."

"I don't know."

"You don't know?"

"My savings have been drained by legal fees and two thousand a month to my estranged wife. I just returned from California and am expecting a check from that job and one completed before leaving for California. The California check is generally late, but the New York work is reliable which could come soon."

James struggled with this and wanted to say, "You must be crazy to think I would give you keys to my property without knowing when you'll pay rent." Before he could speak rationally, something came over him. Had it been Kim, the something would be a person, the person would be spirit, and the spirit would have a name, but this was James suddenly overcome by peace and a desire to help Max moved him to say, "Can you give me something now?"

Max raised his hands and dropped them at his side. He said, "I can't."

James handed over the keys. God continue to fulfill his promise. Family and friends moved through their homes and found living room, dining room, and bedroom furniture. Friends and family bought flatware, dishes, comforters, plants, pots, pans, a microwave, rugs, and televisions. Friends stopped by garage sales and picked up this or that and dropped it off. "I thought of you Max when I saw this bookcase," they said. "This picture had your name on it. If it doesn't work for you, I'll keep it." The house came together as only Providence could decorate it without any initial cost to the renter because friends wisely chose to listen to the Father who made a promise to Max.

Sylvia wondered about his house and its contents; she wondered how one struck down and who left without furnishings continued to rise or gave the impression of one lifted up. "What does he have in his house?" she asked, but Sarah kept the contents to herself. The blue house and what made it a home was Max's story to tell and his alone, so Sylvia enlisted Mark. Still smarting from that fateful night when he yelled, "Why don't you just leave," and reeling from "It's never over until God says it over," he was up for the task.

Home from college for a long weekend, he ascended the stairs to the top of the split level. It was his first time in the house. As he looked around taking it all in, the Lord rose up in Max who was washing dishes in the kitchen. With a plate in his hand and dish towel over his shoulder, he stepped out of the kitchen on the lower level and walked to the bottom of the stairs. Looking up, he said before giving it any thought, "Tell her the high definition television is a flat screen that hangs on a six-foot-high television stand."

"Huh?"

"She sent you here for a report, didn't she?"

Mark looked at Max.

"There's no need to answer, but you can ask me how I know."

"I already know," Mark said.

"Good. Then you have my permission to tell her all that you see came from the Lord. What I sleep on, what you will sleep on, and what Sarah sleeps on was furnished by the All Sufficient One. The plates you ate off tonight, glasses, the utensils, the rug beneath the table you ate from were all gifted to me. Oh, and the microwave that warmed your food as well as the shower curtains in Sarah's bathroom and the one we will use downstairs, gifted too. Tell her all came from the Jesus who promised to furnish my house, and did exactly what he said he would do down to the very pot that cooked the food earlier today. Tell her too though it is none of her business that the Lord put me in this house without rent or deposit. Tell her that his promises are sure, that he did all this out of his inexhaustible funds for his son whose wallet is empty. No, I did not spend the money, the two thousand a month she's expecting. I don't have it. People in education save throughout the school year to make it through the summer, but I haven't been able to save. My lawyer has my money. This life is always about choices and behavior, so when you go back, and she asks tell it all.

Mark listened.

"I'm supposed to pay your tuition. Do you think my lawyer will cover your tuition for me? She didn't think that through." Max went back to washing the new utensils and the dishes he took out of their boxes, so they could be placed in drawers and cabinets. Mark went to bed.

CHAPTER 33

In the spirit, the behavior of a son or daughter of the Most High never followed the world's lead and never recycled its ways. However, God warned of sons dishonoring their fathers, daughters rising up against their mothers, and enemies rising from within one's own home. A warning given to a nation before the birth of Jesus spoke truth to Max and countless other spouses blindsided by darkness through a loved one's heinous act and choice to ignore the spirit of commandments five through ten which still separates those who dress for a marriage feast and those who do not.

At the conclusion of the December divorce, the court decreed the house Max purchased with Sylvia was no longer his. Perhaps the judge had inside information. She somehow knew about the loveseat in the sitting room that was less for love and more for viewing television. He rarely watched. The glider chair Sylvia wanted when pregnant became a cog in the world of laundry; it held the clothes before they were folded and put away. He never used it. None of his clothes hung in the walk-in closet; the mirror atop the dresser, superfluous; the mirror that sat atop the dressing table was too low for him to use. There was little of Max in the bedroom. Perhaps the judge knew this.

His time in the kitchen amounted to little value because the judge could not imagine Sylvia wanted the kitchen at all. Out of his hands, it produced very little culinary art. Her career along with processed food neutered it, and replaced the energy spent creating roadmaps of taste that spurred conversation. The family no longer played games over dessert or created projects immediately after the last bite of blueberry buckle. The kitchen once a four-person expedition of gastronomy and academic pursuit was ill-fitted for three because Sylvia had no use for it, and the judge agreed. Flour, dough, butter—all shunned, and the judge found it inconceivable that a woman initiating divorce in search of her sense of self wanted to revive old shackles. The time spent cooking before playing games in the kitchen accounted for nothing in the divorce ledger.

The work in the yard was Max's too. Perhaps the judge knew that the one who sat rather sullenly before her never worked in the garden, and sufficient alimony would ensure she never would. The art produced in the yard was not commensurate with the time it demanded. Nights proved a bit muggy for roses showing evidence of black spot or lilacs hosting powdery mildew. Only a few gardeners achieved that vivid blue from the hydrangea, but they never discussed the time the plant demanded. Some women found the solitary endeavor therapeutic, but a number of husbands or hired gardeners had yard work now, and the judge not drawn to it herself found it inconceivable that it held any attraction for the one across from her. The hours Max devoted to the landscape had no impact on the judge's estimation of his contribution to family life.

But Virginia courts hope for something more substantial than gardens and kitchens and bedroom furnishings to tack along with the threshold of a year apart, so the judge asked Sylvia, "Why are you here?"

Sylvia thought about it for some time. If he had just touched her that Sunday night or brushed against her as he walked passed her, she could have fallen. There would be no need to search for a reason; she would have it, and it would be documented with an emergency room visit and call to the police, and although it never materialized with "hit me big man," she looked at the judge and said, "He's mean."

The judge caught the look of incredulity on Max's face. She looked again at Sylvia. "I don't see it. Can you give me an example?"

"Well when we lived in New Jersey I had a friend visiting from New York City. I needed something from the grocery store, and I asked Max to pick it up for me, but he refused, and said that we both had cars and I should drive."

The judge furrowed her brow. "I still don't see it," she said. Sylvia provided no context, chose not to describe Max in dirt covered jeans, sweating in the sun bent over lily of the valley on the side of the yard or placing hens and chicks in the crevices among the rocks that defined the driveway and tiered backyard that periodically demanded restacking. She made no mention of a sweaty Max trimming the forsythia hedge or feeding pansies or carrying and emptying bags of soil or mulch for the beds. No context surrounding his refusal and surly behavior that scarred Sylvia for more than ten years of marriage.

His mean streak prompted Sylvia to fight for sole custody of Sarah. During the cross examination, Sylvia denied ever having a conversation with Sarah about fifty percent of her time with mom and fifty percent of the time with dad. She denied ever saying to Mark, "You're old enough. The courts will not tell you where to live," and pretended she did not hear his retort, "No one will tell me where I will and will not live." It was the denial of the topic, not the conversations that Max found unbelievable. She, president of the praise team and devoted church member denied ever talking about living arrangements with Sarah, and she wanted the judge and all listeners to believe that a family ripped by darkness never discussed where all the pieces would land.

The day of auditions for a commercial, Max heard it all beginning with "I want to live with you full time."

Max said, "I don't want a fight honey. Let's go fifty-fifty and be done. It's fair and makes sense, and perhaps we can work around my travel. I can identify ahead of time the weeks I'll be out of town or only travel every other week if colleagues prove flexible. We'll work it out."

With that Sylvia burst into Sarah's room. "I know you're telling him. You tell him everything, and you can tell him that. Now hang up that phone."

"He's already gone," Sarah said, but Max was still on the cell phone and heard the entire exchange before they headed to their auditions.

"Good. I don't want him to know what goes on in this house. It's our business, no one else's. You never tell what you do when you're with him, so I don't want you telling him what goes on here. Is that clear?"

"It won't make a difference at the end of July," Sarah said. "It will be fifty-fifty; I'll be with my dad half of the time."

"That is not what the end of July court date is about. Did he tell you that?"

"No, but that is what I want. I want to be with you half the time and with dad half the time."

"Well it is not for you or him to decide. That is for the courts." With that Max hung up the phone.

During the cross examination, Sylvia remained unyielding when Max's lawyer tried to describe the altercation with Sarah. Max's attorney reminded Sylvia that Max was in California, that she and Sarah had auditions, that Sarah was adamant that she wanted fifty percent of her time with Max.

"I never had a conversation like that with Sarah," Sylvia said. "That's something the kids and I never talked about."

She, a caring, loving parent, contrasted with Max who troubled his children with adult concerns about living here or there. A derelict, he picked the children up late for dinner, dropped them off late, or chose not to show at all. Sylvia dismissed the fact that Max relied on taxis and no matter how early he made a reservation for evening runs, taxis were often late. Sylvia cared nothing about the reason. She entered the time into a color-coded calendar she placed nicely into a binder. Sylvia's attorney handed a binder to Max's attorney and one to the judge. It showed the days Max arrived at the house late for pick up and late for drop off. The binder indicated the days and times she called to find out, "Where are you with my child?" She highlighted those dates in yellow. As the exchanges between parents grew more vitriolic, Max limited communication with her. He kept Sarah abreast of travel difficulties. "I won't be able to get you Tuesday because I'm traveling" or when he knew in advance "I won't make it from Baltimore in time for Thursday dinner. Tell your mom." Sarah would, and Sylvia marked the binder. No pickups and no communication through calls or texts to Sylvia highlighted in red. Green indicated pick up and drop off went as scheduled. Those entries were few.

Sylvia told the court she needed her ailing parents to watch Sarah during the spring because Max was traveling during her annual out-of-state conference. His excessive travel made joint custody impractical.

She shared with the court mother-daughter pampering days which included manicures, pedicures, and facials.

In the courtroom gallery Sylvia's pastor sat still as she provided one uncharacteristic assertion about Max after another. Max was altogether "too spiritual" Sylvia told the judge. The profundity of the phrase was lost on the pastor who weighed the veracity of the union of the adverb and adjective against what he saw week after week, against the description he as shepherd made of each of the sheep he knew. He compiled a tacit list of those who follow and those who obstruct. He knew Max well enough to know that what he heard simply did not add up, but he was no longer Max's pastor and no longer received tithes or offerings from him, so he was under no obligation to serve him. Solely Sylvia's pastor now, he gave the description a fleeting thought.

The judge stumped by the notion of spirituality altogether as a claim for divorce struggled even more with the qualifier "too" and asked for clarification.

Sylvia began, "He acts as if everything is spiritual."

"I still don't understand," the judge said.

"Well everything isn't spiritual. Some things just are," Sylvia said. The judge remained perplexed and no closer to understanding the rift between the two. The enemy understood, and he basked in the collateral damage of these inactive soldiers as he tried to alter the destiny of the two true targets, their children. Max would pay for years of warring in full regalia: helmet, breastplate, shield, sword, and feet shod. Though inactive for quite a while, he would pay for the vast devastation once caused by feet shod, pay for the time he walked as witness to the lost with nothing more than peace and the lamb-like story of grace that fathered it, nothing more.

The dark attack coalesced deep within Sylvia with the clause: I can't. One evening driving around town to avoid that house and his face, lyrics from the radio shaped stories she would never sing in church: songs filled with cheating lovers, all night flirtations, carousing, and fun she no longer had. She imagined bodies dancing with a drink in one hand and the other held high with fingers snapping as bodies moved all around to the song's beat until I can't was longer a thought. Darkness hitched a ride upon the lyrics and rode them forcefully to extend their journey beyond memory and partial recall. It forced their message into the depth of her soul far beyond their usual destination. The lyrics edited the meaning of I can't until it merged with a dark, contemporary version of I won't. She spoke, she thought, only to herself because she drove alone unaware of the imperceptible billowing occurring in her car, unaware of the spiritual nature of darkness rolling like fog all around and in her. "I can't do this anymore; I just can't," she said. Then silence. Finally, she pulled into the driveway, entered the garage, and sat in the car for some time until I can't became a staunch "I won't do this to myself and my children any longer." Resolute in her decision, she walked off plan and onto a heavily traveled, beautiful path leading to a private labyrinth, a spiritual sculpture garden with an endless number of life-like statues of people made of salt.

She came to court in brown. The experience of her legal team dressed her to portray a sullen, humble woman sure to contrast with the power and control a blue suit with red or yellow tie worn by Max would communicate. However, Max too wore brown. Weeks earlier, Jesus tapped the spirit of one of his vessels because he had a word for his son. "The Lord said he will dress you," the little woman by the well said. "He said you will wear a brown suit."

"I don't have a brown suit."

"He knows all. If he knows every hair on your head, surely, he knows the content of your closet. I can only tell you what he gives me to tell you. It's an incredible thing for the Lord to dress you, honey. You are peculiar. Few will understand you, your actions, or the outcomes because down to the level of the automatic decisions people make daily without thought, God will advise you in a number of them. This is one. Can we say thank you Jesus."

"Thank you, Jesus."

"Can we say thank you Jesus."

"All right, I'll buy a suit."

"He'll select brown shoes for you as well, and out of the many neck ties you have in your closet, he said that he'll pick one out for you to wear." Looking toward the outcome of the court decision, Max was encouraged because of the detail with which God orchestrated his court appearance.

Sylvia appeared in court wearing a somber brown skirt, sweater, and jacket and offered a testimony guided on fetid water up and out of the belly and voiced by one posing as both victim and nurturer, one who communicated through eyes, body posture, and the color brown a demure spirit shutdown over the years by an overly spiritual, oppressive man.

Can't and won't found their temporal meaning for half of the union not present the night darkness put on a display of power in a college bible study. The display meant for bad, but the Banner turned it into a master class of sword and shield and deep unfathomable depths of power found in a single name and blood once shed. Max was present when Jehovah Nissi turned the display for good as a finite but powerful source of darkness confronted a bible study teacher armed with an infinite source of light. Max was there, two years before Sylvia arrived on campus when the words won't and can't transformed into cobblestone paths tailored for each member present, and then they merged onto a highway called The Way of Holiness which the unclean shall not pass, and having therefore promises from God, those present chose to cleanse themselves from all filthiness of the flesh and spirit, perfecting holiness in the fear of God. I won't say that; I won't eat today; I won't think on that; I won't drink that… combined with I can't do that, I can't go to that kind of place; I can't watch those movies. Stone laid next to stone laid next to stone created a path of voluntary choices few hear about today, and fewer receive a display of power as invitation to walk therein, and fewer still understand that a specific negative in the spirit multiplied by a negative, that can't times won't leads to a positive invitation and closes doors best not opened and turns the feet of the enthroned King of Kings into to a glorious, restorative gathering place. For Max one half of the union present that bible study night, a finger of living fire wrote the location of the highway upon his heart. There it remained through bouts of hardheartedness, fissure, and erosion.

He sat dressed in a brown suit and new brown shoes because Jesus knowing the story blue contrasted with brown would tell in this courtroom had the ear of a servant who had the ear of Max because he was not spiritual enough to know how to listen to Jesus in the little things. Too spiritual, Max thought. Interesting characterization, but I'll take it.

Max had not seen the Sylvia who appeared on the stand in a long time. The too quiet, soft spoken voice communicated I'm a little shy. The voice, the look suggested she tried for so long to make it work, tried to adjust at the expense of family and self, tried to live a stringent life of sacrifice never required by the Father but exacted by a much too spiritual spouse. While Sylvia spoke, her pastor continued to listen. He attempted to filter a foreign testimony which under the court of law and promise of honesty did not describe what he saw week after week. It was Sylvia who made church functions a surrogate home and avoided the one she shared with Max, Mark, and Sarah. Sylvia stated that Max made no attempt to get joint custody of Sarah once he moved out of the basement and into a rented house. He would have if he really wanted to spend time with Sarah. The custody request according to Sylvia and her lawyer was more a ploy to aggravate her than spend time with Sarah.

Max asked his lawyer to move forward for a change in visitation. His attorney suggested he wait given the short time before the December court date, and Max could barely pay the attorney's fees for the defensive, reactive work needed to counteract Sylvia's attorney.

The pastor stayed through Sylvia's testimony, and before leaving gave her a supportive hug while telling her that she did well. Did well, Max thought and wondered what it meant to do well in the dissolution of a marriage on grounds of hyper spirituality and a terrible disposition given life with an example involving a grocery store from fifteen years ago. The pastor approached Max during the recess, but before he could feign a pastoral desire to grant a brotherly hug in the name of the Lord, Max extended his hand. "How are you, Max?" The pastor asked politely if not genuinely.

"That's an interesting question," Max said with a little edge in his voice. "I'm more than twenty thousand in the hole fighting a divorce I'm still unclear about, and you ask me how I'm doing? In 2009 a parent with no history of drug abuse, child abuse, or spousal abuse; a father with no history of gambling, drinking, or infidelity, and a dad who screamed encouragements throughout his daughter's soccer practices and games, although this testimony would have me derelict on a number of accounts, is fighting for custody, and you ask how I'm doing?" He looked at his former pastor before beginning again. "An example of a mean streak from New Jersey, not Virginia, after all these years here, the best example hails from New Jersey, and that's a well done and hug from you? She's fighting for me to have dinner meetings with Sarah. Dinner meetings! And you ask me how I'm doing? Unbelievable."

"I told her not to put Sarah in the middle by keeping her from you."

"Well, how Christian of you, but the sheep has chosen to ignore her shepherd." He looked at his former pastor and said succinctly, "God is not in it." He repeated, "God is not in it." He straightened the writing pad on the table as he wondered why a pastor would attend a divorce hearing like his and encourage lies with well done. How bizarre. He looked at his former pastor and said, "God is just not in this, and more important he's watching. God is watching." Max turned away. He thought of the email he sent the pastor announcing his leaving the church in which he stated a spirit of divorce had control of the congregation and needed to be fought with spiritual weapons or others, many others would divorce as well. He sent the email in April having moved out of the house in late March. He received a response which simply read, "Wishing you the best." He had no expectation for much, but as a former director of children's church, the youth department, and a former bible study teacher, he expected a little more than mere civility. He clearly did not expect to see his former pastor present in divorce court unless moved in the spirit to be present, but this was not on God's orders because "God certainly was not in this," he said to himself.

The court's ruling wrenched Max. He lost. The judge remained unclear why they were in court, but with work that required days of travel and without reliable transportation, she ruled in the best interest of Sarah. Sylvia would have physical custody. She granted Max every other weekend alternating with every other Wednesday with Sarah. She would revisit once transportation challenges were addressed and travel predictable. He turned down the impractical Wednesday dinner meetings, seeing they encouraged binder entries and impacted work where commuting from Northern Virginia to DC or flying to the Midwest remained unpredictable with or without a decree. A Monday or Friday might be doable, but Wednesday was impossible.

The decree, a decision voiced in the temporal had origins in a well of spiritual darkness. It separated father from daughter, mentor from dreamer. It attempted to thwart Abba's plan for Sarah, a plan for godly offspring built upon the Chief Cornerstone.

In the rented car he called out to the Lord, asking how and why one could win with lies, sing in church on Sunday, and celebrate the victory with a pastor who visited divorce court in favor of one parent over the other. "I dressed for victory because you told me" sounded too much like "Would God that we had died in the land of Egypt! or would God we had died in this wilderness!"[32] Similarities went unnoticed. Neither could he entertain that what a peculiar treasure wears at times serves as a message for temporal and eternal beings watching. His brown suit, shoes, and necktie never equaled a promise of victory at that moment no more than the wooden yoke around Jeremiah's neck exempted the prophet from captivity. The sartorial message told by brown was not for him.

Before driving off he called Sarah and delivered the unfortunate news. "We never had makeup days. That's a bold face lie. She scheduled one this weekend with Ms. Linda and her daughter, and then she canceled it. You've taken me to almost all my soccer practices and games." Both cried.

After the call, Max's anger and disappointment with the Lord rose. He yelled at the Lord and his circumstance, at the twenty thousand and rising legal fees in a losing case, unpaid taxes, and combined alimony and child payment nearing two-thousand a month. "Amazing," Max said, "Amazing. A decree born out of a seat of lies around makeup days, forgotten conversations, dereliction, and a twisted narrative told by a color-coded binder. Tell me how Lord! Tell me how!" He still made no connection behind the biblical circumstances with which God provided flesh to eat in the wilderness for a whole month and his outbursts.

He called the little woman by the well and shocked her with the news. She could only remind Max that God is God and allows what he pleases. "We'll have to pray to understand this, Max, but God is still good! He's still on the throne, and nothing catches him by surprise; he's sovereign, and in your anger don't forget it. Can we say thank you Jesus?"

Max didn't answer.

"Can we say thank you Jesus?"

Max still didn't answer.

"He is still God no matter what either of us see or experience. He is still in control. I'll pray about it, and you do the same. He is God, the Almighty Father. All is in his hands. He does what he wants to do without permission, but because of his lovingkindnesses and tender mercies, we can align ourselves with him and walk in his will because he preserves us. You be blessed. Don't let your faith fail, you hear? Don't let your faith fail. You take care. I love you, but God loves you more. Bye, darling."

Dressed to fail, he thought. Max sat in the rented car and cried, knowing God explained himself to no one, took counsel with no one, and obtained permission from no one. When Peter asked about John's future, Jesus replied, "What is that to you? You follow me." Max could not conceive of receiving news such as Peter's with specifics about a future where others dressed him and carried him where he did not want to go, but he understood that some days following Christ without an interest in the path of others was downright hard.

"That your faith fail not" Evangelist Carter prayed a little more than ten years ago. Not for deliverance or a way out, but for faith rooted in endurance, a way through it all. "That your faith fail not," was a prayer given to Max and Max alone that day. Evangelist Carter covered him as he lay on the floor after she caught a glimpse of what was not. Max tried to change things as Peter had, tried to alter a future he could not see. While the sun still shone, Peter spoke directly to the Lord, telling him I will never deny you, but he did anyway when darkness fell. The Lord could have brought about change and stopped the denials before they happened. He chose instead to wait for the Peter that would emerge on the other side of unbecoming language and denials foretold, wait on the Peter who would be the peculiar light that after a most crushing bout with darkness eventually emerged victoriously. Post denial Peter stood before a crowd after fiery tongues descended and confessed the influence of the Holy Spirit and readied onlookers and the curious for a new kind of wine.

Sylvia won in the natural, and on the other side of the court case, Max immediately embraced anger. His response to the divorce decree proved he was not ready to stand before the masses and confess the influence of the Holy Spirit in building a more honest revelation of God, one not moved by impermanence and the temporal, one who banishes darkness with the brightness of his glory, one who has warned once and again that he will shake the earth and even those who call his name but know him not will fall.

CHAPTER 34

ax picked up Sarah for the second half of the Christmas break.

"Hi, Daddy." She kissed him as always.

"Hi, Princess." We're off to dinner at the Dunston's.

"Ok."

"How was the play? This year they had live animals I understand."

"It's a Christmas church play, and this year more for the camel and sheep herding crowd."

"Ah, but it gave you a chance to meet baby Jesus," Max said with a smile.

"Did you ever meet Jesus at those plays?"

"Of course, they always have a doll in a manger. He'll grow up come Easter, and he'll be a live Jesus. It's astounding the transformations once New Year's Eve comes."

Sarah looked at her dad. "You met Jesus?"

"Sure."

"It's a church play. You cannot expect me to be bowled over because you tell me it is an original piece. The writing lacked imagination. Well, actually it was subpar. The acting was one dimensional, entirely overdone to my mind and the purpose unclear."

"Interesting."

"If the purpose of the play is to win souls it failed. Do you think the church leaders really believed someone would give his or her life to Christ because of that play? If the purpose is to introduce Christ, it failed miserably. Christ is our hero. He's the one. Get him out of the manger and on and off the cross for the person who will only come to church on Christmas. You can't wait for Easter. There is no guarantee those there for Christmas will be back when Easter rolls around."

"Well, perhaps the purpose is to entertain," Max said.

"If the purpose is entertainment which I believe isn't the purpose for Sunday service, it failed on that account as well.

"Wow."

"And then there were the animals, real animals. What is the attraction to nameless animals or more precisely not famous animals? How do you get excited about an animal that isn't rare or isn't famous? The focus should be either spirit or animals, but not both. I mean can we introduce the baby Jesus without goats and sheep?"

"I suspect so."

"Who decides half or whole gospel because it's Christmas? Baby Jesus versus risen Jesus, who decides? Does it have to be either or? It doesn't seem like the church consults Jesus. I suspect that since the planning for these dramas requires a bit of rehearsal time, consulting him might not be what one wants to do two months before the program." She paused. "How will the people know Jesus grew up if they don't get the whole gospel?"

"You're being silly."

"No, I'm not. Meek and gentle Jesus is not so meek and gentle in Revelation. Even the churches that seemed to pass the test got a nevertheless in that book. Some babies grow up to become judges. That's all I'm saying. Jesus turned over money tables and drove the animals and the merchants out of the temple; now in our enlightenment, we bring them back in and pray they don't soil the carpet."

Thinking of the trend in some churches of placing money at the preacher's feet or on the stairs of the pulpit during the delivery of a sermon one thought enlightening, Max looking at Sarah asked, "The money changers or the animals?" He paused. "Anyway, the congregation enjoys such spectacle I'm sure."

"I couldn't really tell who enjoyed it or endured it. I long for the days of fire and brimstone."

"You've never experienced fire and brimstone preaching."

"That's why I long for it," she said embracing a sullen demeanor for effect.

"You're too much."

"No, really! It's like the student approach to Shakespeare."

"I'm lost?"

"We read *Romeo and Juliet* this year, and some students wanted to know why we had to read it. As the argument goes, it's not his best play. How can you know that if you never read it? How will you know if it's the only one you ever read? Is fire and brimstone preaching really bad? I don't know, but I can tell you about walking animals across a sacred pulpit turned into a theater stage for the people, and then with the reappearance of the lectern the pulpit is sacred again. No washing or rewashing. No blood through prayer, just the shifting of furniture and removal of animals."

"And fire and brimstone would...?"

"It's deeper than that, and you know it."

"Have you had a little too much church drama?"

"One could only wonder. I think about what it will be like to see this meek and mild gentle lamb of a baby all grown up with feet like burnished brass, a face like the sun in its strengthen, his eyes like living coals of fire, and his tongue like a two-edged sword."

"How many kids claim Revelation as a favorite book of the moment?"

"Don't know, but I imagine the plastic lectern would melt." She looked at Max with a smile.

Grateful this was not a heavy post-divorce conversation, he smiled back and said, "I imagine it would." He looked at Sarah. "You are beginning to sound more and more like me, my dear. This can't be good. It must give your mother fits, internal if not visible ones."

She hunched her shoulders. "Anyway, we're not taught that we could meet the real Jesus or angels for that matter. At best we might prepare a space for the eternal in case someone shows up on Sunday morning or afternoon."

"And if we get a visit?"

"One third of the congregation would run. The other third would be shocked."

"It leaves a third."

"A mixed bag. Some would attempt to usher Jesus out. The earpiece suited ones who stand on either end of the pulpit like secret service men would throw themselves in front of the pastor just in case. A few would be face down on the floor realizing how unclean they really are when facing the Master. They'd gain a better understanding of the real saving power of the blood."

"I can tell you've given this thought."

"Yes, I have, but for now I will endure cute baby dolls which one can't see from the point of view of the congregation. I'll endure the drama year after year. I'll watch others pretend they are moved on a spiritual level, and that the Holy Spirit has had his way."

"Careful Princess, cynicism is not a lovely path to travel."

"I'm not cynical. Before I woke up this morning I had a dream. Unlike Samuel I didn't hear my name called, and I did not say, 'Here am I.' I wasn't pushed to the next spiritual level as he."

"What did you hear?"

"I remember just two questions though I have a vague sense that I'm very close to recalling the entire dream. One question particularly still haunts me."

"What were the questions?"

"Do they know me? Do you know me? Then I woke up."

"Which is still nagging at you?" Max asked, having confronted the two questions himself.

She looked at Max, and still a little bothered by the suggestion of cynicism turned to look out of the passenger side window. She wondered whether or not children of godly parents walk on streets of cynicism laid out before them by parents taking too lightly the commitment to hold close the peculiar treasure of the Lord. Some seduced by a zealous busyness accept subtle neglect as a cross to bear, but others guided by darkness place the fate of God's young jewels into the hands of a court, a judge, a legal team who remain unaware in the natural but every bit complicit in the spirit in their unauthorized editing of God's plan. Cynicism. After years of being led to believe by both parents that God is in control, one of them moved outside that tenet to find a legal voice bold enough to speak to and for believers nearly two weeks ago without listening to God. Cynicism made itself very accessible. A mother blinded by darkness was unable to see she paid darkness with the desired target, a peculiar and priceless jewel who except for God's grace would experience darkness as reality, choose time over eternity, and at the end of every year find the appearance of live animals and a toy in a crib turned manger more satisfying than seeking the face of the one true King.

Sylvia had her favorite, and Sarah tried to ignore hints until confronted with an unforgettable Christmas dinner a year ago. Sarah the first recipient of Sylvia's Christmas beneficence found ignoring her worked somewhat well, but positives heaped on her brother exposed weaknesses in her sixth-grade coping strategy.

"Sarah, you've just got to do better. You need to study more which you can do if you watch less TV. You've got to take care of yourself and show you care. Pull yourself together; take pride in who you are and how you look." Sylvia paused, and then moved onto the next person. "Mark, oh my Mark, I know you'll never leave me. You are...."

And with that Sarah threw her hands up and blocked out Sylvia's effusive praise. She glanced around the table to see the faces of Max and the dinner guests since the messages to both children verified suspensions. Mom had a favorite, and Sarah was not it. No one asked whether she wanted to be or not. No one gave her a choice, and the fight for custody revolved not around a favorite child or concern for the welfare of a child but simply keeping a daughter away from a father in the temporal. The implications in the spiritual were less than simple.

Sarah wondered if cynicism grew out of the inability to lay it all down or the ability to see zeal masquerading as truth and godly sincerity. Like her father, she noted the hypnotic, rhythmic, melodic sound of earnest voices calling, calling Jesus, calling, calling Jesus in church, but he did not come, or no one saw him or an eternal messenger granting sight like the night of bible study where darkness billowed forward, marriages frayed, and the scene seared itself into memory. She had no visit like that one since, but she did see as others saw husbands and wives in covenant one minute, signing papers to end it all as if the union existed in the temporal only. One spouse initiated the rip to the hypnotic melody, and darkness darned the wound with rejection as backdrop to the rhythmic voices calling.

Like Max, Sarah heard the story about the pastor scattering seeds harvested from the field of darkness into the life of his daughter. "Take him for everything he's got," he said. Such words. Take him for everything on Wednesday and rain on us dear Lord on Sunday. Had the Deliver come bearing gifts, which gifts would he bring? Would he distribute gifts aligned to the spirit that reigned on Wednesday or the one on Sunday? Perhaps mercy kept him away. Or tears of contrition covered too quickly by a message of grace produced too little water to walk upon or perhaps a whiff of something sinister on the inside kept the Spirit at bay and believers from moving beyond an invisible gate into something beautiful.

While she pondered all this, arboreous stretches of land moved along her field of vision, but she did not really notice the perennial towers as individual trees. The car slowed as it entered the more residential neighborhoods. Then she took them in, a sea of branches connected to trunks with evergreens mixed in, groups of mighty, deep rooted trees that grew naturally, permanently knotted and twisted from fighting infection over the years. Scarred by boring insects, these trees held within their trunks the history of local droughts like badges of survival. Craggy, old, and majestically beautiful, storm survivors they were. Like the birds of the air and lilies of the field, they wanted for nothing. She sighed as the car moved passed landscaped yards. Sarah noted the fruit trees, the ornamental trees, the weeping trees all dressed with stakes, hoses, and wires not the least bit thirsty after a summer's drought, but none of the fruit bearing trees would ever produce succulent fruit that could satiate a deep hunger. She thought of figs. She thought of a hungry Jesus approaching shiny leaves of promise. She looked at Max and took in the forced upbeat demeanor he put forth just for her, just for her. Nearly ten days after the decree, she found that in the life of those who know who God is, those that survive drought and the nuisance of boring insects, true beauty is in the crags.

"I was reading *Howards End,* and the character Margaret lamented people generally equate beauty with size. You know, five acres is five times more beautiful than one and ten acres, ten times more beautiful. Is something more beautiful because it's bigger? It may appear more desirable to the eye and flesh, but is it more lovely? And what about the law of diminishing returns?" She paused. "Look at that house there."

Max looked at the house ahead of them in the neighborhood where he and Sarah would celebrate a post-Christmas dinner with friends.

"It's too big. How many bedrooms you think? Five? Six?"

"Where is this going?"

"Is it beautiful? There's nothing unique about it or the rest of them for that matter. They all look alike. I suspect they serve their purpose well, but are they beautiful?"

"And I suspect," Max emphasized the words I suspect, "the current generation of home buyers looks to the utility of the inside space as a determining element of beauty. The tone and feel that people create is included in the notion of beauty. I'm sure similar houses on the outside vary in beauty on the inside. Small, old houses may be cold and empty and less beautiful inside if the people in them never talk, never connect." Max paused and glanced at Sarah quickly to emphasize the word connect. He continued with "never act as family."

Max continued, "I think the whole notion of love is underrated. Going back to the two questions: How can one really know the Father if he or she exhibits little love in the home, yet gives the appearance of loving all when outside the home? People may be fooled, but God isn't. One driving question in the book of Acts is have you receive the Holy Spirit since you believed? It's still driving today, but I think the essential question out of Acts that we need to pay attention to now more than ever is do you know the Father? Cutting through the zeal and showiness leaves one with the question do you know who God is?"

"Mom calls me thunder thighs."

"Are you serious?"

"Yeah."

"What do you do? What do you say?"

"Nothing really?"

"Well does it bother you?"

She looked at Max as if to say that's a silly question.

"Then you need to say something. I can't get involved because it'll only make things worse. Wait till she does it again and say, 'I don't like it when you call me thunder thighs; it's hurtful, and I'd appreciate your calling me by my name.' Make sure you speak calmly and respectfully so the focus is not diverted."

Sarah thought on these words and the idea of love in the home, and the manufactured distance of visitation which made reaching love in the home a challenge, but love overcame the challenge. In his rented house the very few times Sylvia needed her to stay overnight, Sarah went to bed early. She could sleep where Max lived, and she looked forward to such sleep now every other weekend. Max found he woke her up in the late morning when she stayed over because she slept long too, not at all like she described at the old house where she stayed up late and rose early even on weekends. She aptly dubbed the house the judge took from Max, The Castle, more for a sense of the imposing nature it now boasted on the inside as if it had a tower, dungeon, and a moat in the natural that mirrored what the destroyer of the marriage had constructed in the spirit. A decision from the courts that Max could only enter upon Sylvia's invitation and cameras placed within and without the house ensured Sylvia, present or not, controlled the drawbridge. Sarah thought upon the questions. Do you know who I am? Do they know who I am? She thought that if people really knew him, love would abound and permeate every room of a church and every room of a house. She smiled as she thought of houses and churches made of wood, brick, and stone as well as those made of flesh. Whether living or inanimate, she thought every room. Love in every room. She remained silent as they approached the house.

As he pulled alongside the curb and before placing the car in park, he looked at Sarah and said, "Let's avoid updates about the divorce if we can. What say you?"

"Agreed."

CHAPTER 35

Moving quickly between Christmas and Easter, time cleared the memory of dolls and the scent of animals out of the temple in preparation for a goriness that defied entertainment for at least three days when the foolish things of the world took their rightful place to recount the story of the Paschal Lamb and depict the story of the Great White Throne yet to be. A balance, a balance of the past and future is the fulcrum of dreams centered on "Do they know me? Do you know me?"

"There is nothing I start that I cannot finish." The Lord reminded Max of his promise concerning tangible gifts.

"We have a TV in the back seat of our car," a couple over for dinner said. "The army transferred our neighbor, and she left it for us, but we don't need it. Do you want it?" Seven months after the divine promise to furnish the house and two months after the divorce, the Lord had more, but as the year continued, the gifts could not address a growing loneliness hidden from family and friends.

He called the little woman by the well to say hello.

"God Bless you, Brother Max. You know this call is not by accident. I was praying for you and the Lord showed me a book, a worn book. The Lord said that Sylvia tore pages out, and threw the book away.

The hurt is deep. A number walk away from their children, but she ripped yours away. Oh my God!"

Max listened.

"You sit in that rented three-bedroom house and eat in silence without stories from the children of school, friends, or memories. You and the children once sat at the kitchen table eating meals you cooked and completing school projects. You don't talk about it, but the hurt runs deep. You think Sylvia helps with the projects now. God said, 'Not so,' darling. Sarah completes projects alone, and Sylvia remains cloistered in her room."

"You cannot imagine the anger that rose up in her when your daughter asked you to come into the house and connect the printer you bought her because Sylvia would not give her the disc to connect to the one she and Mark used. She has a jealous spirit. She's jealous of the relationship you and your daughter have. That's why you received the letter in mail forbidding you to enter the house without being invited by her directly, and that's why there are cameras in the house. God said, 'But will the cameras see the storm that's on its way?' The Lord said that those ripped pages targeted both children, but really affected your son. However, your son will be back if you hold your tongue and let God handle the restoration."

"You've not let go of the fact that Sylvia lied in court, and you lost time with the children that you'll never get back. You lost it because an empty basket was filled by lies. Do you know what he's talking about?"

"Yes."

"The Lord said you also assumed a mutual friend from New York would call right, right and wrong, wrong, but it didn't happen. The Lord said that it won't, darling. There's always more involved than what you see or experience in the moment. He needs you to know that Sylvia didn't win. You need to know this, this day." The little woman by the well took a deep breath and continued. "God wants you to know that she will not keep that house. I didn't say it; God said it. Do you hear me?"

"Yes."

"God said that you told a member of your former church, that they would not move into the church they're building. Is this God?"

"Yes."

"God said it wasn't you talking. It was him talking through you. They will not move into that building."

She paused before saying, "Pull your money out of the bank." Nearly one year after carrying the TV to his bedroom, the message confused Max and was followed by an equally confusing word. "The Lord said that what you will experience is not going backward and not going in circles. It's all new for you. You need to know this, this day. It may seem like you're going backward to the natural eye, but God said your journey will move you closer to him. And, darling, the Lord said leave those pictures alone. Lust has pulled down a many mighty men of God. Dangerous doors are opening that will take an incredible amount of power to close, and you certainly don't need that now. Repent and close those doors while you can still do it alone. The eye of the Lord is upon them that fear him, upon them that hope in his mercy. He sees all, and his chastisement is righteous and just. Confess and keep it moving. You hear me, darling?

"Yes." Max breathed a little harder that he was found out, but praised the Lord for his discretion.

"Did you hear me, darling?"

"Yes."

"Well you be blessed then, and the Lord said he will not leave you alone. You were divorced; you didn't ask for it; it happened to you. You were thrown away, and the Lord said he has someone for you, so stop saying you won't marry again. It's not your will, but God's will. Can we say thank you Jesus?"

"Thank you, Jesus."

Her voice donned that thunderous quality that made Max sit up a little straighter and listen a little harder. "'She won't keep that house, my son, and you will not always be down looking up! Don't look at what you see. Look up! Look up at what I told you will be, and get out of that stinking hole and stand as a child of the King. I have a house for you that will not flood when the storm comes. Stand! Wash your face and wash your hands and stand as I have commanded you this day! I created the relationship between you and your children. I created the relationship Sylvia tried to destroy, and since I ordained it so, nothing can break it. Do you believe me, son! Where is your faith!'" She broke off in praise. Max could hear her as she walked around her room glorifying God. He waited until she picked up the phone again. "I'll speak to you again when Jesus bids me to do so. You be blessed, and don't trouble yourself about the news you'll receive shortly. Just live in his blessings, and know that you are not going backward."

"Ok, you be blessed too."

Wow, he thought and said, "Thank you, Jesus." He began to pray a prayer of repentance and knew a fast was in order to crucify the flesh. He sat in a chair and meditated on God.

Later that evening he answered a knock at the door. It was James, his landlord.

"Hi, Max, I won't come in or be long. I thought it best to come tell you in person that the bank has foreclosed on the house."

Max said nothing.

"It's not our primary residence, so the bank wouldn't work with us. I don't know how long you'll have in the house, but you'll be able to stay until they contact you and give you a date to move out. It could be one month or five, I don't know. I have a house further south if you need or want it."

"No thanks. I appreciate your telling me, and I thank you for allowing me to rent this house. You've been a good landlord. I've paid this coming month's rent early. Can I get it back?"

"Did you pay it already?"

"Yes, I transferred it into your account."

"Ok, not a problem. I'll check that account and send your money back."

The landlord returned the rent which Max left in the bank to clear and add to that which was already there, but before he could withdraw it, the IRS took it, leaving the account one hundred dollars in the negative. He was warned, so instead of being upset, he celebrated that the Lord loved him enough to give audible directions. Once his account was wiped clean, he received the letter requesting he call the financial institution to negotiate his moving out.

"I need you to move out by the end of March," the representative said. "I'll give you thirteen hundred dollars to move out."

"Ok."

Going smoothly, the representative pushed the day up. "Can you move out the week of the fifteenth? I'll give you eighteen hundred dollars if you can."

"I travel a lot, so let me check." Max pulled his calendar up on the computer, and the fifteenth was doable. "Sure, I can do it."

"The quicker you move out, the quicker I can place the house on the market. Can you move out by the first?"

After a quick look at his calendar Max said, "Yes."

"Ok, can you move out before the end of February?"

"Without looking at my calendar I can tell you that's a heavy travel month. It's too difficult, but March is doable."

The representative pushed, "Can you move out on the twentieth of February?"

"That's tight. I travel earlier that week, and will make it back to complete a move in two days."

"I'll pay you twenty-four hundred dollars."

"Deal." Without savings, he needed money to rent another place, and with the ups and downs surrounding his bank account, heading back to the basement in Maryland was the best option. He called Cynthia and arranged to rent the basement once again. Later that week, the financial institution emailed the paperwork, and to Max's surprise, it added two hundred dollars for a total of twenty-six hundred. Blessing came out of adversity. He found himself back in Maryland with a landlord no longer viewed as a strange woman after the divorce, which allowed Sarah to stay every other weekend after he moved one room's worth of belongings back to Maryland and all else to storage with a word from God that he was not going backward and not going in circles.

CHAPTER 36

ne morning while eating breakfast Sarah said to Max and Cynthia, "This house is peaceful. This is a loving house. I can't remember the last time someone cooked breakfast for me in The Castle."

They went silent.

"No one calls me thunder thighs here."

"Does she still call you that?"

"No, she stopped."

"I did what you suggested. I waited until Mom called me thunder thighs again, and told her I didn't like it. No daughter expects her mother to call her names."

"What'd she say?"

"She said it wasn't a name. It was a term of endearment."

"Did she?"

"I told her the nickname Princess is a term of endearment. Peaches, endearment. Thunder thighs is hurtful. She told me that I was being too sensitive, but she hasn't called me that since, so that's all I care about."

Sarah remained a prize for Sylvia, not a child who needed rearing, love, and care, but someone Max could not see on a daily basis. He since reconciled with the court decree marred in unabashed deceitfulness with a smartly dressed Sylvia who said, "I don't know how I'll make it; I just can't imagine how." He concluded his continued financial struggle was evidence of dark times, and darkness, he began to see, stretched far beyond the reach of the church it inhabited by invitation through the assimilation of worldly ways. No more adjusting the light of life upon entering and exiting church; the light remained dim seven days a week as leadership training replaced discernment, counseling, and deliverance. Experiences and growth models from the world made for a more desirable contemporary church where member felt comfortable saying, "This is who I am" as opposed to "When God gets through with me, I shall come forth like pure gold."

Let your light so shine once directed at individuals now had need to scale up to churches holding fast to godliness and itinerant preachers who preached holiness or hell in the face of rising opposition and people willing to find an accommodating church when a pastor dared to believe the call to Christianity actually demanded more than living a good life. The size of their meetings paled in comparison to those delivering life coach sermons complete with stage props and promised prosperity regardless of lives lived. Worldliness accumulated in so many churches strong in their conviction that the old way kept too many people away.

Max thought of the last men's meetings he attended before leaving his former church. Men sat quietly in the sanctuary watching a DVD on one of two screens that flanked the pulpit. The war movie focused on a soldier in the trenches who eventually came to believe in God and credited God for bringing him home. Though a fitting message, the expletives in the movie mirrored what Max assumed speech found in the trenches sounded like. Max looked around with the first curse, and then decided it was unbelievable with the second. Showing the movie in the sanctuary paid no heed to the sacredness of God's temple and reflected a lack of understanding that for the Holy One of Israel, delivery is as important as the message. No one needed an emissary to see the church had become a dark common place that reflected the ways of the world it was tasked to change.

Max's journey made him more and more peculiar. It melted lead from his eyes and ears as the Spirit shaped one with conviction through "seeing, now see" and his "hearing, now hear." God became front and rear guard, shaping a peculiar treasure traveling through water that could not drown him and fire that could not consume him toward an appointed time when he would sound an alarm of an impending national storm where fire lapped up water and water overcame flame in a land that no longer knew who God was. He worshipped Jesus as he walked around the family room on the main level of the house in Maryland and around the island in the kitchen, exalting the God of All, merciful and mighty, righteous and pure.

His praise brought forth a call from Sister Bett. "Praise the Lord, Brother Max. I was with the Lord and felt you in the spirit. He told me to call you and tell you to call forth the rain."

Max initially thought of metaphor and the beauty of a God who loved language and used words in the act of creation to call forth out of void. Max would break the code of this secret thing revealed and call forth the former and latter rain, speak change to his desert place, and be provided a door in Achor because the Father said to call forth the rain.

"Command the rain, Brother Max, and remember the birds, the wind, the rain all carry messages directly from the throne to his chosen if his chosen listen to him. The Lord wants you to talk to the rain this very day. Remember he controls all, and he said that you once called forth the rain. Do you know what he's talking about?"

Shocked, Max said, "Yes." This was not metaphor.

"You must remember you are a demon chaser—command dark beings to flee, and the darkness will go in the name of Jesus; it will leave. God said for you to go to your doors and your windows this day and say, 'O' Lack, O' Lack, O' Lack you have to go.' The Lord is telling me, you have to talk to the rain, and watch just what he does. 'Try me, son. Try me,' the Lord said. I won't keep you long. I know you have work to do. You be blessed."

"You too."

The Holy Ghost cable from New York to Maryland ignited a fire buried deep within. Gideon like sentiments, "Oh my Lord, if you are indeed with me, why then is all this befallen me?" knocking just beyond the praise dissipated through a fire already ablaze. Max walked from the family room through the kitchen to the morning room and opened the French doors. He called out lack. He walked to the door downstairs in the basement and to all the reachable windows and doors on the main floor and called out, "O' Lack, O' Lack, O' Lack you have to go this day."

Then back to the French doors where he took in the promise of a clear day, the most beautiful blue sky with only a few very high scattered horsetail-like clouds. Thinking on cirrus clouds and reflecting on atmospheric science, his mind escorted him back in memory to late elementary and middle school science, took him back to class and the lessons studied and praying a naturally farfetched request impossible in the natural. A preadolescent who studied the story of Elijah in Sunday school and kept it close to his heart remembered little about oil and cakes, caves and birds. He thought little on the famine, but he never, never let go of the fact that a man who was sometimes strong and sometimes afraid dropped onto the scene as one who walked with God and stopped the rain. Then atop a mountain with only a hand shaped cloud in the sky believed God that at his word three years of drought would end, and the clouds would bring rain again.

That story of truth seems fancy now to many Christians old enough to understand the laws of science and place their faith in computer models that forecast weather, but as a youth in middle school, Max stood along the outside building wall with all others waiting to enter before the start of school. There he told to his friend he had a secret to share. His friend leaned in as cirrus clouds covered blue sky. Max grabbed hold of a heavenly mantle and said quietly, "I can make it rain."

Although a member of a different church, his best friend, Darryl, attended Sunday school regularly. They read the same lesson about Elijah, the same lessons of pursuit, fear, drought, sustenance, and rain. Darryl knew where this came from, and more intrigued then dismissive he asked, "How?"

"I pray and pray and pray until God moves. I wait. I mean I can't make it rain, but I can ask for it to rain, and God answers me when I ask him."

Looking up at the blue morning sky, Darryl said, "Prove it."

"It takes a bit of time."

"We have time."

"What period do you have gym because you won't go outside today." With that they walked into the school and headed in different directions toward their lockers. As they walked, Max began his prayer. Rain was needed before third period if Darryl and all others stayed inside for gym. He prayed through homeroom. Max stopped to say, "Here," when his name was called, and he continued with prayer through the rest of attendance and the reading of the homeroom announcements. He prayed through first period. Tabled Zeus and the golden age myth that wrought a flood to pray and ask for rain. With eyes open, head forward, and hands folded, he prayed and prayed.

After social studies he walked through the clamor of the middle school hallway to English and took his seat. He coasted through the discussion of the mounting singleness of effect and a beating heart encased in wood. It was during the comparison of the Poe's style in "The Pit and the Pendulum" and "Telltale Heart" that Max noticed the first drop of rain on the classroom window. He sighed. Said thank you, Jesus and continued to pray. "I thank you that it's raining, Lord. I thank you that blue sky has turned gray. I thank you for a down pour which will cleanse away doubt and cause others to come to believe." With that he heard the sound of the abundance of rain. The sky whispered at first then released a shout. It momentarily grabbed the breath of a few classmates shocked by the sudden atmospheric change and afraid of thunder and lightning even a distance away. The sound, lighting, and rain guaranteed the gym doors stayed closed because a young boy untainted by science and forecasts believed the history in Kings, believed in the perpetuity of the verb to be when proceeded by the pronoun I to produce a reminder immanent in a name. I Am did it; I Am does it; I Am is doing it. While peers considered Poe's craft in English class, Max engaged past, present, and future tense. I Am sent the rain to fall down from heaven to meet a request rising up out of the heart of a boy learning to wait on God, learning dependence, learning perseverance, and learning to exercise in his youth what he would eventually bury deep in adulthood: God supplied the yea and waited on his children of all ages for the amen.

Word traveled fast among the small circle of school friends. "Can you make it rain today?"

"Watch me," and then the undeniable results eventually won them over. It was childlike faith not sullied by adult constraints of propriety. He simply prayed, "Dear Lord, please let it rain today right now. Please, Lord, they need to believe you control all. That we can have if we ask. Please, Lord, can you let it rain today, right now? They tell us in church that if we only ask, you'll do it for us, so I'm asking, Lord; let it rain please. Thank you, Jesus, for the rain." These were quiet, unassuming prayers with bowed head and folded hands only when there was no audience or a chance reverence would be interpreted as disrespect and disengagement. Eyes were closed if closing them did not bring much attention to him, when there was no blackboard to view or teacher to listen to as he prayed. He prayed slightly more demonstratively reverent during lunch or when in the library. He prayed for rain until the Father answered and drops fell. He would pause and give thanks. Although a start, drops were not enough. He prayed until he heard the sound of abundant rain. This childlike faith carried him until he began to believe too much of what he learned while attending church, that God was not a tool for our use and petty desires. Eventually the message and its varied iterations got through. Rain prayers ceased for decades until he spoke with the little woman by the well who said, "The Lord wants you to talk to the rain."

Standing out on the deck and choosing to ignore the evidence of the eyes, Max prayed. "Dear Lord, bring the rain. Let the clouds gather and quench the thirst of the grass and trees. He asked for rain a little nervous of the memory walk of the young boy sitting quietly at a cafeteria table with few friends. He with eyes closed, some unbelieving, some derisive, but others awaiting the sound. Now nearly fifty, he never forgot he made such requests so early in life, never forgot that he ever asked for something so improbable and got a yes and responded with a thank you, God, and amen. Nearly a half century old, Max was directed back to a time of unmitigated belief in an omnipotent God. He activated a vestigial area of his spirit, a part that could see what was not, see light dispel darkness because a directive from the Master of ocean, earth, and sky granted permission for him to talk to the rain, tap a faith packed away like a youthful secret because he was too old now to believe it himself. Standing on the deck he spoke to the rain that was not, and called on Jesus to send rain bearing clouds. Seeing a few gather, he wondered about Virginia precipitation and called Mark.

"Hi, Pops."

"What's doing?"

"Just relaxing, I'm getting ready to walk down the street to hang out for a while."

"Well move quickly. The rain will be coming soon."

"Really? I was out earlier. It's a clear day."

"It's going to be coming down soon."

"You know something I don't?"

"Just that it's going to rain."

"In Maryland?"

"Here and Virginia. What does your phone say?"

Mark checked. "Clear. No rain at all this week."

"Ok. Talk a little later, jacket or umbrella. Your choice."

Max hung up and prayed. He looked beyond into the spiritual with a youthful faith that an unnatural request was heard. He prayed, and then the sky darkened, the winds picked up, and out of nowhere a drop or two fell on the deck and continued to fall until he could no longer keep track. He celebrated not because today meshed with yesterday, but because he found the Lord was still with him for the drops spoke, "I Am is here, son; I Am is here." Max lifted praise to the King.

He called Mark again. "How's it look now?"

"It's cloudy."

"What's your phone say?"

"Still says sunshine."

"Ok, the sky is going to open up."

Max walked back to the deck, and he called on the Lord to send the rain. He prayed continually as more drops fell. He persisted. "Lord, let the rain pour down; open the sky dear Lord in the mighty name of Jesus," and rain fell in abundance.

Mark called Max, "I can't believe it. It was raining real hard here for ten minutes, and then it stopped."

"It's not done though. Ask me how I know."

"I already know, but the problem with the rain is we have a leak in the living room. I put the bucket down to catch the water."

"Your room's not leaking though, is it?"

"No, the leak appears to have gone around my room. The water either enters from the roof or through the siding, and then travels under my room and comes through the center of the living room."

"As long as the bucket is in place and your room dry, all is well because it's not over. Talk later."

The rain became a drizzle in Maryland, so Max opened the French door to the morning room, walked to the center of the deck and began again. "Lord please hear your humble servant. Lord, I thank you for the rain. I thank you, Jesus, for access to the throne. Thank you, Jesus," Over and over he said, "Thank you, Jesus" with energy and belief that the drizzle would intensify and the rain would last long enough to move out of the realm of chance. He lifted up his voice to the Lord, and the rains returned, steady and long lasting.

A day of rain followed by arid times previously characterized his walk, but his burning thirst now awakened by faith could only be quenched by a constant stream of living water delivered by a servant of the Lord. His spiritual battery discharging through the week ran down unable to sustain the Max of youth who could ask and ask again and again for a display that could shake the natural world and send the dark spirit world into a tailspin. Max felt a little dejected, a little depressed that in moving God to answer a prayer for rain, he could not move God to grant a way out. "A little short of parlor trick," the enemy whispered in reference to rain, "but still no house." Three days after a clear connection with the Father, the enemy added, "And what did it get you?" The question moved Max's sight from agent to act, from God to rain and then from a house lost to a basement rented. He began to look at things, and wonder once again like Gideon that if God were indeed with him, why then had all this befallen him?

CHAPTER 37

He needed the preached word, sound teaching straight from the Bible as a reminder that it is never vain to serve God, for there is profit in keeping his ordinance even when the proud seem happy and they who work wickedness are set up. God hears them that fear him as they speak to one another about what is. He remembers. He hearkens.

Max found a podcast of a teacher his first pastor spoke often about when discussing his deliverance from a debilitating bout with arthritis. The first series for Max, a study on Job, spoke to loss. The teacher grounded all in Scripture; nothing appeared to grow out of the modern day vein of life coach promises. Job could not speak his way out, and the Father was under no obligation to explain himself.

Other scripturally-based teachings followed and fed him in ways his previous church chose not to. He listened to messages on endurance, bitterness, the fear of the Lord, unforgiveness, and worship. In lesson after lesson the podcast addressed his festering hurt of being left alone in the courtroom and pivotal moments after the divorce. The perfect order of topics addressed could only be accomplished by those in sync with one out of time who sees yesterday, today, and tomorrow as one. God's servant who walked closely with him in life decades ago would impact in death the lives of countless people including Max.

Eventually topics focused on blessings and curses, trees planted by the river in Psalms one week and shrubs in parched places in Jeremiah the next. The promises of God's goodness encouraged him, but the teaching on curses stopped him dead. He hit repeat over and over and over to hear the fifth chapter of Zechariah verses one through four. The church spreading darkness and not setting the fractures within families was not free. Those seemly untouched by the fruit of their behavior in this world perched upon a slippery place in the world to come if they did not cry out in repentance and fall in love again with the Master. Max once angry about the outcome of divorce court now asked the Lord to have mercy on Sylvia because of that spoken in Zechariah. "It shall enter into the house of the thief, and into the house of him that sweareth falsely by my name: and it shall remain in the midst of his house, and shall consume it with the timber thereof and the stones thereof."[33]

Sylvia's perjury unleashed a curse upon the house. "I will bring it forth" caused Max to sit up. He heard correctly. God brought it forth. Like the scroll with wings, it entered the house and lodged in the joists, appliances, and the foundation. It rotted them from the inside out. A home cursed could find no peace. Max was stunned by a mystery of Scripture unlocked with revelation granted by God.

The day of the accident, he and Sylvia waited in traffic before reaching a bible study overrun by darkness, but while waiting he missed the reading of Malachi and wondered whether or not it counted toward his goal of covering the Bible in one year. While sitting at the kitchen counter with the morning room to his left and the family room behind him, the teaching and the reading of the Word over the podcast offered words he never heard when reading in private or listening to the MP3 player over the car stereo. He hit rewind and play a number of times until he heard for sure that God himself brought it fourth as written in that book that preceded Malachi. This too was Scripture he did not recall hearing the day of the accident.

The one who swore falsely and proudly said to Max weeks after the decree, "You should have had a better lawyer" invited curse. The dryer was the first to give out. Making no connection between her actions and the dryer's malfunction, Sylvia replaced it. Then the washing machine followed suit. Sarah told Max the dishwasher died and sat unused for some time before eventually being replaced.

"She said that you're not giving her the money you owe her."

"Until the IRS is finished, I suspect I'm not, but you know I'm not interested."

"She said that she can't buy what she needs. It seems to be your fault."

"Still not interested."

The stove joined the appliance strike, and Sylvia replaced it. The fireplace separated from the wall during an earthquake. The living room ceiling leaked during rain. Sylvia called home repair experts and roofers to find and repair it. They looked in all the logical places, but the supernatural source of rot and curse eluded them. Eventually the foyer's ceiling gave way to leak, which also required a bucket during times of rain. The upstairs toilet tank cracked and water flowed down to the main level before Sarah made it home from school and shut the water off. A water pipe in the basement broke and flooded the basement. The house was without water for six days.

The curse claiming the inside traveled to flora on the outside. The rhododendrons on the side of the garage died along with the nearby hardy teacup rosebush that fought before giving in. Portions of the juniper bush near the front porch lost to an invasive winding vine. The juniper gold lace fought the juniper blue star and won, but then succumbed to weeds resembling small trees. The mugo pine hedge along the steps from the driveway to the house traded green for brown and died along with the dogwood and lilac bush. The ornamental weeping cherry tree fought valiantly against boring insects, but it suffered from massive scarring. Seeing the outside when he picked up Sarah for the weekend reminded Max of the words he spoke to a fellow volunteer in the youth ministry shortly after leaving. "What's in the inside of her body and the house will be reflected on the outside of both."

The Lord called out to Sylvia again and again. Jesus tried to break through her sense of success and independence strengthened by a court case that never should have been. She refused to listen, to hearken to his voice. She pulled away; she stopped her ears. Led by the enemy, she made her heart as adamant stone lest she heard the words of the Lord and cried out to him and returned. Calm fled the house too. Cursing and argument between mother and son displaced order and banished peace. Temper tantrums between mother and daughter bled into the store and the car, leaving Sarah to ask, "Just who is the child here?"

"Mom thinks she's been cursed," she said to Max.

"Not interested."

"I know, but there's so much happening, so much that has happened," Sarah said. "There was a dead robin on the front porch with no evidence that it hit a window or the side of the house. Mom wondered how it came to be. She toyed with the notion someone placed it there."

"I had nothing to do with it, but I think I know who did."

"And the spiders and centipedes are everywhere. I hate going into the family room." Although Sarah knew the cause, she maintained silence about that shroud of darkness that overtook a number of bodies the day of the accident. Sylvia was among the number. Still, she never spoke of it, never a word of its uncompromising essence, its prodding and searching, its unsuccessful attempt to gain a foothold in couples emanating light. Heaven granted her a glimpse for one night only, and though the vision passed, she knew the darkness remained.

The Lord provided an eternal strategy to address the seemingly inexorable family destruction, yet none within the church broke the seal with prayer and fasting to glimpse the hidden thing the Father tried to reveal. Members closed their eyes to divine guidance. They sought distractions through new hobbies or resurrected old ones. They took up golf. Operating under temporal principles, the cavalier concern toward divorce barred any possibility of sight. Jehovah Rapha whispered secret things to heal a corporate body's walk gone awry and reignite the char of a do right spirit. Few listened to the only Potentate leading the charge in a battle already won while he reiterated precept upon precept and line upon line, and fewer still who understood made spiritual adjustments, so the Lord poured out a spirit of deep, deep slumber for eyes already closed and heads long since hidden.

It is dangerous to slight a king and an unwise test of grace to slight the King of Kings. Such behavior brought Nebuchadnezzar to his knees and then to a point of acknowledging on the back end of his reign, "All the inhabitants of the earth are reputed as nothing; and he doeth according to his will in the army of heaven, and among the inhabitants of the earth. None can stay his hand, or say unto him, what doest thou?"[34] With no repentance in sight, the Lord God chose their delusion because when he called, none answered, and when he spoke, none heard; all continued in their own way. Before this storm Max once acted as others did that a walk with God could be a casual walk. God's grace for Max was realized through loss, not prosperity. Losing all to ensure a seat at the wedding feast was the true favor of God's grace.

CHAPTER 38

ark visited Max for lunch in Maryland. "Glad you could make it on your day off," Max said.

"You usually come to Virginia to eat with us. It made sense for me to change it up a bit."

"Well I'm glad. I need to tell you that Cynthia has the house on the market which is good for her. This is a big house for one person. She bought a smaller one, a condensed version of this one. Notice the pictures are all down."

Mark looked around and shook his head slowly, now noticing the TV in the kitchen gone as well as small appliances and canisters generally on the kitchen counters.

"Are you moving into that basement?"

"No, I'm not moving with her."

"What are you going to do?"

"Ah the Lord will work it out. I'll wait on him. I'll be here till the house sells, and then I'm out."

"Wow. Ok, I hope it works out for you."

"It always does. It may not feel that way since I'm in the middle of it, but it always does."

While seated at the kitchen counter as Max went back to making sandwiches, Mark said, "Divorce is selfish." He shook his head, and he considered Max's current circumstances and his and Sarah's before emphasizing, "Divorce is just plain selfish, Dad. Erica's parents are getting a divorce."

Max looked up at Mark while building the turkey sandwiches. Mark looked at him in disbelief and said, "Erica found out by reading an email her dad sent her mom. He's moving to Atlanta. Her mom apparently left the email on the desktop. I suspect the email broke something inside her, and she walked away before closing her account."

"When you two took me out to dinner for Father's Day her mom came to the car to meet me while I waited for you and Erica to come out of the house. We never met while members of the church. Her eyes told me she wanted to talk; she needed to tell me something or ask me something, but her husband was washing his car right next to us, and she said nothing of depth. She just stood there after the hello and initial small talk. It was strange, but now it makes sense."

"You know he didn't stay in the house then."

"I had no idea, but I did wonder why he didn't join us. If you think back to a conversation you and I had about Steve and Kara and whether or not he would step down or be sat down, you might better understand my question now. Look at how families have been decimated, particularly those in the music ministry. It's spiritual, more than personalities meshing or whatever reason apart from adultery or abuse church people give these days for calling it quits. The numbers are too high and too concentrated to be circumstance and chance. A spirit has been unleashed. It's pulling strings, and members of the church haven't figured it out." Max walked over to the bar high counter with the sandwiches and juice. "Anyway, why Atlanta? I thought he, I thought they were from the Caribbean."

Mark didn't answer the question. He added, "Mrs. Geri is helping him find a house in Atlanta." He took a sip of juice and then a bite of his sandwich. Holding up the sandwich he said, "This is good."

"Thanks. How is that possible? Is she an agent? She lives here. Is she working on the internet to find him a place?"

Mark didn't answer. He continued to eat like one carrying weight.

"Did her family move to Atlanta? Why Atlanta? Aren't they from the Caribbean too?" Max took a bite.

"No." Mark said.

"Yes, I think they are." He paused and took a bite of his sandwich. Then continued, "Don't ask me how I know, but I think for sure they are."

Max stopped asking questions and looked directly at Mark. "Tell me they're not. Please tell me she didn't."

"Yeah," he said. "She divorced her husband and is with Mr. Lorenzo."

After Max's divorce the devastation continued. Children from teenagers to toddlers were affected by this selfishness as Mark named it. "Is anybody sickened by this? Is any leader speaking out about this? My God have mercy. That music ministry is a mess. How can they minister? How can they usher in the anointing when they are divorcing and then remarrying each other?"

"Right! At first I just ignored what you said. It sounded like something out of a movie, but now this can't be ignored."

"It can't, so let me give you some advice before it latches onto you. "Run, run for your very life!"

Mark laughed uneasily.

"Seriously, you need to quit the band at that church. Find another church that needs a piano or keyboard player, and if they can't pay you, play for free, play for the Lord. He'll bless you for it. I can pray coverage, but you've got to leave if the coverage is going to mean anything." They ate in silence. Max began again, "Spirits hop and lodge and lay dormant for years. They might not raise their head until you no longer think of the connection as spiritual. You'll just see a string of divorces within your circles, and it'll move from generation to generation. Few will recognize the spiritual nature of the problem, and those who find the truth may never know where it began. Since you can see it now, it's time to leave. Those in the throes of it can't see it, so will not fight. The really sad thing is they probably don't know how to fight.

"That's what I don't understand. It is impossible to miss. What is it, seven members from the praise team alone?"

"The church is so large; who hears about it? Some members probably think I'm traveling or just left the church. New members wouldn't know me or those before me who are now divorced. The lack of historical knowledge won't exempt them from harassment by the spirit of divorce. It owns that building, and the children harassed today will feel the weight of the spirit later in life when they marry. It's spiritual Mark. I know it makes no sense in the natural."

"I won't go back. Too much mess for me. There is a church that's asked me to play, and I'll play for them."

"Good. That church lost sight of the holiness of God and became its own measure. Holiness vacillates when measured against other churches or people, particularly people not in the church. Members I spoke too after I left thought nothing of the rising divorce rate. They found ways to excuse it. God's holiness is constant."

"I'm a witness that God will call out to you when you are in sin, but you have to hear him, repent, and get back on plan. He's faithful to forgive, but one can always find another person or group to justify sin by saying, "I'm not as bad as this one or that one." Then nothing changes. That may work now, but it won't stand in the judgment."

"Well I'm not going back, so I'll let them figure it out while I attend another church to get it right on my own. It's a church filled with contradictions, and I'll leave it at that."

"Good."

The visit took something out of Max. After Mark left, Max walked down to the basement and took a nap. In the space between sleep and awake, the Lord spoke to Max's spirit saying, "The Lord will rise up to work an alien work while the bonds of the deaf he once called are made stronger. His people have grown numb to the message of loss and therefore the decree of destruction is given. In an effort to bring them low, voices are coming from the ground and the dust. Thunder, earthquake, whirlwind, tempest, flame. The people draw near with mouths and honor God with lips, but hearts remain distant and the fear of the Lord merely taught by men. Thunder, earthquake, whirlwind, tempest, flame. For those who run in cars and planes to the west or east, thunder, earthquake, whirlwind, tempest, and flame will find them, a thousand fleeing at the threat of one. Return and rest, and you shall be saved. I have shown you the way. Walk in it."

CHAPTER 39

Max transitioned to the Passotel once Cynthia's house sold. The small German boutique hotel located in Virginia, Maryland, and Delaware had the potential for one in any state, and though small, it accommodated Max and his things quite well when not traveling for work. He told Sarah about this arrangement since she saw the contents of his trunk every other weekend. He told no one else. One night while resting on the bed in a Maryland Passotel, the phone rang. "Well praise the Lord, Brother Max. I was talking to your sister, and we both said we hadn't heard from you. What is going on? Where are you?"

"Nothing much going on, I'm in Maryland. God is good, isn't he?"

"Yes he is, and he will do just what he said he would do. Can we say thank you Jesus? A storm is coming. It will come when people think the season is over, but God said he controls the seasons, and they obey him."

As they talked about the goodness of the Lord, the anointing began to fall on them in Maryland and in Long Island. "Praise the Lord, Brother Max, the Lord is showing me your house. I can see Sarah's room, the entrance hall, the floors, and the backyard. Hold on and don't give up. It's on the way. Hallelujah. Hold on." The anointing took her even higher, and she walked away from the phone as she had done so many times. He could hear her in the distance talking with God in tongues and worshipping and praising him. Then she came back to the phone.

"The Lord is pleased with you," she said. "No more mumbling and complaining just a belief that God will do just what he said he would do." Again, the praise rose higher and higher. "The Lord said, 'Don't worry, son. Don't worry about it. Can I not do what I said I would do? Will I not move you from temporary shelter to a home? I'm working it out, working it out, working it out.'" Max generally took notes, but in the dark he listened.

The Lord revealed what Max told no one except Sarah. He lived in the Passotel, but he held onto faith that something better was on its way. In God's time, he would be placed in a house. "Use wisdom and find shelter when you hear the storm is approaching. This won't be regular rain today and then sunshine, so find shelter and use wisdom. The Lord is showing me angels, one on the hood and one on the trunk of your car. Nothing by any means shall hurt or harm you. The Lord said you need to know this, this day. Can we say thank you Jesus?"

"Thank you, Jesus."

"'When the winds blow, ask me, son, Lord is this you? Is this the one? If it is, I will divert the wind from you.' Can we say thank you Jesus?"

"Thank you, Jesus."

"Where are you off to next?"

"Detroit and Memphis with Baltimore in between."

"Let the Spirit lead you. If God tells you not to go, don't go, darling. You hear.

"Yes."

I know it's late, so I won't keep you up long. You be blessed."

Max heard nothing more about a storm until two month later while working in Memphis. His sister called, and began as most calls to Max did. "Where are you?"

"In Memphis again, here until Thursday."

"Oh, that sounds nice. Eating good food?"

"You know it. I'll send pictures—barbeque, fried chicken— beyond words. I fly out at two, and then I have Sarah this weekend. I'll get a roomier hotel of course, larger than the one I use when alone."

"Good. A major storm is coming, and you have to have shelter, the kind that sits on a strong foundation. I know you don't watch TV, and I assume when working and writing you pay little attention to the papers. The reports say this is a big storm, so make sure you have a place to stay. It's a hurricane."

"This time of year? A hurricane? You sure?"

"Yes! And I'm ready. I always have bottled water; you know that. We picked up extra food, and we bought a plastic garbage can today to fill with water as we did when pipes froze on the farm?"

"I remember those days. We learned quite a bit."

"We didn't know it then, but going through hard times prepared us. We'll fill the plastic garbage can with water, and use the water to bath and do the dishes in case the water is shut off or there's a "no use" put into effect. We learned how to hunker down. Who would have thought?

"Who would have thought," he said. "This isn't it. I'm not in my house yet. The Lord said he'd place me first before the storm."

"No, this isn't the storm the Lord told us about. It's a prelude of what is to come, but people don't want to listen. Many link the weather patterns solely to the environment: global warming and pollution."

"In North Carolina a colleague asked me whether or not I thought, given the state of the economy, there would be some uprising of sorts because of the loss of jobs, massive foreclosures, and rising debt. He didn't know it at the time, but the IRS had just finished a second round of taking money from my account. I'd no right to be upset because I owed the taxes. I just couldn't pay them along with everything else and live. We all have bills, but where he assumed a social explosion to remove the overwhelming weight, I know, we know there will be a spiritual explosion, through natural means, yes, but God will be behind it because the earth is full. It can't take anymore. How a regular dad can't see his children except every other weekend and spends twenty-seven thousand in legal fees over six months only to lose when winning would have been fifty-fifty between mom and dad… the earth is full and will vomit up all that's wrong with it.

"That was a spirit, and you know it."

"I told my colleague that I was already in my recession, and when court decisions make rulings that exacerbate what's already wrong with society and impose worldly rulings in families naming Christ, it's not a human uprising I worry about."

"Christians like Sylvia contribute to this sickness and should know better. We should be the buffer on our knees in prayer, fighting Satan and his minions instead of in the courts furthering his work."

"Before leaving for North Carolina, I was praying and worshipping the Lord with Sister Bett, and the Lord sent another word to pull my money out of the bank. I didn't even know I had any in there. Sarah and I went to the bank that Friday. I tried to pull two hundred out."

"Were you successful?"

"No. Nothing. I tried one hundred. Nothing. I said looking at Sarah, 'Ok, let's try twenty.' It worked. I had twenty, so I tried another twenty and then another."

Both laughed.

"In total I pulled out eighty bucks. I needed thirty-two to park the car at the airport; it would be tight, right?"

"If you didn't eat."

"The next day I got a check for eight hundred and seventy-five dollars. I put it in the bank to clear with the idea I'd get it out as soon as it cleared."

"What happened?"

"I went online and found I was negative sixteen thousand in my savings and negative fifteen thousand in my checking."

She gasped.

He continued. "I suspect all stemming from being too spiritual, too mean, and having the gall to fight in court for custody. The explosion won't be social; it will be spiritual."

Max could feel his sister praying silently in the spirit that he would continue to hold on. He sounded good at this moment and recounted the events with clarity as if they just happened yesterday and not months ago. While she prayed, her spirit connected with his. An unbreakable connection from New York to Tennessee emerged, and she knew beyond faith and promise that Max had found his way into a place of peace, a new place in the bosom of Jehovah Shalom.

"We've had more than enough time to get it right, particularly those of us who call Jesus by name. We've failed," Max continued. "Confess the sin, repent, and move on. You can't distinguish the church from the world nowadays. The sad part of it all is that many churches although not all the members in them like it this way."

"Well, look at you and a number of other Christians now casualties of a spirit of divorce hovering over that church. There is no one with a collar speaking against it and binding it up. It seems the leadership accepted it. What kind of spiritual leader shows up in divorce court in the first place and continues to support of a wife making a claim that the husband is mean because ten years ago he didn't pick up something from the store when she asked? That's the example of a mean spouse? He should be ashamed of himself that he sat through that mess, and then call himself counseling your children. It's a farce. Ten years of living in Virginia and not one example to support a mean streak. She just wanted out. The church held open the door of divorce, and she stepped right through it with your pastor as an escort."

"You're right."

"I know I'm right. You visited a small church here in New York to hear a high demon of divorce had control over your church and your wife. That's a shame. Your church sat idly by. That's more of a shame."

"That it is."

"Too many church leaders desire to become megachurches. They want to be on TV and the cover of magazines, worldly magazines to boot that don't care a lick about God, church, or the preacher. They put church leaders on the cover to build them up and increase the attention they receive, so their readership and the nation can tear them down. How these evangelists and pastors have convinced themselves that appearing on a cover to show their wealth furthers the gospel is beyond me. Then they brag about being invited to the White House to pray. Did prophets of old brag about going to the king's house, and was any king ever smug in his ways after a visit? They need water coolers in megachurches, so the leaders can overhear the honest conversations taking place. All this glitz overshadows the real work of the gospel in churches and mission fields all over the world. How did your pastor in New York put it?"

"Preaching the unadulterated Word of God," Max said.

"That's right. The unadulterated Word of God! Where do you hear that in many of the churches that get all the attention?"

"You don't, and that's why my pastor in the Bronx said that many people will bust hell wide open. If you don't believe in God, then don't believe in him. It doesn't make eternity untrue, but for those who say they believe and disregard messages from the Old Testament as trumped by grace or no longer relevant because the law was fulfilled once and for all is worrisome."

"It's dangerous actually," she said.

"Christ didn't eradicate sin; he conquered it. That's why we glory in the cross. He gave us a way out, an advocate with the Father when we fall all because of the work wrought on the cross and his glorious resurrection."

"Where's the holiness?"

"I don't know; I just don't know."

"And where's the power?"

"A crowd sought signs and wonders when Jesus walked the earth, and people still seek them now. Where are they? Praise the Lord for the churches you never hear about, never see on TV that are focused and consistent as they lay hands and cast out demons."

"And thank God for those on TV who preach true biblical revelation for those of us who haven't found a good church home yet, but there are fewer and fewer of them which have not given themselves over to motivational, itchy ear preaching where you seldom hear of the work wrought on the cross."

"My church in the Bronx still has my inhaler suspended from a pipe. There it hangs next to a plastic bag filled with prescription medications, crutches, canes, and wheelchairs. I settled when I moved to Virginia. There really is something to waiting on the Lord."

"I remember that you didn't feel that was the church."

"True, he could preach though."

"That's interesting."

"What do you mean?"

"How do you reconcile that? He could preach, but you didn't feel it in your spirit?"

"He was grounded in the Word when the church was much smaller. He had a fire when he preached. Folks were on their feet before having to leave for the second service."

"Any healings?"

"Not that I witnessed or recall hearing about."

"Any pills or inhalers hanging from pipes on the ceiling?"

"No."

"Anyone speaking in tongues after having joined the church and praying for a Holy Ghost filling? Not those who came filled with the Spirit, but those seeking the Spirit. Any youth retreat legendary for the stories of the Holy Spirit descending and resting on the young with evidence of prophecy, tongues, or healing?"

"No."

"I don't know how you can say he could preach. Seems to me the preaching entertained and energized those in the sanctuary. Did they meet the Father while on retreats? Did they meet him in the sanctuary? Did any who walked up to the altar after service experience a true conversion?"

There was silence.

"Anyway, I'll let you get back to work brother dear; find shelter. I'll call you when you're on the coast. Much love."

"Much love."

CHAPTER 40

In the Memphis airport boarding area, colleagues heading east talked about the coming storm and their preparation for it. Max prepared by extending his stay in the Virginia hotel for his weekend with Sarah. Switching to the Passotel in the immediate aftermath of a storm would not be wise. As he finished amending his reservation online, Mark called.

"Hey, Pops."

"What's up?"

"I don't mean to get into your business and all, but do you plan to pay Mom soon?"

"What?"

"I'm not trying to tell you what to do, but she's really pushing me and Sarah about where you live. She said that she was thinking of getting the courts involved because she isn't getting her money regularly and all."

Max paused. "You know I don't have money stashed away for a rainy day though I suspect this would constitute a rainy day." He thought of the most recent pictures sent to Mark and Sarah from a hotel that was beyond words. The chandelier in the lobby, a massive ship, was a stunning crystal creation complete with crystal masts and raised sails. Max thought about how it looked to Mark.

"You know when I travel for work, I have roof over my head." He felt the silence. Sarah kept his secret. She held close one hotel stay after another and his trunk stuffed with a pillow, blanket, and suitcases of clothes next to hotel laundry bags bursting with dirty clothes in the trunk until their next stay at a hotel with a laundry room. He had to tell Sarah, but Sylvia— spurred on by the spirits that had her purchase surveillance cameras for inside and outside of the house and moved upon her to forbid Mark and Sarah ever touch her mailbox—would move in for total destruction and derive ungodly pleasure from his string of hotels and a car turned bed. She would interpret the valley as a sure sign of Max's spiritual abyss; she would thank God that he led her to cut ties with the nomadic man before he brought her and the children down with him. Sarah never told, and the spirits that sat on the loveseat and then perched on her shoulder watched his car from afar never told either.

Spiritual boundaries existed that Max could not understand. Demons remained an arm's length away from his car turned bed because invisible ministering spirits sent by God kept watch. They stood on hood and trunk. "I am with you, son," the Lord said through his servant. "I'll keep you safe." Dark spirits knew where he slept and in what he slept, but they could not attack, could not get through angelic sentries assigned to keep him safe, and for reasons he did not understand, they remained silent, would not or could not tell Sylvia who was keenly interested in knowing his address.

And she would not dare ask them. There were boundaries that would never be breached except by avowed enemies of the cross of Christ. The price of crossing them placed one's soul in the balance, and the cost was much too high. Saul and the woman of Endor remind all who claim Christ that those who live are forbidden to seek the answers from the dead, and Paul, Silas, and the woman cleansed from a spirit of divination serve as reminders that earthquake trumps jail; the spirit trumps natural; there's holiness or hell. Sylvia would never overtly ask spirits or the dead, "Just where, just where does he live?" She would never move about freely and knowingly in the presence of darkness. What she would not do and what they were forbidden to do resulted in a spiritual stalemate. They would never tell her unless she entreated them to, and the invitation required an inconceivable sacrifice she would not consciously make. A tantalizing stalemate lay between them, a wanting to know and a desire to tell, but neither that of spirit or flesh made the move. Nothing accidental would happen, and nothing incidental, resulting from poor judgment would start the process of moving both closer to each other.

While language shifted and redefined evil and wrong in the natural world, it remained exactly the same in the spiritual world when one third of heaven's inhabitants fell to Earth. In the spirit, the notion of compromise was a myth. Darkness remained as it was and did not gain territory claimed by righteousness or relinquish ground either. Divination, witchcraft, and necromancy were wrong as indicated by the law. Exposure, familiarity, and conversations with loved ones long gone as seen on television and written about in books had no impact on the truth that the dark spirit within a woman crying out an indisputable truth still grieved the Holy Spirit within Paul. Sylvia would not ask. Natural laws could be ignored only with permission from on high; any other way constituted a breach, and a breach though mystifying and uncanny remained subject to one who walked in the Spirit and carried within a Word from the Lord. Natural laws submitted to God and to those who walked closely with the Father.

Sarah who saw family swatches sewn into a dark quilt, ministering spirits in the third row of a van, and darkness billowing in a sacred place never told anyone those things, and she kept his secret surrounding his multipurpose car.

"What do you mean a roof?"

"When I travel, I'm in a hotel. I have to work of course, but I'm in a hotel. When I get Sarah for the weekend, we stay in hotels. During the week when not traveling, I sleep in my car."

"What?"

"Yes, the Passat my good man; it's my roving DC-area hotel."

"You didn't tell me."

"You shouldn't be surprised. You helped me earlier this year when I couldn't pay the phone bill, the storage bill, and my rent for that matter. You didn't help me with my rent, but you sold the flat screen for money to pay the storage, and you used your church check from playing the keyboard to pay the phone bill. I owe taxes. The IRS took the checks, expenses and all. You can say I paid to work, but I owed the money, so I wasn't angry, overwhelmed perhaps, but not angry." The two remained silent until Max began again. "Very few who don't own a company or have parents to lean on can survive a twenty-seven thousand legal bill, twenty thousand to an estranged wife, seven thousand for a car, and twelve thousand in rent in one year. Don't forget, I took you both out to dinner when I came from Maryland." Max could hear Mark's breathing as he continued to share what he previously had not. "Your mom also made a fuss about my working three weeks in Los Angeles every summer. A decent check became a brick in the wall of why I shouldn't have joint custody of Sarah, so I gave it up, and I still lost joint physical custody."

"I didn't know."

"Of course, you didn't. I had a deposition when I returned from my last stint in Los Angeles which meant I had to come up with money to pay my attorney, knowing the July check based on history would not come until October. Still, I had to pay my attorney to join me in a deposition, so her attorney could probe to uncover the many secret places I tuck money away. My attorney used his cell phone while he sat next to me, and all I could think was how surreal this really was. He was clear I'd need to pay him from the minute he entered his car to the minute he finished writing notes in his office after the deposition, and I did. When I worked in DC, I took the bus in, and when I needed to fly out of the region, I rode the Metro or

MARC train to National or Marshall Airport, but your mom made my not having a car an issue in court, so I bought the Passat after I lost the case. I called my attorney. I told him I purchased a car, no longer worked in LA, and would work part-time for my former employer. With this I could guarantee travel on the weeks I didn't have your sister. I addressed all the reasons why I couldn't have Sarah live with me half the time as she wished, but he told me that it would cost another retainer fee of five thousand dollars, and there was no guarantee it would work out. I couldn't believe it. I didn't have the money. I didn't have it because the ball of debt continued to roll.

Mark remained silent.

"I have Jesus. Angels of protection stand guard on the car while I sleep; I don't see them, but I feel them in my spirit."

"Wow," Mark said.

"To the angels or the bed?"

Mark didn't reply.

Max continued, "I sleep at rest stops, generally a different one every night in Maryland, Virginia, New Jersey, or Delaware. The temperature dipped in the thirties only a few times, but I haven't been cold. The hurricane headed our way will set me back. I'll need to pay for a hotel for an extended period of time. I've no car insurance, no health insurance, and the list goes on, but when I feel ill, I recite, 'I shall not die, but live and declare the work of the LORD.'" [35]

Max felt in his spirit that Mark wanted to turn down the help for a used car, so he continued, "You need one thousand dollars for a used car, and I said I'd give it to you. I have two children, not one. You need help too, and I'm giving you the money, so you won't have to walk or take taxis to and from work. Just keep it to yourself. I should have a big check in December, and I'll give her a portion. Her money is held up because she received bad advice, and as it turned out she hurt herself as well as others connected to her. Depositions and exorbitant alimony are for TV drama. It should never be the stuff everyday working people face."

Mark listened.

"I don't think she was the decision maker. I know you and Sarah think I'm crazy when I say such things, but the enemy pulled her strings. I told you to get out of that church because of his influence. He blinded you there. Some of your behavior could be attributed to adolescent individuation, but much was unnatural, and I knew it. The Lord told me to pull back, and he'd open your eyes. You could see God at work when he told me to tell you to stop texting and driving. Remember God told me to say to you Sampson and Delilah. I had no idea your girlfriend tried to trick you with a false pregnancy test, but the Lord knew, and let you know he knew when he chose to tell me through the little woman by the well. The Lord also told me that you wouldn't be returning to school. Christians don't need a prophet's class.

Mark was still speechless.

Max continued, "So here we find ourselves, me with a temporary roof over my head and you learning something new about your dad; don't worry about me; I'm good. Soon this will all be over."

"Wow. I don't know what to say, but I don't think you're crazy. That's why I no longer go to that church. They asked me to come back and play again, but I said, 'No!' Mom took me to meet with Steve when she couldn't convince me to come back. I met with him and told him that there was too much drama there for me."

"What did he say?"

"He didn't. He just lowered his head. I guess someone finally called it what it was. I walked away. I don't think you're crazy. I was more amazed if anything that you knew what Sarah and I did or were thinking of doing, that you told us our dreams as we sat in restaurants to eat dinner. We told no one, but you knew. There's something else. You remember I told you Mrs. Geri and Mr. Lorenzo moved to Atlanta?"

"Yes."

"Well now they are married."

"I assumed they would be, didn't you?"

"I imagine so, but guess who conducted the marriage ceremony?"

"You gotta be kidding me. Our former pastor? I never gave it much thought, but now that you bring it up, I suspect he performed the ceremony for Steve the second time around. It would make sense."

"Yes, but that's not all of it."

"What else can there be?"

"Mr. Lorenzo is going to be ordained as a minister and pastor in Atlanta."

"Oh God!"

"And our former pastor will conduct the installation. He's taking the praise team to minister in song. Mom's going." Mark sat in silence as did Max until Mark said, "I will never go to that church again. This makes me sick. You know Erica, his daughter, says he has no contact with them. How can you be a pastor and not have contact with your children? How do you lead others when you choose not to return the calls or texts from your children?"

Max continued to listened.

"He posted the wedding news online. He even gave credit to the Lord for blessing him with a new start; God this and God that he wrote. His ex-wife had to move back home with her mother in Ohio as he plays house in Atlanta. I don't think God has anything to do with it. No one has seen Ms. Geri's husband. He was always quiet, and he's since left the church. What about him?"

"We might not know where he is, but God does. We can pray for him and the children. The hurt attempts to linger when one doesn't know why."

"I wonder if Mr. Lorenzo believes God will show up during the installation because the music is good or because he gave God credit for something God didn't do."

"Something tells me God's not at all gullible. The created can never manipulate the creator." Max paused needing a little time to digest it all.

Mark thought of the vision of darkness he saw during bible study before his parents divorced. "Dark days lay ahead," he said and laughed uneasily to himself.

Taken aback, Max asked, "What's so funny?"

"No, no I was just thinking about Sunday's sermon. It had nothing to do with the divorces and stuff."

"What about it?"

"The sermon in the church I play for in Manassas centered on 'Thy word is a lamp unto my feet—'"

Max joined him, "and a light unto my path.[36] What about it?"

"I don't know. I was just thinking that when you're really sorry about something your head's down and you reach out to those you've hurt. You reach out for forgiveness, but when you refuse to see your wrongness, is that even a word? Wrongness?"

"It sounds weird, but it's a word. I think you're on safe ground. Anyway, finish your thought."

"Well, when your head is up and you refuse to see your—let me say error."

"Ok, I could live with wrongness, but it's your show."

"Well, you continue to walk in darkness, but if your head is hung down and you're truly sorry, there's a better chance you might just see the light around your feet showing the right path. That's all." It's like sermons mean a little something extra to me these days."

"Interesting. I've never thought of the verse in that context before. The dark times have need for a new revelation, and the Lord has given you insight on this. I'll think of it for sure on the flight to DC. And I've got a plane to catch, so I have to go."

"One other thing."

"What's that?"

"You were right. It's affected the children."

"What are you talking about?"

"Michael and his wife are getting a divorce. They're following in the path of his mother and father, the former bass player of the church band. He and his wife divorced, remember."

"Good Lord, have mercy. I feel like we're sitting on insight on a high-ranking conspiracy, the spiritual collusion between Satan and some Christians, but the devil has duped them in another attempt to undermine the future work of the Lord. No one would believe what's afoot, and very few would be willing to stop it. I'm speechless." Looking at passengers boarding his plane, Max continued, "And I've got a plane to board."

"Love you, Pops."

"Love you too."

After the call Max dwelt on "mom's going." She's still not getting it. Have mercy, Jesus. Then his thoughts moved to the impending storm and the amount the hotel would cost with the extended stay. Max's sister provided a timeframe to the words from the little woman by the well who initially gave a what.

"Don't sleep in your car when word of a storm drops in your spirit, darling. The Lord said, 'He who has an ear, let him hear.' We'll think we're out of hurricane season, but God is who he said he is. Man follows patterns and reads history, but God creates both. Can we say thank you Jesus?"

"Thank you, Jesus."

"Can we say thank you Jesus?"

"Thank you, Jesus."

She repeated, "Don't sleep in your car when the storm comes. The Lord says find shelter, use wisdom. The nation has turned its back on God, but he says, 'If my people, which are called by my name, shall humble themselves, and pray, and seek my face, and turn from their wicked ways; then will I hear from heaven, and will forgive their sin, and will heal their land.'[37] It doesn't seem like his people are willing to listen. God said that it will be as in the book of Joel. 'That which the palmerworm hath left hath the locust eaten; and that which the locust hath left hath the cankerworm eaten; and that which the cankerworm hath left hath the caterpillar eaten.'"[38]

She continued, "Many will be fooled thinking one storm wasn't as bad as predicted, but God said it is the cumulative effect of the disasters. The difficulties will make it so it is best not to leave your house if you don't have to. There will be disease in the air and a shortage of food and people trying to break in houses for food and shelter. The Lord is tired of the zeal. God seeks those who will worship him in spirit and in truth, those who know who he is. Those he'll keep safe in a bubble and guide them if they have learned to hear for themselves what the Spirit of the Lord has to say."

"Can we say thank you Jesus?"

"Thank you, Jesus."

"Can we say thank you Lord?"

"Thank you, Lord."

With those last few words the tone in her voiced changed, meaning as it always had, the word was nearing an end, but not necessarily over.

"Well, I know you're ready for bed, and I'm not going to keep you. God is so good. Where would we be without him? 'The house I have for you will not flood when the waters come,' he said. So hold on, Brother Max. Don't give up, you hear? So many have started this walk, but so few finish because they walk by what they see, not by what the Father promises. You have to walk in the Spirit. Don't give up, dear. Hold on. You be blessed."

"You be blessed too." With that, he hung up.

Many who claimed a relationship with the Father often said, "The Lord told me" just before recounting their actions, but too few heard directly from him because they never learned how he spoke to them as distinct from others; they never waited long enough in silence after they spoke to discover the secrets of spending time with God. Through it all, Max finally learned the Shepherd spoke often and revealed himself as the living road map that for many years went unheeded. Stripped! Max gained the revelation of "hearing, now hear." He attuned both ears for direction, and with this heighten sense of hearing, he secured a room.

God, who knows all, knew Max lived in a car and every night head restraint buttressed pillow that cushioned his head. He took heed to the words, "Find shelter, my son, for the night will come when the wind will blow and the rain will fall and staying in your car will not be wise. I will protect you where you are, but use wisdom. Be guided by the Spirit, for I will come through a land that no longer hears my voice and no longer knows my name. I will blow. Find shelter on that day, but know this is just a prelude of the spiritual storms I will send," so he booked a room and extended the stay at the hotel in Springfield near the highway, forgoing the normal routine of Passotel after a reasonable hotel stay with Sarah.

The hurricane led to school closings. No school meant more time, a precious five additional hours on the back end of a Monday morning as stipulated in the divorce decree. The storm promised empty highways out of common sense and safety, not because of police or town directive. Sarah hoped for another day with dad even if stuck in the hotel room at least she was cooped up with a body in the same room as she, together where proximity communicated parental love. Talking, sometimes quiet and still—it mattered little as long as within the span of talking, listening, and remaining quiet, the parent's presence communicated love, moved beyond the ex-spousal tug-o-war, and saw Sarah as more than a ledger entry that moved between parents with the winner clocking more time. She hoped that the storm would roll in earlier than predicted and common sense and safety in Sylvia prevailed.

The school closing on the front end of the storm extended peace for Sarah with two hours of the extension taken in sleep. No one would expect travel in a storm, but at ten o'clock, two hours before time with Max officially ended, Sylvia sent Sarah a text. "You need to be back here before the storm really starts." At ten-thirty, Max received a text. "Where is my child? Legally I am supposed to know where you live and where you have my child. Check your paperwork."

Max remained calm unlike he did in the past when he received texts from her. He figured a word from the Lord three month ago prepared him. The Lord said that with all she tried to do.... She tried to break Max, and when God said that she couldn't have him, she refused to listen. With blow after blow, his giving up seemed inevitable, but he continued to stand. Max was told that Sylvia was seriously angry, and she did not know why.

He forwarded Sylvia's message to his sister followed by an "Ugh!" Sarah was the recipient of the first text, and he gifted with the second. To his mind the world of Christendom was really at sixes and sevens. This is what frequent visits to the house of the Lord yields, he thought. This is how those who claim to know Christ as King and Lord demonstrate royalty. He dropped Sarah off, and stopped to get gas before heading back to the hotel. Looking into the storm, the Lord brought to mind Solomon, and then brought back the last Christmas dinner in The Castle where all endured the insensitive game before he and both his children refused to play. As usual his mind jumped here and there between Bible and life, between a woman who wanted the top half of a baby and one who demanded a daughter be brought back to her house amid wind and rain and storm.

As he pumped gas and reflected on Sylvia and Sarah and the relationship they had, his phone alerted him to a text. It read:

Send my texts to whomever you want, but be sure to let them know you do not pay child support!!! You

sent text to me by mistake....how funny. You are
consumed with bitterness which will only kill you,
so grow up. You are almost 50. I am so great, and
will be greater when I no longer have to deal with
your bitterness and anger. Send this around.....! like
I care what anyone you associate with thinks about
me. You should be happy you are not in Jail. That's
where they put deadbeat fathers..... Forward this
also...!!!Forward this to the hypocrites who you've
spoken about like a dog in the past who suddenly have
become your best friends.... What a joke. Get a life
and leave me alone!!!

Max had long made it a habit not to respond to the texts that
came at him from Sylvia. Now he understood they came from a
much deeper place. Before the divorce, they came regularly, and
he answered them as soon as they arrived. Sometimes an exchange
lasted nearly thirty minutes until he learned to listen to the Father
and let it all go, let it all go. Now he recited, "No weapon that is formed
against thee shall prosper; and every tongue that shall rise against
thee in judgment thou shalt condemn."[39] He breathed deeply, and
understanding the directive in the New Testament to pray for those
who despitefully used him or tried to harm him, he prayed for Sylvia
and blessed her in the name of Jesus.

Harassed and having to hunker down alone in a hotel, his heart
quickly grasped hold of the chiastic beauty found in the verse he
pondered when delivering a hello to an elderly lady who missed him
dearly and when driving for a slice of pizza thirty minutes from town.
"For my thoughts are not your thoughts, neither are your ways my
ways, saith the LORD. For as the heavens are higher than the earth,
so are my ways higher than your ways, and my thoughts than your
thoughts."[40] In his lack, God proved abundant, and being forgiven

required forgiveness and an understanding of the world's ways as distinct from God's. He was to pray a blessing, not ill will.

His mother would tell her children that if they made their bed, then they would be forced to lie in it. He was to pray for mercy, for God warned of the danger in "houses full of all good things, which thou filledst not, and wells digged, which thou diggedst not, vineyards and olive trees, which thou plantedst not; when thou shalt have eaten and be full, then beware lest though forget the LORD that brought thee forth."[41] He was to pray for mercy.

The court decree, alimony, divided retirement, and child support dismissed this warning along with the charge to teach God's words to Sarah and Mark. "And thou shalt teach them diligently unto thy children, and shalt talk of them when thou sittest in thine house, and when thou walkest by the way, and when thou liest down, and when thou risest up."[42] Talk of Jesus was disrupted by principalities involved in what seemed most natural, the growing apart of husband and wife in the twenty-first century. The disruption barred peace; therefore, Sylvia's search for peace for "just the three of us" remained elusive because the finale directed by the god of this world prevented all forms of healthy communication between mother and son and mother and daughter. Any verbal energy expended focused on repairing a darkened parental relationship, not on teaching God's ways. Counseling sessions with the pastor aimed for superficial healing invoking peace, much peace when there was none to be found. Mercy indeed was needed.

Although Sylvia made a dark bed, money from Max would ensure she would not sleep in it, but "I have stripped you, son," said not so. Max's financial struggles meant Sylvia did not receive nearly two thousand a month from him. She would lie in her bed, and the quality of her attorney would not change that. Had God not stripped him, she would have kept the house and all its furnishings, but "I have stripped you, son," fit into an earlier word. "She will not keep that house" because pits dug fit better the one who held the shovel. He looked up at the sky and took from the grayish color, growing wind, and pelting rain "What will you believe?"

With gas tank full, Max returned the nozzle to the dispenser and got behind the steering wheel of his car. He listened to the wind and rain. As the music of each played he drove off. What did he have but words of promise from a God who is the very promise and cannot lie? He imagined Sarah now at the castle in her room alone while Sylvia remained ensconced in her room on the opposite end of the second floor. She sat satisfied face-to-face communication between father and daughter had been brought to an end.

Driving to the hotel he heard in his spirit, "Hold on, my son. The journey will be over, but not today. I will be your wallet as you settle in." After returning to his hotel room, he spoke with Sarah. She sat alone as he imagined. This left him heavy in spirit thinking again on his loss.

After ten days in the hotel, Max checked out. He reviewed his bill, but never noticed the account number charged was not his when the concierge said, "All is settled sir. Come again."

CHAPTER 41

While he drove to Long Island to wait out the aftermath of the storm under a roof, Sarah called. "She is really getting on my nerve." Sarah donned a cloyingly nasal voice as she said, "Where does he live? Where is he keeping you? I have a right to know." It's driving me crazy. I told her that we stay in a hotel on the weekends, but she still couldn't leave it alone."

According to the paperwork Sylvia had a right to know, but having exchanged a stationary cinderblock foundation for a mobile one of rubber if only temporarily and not by choice made that right to know messy. He would have to send a text every few days and in some cases every day when not traveling for work because "where does he live?" changed with each hotel and rest stop used. Foxes have holes and birds, nests, he knew this, had read this, but now he experienced the profundity of the Master's words.

The Lord was clear. Max was not to tell everyone he turned the car trunk into a chest of drawers, the back seat into a file cabinet, and the driver's seat into a bed. He had become an alchemist, if not of compounds and minerals, then of large unwieldy things; if not in reality, then in metaphor. A vehicle by day became bedroom by night. The glove compartment became a medicine cabinet and held mouthwash, toothbrush, and other essentials. He brushed his teeth while parked in lots and rest stops and rinsed with mouthwash before heading to the men's room. Soap, hot water, and a washcloth were all he needed to wash up during his time on the road as he called it.

Eateries with private bathrooms proved best for morning washing since they accommodated one guest at a time. Childhood on the potato farm provided clarity about necessities and luxuries, so the stint in the car and public restrooms did not undo him. With a change of underclothes in one pocket of his shorts or jeans and deodorant and soap in the other, he made it work. Enter an establishment unwashed and exit clean with coffee in one hand and bagel or muffin in the other. When a restroom was not available, unscented wipes worked best. Scented, perhaps good for babies, spoke too loudly for adults and betrayed them.

Childhood made him a master of small spaces, an artisan of making it work. A one-bathroom house and a mother and five children sleeping in a room with two beds, he could make it work. Move pillow to trunk, shift papers from the backseat to the front, and work out of the makeshift office. He pulled on experience, mixed what he knew with what he learned in the spirit. He learned to see the miraculous, hear divine whispers, and attend to a most subtle message as reminder that those who know the Father have never seen the righteous forsaken.

The Lord, he found, sent subtle messages of encouragement to the seeing and hearing. Late one night the Lord directed a one act play while Max sat in a coffee shop in Columbia, Maryland. He was at once in a cave, the only customer in the back corner of the dimly lit coffee shop made darker as closing approached and by a brook, a portion of the floor he did not occupy freshly mopped and difficult to cross without tracking. He was fed by a raven, a young man dressed in black with the bill of his cap pointing forward as he leapt over the wet floor to deliver an unopened loaf of banana chocolate chip cake soon to expire but still fresh. A gift from above in the form of an Old

Testament story performed on an earthly stage for an audience of one. Max feeling the hand of God said, "Bless you" to the raven as he left the coffee shop, and "Thank you" to the Director before parking his car at a rest stop for the night.

In the morning he rose, starting his routine with, "Thank you, Jesus." Those in Detroit, Memphis, or Baltimore never knew he was homeless. Stripped! He worked during the day, and closed his eyes at night after reciting his list of proclamations. With God's promises in mind, he said among others, "For as the rain cometh down, and the snow from heaven, and returneth not thither, but watereth the earth, and maketh it bring forth and bud, that it may give seed to the sower, and bread to the eater: So shall my word be that goeth forth out of my mouth: it shall not return unto me void, but it shall accomplish that which I please, and it shall prosper in the thing whereto I sent it."[43] Then sleep, turning many times in the middle of the night and saying, "Thank you, Jesus" before falling back to sleep in the most unnatural and cramp producing positions constrained by gas and brake pedals and a chair that no matter how far the back reclined could not lay straight. Max would wake in the morning, grab his proclamations, and say, "O LORD, I will praise thee: though thou was angry with me, thine anger is turned away, and thou comforts me. Behold, God is my salvation; I will trust, and not be afraid: for the LORD JEHOVAH is my strength and my song; he also is become my salvation. Therefore with joy I draw water out of the wells of salvation."[44]

The practice of reciting the ever-growing list before going to bed in the basement rental continued before going to bed in his car. When courting despair, "Why art thou cast down, O my soul? and why art thou disquieted within me? hope thou in God: for I shall yet praise him, who is the health of my countenance, and my God."[45] One evening he arrived at the rest stop too early for sleep, so he read First Corinthians chapter four. "For who maketh thee to differ from another? and what hast thou that thou didst not receive? now if thou didst receive it, why dost thou glory, as if thou hadst not received it?[46] Even to this present hour we both hunger, and thirst, and are naked, and are buffeted, and have no certain dwellingplace."[47] He put his head back and closed his eyes, and as if Paul appeared in one hand and in rotation some of the most famous preachers of today in the other with their compounds, runways, tailors, jewelry, and empires, Max saw favor today looked so very different than it did then, so very different. He opened his eyes and breathed deeply and continued to read. He concluded he had many instructors in the gospel, some good and some not so, but as Paul intimated in chapter four, he had only one father in the gospel and for Max, that father lived in the Bronx. His father in the gospel would never have exchanged things eternal for those which could be shaken as Max and Sylvia had. Max recalled the words, "be ye followers of me," words extremely important now in a mobile society where people who moved to a different state or city had need of a new church home, and sat through hours upon hours of new member's class when they found it.

Max laid much of his early teachings down, and chapters one through four of First Corinthians admonished him to pick them up again because "the natural man receiveth not the things of the Spirit of God: for they are foolishness unto him: neither can he know them, because they are spiritually discerned."[48] Seek God's face, pick up sustained prayer, pick up fasting, covet the best gifts, and begin to tear Satan's kingdom down. This was the teaching from his first church, a Bible believing church of Christ.

Darkness failed to overwhelm Max. The destroyer that tore his marriage apart was granted entry, but it could not make a home within him. Max refused the initial weight. Darkness fitted him for doubt, rejection, and bitterness only to find it sized him wrong as his faith grew. Doubt, rejection, and bitterness fell off. Darkness tried again after resizing Max only to see a repeat of what had gone on before. The destroyer sized Max for depression, but it too slipped off even though he slept in his car each night with an angelic security system, including two with unsheathed swords seen in the spirit by the demonic. It kept its distance since the power lay not in the unsheathed, but spoken words reminiscent of the dispute over the body of Moses.

For the first time in a long time Max felt lighter though not attributable to his loss of family or things. Had the invisible weight fit him correctly it would have destroyed him. Men jumped off buildings and bridges to end it all, drove cars into guardrails, or offered their last stroke to a nearly imperceptible undertow when weighted down by the invisible. Max considered such endings, but the Spirit pulled him ever forward into a place where his struggles, his loss, and his heartbreak became a light affliction, an artist's tool for a spiritual rendering in the eternal landscape. The work on him lasted longer than a moment, but each artistic stroke with hammer and chisel spoke to a promise of a far more exceeding and eternal weight of glory.

Before and for some time after his divorce he carried an invisible albatross around his neck, and it would have remained there, fluttering about and defeating him by the sheer weight of it all if he had not learned to listen to the Father's voice. By all accounts, this was his lot as it was his parents and grandparents. His mother besieged by diabetes, ulcerous legs, glaucoma, cataracts, breast cancer, and lung cancer would say with resignation, "One day my ship is going to come in." But it never did, and she walked about the house in the dark for the most part because her eyes succumbed to the weight of it all before the rest of her body did. Legal blindness doctors called it. A Long Islander through and through, she channeled Samuel Taylor Coleridge's an ancient mariner's rime when she stood on the back porch of his childhood home and said, "Water, water everywhere and not a drop to drink." She waited as an albatross clung about her neck while she stood on a spiritual deck in rough, rough seas. A fleeting hope anchored in the temporal—grasping, she believed things would get better. When she died, blessings and curses bequeathed to her followed their temporal course. A bundled inheritance of hope and clouded eyes, faith and diabetic promise, and hardiness and dormant cancer cells passed to her children as they had been handed down to her from a paraplegic father and a cancer-ridden mother, a course followed generation after generation.

All her children accepted the hope inherited, but two of the five after private bouts with darkness shifted that hope into the eternal and eventually refused the albatross of disease, affliction, and penury. The two, Max and his sister, chose instead to live in the spirit, to live with things not yet evident in this world as though they had them already, to live as though the unsettling wind, the clamor, the debilitation belonged to someone else. They shod their feet with good news amid turbulence and upheaval, built-in depreciation and an ever-present but distant albatross spurned and still smarting from their rejection. "No, that's not mine" to lupus. To asthma, "this is not your home." To the doctor reading with natural eyes test results suggesting diabetes, "You're fired." She'd eat a piece of cake, and then search for a new doctor with a little better vision than the previous one. Passotel notwithstanding, Max exchanged homelessness in the temporal for a home selected by God in the spiritual, not a room in a mansion in the sweet by-and-by, but a home here, not yet seen but here nonetheless. A promise is a promise, and God who swore by no other than himself promised and settled it in heaven. "I will bring you out, son, and you will say, 'Look what the Lord has done.'" He came to believe that crippling debt in the natural atrophied and withered in the spirit when one claimed Jehovah-Jireh as source.

When he lost sight of the eternal and became overwhelmed by the evidence of the temporal that suggested Satan won (five months of work without money, spousal texts which threatening incarceration for lack of payment, an uneven bed, and the eternal promises not meshing with the everyday), God through his mercy and grace would send a word. "I told you to wait on me, to trust me. Just say thank you Lord Jesus. If I am your Father, why are you weeping? Everything I promised you will come to pass. Tonight, you need to know this."

In prayer with the little woman by the well, the Lord said, "The enemy didn't strip you. I stripped you." God showed Max how his and Sylvia's choices brought them to where they were, one still under the aegis of darkness, the other stripped to remove it. The new members' class encouraged Max and Sylvia to hoist anchor and exchange it for a later model. They laid aside deliverance and notions of holiness; they shut up the expectation of tongues spoken and the Holy Spirit operating. Week after week the Tuesday night new members' class reminded prospective members to put away the vision and teachings of their previous pastors and accept the tenets of the current one, and Max and Sylvia let go and conformed. Any gifts from God that could not double as entertainment, they and other families laid them down as body and soul rose up within and attempted to do the work of the spirit. They began to believe or tried to convince themselves that in the words of one member, "It didn't take all that."

In his first church when soul and flesh fought the spirit for prominence in a choir feeling a little too much of itself living in the riffs, dwelling in the harmonies, and swaying as if lost in the rhythm it created, the bishop sat the offenders down. Invited into the assembly by pride, the darkness appeared suddenly and floated all around the group until confident enough to begin a desultory run toward the unsuspecting congregants listening with carnal ears to the lyrics praising God's mercy while oblivious to the invisible self-glorification put forth by the flesh. "Look how wonderful we are and how glorious we sound."

Sensing the errant praise, the pastor opened his eyes, rose, and walked out of the pulpit and stood between the choir and the congregation. He blocked the darkness promising a stranglehold if not brought to the light. He spoke directly to it, "Entertainment, the blood of Jesus is against you. You will not trump anointing in this house," and then he spoke directly to the choir. "This is God's house, and we sing to him and for him only." Referring to the choir's antics, "This is flesh at work, a portent of dark days ahead, but not in this house. It is not of God." He sat the choir down for a month. A few choir members saw their error and understood that true worship like a sweet-smelling savor travels vertically, travels upward. Many took the reprimand to be the antics of an aging man out of touch and doggedly hanging on to a romanticized notion of sanctification that characterized the old ways in a sea of contemporary change, so some left the church. They likened the pastor's actions to those who forbade guitars and drums in the house of God as if the instruments themselves opened the door for Satan. It was never the instruments, those crafted by people: guitars, drums, organs or that crafted by God, the human voice. The pastor knew it was misplaced entertainment, a gift offered to flesh and soul in a house of worship while a jealous God watched.

That was then, a church with a guardian of the old way at the helm who held deliverance prayer breakfasts, spoke of holiness as a way of life, expected signs and wonders from a prayer line, spoke in tongues, and used hymnals. Too many now believed that was for then, a relic of robes and rules, a vision for yesterday to be put away and exchanged for a contemporary vision as if the first church's trappings now belittled or reduce to mere legalism never ever had their origins in spiritual warfare, as if spiritual war never really existed.

God expected much more from Sylvia and Max. They were to influence and not be swayed; they were to fill fruit baskets by taking the emptiness out of bind and loose, decree and declare and give them meaning in a church having heard the words and desirous to use them, but knew them not. Sylvia and Max drifted while working very hard in a church that demanded much visible work for this temporal world and less and less of the closeted work eventually tried by a consuming fire after the dead in Christ rise and the living do too. They participated in back-to-school backpack distributions in August, harvest festivals in October, and retreats. Programs and more programs yielded less and less discernment, spiritual warfare, and growth until there was none in the body to tap. God who searches the heart found the dire situation required intervention, so he stripped them.

God stripped the natural because the two like many in the congregation willingly shed nearly all evidence of the spiritual. It was a golden calf in the making, and it warranted a stern reaction from the Father. The stripping served as a loving call to come back to their first love because the Lord who spoke through Old Testament prophets would use no new words to further reprimand living art who after repeated warnings not to do so attempted to take back their hearts from the Divine Artist who held them. Straight from his Word came the stern response: Cursed be the man that trusts in man, and maketh flesh his arm, and whose heart departeth from the LORD. For he shall be like the heath in the desert, and shall not see when good cometh; but shall inhabit the parched places in the wilderness, in a salt land and not inhabited.[49]

"The enemy did not strip you, I stripped you!" This was a revelation to Max, a tough saying because he worked hard, and like so many, he worked as though it would in fact ensure him residence in heaven. He knew that was impossible, yet his understanding darkened, his actions fought against truth. He worked until stripped of all he had left after Sylvia decided she was finished. He landed in a place where the car's head restraint posed as headboard and dew and frost on windows served as shades between his life on the inside of the Passotel and the lives of those on the outside who walked by a rather ordinary car.

Chapter 42

Homeless and alone, Max felt lighter and more content than ever that he was safe in the Master's hands. Work would not be driven by a natural assignment. It would be Ruthian in nature: Jesus, Dear Jesus, whither thou goest…, and Jesus, Dear Jesus, whither thou lodgest…. Jesus chose. His heart returned to the Divine Artist's hands, and his eyes observed God's ways. Max fell in love with God again, and asked without trembling, without astonishment, "Lord Jesus, what do you want me to do?"

Reclined behind the steering wheel of his car parked at a Maryland rest stop, his mind went back to the night he wrote a report and the cell phone provider cut the service for lack of payment. He wanted to work until midnight before going to bed, but his phone flashed. He picked it up, looked at it, and then sent a text to himself. It failed to go through. He called Mark twice, but when the service provider rerouted each call to billing, he hung up. He worked until five in the morning.

Already resigned to the loss of his possessions slated for auction in less than forty-eight hours, Max felt overwhelmed. He shut down the computer and walked to the bathroom to brush his teeth, but before he turned the doorknob, he forgot why he headed that way. He turned around and walked to his bedroom only to remember he forgot to brush his teeth. Heading back to the bathroom, he thought he left his laptop on, so he entered the TV room to shut it down. Finding it off, he shook his head, and then he took a deep breath. Max turned to walk back to the bathroom, but his body realizing it moved in circles stopped. His mind, however, continued moving and calculating. It called up bills that needed payment. It ran over to teeth that needed brushing in a bathroom that appeared to be a mile way. His mind called to a body that craved sleep though torn by the need to work to dig itself out of the financial clutches that held him.

His mind whirled around the storage unit and gas to get to the airport but none to make it home. His mind insisted his body remained in motion, but his feet yelled back in defiance. His mind continued jumping here and there. Tears fell, and absent a tall building, guard rail, or undertow to stop them, they fell uninterrupted for some time until his spirit pushed out the proclamation based on Jeremiah 29:11: Lord I thank you that I know the plans you have for me, plans of peace and not of evil, plans of prosperity and not of calamity to give me a future and a hope. He needed the personalization he applied to the verse. Over and over he repeated the proclamation in his mind until his lips moved, and then he spoke as directed by his spirit.

Finally, his heart heard what his feet yelled up all along and believed what eyes revealed. His body stood in one spot though utterly wiped clean of energy. He continued to recite like a soul on automatic, "Lord I thank you that I know the plans you have for me, plans of peace and not of evil, plans of prosperity and not of calamity to give me a future and a hope." Over and over until the body settled down and his heart believed what his mouth now said: I shall not die, but live, and declare the works of the LORD.[50] With that he wiped his face, turned to the bedroom, unrolled the plastic that in times past was an air mattress, and fell asleep.

He slept until his ringing phone woke him. Seeing Sylvia's name, he hit the red button to end the call and turned to go back to sleep. "I don't have the energy for her right now," he said. It rang again, and he hit the red button to end the ringing. The phone rang a third time. "Satan sure is persistent," he said. He looked, saw it was Mark, and picked up the phone.

"Hello."

"Hey, Pops, I figured you didn't pick up because it was the house phone, so I called you using my cell phone."

"Wait a minute. How are you calling me? The phone is dead."

"I paid the bill this morning, well half of it. I'll pay the other half when I get paid. The phone company said you were a good customer, so they let the phones stay on for three month or so, but couldn't let the account go on without some payment any longer. They said they'd work with you."

"Wow. Thanks."

"Oh, and I sold that flat screen TV in storage. I hope you're not upset."

"No not at all."

"Good. I sold it for the amount of money you owed, so they won't auction the storage unit tomorrow; it's paid up. They called me when they couldn't reach you. I guess you're not picking up the phone, huh?"

"Wouldn't change much if I did. He had nothing else to say except "I'm proud of you, but I'm too full at this moment to talk any further. He began to well up. "I can't talk right now. I'm too full. Proud, thankful, and full." He hung up.

Max turned on the floor and cried. Different tears this side of the call. He cried until he fell asleep. A sweet short sleep fell on him before he woke up to finish his report.

Thank you, Jesus, you are so good he thought while sitting behind the steering wheel, but he did not always think so. Early in this journey Max fed the goat that rose within and complained often. He complained when the favor received did not meet his expectation because the manna had become all too familiar, and its timing almost always in the morning after a dark, dark night. Stripped! Absent house, money, and things, there was nothing left to muffle the Master's voice. Carried through divorce and being made whole post-divorce, Max spoke what lived in his heart. "Be not a terror unto me: thou art my hope in the day of evil."[51] The words of Jeremiah became real to him once stripped and unable to say, "I lost this here, and I lost that there." Unable to see a beginning or end to the trial, he held close to his heart words of hope from Jeremiah. "For behold, days are coming, declares the LORD, when I will restore the fortunes of my people."[52] For Israel and Judah, yes, but on the day Max opened his computer expecting to resume a study of Kings, the thirtieth chapter of Jeremiah appeared with a brief commentary for the verse that consisted of nothing more than the verse itself, a message to Max. Thank you, Jesus he thought, "For behold the days are coming." He added that verse to his daily proclamations.

CHAPTER 43

With little and no one nearby to lean on until those days came, Max learned the benefit of asking God's direction and permission. "Lord should I go to this gas station? This grocery store?" He found pedestrian errands turning points in unnamed battles in the spiritual lives of those he knew only in passing or not at all.

One morning when he woke, he had a desire for pizza. He cleaned up at a coffee shop and walked around the strip mall for exercise and a need to kill time. None of the pizzerias in the mall or those nearby spoke to him, so he drove to Virginia. He didn't stop until he reached a pizzeria in Manassas. He had never been there before and heard nothing about pizza there, but he knew in his spirit this one was it.

Leaving the pizzeria, he nodded as he held the door for an older gentleman with a cane. In that brief moment of eye contact Max caught the despair, but carrying enough weight of his own, he was grateful he walked in the opposite direction to his car. Pushing the unlock button on the key fob and singing to the MP3 selection, he miraculously heard through his earphones one yelling, "Sir! Sir!" He turned around to see him, the man with cane carrying a small pizza box. "Can I trouble you for a ride?"

He looked around as if the simple yes or no would come through a committee of parking lot onlookers of which there were none, but hearing a single voice within saying give him a ride, he said, "Sure, where to?"

"The homeless shelter. It's not too far when driving, but walking with a cane and a box of pizza, it might as well be."

"No problem. Put the pizza on the back seat and get in."

"My name's Percy," he said while extending his hand.

"I'm Max."

"I saw kindness in your face, Max. I didn't see it in the others except the owner who gave me the free slices. I didn't have the energy to walk back to the shelter, so I called out to you. God bless you, sir."

"God bless you too, Percy." Max changed the song on the MP3 player to Vanessa Bell Armstrong's "Peace Be Still" before connecting it to the car auxiliary stereo port.

"I can't believe you heard me through those earphones. Young people don't generally hear through those things."

"I'm not that young." He laughed.

They sat in silence as the words to the song began with a call to the Master as a tempest raged on and the occupants wondered if Jesus cared whether they perished.

"I'm staying at the homeless shelter. I have people in North Carolina, but I've not been able to get down there." The kindness, free pizza, and ride to the shelter cordoned off despair. "We're, my wife and I, we're at the shelter. They're good people there. She's clean too. It's tough you know." He paused and listened quietly to the music before sharing, "I have HIV, and we lost our home. It's tough." Max thought about how comfortably disease and material loss sat side by side, that pounding after pounding brought resignation, resignation brought acceptance, and acceptance led to no will to fight. He sent up a silent prayer broken by Percy saying, "We've done much in our younger days that's come back for payment now." They listened to the song. "This song, the words and that voice, my God." He shuttered. He tapped his heart as he said, "Just hits me, you know?"

Max nodded and said, "It's beautiful, isn't it? Jesus hits the spot when and where you need God most?"

Pointing, Percy said, "Right there, that building across the street." Max pulled into the parking lot and turned the car off but not the player so that Percy could hear more about the wind and the waves obeying God's will and how no ocean could swallow a ship the Master boarded.

"Do you know the Master, Percy?"

"Yes, it took a while, but now I do."

"Good, Jesus is always listening. Talk to him and tell him all about it. He listens when no one else does, and according to your faith, Percy, North Carolina is closer than you think." He unbuckled his seatbelt and reached for his wallet in the natural while standing unbridled in the spirit at the shoreline of a sea casting bread with both hands.

"No, no, I didn't tell you all this for money," Percy said as he placed his hand on Max's shoulder.

"I know, but I'm learning to move according to the Father's directives, not my own." Max pulled his wallet out of his back pocket. Taking out money, he folded it without counting it. Still holding the money, he said, "Here, I don't have much; it won't get you to North Carolina, but let it be a blessing and a reminder that God has not forgotten you. I traveled a slight distance for this pizza, passing many options. Now I know it was to meet you. I'm to give you this and remind you that it will be all right, Percy; it will be all right."

Percy thanked him and welling with tears grabbed the hand with the money in both his and just held it, shaking it, shaking it. "God does care," he said. He paused and looked Max straight in the eye and repeated, "God really, really cares." He got out of the car.

Max drove to a nearby shopping center and parked. He prayed an intercessory prayer of peace, standing with the past before him and Percy and his wife behind him, Max held up in the spirit proof of a check written with pen of wood and ink of blood that read paid in full. Looking ahead at Percy's past, he bound HIV and despondency. Looking behind he prayed for Percy and his wife, and continued with a prayer that the Lord would send others as migrant gardeners tending in the spirit the moment of their meeting this fragile garden threatened by aggressive weeds fertilized daily by a mind tethered to remember when.

CHAPTER 44

Reacquainting Max to the ways of spiritual warfare began in the basement but matured while on the road. "I see a grocery store, and the Lord is telling me the old lady misses you," the little woman by the well said.

"I didn't speak to an old lady at the grocery store when I lived in Virginia. I wouldn't consider the people who rung me up old," Max said.

"The Lord said the old lady misses you. I can only give you what he gives me. Lay before him this night, and he'll make it plain," she said.

He racked his brain over this old lady but couldn't figure it out. "I need your help Lord. I don't have a clue. A little less mystery perhaps." Two weeks later on his way to pick up Sarah for the weekend, he stopped by the grocery store for a few things. No one he spoke with was old. Exiting the store, he decided to drive the back way to the house and retrace his former walking route from the days when the family was still intact. Driving down the street just before the turn into his former neighborhood, he saw the empty rocker on the porch of the woman he spoke with as he walked to the grocery store when he lived in the gray house. The store was a measure of distance when he walked, not a holder of goods, so he made no connection between the old woman in the rocker and the grocery store. "Lord you could have made this easier, no? But I suppose if I learn to listen more effectively, you can come to me directly. Not a problem." Max made a U-turn and then another to park right in front of the house. He got out of the car and knocked on the door. He was greeted by a radiant smile. "I thought you moved. I was wondering where you've been. I told my daughter that I hadn't seen that nice young man in a long time. Where have you been?"

His everyday routines seemed rather unimportant in the temporal, but in the eternal, they donned gloves, watering pails, and hoes for sowing, watering, or tilling a private garden for the Lord. "Guide me as I drive, Lord. Tell me where and tell me when to stop." Out of all the choices he could make, he began to ask God before converting the Passotel into a car. He would hear voices say, "Max, just go to the gas station here or that grocery store is too far away." Stripped! Max learned Jesus had a voice and dispensed orders, but many seldom gave him an ear except in emergencies or catastrophes or anxiety ridden moments when listening was the only option for a small number who could hear.

Hearing he learned is as important as obedience and exactness. Once after dropping Sarah off at school, he needed gas. He figured forty dollars in the tank would allow him a couple of rest stop nights as he waited on the Lord. He asked Jesus which gas station before he pulled into the one next to the highway entrance that made sense. He felt in his spirit the Lord wanted him to go to the gas station across from the hotel he and Sarah just left. "Lord," he said, "You couldn't have had me get up a little earlier and get gas immediately after checking out this morning?" He waited, "All right, Jesus, I guess not. Someone in that station needs a word of encouragement, right? I get it, better to have me alter my route than someone who doesn't fully understand your hand in the itinerary changing business to rearrange theirs."

But people did alter schedules for him, and the Lord reminded Max of this. He forgot about the day he returned from a Midwest business trip and his debit card read insufficient funds when ye tried to pay for long term parking. He called Mark. Mark picked him up and dropped him off in Maryland. He decided to wait until his next check arrived to pay the parking fee and get his car. The bill would be much higher, but he would have the money, and waiting for a check meant no need to borrow. Before lying on the floor to sleep, Max recited his proclamations and meditated on one in particular. "And God is able to make all grace abound toward you; that ye, always having all sufficiency in all things, may abound to every good work."[53] He slept through the night.

In the morning, Cynthia left for work but returned shortly thereafter. When she entered the house, she heard someone downstairs. Max hearing someone walking on the main floor prepared to go check when Cynthia called down to him. "Max, is that you?"

"Yes. What are you doing home?"

"Never mind that. I don't recall seeing your car outside. Where's your car, Max?"

"At the airport."

"What, did it break down? I didn't hear you come in last night. How did you get here?"

"Mark."

"Did your car breakdown?"

"No, I didn't have the money to get it out of the long-term parking lot, so I called Mark to get me. I'll pick it up when I get paid."

"When's that?"

"End of the month."

"That's about twenty days away. That's going to be a lot of money. How much is it today?"

"Forty dollars."

She reached into her pocketbook and pulled out fifty dollars. "Here, take this money and get your car out."

"It's all right. I can wait."

"Stop being silly and take this money. Call your son and have him take you to pick up your car. I have to go back to the school."

"Thank you. I appreciate this."

"You're welcome. I came home because I wasn't sure I turned the stove off. Now I see God wanted me to come back here to give you this. God is so good."

"That he is."

Driving to the gas station he said to the Lord, "All right, not just me, sorry about that."

He arrived at the service station and parked by a pump, but seeing no one pumping gas and no one in the convenience store except the one behind the counter, he wondered whether or not he heard correctly. He got out of the car and walked to the convenience store. One he presumed homeless rounded the corner and asked for a dollar. "I don't have it," Max said. Heading toward the counter to pay for gas he heard, "Hearing, now do" in his spirit.

The attendant asked, "How much?"

"Shouldn't it be hearing now hear?" Max said aloud.

"Excuse me," the man behind the counter said.

Max looked at the man and said, "Never mind." He looked at the contents of his wallet. Then looked at the man again, and instead of asking for forty dollars' worth, he asked for thirty-five of regular. He paid the attendant and walked outside in time to hear another customer turn away the one who asked him for a dollar moments ago. "Sir," Max called. The man jogged over to him, and Max gave him five dollars.

"God bless you sir," he said.

"God bless you too," Max said. He had nothing else to share." He pumped his gas and watched the man walk along the side of the hotel and disappear into the trees. The customer who turned him away watched as well and put his head down when he caught Max looking his way. "Ok, timing is important. I get it. My ways are not your ways. No arguing that," he said.

He reenlisted for active duty and fought once again in the army. After pumping gas, he headed to a coffee shop to write.

Sylvia reveled in Max's seemingly downward spiral. The Lord told him as much, and Sarah confirmed it. Bypassing a line from Paul, John, Moses, Abraham, and numerous Psalms, Sylvia chose a movie as she looked Sarah squarely in the eye one day and said, "Until your father does right by me...."

Sarah shocked said, "A movie! Are you kidding me? Sixty-six books hopefully read or at least referenced in church on Tuesday, Thursday, Friday, and Sunday and you chose a movie to lay down a curse. Interesting."

"You're being disrespectful, young lady," Sylvia said.

"That's what she said, Daddy.

"Not interested in channeling movie characters, but once again you have to remember she is your mother and what the Bible says about honor. I'm old enough to take care of myself. There's no need to defend me."

"But she—"

"I'm not interested."

"It's funny."

"What is?"

"She thinks we talk about her, and I only listen to you talking about her and won't allow her the same courtesy."

"Well we don't, and I'm not interested in what she says about me." Having come through the fire, Max was not to do the same to Sylvia. God was clear with Max that God's children forgave as they had been forgiven, that things turned around when they humbled themselves and prayed for and forgave those who despitefully used them or took advantage of them or tried to destroy them. Max prayed for Sylvia; he prayed for the Lord to send mercy her way. He stood more firmly planted in the Lord now though all around him in the natural still suggested sinking.

Sylvia continued in her attempt to turn Mark and Sarah on him. "He has you both wrapped around his finger. He's manipulating you two; he's brainwashed you both and neither of you know half. I shouldn't have to bear the financial burden of you two alone. He's given me nothing, and he's given you two excuses."

"We stay in hotels for Pete's sake," Sarah said.

"Hotels cost money and take away from the money due to me."

"He lives in his car."

"Well he's grown with two degrees. He should get a job."

Max understood the frustration. The cost of the conflict that took place between leaving the house and being legally divorced reached sixty-six thousand in six months. Only Jesus could get him out of this, and he would have to wait on the Lord for his appointed time. Mark and Sarah wanted no part of the bickering, no part of at all, and Max made it clear that he didn't either. The less he heard from the two children, the better, so he made that clear every time they started a story. Their conversations had to be about other things.

"I'm listening to the podcast on Jonah again," Sarah said when speaking to Max on the phone as he sat in the Delaware rest stop writing.

"You are. Cool. What stands out for you?" Max asked.

"A lot but I'm reminded at this moment that many confuse God's justice and judgment with a strong desire for revenge. The message moves listeners to think about whether or not Jonah really knew God. By extension, if we can't forgive, show compassion, and move on, do we really know who God is?"

"Ah, your two questions, do you remember? Do you know me?"

"And do they know me? It's been two years since that dream, but how could I forget?"

From the blue house back to the basement and now behind the driver's seat of his car the questions remained unchanged. They were the same in the Old Testament where friends pondered divine justice and hidden sin in a wealthy and righteous man surrounded by loss and death. They were the same for one who sat comfortably under a shade producing gourd for a short time, and the same beneath the question, "Who do men say that I am?" The questions remained the same, "Do you know who I am? Do they know who I am?"

CHAPTER 45

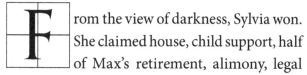rom the view of darkness, Sylvia won. She claimed house, child support, half of Max's retirement, alimony, legal fees, and nestled within all her spoils sat homage to poor judgment, a peculiar acquisition out of place like the Ark in Ashdod measured more by time not spent with dad then time in the presence of mom. That one act more than the others courted a heavy eternal hand.

From a heavenly perspective darkness lost. Max had no need to say, "I've read the end of the book" to remind himself things would get better, and he would live to see a day where he would sleep under a sky light, not a sunroof and on top a mattress, not a car seat. He held an eternal promise and came to understand that his struggle served to pry him out of a temporal seat that claimed him. He saw the mystery of the eternal embedded in subtleties like the dance between the fifth verse of Isaiah fifty-three and first Peter. Both used interchangeably without the understanding of the nuance and the distinct melodies created by the three-part harmony of what was, what is, and what is to come.

The Lord God always, always in the midst of his children covered Max at the rest stops, in the basement, in the courthouse, on every plane, in the bank. He was always present and always mighty to deliver and save with an offer of rest wrapped in a choice to claim rest now on earth or later in the eternal, today or tomorrow the choice balanced on a unique name that consisted of a first-person pronoun and a ubiquitous verb. Max internalized the question behind Isaiah and Peter's discussion of stripes and healing as which side of the transaction will you live on? Which side? Stripes ye were or stripes we are, which side works best for you? Already done or yet to happen. Which side? Whether healing, deliverance, or a change of circumstances, the question of stripes asked of Max, "Done or yet to happen, which works best for you?" Still no house, living in a car, no money, and hampered by the threat of jail because money in the twenty-first century did not sit in the mouths of fish awaiting catch for tax purposes. Which side?

He chose done and sealed the choice with faith that the natural would eventually reflect the reality of the spiritual, and that which was not in this world would in fact materialize, but he had need of patience.

The little woman by the well, to Max's chagrin, often said, "According to your faith." For Max living in his car, according to your faith meant not yet in the natural since he possessed no key that opened the door to his own house. While the Lord ensured he was not on the street or in the woods, he lived the harsh reality that his car by any word he coined was still a car, and "I have placed you in a house according to your faith" was followed by night after night of mobile sleep, interrupted by a stay here and there in hotels.

The promise "I have placed you in a house" kept him going. Three years in the making with gifted goods in storage and no home, he held on tightly to the divine promise and the belief that Peter's assertion confirmed Isaiah's prophetic utterance and the promise was already done in Jesus.

One weekend he and Sarah attended an open house wondering, "Lord, can this be it?" He tried to seal the house with a Scripture. He placed the house number in the notes section of his electronic Bible.

He drove by the house three times and read the first verse of the first Psalm aloud each time. The house having been on the market for some time eventually sold. Max wondered what it meant to have faith, what it meant to wait on the Lord, so he and Sarah walked through another four weeks later. The house had slight water views with a sloping backyard that gave the illusion of a high hill from the deck. Remembering the words, "Your house will not flood in the storm" Max asked in his spirit, "Lord, is this the one?" But it was not. Would he have to wait ten years or so to say, "Look what the Lord has done?" Would he be sixty or more? Would the Lord use Max to redefine the word nothing by losing even more of what he did not have?

He scoured online real estate websites for houses. "Is this two-bedroom townhouse okay, Lord?" Summer nights became fall nights and required a trip to a department store for a blanket. He refined the search thinking perhaps something bigger, a blessing befitting a spiritual remaking from the King of Kings, something with grandeur, something eye-popping, and something unexpected. "Is this one it, Lord?"

But nothing changed. He slept in the Passotel. He prayed for heat when the temperature outside registered thirty-five degrees. "Am I to die in the car? Are you ready to take me home?" If I die in the Passotel will it be deemed exposure? Turning fifty soon meant his license would expire. He was denied a passport and the opportunity for summer work in China because he was in arrears; "a dead-beat dad" Sylvia called him after alerting the Internal Revenue Service that the responsibility of her tax preparation error for the withdrawal of retirement funds while married belonged solely to him according to the divorce decree. Her refund was not to be touched, so they took every check he worked for along with expenses from October through January. He could not catch up, and after his birthday, he would not renew his license for fear of losing it, resulting in his inability to travel on planes for work.

He wondered where he would sleep without his uninsured car. How would he, how would he insure it without an address or license? What did it mean to sit in a coffee shop all day reading and writing, sometimes unwashed and alone because there simply was nowhere else to go?

During a December afternoon in the Charlotte, North Carolina airport, Max wondered how one recovered without the Lord and how one hung on until the Lord knowing how much one could bear moved mountains.

"If you'd just turn these stones into bread, Lord," he mumbled.

Sitting in a chair at his gate, his mind went back to coffee shops as the morning shift transitioned into the afternoon shift, "How long, Lord? How long do you expect me to hang on?" No one was expected to endure what Job did. He understood this, had not lost children to grave and had not suffered ill health, but in the larger scheme of things, vetting the degree of loss seemed pointless. "How long, Lord, how long?"

His loss was not a result of divine justice though the loss of his possessions came with permission from above. God removed the distractions from his life, so he would see more clearly the Great I Am, breathe in the complexity and power of the simple pronoun I in union with the verb to be, the embodiment of past, present, and future—all seeing, all knowing, all powerful. "I have stripped you, son," the little woman by the well said, "so seeing, you might see clearly; I have carved away the bewitching accumulation of things, so you would come to know me, I Am."

Max breathed in deeply and thought of John Newton's poem "I Asked the Lord that I Might Grow" as eighteenth-century counterpoint to a perverted twenty-first-century theology that approached fiery trails as strange. Thank God for the wisdom of the old saints reminding us we are not alone in trials.

Hearing his zone called, he rose rather mechanically to board the plane. He found his seat, an aisle seat near the back. He buckled himself in along with a stowaway of heaviness pulling him down until Sarah called before he sunk too low for rescue and too low for sleep.

"Hi, Daddy."

"Hi, Sweetie."

A discussion of school and home shifted into a strange, unexpected conversation where she spoke of overcoming darkness. "It's really much larger than we are, isn't it, Daddy? Larger than whether someone calls me a name or about whether or when the name calling stops, isn't it?" Max listened intently. He knew this was a word sent by God. "It is not whether we are both weary, and we are tired, bone tired or why you were discarded like trash. All this will pass away, the desires, the hurts, the compromises, and the slights behind the actions; all this can be seen or felt or sensed, and this will pass away. It's what we can't see with the natural eye or sense with the body or react to with emotion that stands fast when the shaking starts. That's real. The darkness holding up things in this world will fail along with those things that seem sound but don't stand fast in God. It's not important whether there is logic to our stories or a sense of coherence—a beginning, middle, and end that needs uncovering or whether justice is meted out in this life. All this can be seen. While Stephen was stoned God gave him a glimpse of the eternal." She thought about what she saw in the church, the impenetrable light that refused entry to the darkness and the docent who provided spiritual insight on the invisible. She continued, "Heaven opened for Stephen. He saw Jesus standing on the right hand of God. No one else saw what he did. All others heard only words from the crowd, saw bloody flesh gnarled by stones, and witnessed garments laid at the feet of Saul, but the Lord blessed Stephen with a glimpse."

Max listened intently.

Sarah paused and then continued with a profound statement. "Daddy, I stand not on myself, but on he who sups within me." As a clear profession of faith, Sarah continued, "And I choose to stand on what I can't see."

Max listened and thought of the previous week where he closed a coffee shop in Laurel. The night before that one, he drove through Fort Washington, sipped coffee, and wrote a report. Growing tired, he drove to Columbia, sat, and wrote until the manager delivered the "store will be closing in ten minutes" line. He slept in Maryland at a rest stop, opened a bottle of over the counter pills, but then closed it, choosing to stand on what he could not see.

Max interrupted Sarah and said, "Until my heart believes what flesh refuses. Until it's no longer a choice, but just is. I thank you, Jesus." He said goodbye after the flight attendant's request to turn off all electronic devices with an on and off switch. Max said to himself, "I stand against an army of darkness, against a spiritual troop that relentlessly tries to destroy me." He closed his eyes and slept until he landed in Baltimore.

While walking through the airport, Max looked at others heading to their homes if returning or to hotels if arriving. They would lay their heads on beds twenty minutes or an hour away. His home awaited him in the long-term B parking lot. Walking toward ground transportation, he sent three texts. To his brother-in-law, "I left my coat in the rental car while traveling in Detroit. My colleague needs to send it to me. Can I have it sent to your house?" The others he sent to Mark and Sarah. Mark sent a text back with his usual amen after receiving the paternal blessing: "The Lord bless you and keep you. The Lord make his face shine upon you, and be gracious unto you. The Lord lift up his countenance unto you and give you peace."[54]

Mark followed his amen with "What are you up to tonight?"

Max said, "I am going to bed." Mark was not sure how to reply.

Bed of course meant car at a rest stop of Max's choosing. Walking in the spirit in this body meant hiking on the mountain peak one day and trudging through the valley of the shadow of death the next. Max thought about Carlyle while heading to his car. He thought it strange that Victorian prose and poetry which few read or thought of today would pop into his head while walking through Thurgood Marshall Airport heading home to a car and nothing else, nothing else.

The shuttle ride from the airport to the parking lot was a literary feast of eighteenth-, nineteenth-, and twentieth-century works. With eyes closed, he turned page after page in the spirit and recalled favorite lines he memorized long ago. He opened *Cane* and rested with Toomer, "Call them from their houses, and teach them to dream." He had to dream about things as other than they were, so he rested there for a short while. He moved to Pope, "Hope springs eternal in the human breast." He smiled and sipped on that slowly. He heard the automated system on the bus say, "We are approaching stop one please check around your seat for your belongings." He blocked the rest of the message out and the message for each subsequent stop until approaching his. His stop was ten, always ten. With nine stops to go, he thought of West's, "Only those who still have hope can benefit from tears." He wallowed privately in the message. When in doubt a quotation, and when brought to tears, hope. With "We are approaching stop ten," he closed the books in his mind, got up, collected his luggage, and exited the shuttle when it stopped. He walked to his car.

He entered his mobile home and sat behind the steering wheel in his car turned bed, a quiet sanctuary, a place of prayer and worship no matter what role it played. Though grateful for the messages of hope, he sat fighting despair and a simple human desire to know when it would all be over. It was not the quotations or the thinkers of old the Spirit sought from memory. It was the notes embedded deep within those books. Max had written stealth notes to himself, and he needed to leaf through the books mentally, pass through the authors' words, read a signpost on hope here and there to nestle down deep near the bindings for the prize. In this valley of shadow, the Lord brought back the notes he placed in Carlyle, in Donne, in Toomer. He thought about those words of encouragement sent a little more than thirty years ago.

For years he engaged in stealth witnessing in books, wrote short missives of God's love and concern directed toward an English major he thought he would never formally meet. The university was a large one, and notes addressed to readers of Dryden, Toomer, West, and Swift were written to an esoteric group; thinkers who considered the eternal vastness one minute and felt an overwhelming emptiness the next. Max wrote notes to them about Jesus in areas of the books not easily seen by the bookstore retailers assigned to review used books and reject those with too much annotation or doodling.

As he sat in the car and contemplated yet another night of mobile sleep and another night alone, the Lord began with notes embedded near the bindings of Carlyle and Swift, notes directed by the Father who sees yesterday and tomorrow side by side. Fifty years old in eight days, he sat in his car and closed his eyes, not to pray or give thanks but to read a letter in the spirit that he wrote to himself. Thirty years in the past over three years during the fall, winter, and, spring, Max wrote. Thinking some thirty years earlier it was for someone he had not met and probably never would. He believed he would pass her by on the podium of the campus or sit next to him in class, but they would never meet as axiom writer and reader, as bearer of hope for one weighted by tears. He was right.

It was his future self, spliced and edited before him. He read, "Jesus is the Everlasting Yea, an exemplary editor whose best work emerges as flesh and soul lay on the floor to release a spirit that soars without wings, soars." He opened his eyes and could see in the spirit another note to self as if etched in the glass of the windshield, "Let us not be weary in well doing: for in due season we shall reap, if we faint not."[55] He smiled and then read, "The Lord is a keeper. Even green pastures turn brown in the winter months. Remember, the

Lord is your Shepherd who leads you to still water when you're thirsty, when you need peace. His rod and staff will comfort you. Read his Word, Read!" He thought it clever then; found it needful now. In this moment proof emerged the Lord never for one second left him alone, had him write letters for today, not in a journal with pen and pencil but in the spirit yesterday.

"Thank you, God." The only goods Max knew no one could ever take away, and so he gave as sacrifice to a loving Father who would never refuse such from one of his children. Time in the car confirmed that the tangible measures of worldly success could never enter the sanctuary within him, would not be pulled along in a wagon behind him as he walked down streets of gold. The temporal, shakable things never reached the Father and Son who supped within and shone inside with a force of glory.

Lawyers searched for that which is unknowable in the flesh, searched for that very special treasure that once caused a leap within a womb at the sound of a salutation. The court room mistook the Spirit for worldly treasure, and so took worldly things under the Sovereign's approval. They searched unknowingly for that blessed jolt that occurs in the spirit when two strangers who are saints pass each other on the street. They hug in the spirit, Holy Ghost to Holy Ghost, but their feet remain in continual motion, obeying focused flesh and soul in a hurry. The two move further and further away from each other, having shared only a brief nod, a friendly smile, and possibly a good morning as they walk ever forward, perhaps unaware of the powerful embrace in the eternal between the unspeakable treasure in both, treasure priceless and not for sale.

Law firm and ex-wife searched for hidden wealth, caught glimpses and thought perhaps a Swiss account, a different bank, clandestine funds in the Cayman Islands or a healthy contract postponed till after the divorce. They took what they could find and sought out the wealth they could not and did not know where to look because the invisible

God placed a resplendent, eternal treasure inside his earthen vessel, visible in the eternal realm only, closed off to the natural eye save a twinkle, a hint of what is but nothing more.

Just where was that wealth that even a deposition could not uncover? Sylvia, the lawyers, and the judge caught hints of a fulgent treasure buried in an earthen vessel more than forty years in the making, worn thin in spots through sporadic fasting over twenty-five years and weather-beaten over the last five. Their search left Max perplexed until now where sitting behind the steering wheel he read, "We have this treasure in earthen vessels, that the excellency of the power may be of God, and not of us. We are troubled on every side, yet not distressed; we are perplexed, but not in despair; Persecuted, but not forsaken; cast down, but not destroyed."[56] Max paused since after reading that letter written to himself much of what remained a mystery began to make sense. He continued reading:

> Always bearing about in the body the dying of the Lord Jesus, that the life also of Jesus might be made manifest in our body. Though our outward man perish, yet the inward man is renewed day by day. For our light affliction, which is but for a moment, worketh for us a far more exceeding and eternal weight of glory; while we look not at the things which are seen, but at the things which are not seen: for the things which are seen are temporal; but the things which are not seen are eternal.[57]

It became clear to Max that they searched for something Simeon and all his sorcery eventually found was not for sale.

The mystery of clay bearing the eternal, a body selected to carry within a treasure, an unspeakable gift eventually caught up in the air where the body glorified reflects the glory within told Max his life and all others not enemies of the cross of Christ were not their own.

They carry Truth, not a bundle of Scripture and a notion of right and wrong. They carry within a supping Jesus, Father, and Holy Spirit who work from the inside preparing the temple for a wedding feast.

He turned the ignition key to his house and read another written letter to self pulled right out of Romans eight which now appeared as if etched in the rearview mirror:

> Who shall separate us from the love of Christ? shall tribulation, or distress, or persecution, or famine, or nakedness, or peril, or sword? As it is written, For thy sake we are killed all the day long; we are accounted as sheep for the slaughter. Nay, in all these things we are more than conquerors through him that loved us. For I am persuaded, that neither death, nor life, nor angels, nor principalities, nor powers, nor things present, nor things to come, Nor height, nor depth, nor any other creature, shall be able to separate us from the love of God, which is in Christ Jesus our Lord.[58]

Max laughed to himself. He offered thanks for the pages of Jean Toomer that held such a pearl. He had not cast them before swine but sent them to himself down a straight and narrow path, one measured in years not miles. Before putting the car in reverse, he looked hard into the rearview mirror squinting with his natural eyes just in case another message appeared. Seeing none, he began the transformation of car to bed by driving to a rest stop in Maryland for one night only before his visit to New York to see family. No need for coffee. He drank words of life.

He felt nothing special walking down the jetway and making his way to his car, but sitting behind the steering wheel he read the words from a herald sent more than twenty years ago, words that finally reached their destination as they cut through despair and doubt with an announcement of a covenant, a reminder that a wedding is coming, a wedding is coming, a reminder to ensure his attendance in appropriate attire having made it through this journey tattered and worn. Washing at the lever and exchanging the garment of heaviness which he wore at times for the spirit of praise began with "Thank you, Jesus," and continued until he parked at the rest stop where invisible sentries took their posts to protected a member of the royal priesthood that friends disliked, to keep safe the peculiar treasure Max discovered he was.

CHAPTER 46

The next morning, Max thought heavily on being a peculiar treasure of the Lord. His mind fell on Joshua and Peter. Joshua said yes and Peter too, both of them nurtured in a line of yes. The line for Peter became apparent since sacrifices and burnt offerings ran their course and a prepared body filled with a yes left heaven because God wouldest not; he wouldest not. The other nurtured under one who murdered an Egyptian and renounced the glory of pyramids and Egyptian civilization for a consuming fire resting on a bush with no need of bark or wood as fuel brought forth a yes in the form of "I'll go."

The Lord of all taught waiting, and Moses taught it too. Each taught followers through action and word, followers willing to grow and wait. Joshua and Peter each learned to wait, Joshua for a land teeming with milk and honey and Peter for the Comforter who still kept his promise after repeated denials.

Through humility, awe, and obedience, Joshua and Peter walked in a line of yes, and water ignored natural laws, took on the characteristic of a solid, and forbade sinking for one and allowed stacking for the other. One knew in the spirit that as God was with the yes before him, God would not fail him. The other felt the yes grab his hand as he started to sink and was reminded in the spirit that water bowed to the Lord who would never leave and never forsake him. Both men had the testimony that they walked with God, and each had a story about water to prove it—one on top and one through it. Joshua, who once waded through a month's worth of weeping, full of the spirit of wisdom and courage split water, stood in the Jordan, and walked across on dry ground. Peter walked on water and eventually brought forth an invitation for repentance, baptism, and receiving the Holy Spirit. Both were told to be to be strong, of good courage, and not to fear. One witnessed the power of The Rod and the other stretched toward him, toward Jesus in route to a promise. Herein lies the faith of Joshua moving past Moses; herein lies the faith of Peter moving toward Jesus and the promise of greater works if his faith failed not.

These bold peculiar treasures for the Lord confronted disobedience, theft, and lies from those under them. Achan tried but could not get away with hidden bounty buried in the earth beneath his tent beyond the scope of Joshua's sight, but not God's. Ananias tried but could not get away with artifice though two touched and agreed before standing in front of Peter who severed intentions of the heart from the root of deceit with a two-edged sword. Evidence pulled out of dirt and excised from the heart, no hiding place, no hiding place. Sin made plain.

Much might have been theirs had Ananais and Achan humbled themselves and waited, cut greed clean through with prayer and fasting, embraced patience, learned temperance, and waited, communicated humility through silence and amen, and held trust hard until they embraced the belief that the one who made the promise would do exactly what he said he would do.

Just how many ways did the Word demand patience and then promise deliverance and support if followers waited? God would keep his word; he would make the sun stand still rather than break it. The Spirit by which all things which were not came to be remained true in the camp of Achan and community of Ananais and would benefit both of them had they waited and respected their leaders, if they could have for more than a moment been still and knew that I Am is God, and he demanded a yes.

There were plans much larger than either knew, but neither cut loose greed and denied self. One knew better than to ask for treasure, so he took it. The other never asked. He made an offer and reneged on it. Both died. One without the camp and one carried out of it dead. Had they waited, mounted up on wings and waited, peace and hope would have been theirs too. One would become an heir and recipient because of a promise made to his leader, and the other would become an heir because the eternal promise was the leader and passed as pilgrim through a strange, strange land. Both Achan on the other side of the Jordan and Ananais on the other side of Pentecost stood alone on their own two feet and paid a price for having refused the wings of eagles.

Max thought on the warning their deaths imparted. Mark told him that the organist Lorenzo married Geri the soprano; both divorced spouses while attending his former church that promised new life. Neither cried out to the Lord, "Forgive me, forgive me I took another man's wife" or "I took another woman's husband." Both stole that devout thing once dedicated to the Lord; did demonic division of the darkest kind and hid the bounty for a short time under the argument of modern times, the linguistic dance of nobody's business, and the argument of the privacy of my own home. They hid the act under tent and earth made of voice and keyboard that combined for a bewitching horizontal, counterfeit heavenly sound that could not rise.

CHAPTER 47

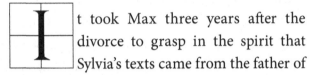t took Max three years after the divorce to grasp in the spirit that Sylvia's texts came from the father of lies spewing dark, fetid water up from the belly, pretending to carry the weight and power of an inspired *rhema*. It took more than three years to understand a hint of what Daniel knew before resting his head on the abdomen of a hungry lion, what the fourth told the three as they walked on the bottom of a furnace bejeweled in flames, what a dreamer declared about evil turned to good.

A trip from New York for a weekend with Sarah took ten hours instead of the normal five to six. Max said, "Lord, I can't do this much longer." He arrived at seven thirty at night to pick her up. After hugs and an update on school, Max said, "Your mom sent me a text that you need money for dental work."

"Yeah, she told me she sent it, but you didn't answer. She doesn't have the money, and you've not given her any she said. She said that you also need to pay for my lacrosse head."

"I asked you about that when I had money. You said that you didn't need one."

"I didn't think I did at the time, but it can wait. Besides the mail order clothes still keep coming for her. I suspect that if I make it big one day, I'll talk little about the sacrifice made for me in my single parent home. She had the house, you have a car. She should be content. Anyway, we're off to New Jersey, right?"

"Wait a minute. You said had, past tense."

"I'm not supposed to tell you, but she can't afford to keep the house. Somebody from New York is coming down to get the appliances, and we're moving into a townhouse, but you didn't hear that from me."

"Interesting, but didn't either of you think I'd figure it out when I picked you up for the weekend?"

"Not for me to dwell on such things. We're off to New Jersey, right?"

"Tomorrow morning. I don't have the stamina or concentration this late at night after ten hours of driving. I'm afraid we wouldn't make it. The Lord has promised me a house. I can't wait."

"I can't either. I'll be old enough to drive over."

"That you will." Grounding the tenor of the conversation in the now, Max said, "When my next check comes, if all works according to plan, I'll send some money to the child support agency. I'll let you know when. It should cover your teeth. We'll work on getting a head for lacrosse directly from me."

Sarah nodded. "It's President's weekend, so we have an extra day."

"Right, I think that we'll need to stay in Jersey through Monday, leaving Tuesday early in the morning to get you to school on time. Since we'll stay in the hotel on the front end of the weekend which was not my plan, I don't have the money for a hotel on the back end. We'll leave about two-thirty in the morning. You'll need to go to bed around nine Monday night, all right?"

"Ok."

"We'll fine tune the travel plans as Monday approaches."

CHAPTER 48

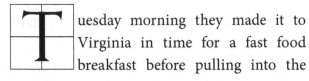uesday morning they made it to Virginia in time for a fast food breakfast before pulling into the school parking lot.

"All right, dearest. Have a good day," Max said. "We'll talk later."

"Bye, Daddy," Sarah said and reached over and kissed him before grabbing her cup of orange juice. She picked her backpack off the floor and opened the door to get out, but resignation remained after she closed the door. Max drove to a coffee shop and worked through the evening on a report. Before leaving the parking lot for a Maryland rest stop, he took his blanket and sweatshirt out of the trunk and threw them on the passenger seat. The temperature on the dashboard read twenty-seven degrees outside, but determined not to change course until he received answers, Max said aloud, "If I die Lord, then I die. I will sleep here tonight, tomorrow, and the next day until I hear from you." He pulled the blanket over his head and under his shoes. Where able, he tucked it between his body and his reclined car seat. He talked to God until he fell asleep, waking periodically when he felt pain in his knees from either their cramped position or the cold. He would feel around the console for his phone to read the temperature without pulling his head from under the blanket. At three in the morning the temperature registered twenty-three degrees. Frost covered the windows. His toes were numb, but he said, "It's me and you, only us" before turning on his side to go back to sleep.

At seven thirty in the morning he brushed his teeth and rinsed with mouthwash before getting out of the car to use the rest room. He spat the mouthwash on the ground, locked the car, and headed for the building. When he returned to his car, he checked his phone and read a colleague's email seeking status on the progress of the report. "Will send tonight," he wrote back before driving to a coffee shop to begin work, and then another much later that afternoon to work well into the evening writing. He emailed it at eight before leaving. He bought fast food with quarters he cobbled together from the astray and console. "Lord, life would be so much easier if I had a house. I could write; I could eat without spending money every day, and I could even have a conversation with a flesh and blood person if I haven't forgotten how to be conversant in subjects other than report writing and high school angst. No offense" He sat eating his burger. "Conversation means it's your turn to talk." He waited. "All right then don't say anything. I'm going to find a place to sleep." He drove to the rest stop.

Pulling into a spot he said, "Help me here and now or take me home." He pulled the blanket from the back seat and covered his head and shoes as best he could. The temperature registered twenty-seven outside. He spent the first half of the night turning the engine on and off, battling cold made worse by wind. Somewhere during the night, he fell into an uninterrupted sleep.

In the morning he woke and marveled at the amount of time he needed to unwrap himself. The wind made the night nearly unbearable. With fingers purple, toes numb, and his left knee stiff and swollen, he wondered whether he could endure another night like last night. He turned the engine on to warm the car and himself before stepping outside and quickly making his way to the men's room.

The mirror and windshield showed evidence of warming before fingers and toes, and so he waited. He looked up and to his surprise a note began to emerging. The slow process of defrosting began in the middle of the mirror and worked outward. Squinting as if it would make the note more visible, he made out the phrase, "When he has" and just above that phrase the word, "proud" and just below it "crown of."

"I wonder what... all right, all right." He paused. "I'm not a contestant on a game show; no guessing, I can wait." He closed his eyes, assuming it would be best to read the message in its entirety instead of piecemeal as the car warmed up. He sat silently though filled with anticipation for an answer concerning his way out. He opened his eyes and read, "Blessed is the man who maketh the LORD his trust and not the proud, who remains steadfast under trial, for when he has stood the test he will receive the crown of life, which God has promised to those who love him."[59] He sighed, bowed his head and closed his eyes again for a moment. He remembered writing the verse while sitting on his bed surrounded by Larsen, Dryden, O'Neil, and urban economics textbooks. "What was the trial back then that made this verse so important to me?" he wondered aloud. He tried but could not recall. "Was it just the beauty of the verse that spoke to me then, and what does it mean now?" He looked at the mirror again for a second read, but the verse was gone. "Ok God what does it mean to remain steadfast in a car with temperatures below freezing? I am at a loss here. Have I withstood the test?" But he saw nothing else in the mirror.

He lowered his head. Doubt sought entry through the verbal door of, "Ok, maybe I've imagined all this. I've spent way too much time alone since I see verses in my rearview mirror and windshield. Perhaps I'm losing it." Rubbing his eyes with his right hand, he said, "Maybe I want so badly to know you're really here, and I'm worth your time that I see notes that don't exist." Max raised his head, and then lowered it again into both hands. "Maybe I just have to figure this out myself. This is nuts."

He opened his eyes and threw the car in reverse with no clear destination planned. With his left hand on the steering wheel, he swung his right hand over the passenger head restraint and looked out the rear window now defrosted enough for him to see through it. In his quick motion spurred by a desire to leave, he realized he missed another note appearing in the mirror. He turned, pulled the car forward, and placed it in park. Looking squarely into the mirror, he read, "For, yet a little while and he that will come will come. He will not tarry."[60] But he did not recall penning that one. He flipped through the mental bindings of Attaway, Pope, Hurston, Swift. Then put those down, as it were, and opened Larsen, Mills, Shakespeare, Olsen, but nothing.

The verse unearthed no recognition deep within as others had. It held no nostalgic attachment between yesterday and today, no connection from a college dorm in the eighties to a car seat in 2013 to reach a child of God wanting badly to go home, put on a white robe, sit at the feet of Jesus in a verdant field, and tell his story. Tell it at home, not in a car, hotel, or relative's place, but recount his story beneath a special tree that dropped curative leaves atop a weary soldier's soul.

"I never wrote that, not on a gum wrapper, in the margins of a notebook, in the sand. I, didn't… it's not… no—not mine. You picked that one," he said to God. "That's not one of mine."

Max looked up again and there it sat for another read, "For, yet a little while and he that will come will come. He will not tarry." God sent his Word to one of his own aching for the cleanliness of precious metal streets and the healing from a species of tree too lovely, too precious for the current earth. The personal letter written in light he hoped would encourage him mixed instead with sheer exhaustion, for the words "For, yet a little while" implied not quite over. His composure fled. He cried until the voice belonging to the invisible holy curator of spiritual video and conversion photography not heard since the week of that fateful bible study when God asked Max, "What will you give up for me?" on Tuesday and told him, "I only lead sheep" on Sunday. That voice now called him by name.

"Max."

Startled, he looked up into the rearview mirror. The verse was gone. He turned around to make sure that the angels on hood and trunk had not left their watch, and no one he somehow missed when preparing to back up broke into his house in the middle of the frigid night. Seeing no one, he settled down internally and allowed body and soul to follow spirit into a godly stillness where soul got behind spirit and body followed too into a quiet reverence befitting the divine still small voice. Then the Lord called again, "Max."

And with bowed head and prostrate spirit and soul Max said, "Yes, Lord."

CHAPTER 49

The Lord as if pointing to a younger Max said, "That was Max then. One who in seventh grade could pray for rain, and I sent the rain because you prayed fervently. That Max," as if pointing to the adult Max who stared back at him in the rearview mirror, "is a Max who whined through trials, through storms and did not always follow my directions with precision. I told you to anoint hands and feet with oil, and you did inconsistently. The oil was to serve as gloves and boots for your time in this car. My ways are not your ways. This Max," as if referring to a Max he was finished with but one who did not yet exist "became like the Max back then. This Max is the Max who knows how to walk in the spirit, how to listen, how to follow directions, and how to pray till rain falls down."

"I had to take care in releasing the Max long since missing. I had to chip away flesh in the spirit to reach the one who existed before the wedding proposal, bring forth the Max that lived before you formally knew who I was. I needed the Max who tapped the Holy Spirit as a child. I was willing to leave ninety-nine in the wilderness to go after the Max who was lost and bring him back on my shoulders. That young Max stood around a wooden stool hand-in-hand with his brother and sang about tearing Satan's kingdom down. It was a dream, but the earth shook. You woke to a bed shaking. I sent that dream to a young boy. That Max has what I seek.

Max listened. He wanted to write down what he heard so that he would not forget any of it, but the Lord spoke directly to his spirit without a seer or prophet and called him by name. There was no need to write.

"I sent messages while you lived in the blue house that I stood right beside you, and I would never leave you, but you continued to whine. You asked, 'Why Lord? Why?' I need the faith in the old Max to connect with the present knowledge and humility in the current Max. That Max sees me as the only viable object of faith. That is the Max I want. Not the old one. Not the current one. I seek the Max resulting from the merger. I gave no explanation, but stripped you again. After you asked me why, you never listened; you never waited long enough; you would not remain still to hear my reply, to know that I am God. I needed a brave soldier who personified humility after sleeping on the floor in a basement and the windy nights of twenty-three degrees in your car with only my name and a promise of anointing oil on hands and feet to keep you warm. This level of adversity shapes a prophet that I have chosen to honor with revelations. One who will not be puffed up by the mysteries I reveal. One who will speak to my people and speak to the rain. I need the one who once spoke to the rain. The one who could see what was not and pull it into being, a Max who once wrote in the margin of books 'We having the same spirit of faith, according as it is written, I believed, and therefore have I spoken; we also believe, and therefore speak.' You recall that letter you wrote in college, my son, a pure unadulterated letter written to yourself.

"When I put you in the blue house, you wanted to invite friends and the curious to a "Look What the Lord Has Done Party," but I said no, and sent word through the little woman by the well to tell you it was not your time because the carving was not over, the buried Max still called out to me. That Max who could place clouds in a clear blue sky with a word and faith, who continued to pray like Elijah did still called. That Max prayed till the rain came down even when it meant praying and praying again. I had to dig deep over time for him. Some things flesh cannot endure in concentration. Some things flesh cannot survive within a short timeframe. I needed the Max who would not settle with working for the Lord, but yearned for a closer walk where hearing only from me satisfied him and set him on course for work I authorized. I needed the Max who walked for hours in the garden alone and refused to leave until he met me there. It took time to reach him, a young, peculiar will-doer who understood what it meant to eat and drink from my table. This was not an overnight process. Flesh as you well know is not marble.

"The enemy locked you up, and I needed the one the enemy locked up behind a desperate need to belong. You shunned difference, buried the peculiar, and submerged the person I made you to be, and the enemy locked the door. He locked you up with the drugs you smoked in eighth grade and pulled you in with that magazine you opened in the grocery store in middle school that called to you after divorce these many years through the internet during lonely times. Pre-locked down and post-locked down. I needed the pre-locked down Max who brought down rain when seated at a lunchroom table and when seated in front of a history textbook by asking, 'Lord let it rain; please let it rain.' Simple and earnest prayer for forty minutes or longer if needed, a Max not satisfied with clouds or drizzle. The one that friends asked, 'Can you get it to rain today?' You replied, 'Sure, I'll ask.' Then you did for forty minutes or more until water hit dry windows. I sent rain for you because you asked with a child-like faith which could move the wind and redirected clouds.

"There were remnants after you read the letter written in light in college and accepted my invitation to the future wedding feast but only remnants, only remnants. When people look at you now as they did then and tell you that I have so much more for you, they speak truth because I do have more. You are peculiar and rarely will be understood even by those who walk with me. They have no idea how much more I have for you, and neither do you. Therefore, I sent the little woman by the well. She gave you direction, but you could not hear fully. When she told you to go back to the beginning, you thought of college where you prayed, and I answered. I fixed knees and healed lungs; I sent dreams and wrought miracles, but I needed to wake up the Max that formed clouds in blue sky with words of faith, words wrapped in belief. In the gray house, that Max called out to me from beneath dead flesh that found life again and became living adamant stone, so like the woman searching for a lost piece of silver, I lit a candle, and I swept the house until I found it.

"Remember, Max. Remember when Donald's car would not start. He had to work, and with no time to wait for a mechanic, he came back to the dorm room and got you. You knew very little about cars, but he knew you knew me, and I know all. You told him about my goodness, about my love, and about how I would fix his car for him. You laid hands on it, prayed aloud, and the car started. To his amazement and your suitemates' amazement, I started that car, but not for him; you were wrong. I did it for you, so you would keep the faith in what could be, Max.

"When your engine light came on while you lived in the basement and your anxiety grew because of it, I had the little woman by the well tell you to lay hands on your car and speak it fixed like you once did instinctively, and when you did the light disappeared. A month later when the engine light returned, I had her tell you where the problem was and how I sent an angel to fix it according to your faith. As you drove from Long Island to Virginia, the engine light turned off on the turnpike. When you moved thoughts from the engine and worshipped me in your car, the angel I sent had free reign to do what I charged him to do. Remnants, Max, only remnants.

"When vending machines took your money in college, you laid hands on them, and what you paid for came out. Remember when it happened in front of the one I wrote on with pure light for you to read? You both lost money so it seemed, but you laid hands on the machine. Yet, when nothing happened, you walked to your room in faith, believing the vending machine would give you what you bought. You believed that I would place in the bin a roll of wintergreen and a roll of peppermint candy, and I did. An hour later in the vending machine they were there just for the two of you. No one else could see them. Because of prayer, I gave you candy back then and gave you extra mileage now. While in Maryland when you were driving from the airport and needed gas but had no money, did I not increase the mileage one gets from gas as you drove? Did you not see the digital readout defy reality and increase significantly after you prayed? Remnants, and I need a Max that does not exist for such moments because he lives them and has learned to look beyond them to see me, I Am. My gifts, miraculous to others, should be nothing out of the ordinary to you, nothing out of the ordinary.

"I sent you a bird, but you would not see. You tried to feed it. It refused your gift because it was sent to feed you. I told you I would send a bird, and you would know it was me, son; you would know I was with you. I sent the bird that followed you as you cut the grass. You were afraid at first because the bird did not fly away. It hearkened to my command. It stood still when you started the lawn mower. You tried to shoo my messenger away, but it held firm; it could not leave. It followed you from the front to the side of the house, walked behind you and on the side of you, and watched you watch it. It watched over you as I have, as I do. When the lawn mower began to smoke while you cut the grass on the side of the house, you turned it off and walked into the utility room to get oil. I caused the mower to smoke; it was not a lack of maintenance, Max. I called forth smoke because you were not seeing; you remained in the natural and would not see that the grayish-brown bird as you described it, the catbird, was a messenger sent by God. I caused the smoking to break your routine so that you could see from the beginning again. When you returned, you found the bird comfortably perched on the handlebar. Remember? I commanded the bird to alight there. It frightened you; it confused you. You went back into the house and brought out crackers and bread to feed it, feed my messenger with temporal goods when you should have opened yourself up and been fed in the spirit by it. You spread the bread and crackers around, but it looked at you and remained on the handle bar. You shooed it, but it only jumped from the bar to the ground. I watched you watching it. Finally, you furrowed your brow, and then recalled my words. The little woman by the well told you that I said I would send you a bird, my son.

"You looked at the bluebird, and because of the vibrant blue and orange feathers, you asked, 'Lord, is that you?' You looked at the cardinal with its red easily seen in a sea of green as it flew from one tree to the next, and you asked, 'Lord, is that you?' You looked up at the blue jay and asked the same question of me. I did not send them for you. They moved naturally, and you needed a supernatural message sent from above to know I am with you, that I walk with you, ride alongside you, and will drive if you let me. I am no shorter than my word which cannot be broken and cannot lie. Just walk upright before me.

"I sent you an unassuming catbird from the hedges, not high trees, the hedges so that you would know I Am was and is right there with you always. When you do right and when you do wrong, I see it all. My messenger ignored your food, paid no attention to your crackers, and refused your bread because I sent it to feed you in the spirit. I said, 'I will send you a bird.' It followed as you cut the entire yard. It walked right beside you near the loud lawn mower and did not take to flight. I commanded it not leave until you were done. You marveled, marveled that it followed you to the final side of the yard and perched on the wooden fence and kept watch over you. When you turned the lawn mower off, you looked at my messenger and said, 'I'm done.' Then it flew off. I kept my word. I am my promises. You were not and will never be alone.

"It was I who put you in that blue house, but it was not your house because you were not the Max I wanted, the Max who could speak to the wind and the rain and bend them both as I allowed. Only I, only I could have one walk into a house without a security deposit or rent and say to the landlord, 'I don't have it yet.' Only I could do that, and I did it for you. You walked into a house empty handed to claim a house. I said yes, and you said amen. I placed a yes in your spirit and a yes in the landlord's and amen in your heart. What is faith without a test? What good is a test if there is no challenge? Did I not send word that I would furnish your house? Yet, you still doubted me.

"You said to yourself, 'I guess that means I'll have to buy my furniture, and then tell everyone the Lord blessed me.' I heard you, heard disbelief come from a Max that was not the Max I needed, heard from him who worked hard in a church but could no longer bring rain. One who would pray today and whine tomorrow. Still I had mercy. Did I not furnish your house down to plants and pictures? Did I not do this for you who believed me not? I gave you table and chairs for eating, gave you couch and loveseat for sitting, gave you a flat screen TV for viewing, and gave you beds for sleeping. I put flatware in the kitchen drawers and plates in the cabinets. While you were out shopping for pots for the house, did I not send a call and have your friend ask, 'Where are you and what are you doing?' Think about that question. Now see it coming directly from me, not friends. 'Where are you, Max, and what are you doing?' Your Heavenly Father has inquired. You and Sarah were in the store buying pots, but I never told you to buy them. 'Where are you and what are you doing?' Now imagine I asked that question not about your location and what you picked up from the shelves, but about your spiritual walk and what you picked up with your eyes and ears? Still, after all I had done, this was not the Max I needed.

"I sent that message for you to put the pots back, and I gave you pots and knives for your house. I put canisters in place. I cleaned your house from top to bottom so you could move in, my son. Did I not supply end tables? Before you noted the wear and tear of the dining room floor with the yellow glue bleeding through the linoleum, I supplied an oriental rug. I had those who gave you the end tables they no longer needed drive by a garage sale and pick up the rug for free. That rug fit perfectly. Your sister gave you flatware and dishes and your father, Sarah's bed. Only through me could you enter a house and pay nothing, but the blue house was merely a temporary shelter where I fed you.

"Yet, the Max who stood before me though grateful still stood amid disbelief. The house was your cave, the furnishings, food, and support, your brook, and then when you grew weary and began to believe once again you were all alone, I sent a bird, but you could not see, so I stripped you again. Forbade party and celebration reserved for a house. You wanted to celebrate while you were in your cave. That was not your house, and since you had not fully crucified the flesh but presented what should have been dead, I stripped you again. Sent word for you to listen to wind and rain and ask, 'Lord is that you?' I told you to anoint your feet every morning and ask me which way you should go, but you started much of what you would not finish.

"That night when Sylvia raged and Mark did too, she told you to run, 'Go ahead and run away like you always do.' Remember, son? Who in my Word spoke to the rain so that it rained not? Then spoke to the sky so that it rained on his word. Who? Who fled Samaria at my word and hid under a tree, by a brook, in a cave, and finally took shelter in a widow's house? Who, my son? When she said, 'Go ahead and run away like you always do,' she spoke out of something much deeper than both of you know, which tried to relay a message not to you but to something even deeper still that I placed in you. I had to send trial after trial and storm after storm to release it and make it live again, a spirit I imparted long ago before you and your brother stood around a wooden stool and sang of war inside a dream. You began to call down rain before you sat in Sunday school during your college days to learn about my ways.

"When in the basement your money withered and you had no food to eat, did I not command a widow woman there to feed you? After not eating and living off water and the Word when you said enough is enough, did she not leave you a note, son? Did the note not say, 'There is a bag of frozen chicken breasts and a bag of frozen Italian meatballs in the freezer and noodles in the pantry; all I have is yours?' Did she not say, 'We will get through this together?' I placed her. I placed you, and I put my treasure in you, an earthen vessel that the excellency of the power may be of me, God, and not of you.

"I sent a bird, and I prepared a widow woman too. For whom in the Word, Max? For whom in the Word did I do such a thing? I commanded the bird to feed thee there, and in the basement, I commanded the widow woman to feed you there. I am who I said I am, and my promises are sure. I am I Am. There is nothing stripped that I cannot replace, chariots that I cannot have you outrun. I need more than remnants from you, more than stories of the past tapped to get you through to the next test. Recall how you spoke reverently to me in your youth before you thought you knew me. You knew enough of me then to come humbly, to ask until it was done, to turn neither left nor right, but to press until you heard from me. The rain was my answer, Max. You spoke then, and I answered, but now I need a Max that speaks, expects, waits, and listens. I need a mature Max. The past must be now. The soldier who prayed for his mother's ankle at my word before the cast iron pan fell on it during spring break, I need him back. The young man who laid hands on the plumbing when the plumbing backed up, I need him back. The young man who listened to a dream and told his childhood pastor he saw an ant eating around the edge of a cracker and shared that dream as warning before the pastor's death, I need that Max back. No need to worry about your shortcomings. I will take those too.

"I told you I would bless Cynthia because she blessed you. I told you when you left for the Midwest to shake the dust off your feet because you would never return to that basement when I moved you out this time, and your heart grew heavy for her because shaking off the dust is never good. I told you to shake the dust when you left your gray house. Now it suffers from leak upon leak, an unnatural depreciation of all things mechanical, insects, and spiders. Trees suffer, and some die while border shrubs are overrun with weed. Before you left, I told you the outside would resemble the inside, but you could not see what I see. I showed you insects and spiders claiming the house. I sent Sarah a vision of insects marching, and as they got closer to her, she saw faces, human faces. The emptiness of the inside and the lack of hearing there wrought desolation on the outside. You shook the dust, and I pulled the covering.

"The insects and spiders never cross the blood-stained frames of Sarah and Mark's bedroom doors because you prayed in the dark hours of the night, and to this day I honor that prayer. For your ears, did I not have the little woman by the well call you at five in the morning, waking you to say that I heard your prayer last night? She told you that your prayer reached the third heaven. I had her tell you that I placed angels next to their beds, and since you covered the doorposts of Mark and Sarah's bedrooms with the blood of Jesus, insects would not enter their rooms and rot and depreciation would stay away. However, insects, spiders, and rot had unrestricted access in all other areas of that house. The little woman by the well told you that I remember the fallen dust from the soles of my people and the unspoken stories that rise up to my throne after that dust speaks to the ground; therefore, the curse shall remain in the midst of that house and shall consume it with the timber thereof and the stones thereof until I take it away, the result of the perjury in the courtroom and the fallen dust from the shoe of an unwelcomed peculiar vessel carrying my treasure. You shook the dust as you were directed both times, but did I not move your landlord out, put her in another house—she who took care of mine?

"I see you sleeping in your car with temperature registering twenty-three degrees. I tucked you in last night when you could not seem to wrap yourself just right. You tossed and turned until I tucked you in, and then you slept until the morning. It took you a great deal of time to unwrap yourself. I see. I see. I see the weariness. I know your thoughts: Save for my kids you can take me now, and I hear your fears of being a burden. Remember, perfect love casts away all fear. Move in me, and fear not. This will not take much longer. Let the Max who called down rain call that home into being. I had my young servant tell you, 'Don't you stop running, Max. Keep on running.' That message was for now, so tuck in your cloak and outrun your Ahab. Leave Jezebel speechless, and bind those demons that kept you buried.

"When you have your house, place a mat at the front door that reads, "Look what the Lord has done." You will glorify me, and I will honor you. You have walked a path of divorce, separation from children, homelessness, debilitating debt, hunger, stress, and loss much, much loss. These are your shoes, and no one else can walk in them. Now your time of famine is over. Bouncing from hotel to car is over, so pull down that rain, the latter rain, and I will make the places you rest a blessing, and I will reserve the shower of blessing for you to pull down by your word. It will rain in the spirit over you, and your cup will never run dry again, for I have spoken, the I Am you have grown to know wills it so. Bring down the latter rain! Let that young Max and the Max of wisdom combine to call down rain that cannot be seen with the natural eye, for you confessed to me, your Father, as the prodigal did to his, 'Father, I have sinned against heaven, and in thy sight, and am no more worthy to be called thy son.'[61] As that father did, so too have I commanded my servants, 'Bring forth the best robe, and put it on him; and put a ring on his hand, and shoes on his feet: And bring hither the fatted calf, and kill it; and let us eat, and be merry: For this my son was dead, and is alive again; he was lost, and is found.'[62] For you, Max, I do this for you, my son. For I, Jehovah Perazim, have commanded the darkness: O' darkness, darkness! My son shall pass!

"Fear not, Max; let your hands be strong. Then speak to the rain and watch what I do."

ENDNOTES

Chapter 1
1   Matt 19:30 KJV

Chapter 10
2   Matt 19:25 KJV

Chapter 13
3   Prov 27:1 KJV
4   Prov 27:7 KJV
5   Mal 12:5 KJV
6   Jer 4:20 ESV
7   Jer 6:19 ESV
8   Isa 55:3 KJV

Chapter 15
9   Jer 1:5 ESV

Chapter 16
10   Jn 10:28 KJV
11   Ps 25:14 KJV

Chapter 17
12   Num 14:9 KJV
13   Newell, William. "At Calvary."1895
14   Foote. John. "When I See the Blood."

Chapter 19
15 Jn 6:39 KJV
16 Isa 12:1-3 KJV

Chapter 21
17 Lam 3:15,17 & 18 KJV

Chapter 26
18 Prov 27:7 KJV
19 Isa 58:14 KJV
20 Isa 58:10 KJV
21 Jn 4:32 KJV
22 Jn 4:34 KJV
23 Hos 6:4 ESV
24 Hos 6:6 ESV

Chapter 27
25 Ezek 37:4 KJV
26 Acts 20:28 KJV
27 Ezek 34:2-5 KJV

Chapter 28
28 Isa 55:3 KJV
29 Jn 1:1 KJV
30 Matt 16:16 KJV
31 Featherston, William. "My Jesus I Love Thee." 1864.

Chapter 32
32 Num 14:2 KJV

Chapter 36
33 Zach 5:4 KJV
34 Dan 4:35 KJV

Chapter 39
35 Ps 118:17 KJV
36 Ps 119:105 KJV
37 2 Chr 7:14 KJV

38 Joel 1:4 KJV
39 Isa 54:17 KJV
40 Isa 55:8-9 KJV
41 Deut 6:11-12 KJV
42 Deut 6:7 KJV

Chapter 40
43 Isa 55:10-11 KJV
44 Isa 12:1-2 KJV
45 Ps 42:11 KJV
46 1 Cor 4:7 KJV
47 1 Cor 4:11 KJV
48 1 Cor 2:14 KJV
49 Jer 17:5-6 KJV

Chapter 41
50 Ps 118:17 KJV
51 Jer 17:17 KJV
52 Jere 30:3 ESV

Chapter 43
53 2 Cor 9:8 KJV

Chapter 44
54 Num 6:42-26 KJV
55 Gal 6:9 KJV
56 2 Cor 4:7-9 KJV
57 2 Cor 4:10, 16-18 KJV
58 Rom 8:35-39 KJV

Chapter 47
59 Jas 1:12 ESV
60 Heb 10:37 KJV

Chapter 58-59
61 Lk 15:21KJV
62 Lk 15:22-24 KJV

Printed in the United States
By Bookmasters